Tangled Games

USA TODAY BESTSELLING AUTHOR

T.K. LEIGH

TANGLED GAMES

Published by Carpe Per Diem, Inc

Edited by Kim Young, Kim's Editing Services

Cover Design: Cat Head Biscuit, Inc.

Cover assets:

© dor-iss

Used under license from iStock.

Books by T.K. Leigh

For a full list of all of T.K. Leigh's books, including recommended reading order, please visit her website: www.tkleighauthor.com

Books and reading order for hers small town romance alter ego, Tracy Leigh, can be found here: www.tracyleighbooks.com

For a free eBook, sign up for T.K.'s newsletter.

Some of T.K. Leigh's books may contain content that could be triggering for sensitive readers. For a full list of content warnings for each book and/or series, please visit her website by scanning the code below.

One

Nora

I don't have many memories of my father.

Not only did he die when I was young, but even when he was alive, he was often deployed. Despite that, some memories occasionally find their way to the surface.

Like when he came into my room and woke me up with an offer to make pancakes in the shape of my favorite animated character.

Or the way he'd tell me he loved me out of the blue, something I longed to hear from anyone after he died.

Or the way I can't look at a book without thinking of his passion for the written word, memories of the hours I spent with him at the library as clear as if it were just yesterday. Instead, over twenty-five years have passed since I watched his flag-covered casket being lowered into the ground.

As I run my fingers along the spines of the hardcover novels while perusing the shelves of my favorite Manhattan bookstore, I feel his presence. Then again, I feel him whenever I walk into a bookstore or library. Maybe that's why I was drawn to this place today when I have a long list of things I should be doing instead.

Maybe I wanted to feel my dad's presence again.

His reassurance.

His love.

When my hand glides over a familiar title, I stop, a nostalgic smile curving my lips.

Everyone remembers the book that sparked their love of reading. For some, it was Nancy Drew. For others, the *Babysitters Club* series. For others still, it was V.C. Andrews' *Flowers in the Attic*.

But for me, it was something else entirely.

I fell in love with Maxim de Winter from Daphne du Maurier's *Rebecca*. I don't know what attracted me to the story about a young woman who married a wealthy older widower, only to discover the happily ever after she thought she'd have would come at a steep price. But ever since my teenage years, I often return to the tragic tale.

How did the unnamed narrator feel when she went from being a lady's companion to the lady of an English manor? Such a drastic change, one she never fathomed happening to her. Yet Maxim fell for her, regardless that she was an ordinary girl, at least in her eyes. In Maxim's, she was fascinating.

Maybe that's why I've always loved this story.

Because Maxim made her feel extraordinary, not the stupid little girl her employer made her out to be.

For the longest time, it gave me hope I'd find something remarkable, too.

Sliding the book off the shelf, I flip to the first page. A

warmth rushes through me as I read the opening line. It's like seeing an old friend after spending years apart.

"'Last night, I dreamed I went to Manderley again.'"

I stiffen at the deep, guttural voice reciting the first sentence. It sends a shiver down my spine, the subtle British accent the perfect inflection to set the tone.

Slowly, I turn around. A tiny breath manages to escape in response to the pair of blazing blue eyes staring back, the corner of his full lips quirked up into a mischievous smirk. I trace my gaze over his face…the scruff along his jaw, his chiseled nose, his smoldering stare. My pulse kicks up, skin tingling with a vulnerability I didn't think possible from a look alone.

"It's quite refreshing to meet a woman who appreciates a physical book," he continues smoothly when I remain mute. "Most people these days seem to prefer the convenience of an e-reader."

I swallow. "While I can understand that…" My tone turns sultry, "there's no replacement for the feel of a real book." I close *Rebecca*, running a lithe finger along the cover.

Emboldened by the raw hunger covering every inch of him, I curve toward him, acting incredibly out of character for me. But isn't this every woman's fantasy? Or at least every bookworm's fantasy? Running into a handsome, well-dressed man in a bookstore, one who appreciates books for the gift they are?

"Or the scent," I continue in a low voice, "of a real book." I linger near his neck for a moment, inhaling deeply. "It's incredibly…intoxicating." I pull back, eyes locking with his.

Silence stretches between us as he focuses on me in a way that pierces my soul, as if able to read my thoughts, learn my deepest, darkest desires.

With that one look, everything else disappears. Gone is the background chatter, nearby sirens, whirring of the air conditioning. I'm in a vacuum, an alternate universe where nothing exists outside of me, this man, and this arresting lust rioting through me, leaving me mindless, breathless…and perhaps a bit reckless.

When he lifts his hand, my heart hammers in my chest, the hairs on my nape standing on end. I moisten my lips as I brace to feel his skin against mine. His body against mine. His *anything* against mine.

Instead, he gingerly takes the book from my hand. Disappointment ripples inside me. It lasts less than a second before he grips my hip, harsh and invigorating. A gasp tumbles from my mouth when he yanks my body against his. I barely have time to register what's happening as his other hand burrows into my strawberry blonde waves. This is all surreal, like I'm in the presence of Maxim de Winter himself, my deepest fantasy coming to life in the aisle of a Manhattan bookstore.

With unhurried movements, his lips descend toward mine. Each prolonged second is excruciating, ratcheting up my desire to a smoldering level, burning through me.

"'If only there could be an invention that bottled up a memory,'" he murmurs in a husky voice, his breath caressing my mouth.

"And now you've quoted yet another one of my favorite lines from *Rebecca*. Start quoting *Lady Chatterley's Lover* and we'll have to find somewhere more…private."

He cocks his head to the side. "Is that a promise?"

I eye him. There's no way he's read that book. Or if, by some fluke, he has, he won't be familiar enough with it to pull a quote out of thin air.

I think.

With a slight nod, I murmur, "It is."

"Well then…" He adjusts his stance, his arousal pushing against my abdomen, his lips skimming my neck. "'I believe in having a good heart, a chirpy penis, a lively intelligence, and the courage to say shit in front of a lady.'"

I burst out laughing. The sound carries through the aisles, attracting several curious stares, but only for a heartbeat. It's one of the things that drew me to Manhattan in the first place.

Here, no one cares about anyone besides themselves.

Here, I can disappear into the background.

Here, I can be a nobody.

But I don't feel like that right now. Not with the intensity in this man's gaze.

"Why did I have a feeling you'd quote that particular line?" I muse.

"I've been carrying that gem around in my back pocket for ages, waiting for the perfect opportunity to woo a beautiful woman perusing the Literary Classics section of a bookstore."

"If that was your game plan, the odds were stacked against you."

"Perhaps." He shrugs slightly, his eyes dancing with amusement. "But it worked on you, didn't it?"

"Jury's still out."

His expression darkens once more. "I suppose I need to figure out another way to woo you then."

"And what would that be?"

"This."

He crashes his lips to mine, the kiss surprising, yet addictive.

I stiffen, taken aback by his forwardness, especially in such a public place. But that's short-lived, a burning lust for more making me blind to everything else.

This is one of the most spontaneous things I've done in quite some time. I've never been one for overt displays of affection. At least not in places that are so…public. A busy Manhattan bookstore is the definition of public. But that doesn't bother me right now.

And it obviously doesn't bother him, either.

Instead of pulling away at the sound of nearby whispers and snickers, he deepens the kiss, his hand on my waist steering me down the aisle until my back comes into contact with the wall.

He moves his hips, his erection grinding against me. A low groan rumbles from his throat as I dig my hands into his thick hair that's a cacophony of shades, from brown to copper and even a few hints of blond at the ends.

When he tears away, our ragged breathing pervades the space between us. "Let's get out of here."

"And where shall we go?" I zero in on his plump lips that shine with the remnants of my gloss.

"Somewhere more private."

I arch a brow. "Private?"

With a slow nod, he lowers his mouth toward my neck. His breath on my skin is intoxicating, causing a pleasurable ache to build deep within me. One I doubt will be satisfied until I have him.

All of him.

"Yes, gorgeous." His lips skim against the sensitive flesh where my neck meets my shoulder. "Somewhere I can take my time indulging in every single inch of you." He nibbles my earlobe, eliciting a whimper from me, one as innate and uncontrollable as breathing. "Where I can make you scream without having to worry who will overhear."

Needing to maintain some semblance of control, which escapes me with every word he speaks, I place a hand on his chest and gently push him away. "And here I thought you didn't mind making a scene in public. Why else would you have shoved your tongue down my throat, then groped me for everyone to see?"

He smirks. "I didn't hear any complaints."

"That's because there were none to be had."

"Even so, I know where to draw the line." His tone had dropped to that toe-curling decibel once more.

He leans closer but doesn't touch me, maintaining his distance, regardless of how slight.

"And I most certainly draw the line at allowing anyone else to witness your blissful expression when I make you come. Over. And over. And over. Until you beg me to stop. But even then, I won't stop making you feel good."

Playing the part of the vixen to his fox, I trail my fingers down the buttons of his shirt and grab his tie, pulling his mouth to within a whisper of mine.

"Then let's go somewhere so you can make me scream."

His pupils dilate, nostrils flaring. He clutches my cheeks in his calloused hands, slamming his lips against mine in a punishing kiss that leaves me breathless once more.

Breaking away sooner than I'd like, he grasps my hand, not allowing me to catch my breath as he pulls me through the aisles. I do my best to keep up with his determined strides, but it takes two of my steps to meet one of his, my five-four frame no match for his estimated six-four stature. Still, the conviction and resolve in his movements send a thrill through me.

"I almost forgot." He spins around, nearly giving me whiplash as he changes direction.

"What is it?" I ask, my skin warming from the stares and snickers coming from those who witnessed our…moment.

"Why this, of course."

He stops at the proverbial scene of the crime and picks up my abandoned copy of *Rebecca*.

"What about it?"

"You should have it. I'm buying it for you." He pauses, brows furrowed. "You don't already own it, do you?"

"Actually, no."

As much as I adore this book, you'd think I'd own a copy. Having spent the better part of the last decade living in a tiny Manhattan apartment, I've learned to only buy the essentials.

"Now you will." He squeezes my hand and leads me toward the cashier.

"You sure know the way to a woman's heart. Books and the promise of sex? What did I do to win the jackpot?"

He edges toward me. "More than you'll ever know, gorgeous."

There's that word again. The one that turns my insides to jelly. He must sense it, too, wrapping an arm around my waist to support me as we wait our turn. If I didn't love books as much as I do, I'd tell him to forget about it and take me to bed, to hell with waiting in line.

But I want this reminder of today. One I know I'll cherish in the months ahead.

After what feels like an eternity, he pays for my book, then steers me toward the large, glass door, holding it for me as I step out onto the busy Greenwich Village sidewalk.

Finding my hand once again, he wraps his around it, pulling me toward the nearest corner as a dark SUV pulls up. He approaches and opens the rear passenger door.

"Is this your ride?" I ask playfully.

"It is."

I'm about to climb in when he stops me, pinching my chin. He urges my mouth toward his, running his thumb along my bottom lip. "I can't get enough of these lips." He dips his head toward me, tasting them in a soft kiss.

"Let's go so you can have more of them. And then some." I waggle my brows.

He all but tosses me into the back of the SUV, giving a small smile to the man behind the wheel as he merges into the early evening traffic.

"Eager much?" I jest.

He wraps an arm around my shoulders, pulling me into his embrace as he buries his head in my neck. "You have no idea, gorgeous."

I sigh, melting into him, savoring every second of the twenty-minute drive to the Upper West Side. I want nothing more than to get out of this SUV and continue where we left off in the bookstore, but at the same time, I want to stay here, too. It's a strange sensation to be pulled in so many directions at once. To yearn for the future, but also want to live in the present. To want to hurry up, yet also slow down.

When the SUV pulls up in front of a tall apartment building in a quiet neighborhood, he turns toward me, a single brow raised. "You sure you don't want to change your mind? Go back to the bookstore? Pick out a different book? Perhaps one with less…complications?"

I shake my head, brushing my lips against his. "Not a chance in hell."

He presses a chaste, yet invigorating kiss to my mouth. Once he slides out of the SUV, he helps me to the ground. Hand on the small of my back, he leads me toward the lobby of a building at which I could never fathom being able to afford to live.

The doorman offers us a warm greeting as he opens the glass doors, then runs ahead to call for an elevator. One arrives immediately. We step inside, the steel doors sliding closed, shutting out the rest of the world.

I attempt to step away, but he tightens his grip.

"Don't think you're getting away from me that easily," he croons into my ear.

I glance up at him. "Is that right?"

"Now that I've brought you back to my lair, you're mine." He grins, a devilish glint in his eye.

"How very primitive of you." I adjust his tie, smoothing it down his body, able to make out the defined chest and abdominal muscles underneath.

"Just you wait…" He nuzzles my neck, the scraping of his unshaven jaw against my flesh igniting a flame inside me. "You're about to find out exactly how primitive I can be."

The elevator dings and stops, announcing our arrival. He nips my skin before linking his fingers with mine. He leads me down the hall, approaching the only door on this floor.

"So this is home?" I ask flirtatiously as he inputs a code into a keypad above the doorknob.

He's about to press the final number when he pauses, a breathtaking smile crossing his lips. It's no longer mischievous or salacious. It's peaceful, serene.

It brings me peace, too.

"No, love." He grabs my left hand, bringing it up to his mouth, feathering a kiss on my fourth finger where a diamond ring typically sits. "*You* are my home, Nora."

I sigh, draping my arms over his shoulders. "You're my home, too, Anderson."

Two

Nora

"S urprise!"

I come to an abrupt stop the second I step into the apartment I've shared with Anderson the past few months. After I'd agreed to make the move to his home country of Belmont, he bought it so I'd still have somewhere to call home here in the States.

I dart my eyes toward the open living space off the entry where my three best friends, Chloe, Evie, and Izzy, stand beneath giant balloons that spell out *Engaged A.F.*

It reminds me of the Ding Dong Divorced party they threw me around this time last year. Back then, falling in love again was the last thing I wanted.

That was before my path crossed Anderson's, something that never would have happened if my three best girls hadn't encouraged me to take the trip on Route 66 I'd put off for years.

I marvel at all the pieces that had to snap into place for us to meet and fall in love. It wasn't an easy journey, and I'm sure we'll have more than our fair share of struggles ahead, but Anderson's worth it.

"What's going on?" I glance at him.

In the few days since he surprised me with a proposal, I've tried to remain cognizant of Anderson's desire that we keep our engagement to ourselves until he has a chance to talk to his father. After all, he's crown prince. As heir apparent, the king's approval is required for all marriages. He'd already bought the ring so he'd have it when the time was right. Apparently, that was the other day, despite the lack of formality. Then again, that's typical Anderson. From the moment we met, he's always been spontaneous.

"Your engagement party, of course," he says with a wink.

"But—"

He swallows my protest with a kiss. Then he reaches into the inner pocket of his suit jacket, retrieving a familiar, velvet box. With minimal fanfare, he pops it open and slides the stunning ring with a vintage flair onto my finger.

Taking my hands in his, he runs his thumb along my knuckles. It's only been a matter of days, but every time I leave the apartment and have to take off my ring, I feel like a piece of myself is missing.

"It wasn't fair of me to ask you to not share this with your friends."

"You had your reasons," I insist in a low voice.

"True. But when I proposed, I promised to give you everything you ever wanted." He nods toward the living area where my friends wait, their own significant others close by. "That's what I'm doing. You deserve to celebrate this important milestone with your best friends, not be forced to keep it a secret. They know not to tell anyone until there's a formal announcement. You're about to leave the only place you've called home to start over in a new country. And not merely as another face in the crowd, but as Prince Gabriel Anderson Wellingston's American fiancée. You deserve one last taste of normalcy. We both do."

I lift myself onto my toes, draping my arms around his neck, peering into those eyes that mesmerized me from the beginning.

"Thank you," I murmur against his lips.

"I love you."

"And I love you." I gently touch my mouth to his.

"For crying out loud. Will you stop making out so we can see the ring?" Evie exclaims excitedly.

I laugh against Anderson's mouth, then pull away. My friends quickly advance on me, grasping my hand to admire the setting.

"Oh, Nora. It's breathtaking," Izzy exhales as Anderson approaches the men, each of them offering him their own congratulations.

A few years ago, I never could have imagined this scene. Evie was still hopefully devoted to her ex, Trevor, which was to her detriment. Chloe was still vehemently anti-relationship. Izzy was still trying to convince all of us that, as a nurse who worked strange hours, she didn't have time for a relationship. And I was engaged to the man I'd hoped would help me come to terms with losing Hunter, my first love.

Everything's changed.

Julian taught Evie she shouldn't have to sacrifice who

she is for someone to love her. Lincoln helped Chloe see she's worthy of love. Izzy learned she could run from love all she wants, but it will eventually come back for her, like happened with Asher. And I learned it's okay to be vulnerable. To be less than perfect.

To be human.

"Have you discussed a date?" Evie grabs my elbow, leading me toward the kitchen island where a wide variety of finger foods have been set out.

I don't have to ask who put this all together on such short notice. It has Evie written all over it. After all, she was the one who organized my Ding Dong Divorced party, including the rather macabre wedding cake featuring a bride pushing her groom off the top tier to his bloody demise. This time, instead of a cake, there's an assortment of cupcakes arranged in the shape of a giant diamond ring.

"Not really." I grit a smile. "We may not have much control as to when, but I told him I wanted to wait until you two can travel again." I gesture between Chloe and Evie, both of them six months pregnant. "I'd like a long engagement anyway. That will give me time to get adjusted to life over there."

"Are you *ready* for life over there?" Chloe presses. "For him to finally go public with your relationship?"

"Is anyone ever ready to be in the spotlight?" I joke, hoping my light tone masks my nerves.

It's part of the reason he hasn't brought me back home yet. He wanted to wait until we'd been together longer than a few months. Wanted to give us more time to be us — two strangers who met on a road trip and ended up falling in love. Because once we land in Belmont, I'll become the American girl who stole the crown prince. A few photographers have snapped shots of us together, but thanks to recent drama in the British Royal Family, any that were published have been buried in the headlines.

"Just ignore everything," Evie suggests with a wave of her hand, pushing a few locks of her vibrant red hair behind her ear.

She and Chloe know personally how brutal celebrity gossip can be. After all, they both work in the magazine industry, Chloe having been on the gossip column herself before being promoted to the current affairs desk.

"Exactly." Izzy gives me an encouraging smile. "It's all just noise."

If anyone's had a taste of what I'm about to go through, it's Izzy. Her husband is Asher York, rock god who sells out stadiums nightly. I have no doubt there have been quite a few stories written about the woman married to the man who was once rock 'n' roll's most eligible bachelor. But Izzy's never cared what anyone thought of her. Although she's adopted, she grew up with the unwavering support of two loving parents. They never berated her or made her feel like she'll never measure up. Like she's a complete failure at everything she does.

Like my mother has always made me feel.

"All that matters is that he chose you," Evie adds. "That he loves you. That he wants your pussy for the rest of his life."

I burst out laughing.

This is one of the many reasons these girls are my family, my soul mates. No matter what happens in my life, they have my back.

When I told them I'd agreed to marry my now-ex, Jeremy, after only a few months, they offered their unwavering support, once they made sure it was what I wanted. It wasn't, but that didn't make them turn their backs. It only made them support me even more.

When I told them I'd discovered Jeremy in bed with another man, they helped me drown my sorrows in a bottle of wine. Not once did they question what I did to make Jeremy stray, like my mother did. They happily helped me navigate my divorce.

And once my divorce was finalized, they threw me a party to celebrate the next stage of my life. It was at that party they opened my eyes to the fact I married Jeremy to try and patch a wound that still hadn't healed.

That I was still holding onto Hunter.

That I needed to let him go in order to find the happiness I deserved.

So I set out to do just that. Never did I expect to meet a man like Anderson along the way.

I truly believe some higher power played a hand in our meeting. Knew that we were two lost souls in need of something… In need of each other.

When I glance across the room to where he laughs and jokes with Lincoln, Asher, and Julian, my heart expands. Over the past months, they've welcomed him into their fold, treating him like he's just one of the guys, not the heir to the throne of the European Nation of Belmont.

I hope that doesn't change.

As if able to sense me staring, his eyes find mine. Every time our gazes lock like this, it feels like the first time I glanced up in a Downtown Chicago diner to see him staring at me. I still feel my surprise when I left the pool at my motel on Route 66 and ran into him…literally. I still feel the awe and wonder when he told me I was beautiful the first time.

It's these mundane events that will always hold a special place in my heart. The foundation of who we are as a couple. I have to believe these building blocks of our relationship are strong enough to help us navigate the uncertainty of our future.

At least the uncertainty of *my* future.

Anderson's future has been written since he was born. I just hope there's a place in it for me, too.

"Can I have your attention please?" Evie calls out.

I snap my gaze to where she stands in the center of the room, the picture of the perfect hostess.

"It's not an engagement party without a toast." She nods at Izzy, who walks around with a tray, offering a glass to everyone, specifying which ones have alcohol and which don't.

Anderson approaches with two flutes, extending one toward me. "One tiny sip won't hurt," he murmurs so no one can hear as I wrap my fingers around the flute.

I nod in agreement. He isn't a big drinker these days. Not after his doctors recommended avoiding alcohol to help prevent any multiple sclerosis flareups.

"Okay, you love birds," Chloe teases. "If you can keep your hands off each other for a minute or two, I'd like to say a few words."

He pulls away, but keeps me in his embrace, a finger tracing a light circle on my bicep. It's a simple gesture, but it still lights me on fire. It doesn't help I thought we'd be having sex once we got back here, not walking into a surprise engagement party. Talk about being cock blocked. Or, in my case, clam jammed.

"I met Nora during our freshman year of college," Chloe begins, a nostalgic smile on her face. "We were both scared. Both in a strange place. Both forced to grow up pretty damn quickly, although the jury's still out on whether we've succeeded in that."

"Growing up is overrated," Anderson states with a chuckle.

"I'll drink to that." Evie raises her glass but doesn't take a sip.

"As her roommate," Chloe continues, "I witnessed a lot of her ups and downs. I was there when she got home from that first date with Hunter. I listened to her gush and swoon over everything he did and said. At the time, I was convinced they were soul mates." She pauses. "Until she FaceTimed me and told me she'd agreed to travel Route 66 with a complete stranger after her rental car broke down." Her eyes lock with mine. "You may have just met him, may not have known anything about him, but in those few moments, I knew this was different. Knew this man would change everything. Knew you'd found your true soul mate."

She smiles at me before clearing her throat and turning to address everyone else once more.

"They say most people fall in love three times during their lifetimes. That each of these loves serves a different purpose."

Evie appears quite pleased by this, considering her

obsession with the number three.

"Your first love typically happens when you're young. Around high school." Chloe gives me a pointed look, and I know all too well to whom she's referring.

Now that I'm older, I consider my first love to be Hunter, but before him was Aaron, my high school sweetheart. And the person I was dating when I got a wrong number text from Hunter.

"While this love is more akin to infatuation, you can't dismiss it altogether. This first love teaches you what love can be. It's not all-consuming. It's merely your first exposure to this strange sensation. Think about the ocean. It's like dipping your toes into the water to test it, but you don't venture out too far yet.

"Now, your second love is challenging. This is the one that teaches us what a broken heart feels like. Teaches us lessons about life. Makes us stronger. In this second love, there's great pain." She swallows hard, her expression falling. "And great loss. But with this love, we grow. We learn more about love. What it's like to fall in love. What it's like to lose that love. Because we experienced this second, heartbreaking love, we're able to figure out who we are and what we want in life. We're finally ready to experience real love."

Anderson pulls me closer as I swallow past the lump in my throat over the reminder of Hunter. Of exploding with joy when he got down on one knee and asked me to marry him. Of planning our life together. Of losing him and our unborn baby in the car accident I survived.

Of the years I spent wishing I hadn't.

"And that brings us to the third love." Her expression

and tone brighten. "This is the love that takes you by surprise. Finds you when you least expect it. Probably at a time in your life when love is the last thing you want. You fight it with everything you have. But before you know it, you can't imagine your life without this person, even though you barely know a thing about them."

She lifts her gaze to Lincoln, who towers over her by more than a foot. On the outside, they're as different as two people can be. But outward differences don't matter where the heart is concerned. I've learned that lesson with Anderson.

"You somehow find the ability to look past all his imperfections, all his faults." She pauses, then adds. "All his regrets."

I nod, swiping at the tears sliding down my cheek.

"At the end of the day, those things don't matter. All that does is the understanding in your heart that you've finally arrived. That you've finally found peace. That you've finally found a home. And no matter where you go, no matter the miles you travel, as long as you're together, you will be home."

She raises her glass, and everyone else follows suit, this mishmashed group of people that has somehow become my family toasting us.

"I'm thrilled beyond belief you've finally found your way home. To Nora and Anderson."

"Nora and Anderson," everyone repeats.

I look at Anderson, who tips his flute toward mine. He curves into me, his breath warm on my lips.

"Here's to our next adventure, love."

I clink his glass. "To our next adventure."

Three

Anderson

"Nora, darling," I murmur into her neck, rousing her from sleep.

"We can't be there already," she replies in a scratchy voice.

"Almost. We'll be landing in about an hour. I thought you might want to take the opportunity to freshen up beforehand."

She groans, her eyes remaining closed. "It's frowned upon to step off a plane with bedhead, isn't it?"

I chuckle, brushing my lips against her temple. "You're still gorgeous. While I doubt there will be many reporters at the airfield when we land, being in this life means always looking the part."

She rolls over in the bed in the rear cabin of the private jet, her gaze meeting mine. "I'd prefer to play the part of an unknown New Yorker a little while longer."

"Wouldn't we all?" I smooth a few of her waves away from her face, cupping her cheek. "Are you nervous?"

"What do I have to be nervous about? It's not like I'm flying in the royal family's jet and moving to a country I've never been where I'll have to trade my privacy and anonymity for the spotlight as the crown prince's girl-friend, and eventually fiancée once you speak with your father."

"Exactly," I retort playfully. "You have absolutely nothing to be nervous about."

Her laughter fills the space before her expression turns serene. "Even so, one thing is certain."

"What's that?"

"You're worth any nerves I may experience."

"I'm glad you think so." I place a gentle kiss on her lips before standing and buttoning my suit jacket.

When she sees I'm already dressed, she furrows her brow. "How long have you been awake?"

"Not too long. I'll give you some privacy to freshen up. I'll have breakfast waiting when you're ready." I bend down and kiss her once more before walking toward the door.

My hand on the knob, I pause to appreciate her beauty one last time while she's still the woman I met on Route 66. I can't shake the premonition that the second this plane lands at the airfield in Belmont, everything will change. *Nora* will change.

On a long sigh, I slip out of the bedroom and into the bright cabin.

"Sir," a voice says once I close the door.

I look up as Creed strides toward me, his dark eyes urgent. A military man with special ops training, he's typi-cally calm and collected, nothing usually causing him concern. Immediately, I know something's wrong. Something I won't like.

"What happened?"

He licks his lips, an uneasiness about him. "This just hit the wires about fifteen minutes ago." He holds out his tablet.

I take it from him and read the headline. A wave of nausea pummels through me as I waver on my legs. I quickly place a hand on the top of a nearby seat, attempting to steady myself.

"Are you okay, Anders?" Creed asks in a low voice, shifting from my chief protection officer to childhood friend.

"Fuck," I hiss under my breath, jaw tightening. "We were careful. I didn't think anyone would even recognize me."

"It appears it was simply a case of right place at the right time," he answers, all business once more. "Or perhaps wrong place at the wrong time."

I swallow hard, staring at the photo below the headline announcing to the world something I'd hoped to keep to myself a little longer. But that's impossible now, especially when the photographer was able to capture the perfect angle, Nora's left hand cupping my face as I kissed her on the sidewalk in front of our Upper West Side apartment building, a large diamond ring on a very important finger.

She'd started to take it off before we left our apartment, but I insisted she keep it on, give her a few more minutes to wear it before we needed to keep it a secret again.

I should have known better.

"Do I want to know what kind of backlash we're facing?" I give the tablet back to Creed.

"Public perception is mixed. Some people aren't thrilled at the idea of you being engaged to a foreigner. The American press is positive, so that's a good thing. Unfortunately, Europe is a different story."

"I figured as much." I pinch the bridge of my nose and squeeze my eyes shut. A muscle in my shoulder twitches, so I shift my stance, trying to shake it off.

"Sir, are you sure—"

"Anything else I need to be concerned about?" I interrupt before Creed can finish his question. I don't want to hear it. Don't want him verbalizing my own fears. That he's noticed more and more signs of a potential flareup in my MS. Or worse, that my condition is deteriorating.

"There's also the matter of the media."

"The media?"

"A media contingent has assembled at the airport and is awaiting your arrival. I have a team handling it as we speak."

I run a hand over my face, cursing myself for being so careless. I just wanted one last moment of feeling like a normal couple. But we're not even on the ground yet and are already in the thick of it.

"I can arrange for your flight to be diverted to a different airfield."

I vehemently shake my head. "That will look like I'm trying to hide something. We're already on the defensive. No sense in giving them even more fodder to speculate on."

"Agreed. So we'll keep to our original plan, but there

will be additional security present. Your private secretary, Lieutenant Colonel Bridge, will meet the plane to go over a game plan for your arrival."

I inhale a deep breath I hope will calm me. All it does is increase my anxiety.

"What's wrong?"

I snap my head up, my gaze settling on Nora standing in the doorway of the back cabin. She's dressed in a knee-length, floral wrap dress, her hair in loose waves, makeup freshly applied.

How do I tell her our secret's out? That the European media already seems to loathe her before we've even landed in Belmont?

"I'll give you two some privacy." Creed looks at Nora. "Ma'am." Then he turns to me and bows his head. "Sir." Spinning, he stalks toward the front of the plane, disappearing from view.

"Anders, what's going on?"

I refocus my gaze on her. What I wouldn't give to rewind the clocks to that moment in our New York apartment before we left. When I pinned her against the wall and kissed her like it was the last time I would. Now I fear it was. At least the last time she kissed Anderson North, the alter ego I travel under when I don't want people to know who I am.

And the man Nora first met on Route 66 before I told her the truth.

I gesture to a nearby table. "Let's sit."

"I'm not sure I want to." She pushes out a nervous laugh. "In my experience, nothing good follows a request to sit. Especially considering your morose expression. You look like you just learned someone died."

"No one died," I assure her, although it feels like *some-thing* has.

It's not our engagement being public knowledge that has me on edge. It's the fact it was leaked before I had a chance to speak to my father. Before I had an opportunity to go through the typical procedure required of all members of the royal family. Or at least the first five people in the line of succession.

I help her into a chair, then skirt around to the other side of the table and sit. Taking her hand in mine once more, I toy with her empty ring finger. If there's one positive thing to come from this, she can now wear her ring all the time. At least I think she can. I'll need to talk to my private secretary before confirming anything.

"I messed up, Nora," I admit softly.

She blinks. "What are you talking about?"

Pulling my phone out of the inside pocket of my suit jacket, I navigate to the website Creed had shown me. Then I hand it to Nora, allowing her to see the headline and the photo of us in an intimate kiss, her ring prominent. Below that are more photos taken after she pulled out of the kiss, her face visible.

"'An American Princess'?" Nora reads, snapping up her head to meet my gaze, confusion etched in her brow. "How? I thought—"

"It's my fault," I assure her, not wanting her to burden herself with even a hint of the blame. "I'd grown complacent. Didn't think anyone would recognize me. It's not like I'm a member of the British Royal Family or anything."

"But some people still know who you are."

"All the more reason I should have been more careful, shouldn't have insisted it was okay for you to wear your ring. It was selfish of me. I hate looking at your finger and not seeing a ring." I glance at her still vacant hand. "Once we boarded this plane, I knew you wouldn't be able to wear it, even at home, until we went through the proper channels. When I put the ring back on your finger the other night, your face lit up, Nora. I hated depriving you of that again. Now my carelessness may cost us. This story is making headlines everywhere. Not only in my home country, but also all over Europe. And America."

Nora sits with her spine straight, not reacting as she processes this news. I wish she would. Wish I knew what she was thinking.

"When we land, we'll have to face the media. According to Creed, there's already a frenzy waiting."

She nods, glancing out the window, nothing but miles of clear, blue sky surrounding us. "I guess this is one way of ripping off the bandage, so to speak." She laughs under her breath, but it's laced with anxiety.

To say she's been apprehensive about being thrust into the spotlight would be an understatement. Despite her assurances that I'm worth the lack of obscurity she once craved, I didn't want it to happen like this.

"I can't tell you how sorry I am about this, Nora. This isn't how I'd hoped to introduce you to my world, my life."

"I know." She treats me to a smile, but it doesn't reach her eyes. "If this past year has taught me anything, it's that you'll always be by my side. As long as you promise to stay true to that, we'll get through whatever awaits us."

"And I will. No matter what happens. No matter what

people do to try to break us apart, I will always be by your side." I bring her hand to my lips, feathering a kiss along her knuckles. "Promise."

She swallows hard and repeats, "Promise."

But regardless of our affirmations to one another, I still can't shake the feeling that we're about to set sail on uncharted waters.

That life as we know it is about to change.

That our *love* as we know it is about to change.

Four

Nora

My stomach is in knots.

I don't want Anderson to worry any more than he already is, but I can't shake off the unsettling feeling winding through me over what awaits me — *us* — when we land.

Is our love strong enough to endure the storm I sense brewing offshore?

Or will this life pull us into its riptide until we drown?

Perhaps I didn't give this scenario the careful consideration it deserves. I've known *who* Anderson is from almost the beginning. Yet I haven't been exposed to *what* he is. Not in this world. Isn't that why I agreed to move here with him? To get to know that part of him, too?

Why do I feel like it's all falling apart before I've even stepped foot in Belmont?

"Those are the canals I told you about." Anderson's voice cuts through my thoughts. He nods toward the window.

I follow his line of sight, peering a thousand feet below as the plane grows closer and closer to the ground. Everything is green and vibrant, small canals lining historic, brick buildings. Exactly like I pictured his home country and the capital city of Montrose.

"Wow," I exhale.

It doesn't matter how many times Anderson has shown me photos of what is now my new home, or the multitude of images I've looked at during another online search. Nothing could have prepared me for how beautiful it is. How *different* it is from the hustle of the concrete jungle we left eight hours ago.

"What do you think?" he asks. "She's a sight, isn't she?"

The love he has for his homeland is clear in both his tone and the small smile that tugs on his lips as he admires the ground below us. It's the look of a man coming home. The same one my father bestowed on me whenever he returned from deployment.

"It's gorgeous," I tell him. "So…European."

He chuckles, brushing a soft kiss against my knuckles. "Good thing, because this *is* part of Europe. There *are* countries besides England and France, you know."

"I know." I roll my eyes playfully before looking back out the window. "But this is different. It's old, charming. And I'm only seeing it from up above."

"I can't wait to give you the grand tour."

"Me, either."

He peers down at our intertwined fingers. "Have you read up on the royal family at all?" he asks after a beat.

"Not really. I know a little, but I'm not like Chloe, who

can write books about your family's history." I laugh nervously. "Hell, she probably knows more about your family than you do."

"Probably." He pauses. "Do you know how my father came to be king?"

"I assume because your grandfather passed away. Isn't that how these things work?"

"Usually. Although in Belmont, there's a tradition for the king to voluntarily abdicate around his sixty-fifth birthday. But you're right. My grandfather *did* die. However, my father was only supposed to be 'the spare'."

I tilt my head, brow furrowed. "The spare?"

"It's an unspoken obligation in the family. You need to have an heir and a spare. Two kids in case one..." He gives me a knowing look. "You have a backup. My grandmother, being the overachiever she is, had four spares."

"Makes it sound like kids are commodities. Not living, breathing humans."

"Welcome to my world, Nora." He smiles, but it oozes with sarcasm. "I don't remember much about my Uncle Nicholas. I was young when he died. Only eight."

"What happened?"

"He and his family went to the mountains for a skiing holiday one Christmas. An unexpected avalanche came over them. Killed him, his wife, and their four children."

I cover my mouth with my hand, shaking my head. "Oh, my god."

"It made headlines back then, but considering you were probably only two or three at the time, I doubt you remember it. Needless to say, it affected the entire family. Hell, the country. In the blink of an eye, not only did the heir apparent perish, but so did the second, third, fourth, and fifth in line to the crown. Until that point, I was content with the fact I'd never be king. That I'd never come remotely close to being king. I got to have a normal childhood, unlike my older cousin, who had to go through all this extra tutoring to learn about our government and the monarchy. To learn how to rule. Then it all changed."

He swallows hard, a pensive look crossing his face. "This will probably come out as extremely insensitive, but when I heard the news, I cried. Not for my cousins or aunt or uncle. But because I saw their deaths as mine, too."

"Anders…," I sigh.

"You'll hear the word 'duty' being tossed around a lot in the coming weeks. After the accident, I had it thrown at me from every direction. Their bodies were still warm when I was ripped out of my old school in the country and placed in a new one in London where I'd learn how to be an effective leader, in addition to everything else expected of me. It all happened so quickly. One day, I was just a kid most people barely recognized. The next, my face was all over the media as the future king. From seventh in line to second." His Adam's apple bobs up and down. "And within a month, I went from second in line to heir apparent."

I close my eyes, my heart breaking for the boy he once was. It sounds crazy, considering the picture popular fiction paints of royalty. But I can see the truth plastered all over Anderson's face. This life isn't as charmed as everyone believes.

"I'm not telling you this because I want your sympathy. I've made peace with the circumstances that led to this point in my life. I'm telling you this because I know how it feels to be an outsider. Maybe not to the extent you're considered an outsider, but I can relate. The first eight years of my life, I was…normal, apart from my grandfather being king. I went to a normal school. Had normal friends. Played normal sports. Then all that changed. The entire country's attention seemed to be focused on my father and me. And, to a lesser degree, my sister, as well as the rest of my cousins. Granted, it's not the same thing as what you'll go through as you get adjusted, but—"

"You're right."

Cupping his cheek, I brush my thumb against the smooth skin. It makes me miss his usual scruff. Something else I'll have to get used to. Anderson's made his distaste for the rules regarding his appearance quite clear.

"It *isn't* the same. You had this life thrust upon you. You had no choice but to acclimate." I crane my mouth closer to his. "But I do, Anderson. And despite knowing it won't be easy, that there will be quite a few people who don't like the idea of their future king marrying someone like me, I still choose this." My lips skim his. "Still choose you."

He digs his fingers into my hair, pulling me closer. Or as close as possible with an armrest separating us. The plane jostles as the wheels hit the ground, but neither of us breaks away. He swipes his tongue against my lips, and I open for him, not caring who might see us. That doesn't matter, not when I'll have to share Anderson with the rest of the world in a matter of seconds. For now, I'll take every last heartbeat he'll give me.

As the plane slows and turns off the runway, he brings

the kiss to an end. Without saying a word, he reaches past me and lowers my window shade.

"For privacy," he answers my unspoken question. "You'll learn to take what you can get."

"Oh… Of course."

I stare straight ahead, a bout of nausea rolling over me, which only increases the second the plane comes to a stop, the few members of the cabin crew jumping up from their seats. I study Anderson, taking my cues from him. He remains sitting in the plush chair that's a far cry from any commercial airline seat, but he does unbuckle his seat belt, so I do the same.

I peer at the shaded window, wishing I could see what's going on outside. Then again, it's probably best I don't, especially when the attendant opens the cabin door and I'm able to make out the sound of a crowd assembled nearby. I inhale several deep breaths, practicing the meditation techniques I once taught on a daily basis in the yoga studio I used to run.

Positive energy in. Negative energy out.

But no amount of breathing can help ward off the nerves filling me.

When I feel him squeeze my hand, I bring my gaze to Anderson, who gives me an encouraging smile. Noticing movement out of the corner of my eye, I look forward as a man in a dark suit enters the cabin. Creed greets him with a curt nod before they make their way toward us.

"Your Highness," the man says, bowing his head toward Anderson.

He has a no-nonsense attitude. Much like Creed, something about him screams former military. But his frame isn't nearly as formidable as Creed's, who easily towers over him by at least a half-foot. Then again, being the same height as Anderson's six-four, Creed easily towers over most people.

"Welcome home."

"Thank you, Nathan," Anderson says in an even tone I've only heard on occasion. It's his business voice. His *royal* voice. His Prince Gabriel voice. "May I introduce you to Ms. Nora Tremblay. Nora, this is my private secretary, Lieutenant Colonel Nathan Bridge."

The man looks at me, nodding slightly. "Pleasure, ma'am."

"Likewise."

When Anderson first mentioned his private secretary was former military, I was confused why someone with that background would take a job as a secretary. It seemed like a waste of his qualifications. Then he explained that as the private secretary to a member of the royal family, Lieutenant Colonel Bridge is often the first line of communication between Anderson, as heir to the throne, and the rest of the government and royal household, as well as the media. He's also in charge of planning Anderson's day-to-day schedule. Apparently, those working as private secretaries, or assistant private secretaries, yield a considerable amount of influence. Even Creed, Anderson's chief protection officer, must report all of Anderson's movements to Lieutenant Colonel Bridge.

"As Captain Lawson has advised you," Bridge begins, glancing at Creed before returning his attention to Anderson, "there's quite a large press presence here, in addition to a considerable number of civilians lining the road."

"Good? Bad?" Anderson inquires.

"A mixture of both. You're aware there's a small, yet rather vocal minority of the populace who are vehemently anti-foreigner. Particularly anti-American."

Sensing my growing unease, Anderson grabs my hand in his once more and gives it a squeeze.

"I am."

"Captain Lawson has arranged for increased security not only here at the airfield, but also along the route to your residence. I'm in the process of coordinating a response with His Majesty. In the meantime, I'd advise both of you to remain silent." He glances my way. "And if I might, I suggest Ms. Tremblay keep her left hand hidden. That way, no one sees you with or without a ring."

Out of instinct, I move my left hand from the armrest, pulling it toward me, as if I should be ashamed.

"At least until we've had more time to discuss this with the royal household," he adds with a trite smile.

"Captain Lawson and myself will exit the aircraft first. Once we reach the tarmac, you two will step out together, your right hand holding her left. You'll pause at the top. Smile. Wave." He pins me with a stare. "And I can't stress this enough. No matter what you may hear shouted at you, you smile. You wave. You remain the picture of poise and sophistication."

A queasiness overtakes me, my stomach roiling. What could anyone possibly say to warrant this sort of admonition?

"It'll be okay." Anderson touches my chin, turning my eyes toward him. "Like I told you… I'll be by your side the entire time. You'll eventually learn to tune out the noise.

And that's precisely what this is. Just noise."

"If you say so…"

He steals a quick kiss, then turns his attention back to Bridge, awaiting his next instructions. I find this all a bit odd. One day soon, Anderson will lead this country, yet right now, he's taking orders from his private secretary. Just shows how ignorant I am about how this world works.

"After a few seconds, you'll descend the stairs and walk casually, yet briskly toward the waiting SUV," Bridge continues. "You'll help Ms. Tremblay in first, mindful to keep her left hand hidden from view. Once she's inside, you'll pause, giving the crowd one last wave. Then we'll depart for Wintervale."

I look at Anderson. "Wintervale?"

"It's the name of my residence."

"Oh. Right."

Bridge looks at me with something that borders on disapproval, as if I should have known this. Why would I? It's not like it's ever come up in conversation. We typically steer clear of any discussion of his role as the future monarch.

Now I wonder if we were setting ourselves up for failure by ignoring the reality of who he is.

And who I am.

A commoner who fell in love with a prince.

"We're ready when you are, sir," Bridge states.

"Thank you. I'd like a moment with Ms. Tremblay."

"Of course, Your Highness." He bows, then spins, walking purposefully up the aisle, Creed following.

Anderson turns to me, his expression urgent. "I need you to promise me something."

"What's that?"

He grabs both my hands. "That no matter what happens, you won't shut me out."

"I'd never. I—"

"I know you, Nora. You lock up your feelings, not wanting people to use them against you, as your mother so often did. I get it. Trust me. I did the same thing. In this world, in this family, feelings are a commodity to be used against you. You learn at an early age to keep them to yourself. It's the only way to survive."

He drops his hold on my hands and cups my cheeks, edging toward me, his breath dancing on my lips.

"But I don't want you to do that with me. Not now. Not with this world you're about to enter. It will eat you up and spit you out, if for no other reason than because it can. Because it's powerful. Because it's bloody ruthless. When I was thrust into it, the only thing that helped me was my sister. Esme and I had each other. Were able to share our true feelings. And we still do.

"So I need you to promise me that you will *always* talk to me. That you won't shut me out because you're worried I'll find your struggles to be a sign of weakness. Nothing could be further from the truth. You, Nora Jean Tremblay, are one of the strongest women I know. Despite all my warnings about what you'll have to give up, what you'll have to endure, you still chose to walk away from the only life you've ever known to join me in mine. I'll never be able to repay you for this. For everything you've given me."

"You did get me a nice apartment on the Upper West Side to call home," I remind him, trying to break through the tension. "Not to mention all the clothes and jewelry you've spoiled me with."

"Those are material things. They can be replaced. But I hope you feel that my love for you is irreplaceable. Because your love for me will never be replaced."

"And your love for me will never be replaced." I graze my lips over his, our kiss light but still exhilarating. "I promise I won't shut you out."

He deepens the kiss, then reluctantly pulls away and stands before helping me to my feet. The instant I'm up, Anderson grips my face in his hands. "I love you so fucking much." His gaze sears into me, not a touch of hesitation within his brilliant blue orbs. "Never forget that."

"You won't let me."

"Damn straight, gorgeous." He treats me to one last kiss. "Now, let's get this dog and pony show over with."

We position ourselves as Bridge instructed, Anderson's right hand wrapped around my left. He brings it up to his mouth, kissing my vacant ring finger.

"I'm sorry about all of this. But for now, it's best we don't give them any more fuel for the fire, I suppose."

"I understand."

He kisses my knuckles again, then lowers my hand, clasping it in what feels like a death grip. As he leads me toward the front of the plane, my pulse steadily increases with each step, echoing in my ears.

Why do I feel like a condemned prisoner headed to the gallows? A small voice inside of me tells me that maybe it's because, deep down, I realize I'm not good enough for Anderson. That he'd be better off with someone more appropriate. Someone from his typical social circles. Someone who can handle the spotlight. Someone you'd expect to see with a future king.

I do everything to silence that voice, but after a lifetime of being made to feel inadequate by my own mother, it's difficult.

As we approach the open door, sunlight streams into the cabin. It feels like my legs are about to give out beneath me. And I'm not the only one anxious about this, either. When I notice a tremble in my hand, I glance to where it's joined with Anderson's, observing a subtle twitch.

"Are you okay?" I ask.

"It's fine. Don't worry."

I part my lips, about to tell him it's my job to worry about him, but I'm cut off by Lieutenant Colonel Bridge.

"Ready, sir?" he asks.

Instead of answering, Anderson looks at me, a single brow arched.

Not wanting this country's first impression of me to be of weakness, I hold my head high, my expression determined. "Ready."

Five

Nora

Have you ever had one of those dreams where you're walking into work or school and everyone's looking at you, but you have no idea why? You don't want to let your insecurities show, so instead of trying to figure out why everyone stops to stare, gawk, perhaps laugh, you continue on the path you've taken every day prior without incident?

That's how it feels the moment I step out of the airplane, Anderson at my side. The lights and flashes from dozens of cameras blind me, my irises burning. What I wouldn't give to hide behind a pair of sunglasses, but according to Anderson, those are a big no-no during official events. And this is now an official event.

I do everything to maintain my composure and act as if this is just another day. That I'm not being put on display for the world to critique and evaluate.

There's so much noise and commotion, I can't decipher a single question or comment shouted at us. But in the midst of it all, I draw strength from Anderson's unwa-vering hold, his hand still intertwined with mine.

I glance at him, giving him a smile as he raises his free hand to wave at the crowd, his motions practiced. Remembering Bridge's instructions, I do the same. I hope I don't appear foolish. I never thought much about how to wave. Now I'm overly critical of myself. Is it too enthusias-tic? Too indifferent? Too much? Not enough?

When Anderson squeezes my hand, I know that's my signal for us to start walking down the stairs. Placing my free hand on the railing, I carefully descend the steps. I do my best to keep smiling, although it's becoming more and more difficult, particularly when I'm able to decipher some of their questions.

"Is she pregnant, Your Highness?"

"Are you worried she's only marrying you because of your money?"

"What does this mean for your relationship with Caroline DeVries, Your Highness?"

"What makes you think you're better than someone from this country?"

"She's not even that pretty, Your Highness. You can do much better."

Anderson tightens his grip on me, silently telling me to ignore them. I can't believe the balls some of these reporters have to ask such horrific questions and make such derogatory comments. We're living in the age of social media. I've read my fair share of awful things. But you must have a serious lack of conscience to tell someone they're a gold digger to their face when you know nothing about them.

By the time we reach the SUV, my nerves are frayed, each insult flung at me another scar against my skin. Sensing my agitation, Anderson's quick to help me inside. Then, as instructed, he gives one final smile and wave before ducking in beside me.

Keeping my eyes focused straight ahead, I don't take a breath until the airfield is far behind us. At least the crowd lining the streets from the airport seems a bit more supportive than the press, many of them holding signs congratulating us on our engagement. There are a few accusing Anderson of selling out his nationality, but the majority seem happy for him. I try to find comfort in that, but it's difficult. How am I going to survive life in the spotlight as Anderson's wife and a goddamn princess when I could barely handle the few seconds it took me to walk off the plane and to the car?

"You did great, Nora," Anderson reassures me.

"Is it always like this for you?"

"Not usually." He runs his fingers through his hair. "Yes, I'm often hassled by reporters or photographers when in public, but this kind of thing only happens when there's been a big news story about the monarchy."

I nod, gazing out of the window, not even able to appreciate my surroundings. The historic architecture. The cobblestone roads. The flower-adorned railings on the bridges across the canals. All I can think about is if we'll ever be a normal couple again.

"Would you rather live your entire life in virtual reality where all your wishes are granted and dreams come true…," Anderson begins after a long silence. "Or live in the real world where you may face things that frighten or scare you?"

I scrunch my brows at him. "What are you doing?"

He shrugs. "Would You Rather. Like when we were two strangers crazy enough to go on a road trip together. It seemed to break the tension back then." He waves his hand. "I'd hoped it would break the tension between us now, too."

I reach across the seat and squeeze his thigh. "As much as I hate the real world sometimes, I wouldn't trade it for anything."

"Either would I." His shoulders relax as he exhales a long breath, a slow smile playing on his full lips. "Your turn."

"My turn?"

"Have you forgotten how the game's played? It's been a while, but—"

"Okay. Okay," I interrupt. "Just give me a minute."

I chew on my lower lip, trying to come up with an appropriate scenario. It brings back memories of our early days together. Of the endless stretch of road as we traveled Route 66. Of gradually transitioning from complete strangers to friends. Then to something more than friends.

They are some of the happiest moments.

"Would you rather spend a year traveling the world on a shoestring budget, or spend a year living in luxury but be forced to remain in one country?"

"Is that even a question? A year traveling. Without a doubt." He brings my hand to his lips. "Preferably on Route 66 so I can meet you for the first time all over again. Although, I must confess…"

"What's that?" I tilt my head.

"Every day I wake up with you in my life feels like the morning after we first met. I still experience the same excitement. The same wonder. The same…faith."

I sigh, losing myself in his eyes. In that one look, all my anxiety evaporates. "I don't know how you do it, Anderson. But I manage to fall in love with you all over again every day. Even when you piss me off."

He throws his head back, his laughter filling the small space. "I'll try not to 'piss' you off. Although, you should be aware that piss has a different meaning here."

"And what's that?"

"Legless."

"Legless?"

"Drunk."

"Ah… Of course. I'll have to remember that. I'm sure there's a lot I'll need to learn in the coming weeks and months." I peer at him thoughtfully, then settle back into the seat, welcoming the distraction from the people lining the streets. "Tell me some of it."

"What do you mean?"

"I'm pretty new to this whole royalty thing. What are some of the rules I'll have to adhere to? Other than the few you've already shared, like no sushi, which I've only agreed to because I like your dick too much."

Creed laughs from the front seat, yet tries to cover it

with a cough.

"I'm happy to hear that." Anderson winks, then stares ahead, expression pinched in contemplation. "Here's one you made me break on our road trip."

"What? No associating with commoners?"

"No selfies."

"You're joking. That's actually a rule?"

"'Fraid so."

"What's the reason behind it?"

"I ask myself that regarding a lot of these rules. Some I can understand. For example, once my father became king, I was no longer able to travel with him. I couldn't even ride in the same car."

"Is that because of what happened to your uncle and cousins?"

"Actually, no. That's been a rule as long as I can remember. The heir apparent can never travel with the monarch. Once we arrived at our final destination, we could be together, but we couldn't fly on the same plane or anything like that."

"I can kind of understand that. Must make planning a vacation a nightmare, though," I add in jest as the SUV pulls off a quaint road and comes to a stop in front of a gate.

A man dressed in a dark suit steps out of the guard-house, bowing toward the back seat where he must know Anderson sits, despite all the windows being tinted black. Then the gate opens and Creed maneuvers the SUV up a winding drive shaded by mature trees.

I gawk at my surroundings. "Is this Wintervale?"

Flowers and perfectly manicured grass line the long

driveway, everything full of color and well maintained. I can't remember the last time I've lived somewhere with grass. It's one of those things you take for granted until you move somewhere like Manhattan and have to go to Central Park to enjoy it.

"It's the residence of the heir apparent. Well, technically, it's supposed to be the heir apparent's residence upon his marriage, but I kind of broke the rules on that front."

"How so?"

"Most members of the royal family are married before they're thirty. It's…encouraged in order to produce an heir."

"And a spare. Don't forget the spare."

"Never." He winks. "But after I lost Kendall…" He smiles sadly.

I squeeze his hand, knowing all too well how he feels. It doesn't matter how many years have passed. Like Hunter, Kendall was Anderson's first love. And was also someone who wasn't supposed to die young. Whereas I lost Hunter in a car accident, he watched Kendall collapse during a volleyball tournament, then spent months blaming himself after learning she had an undiagnosed heart condition that caused her to have a heart attack and die before her thirtieth birthday. At least I was able to mourn Hunter in private. Anderson wasn't. Instead, he was forced to say goodbye to the woman he hoped to marry while the paparazzi attempted to cash in on his grief.

"My father 'gifted' it to me," he continues. "Hoped it would remind me of my place in this world."

"Did it?"

"At first, I decided the best thing was to focus on my role as heir and future monarch. When I received an invitation to speak at the opening of a volleyball training center in Long Island that was named for her, I returned to the U.S. for the first time since her death. And that was where I was diagnosed with MS. I thought it was heat stroke or the stress of being surrounded by memories of Kendall. Even told Creed that was the reason I'd fainted."

"But it wasn't."

"It wasn't. So instead of hopping on a plane to Los Angeles, where I'd planned to spend a few weeks before returning home, I decided to drive." He leans toward me, brushing his lips against mine. "And one fateful day, I glanced up from my coffee in a loud, greasy diner in Chicago and saw this woman meditating."

I laugh under my breath. "Not the most conducive spot to clear your mind."

"True. But I knew I had to find out more about her. And I can't tell you how grateful I am for every day I get to know you."

He presses a chaste kiss to my lips as the car slows to a stop, then gestures out the window toward a palatial brick building that looks like it belongs on the set of a period romance. "Welcome to Wintervale, Nora."

Blinking, I slowly slide out of the car after a valet opens my door and drink it all in. Vines snake around the façade of the massive three-story building. Not in an overgrown manner, but in a way that adds a historic feel to this impressive estate. I want to pinch myself. This can't be real. Can it? A year ago, my divorce had just been finalized and I was unsure what my future held.

Never could I have imagined I'd be engaged to a prince. That I'd be the future queen consort of a European country. It feels like I'm living a fairy tale. Like I'm the unnamed narrator in *Rebecca* seeing Manderley for the first time.

Just like she'd encountered a rude awakening once she was thrust into a life she never imagined, I know I'll face the same. For now, I want to bask in this brief slice of happiness. Of the sun warming my skin. The birds chirping. The fresh air surrounding me.

The feeling of hope.

"What do you think?"

"It's nice." I shrug, feigning indifference. "I've seen bigger. I mean, the fountain is a bit unimpressive." I nod toward a gorgeous three-tiered fountain in the center of the circular drive.

Anderson slings an arm over my shoulders, kissing my cheek. "Well, for you, my beautiful Nora, I'll have an even bigger one put in. Now, come on. I have plans for you." He waggles his brows.

"Plans?"

When his eyes darken, a thrill shoots through me. "Oh yes. Big plans. And they involve me, you, a bed, and absolutely no distractions."

I tilt my head back and relish in the warmth of his lips on mine. "I like the sound of that."

Six

Anderson

I don't think I've ever seen Nora's eyes as wide as they are now. She's always had a sort of doe-eyed appearance, her face reminding me of the way many animators seem to draw princesses. Soft features. Pouty lips. Bright eyes.

But as I introduce Nora to her new home, I'm confident they're about to pop out of her head. Between the spacious library, private yoga studio I had designed, and lush gardens where Nora plans to spend a great deal of time meditating, she's on cloud nine.

It takes longer than I'd anticipated to show her around the grounds and introduce her to the staff. Or maybe it feels that way because I'm desperate to be alone with her after having to share her for the past few hours. I'm done sharing. And when we finally make it to the bedroom, I'm rather short with Richard, my personal butler, dismissing him with an order that I'm not to be disturbed for the rest of the day.

Once we're alone, Nora gives me a coy look. "Does everyone here always do whatever you tell them?"

"If they want to keep their job, they do," I answer, although that's not entirely true. Half the time, *I'm* the one being told what to do, not the other way around.

Hips swaying, she saunters up to me, her gaze darkening. In a heartbeat, I forget everything else, my body buzzing to life. My pulse increases, a dizzying sensation consuming me, my fingers aching to reach out and touch every inch of her.

"And what about me?" She curves toward me, wrapping her hand around my tie, urging my mouth closer to hers. But there's still too much space between us.

I want to consume her, devour her, lose myself in her to the point where I'll no longer be able to tell where I end and she begins, our souls intertwined for all eternity, nothing about to come between us.

"What about you?"

"Do *I* have to do everything you tell me to?" Her tone is husky.

"Do you want to?" I chase after her kiss, but she remains out of reach, my desperation for her growing with every pounding heartbeat.

"That depends."

"On what?"

She brings her mouth to within a whisper of mine. "On what my punishment will be if I disobey."

Growling, I dig my fingers into her hair, my hold on her resolute. I crush my lips against hers, coaxing her mouth open. When my tongue sweeps against hers, she whimpers, our kiss wild and filled with lust. Teeth clashing.

Hands roaming. Bodies wanting. This is exactly what I need today. This connection. This addiction. This love.

Gripping her hips, I move her backward across the room and toward the bed. I don't break our connection. I can't. She's my one source of sustenance. My lifeline. Without the elixir in her kiss, I'd perish and die.

When the back of her legs hit the bed, I scoop her up and gently toss her onto the mattress. Her eyes narrow hungrily, watching my every move as I shrug off my jacket and drop it onto the floor, my tie quickly joining it. I crawl up her body and cover her mouth once more, pulsing against her as she wraps her legs around my waist.

"Do you feel what you do to me?" I ask through my heavy breathing. "How much I need you?"

"I do," she pants, threading her fingers into my hair.

I snake down her frame, my hands exploring this body I know so intimately.

"You should feel how much *I* need *you*."

"I plan on it." I pause and lift my eyes to hers, the awe and wonder of minutes ago replaced with a burning desire. "Actually, I'd rather *taste* how much you need me. Would you like that?"

"God yes," she moans as I wrap my mouth around her nipple through her dress, the material a rather unwelcome barrier. "I need that so much right now."

I continue down her body, trailing soft kisses along the way. When I settle between her legs, I pause to admire her ragged breathing, her chest heaving. I push the skirt of her dress up around her waist and reveal a sexy pair of pink panties.

"I don't recognize these," I comment, grazing my

thumb over the lace material.

"They're new."

"Is that right?"

Chewing on her lower lip, she nods. "You should see what else I got."

"I can't bloody wait. For now, I'd love nothing more than to rip these damn knickers off you."

"Then what are you waiting for?" She lifts her hips in invitation.

I hook my fingers into the waistband of her panties, fumbling to rid her of them as quickly as possible. Once I toss them aside, I return to her, stealing a glance at her expression. Lips parted. Eyes closed. Expression flushed. I'm not even touching her yet, but that doesn't matter. The promise of what's to come is enough to ignite the flames within.

Gripping her thighs, I spread them apart, pressing my mouth against her, my tongue circling her clit. A moan slips from her throat as she throbs against me, urging me to go faster, deeper, harder.

"God, I love you," she exhales, digging her nails into my scalp.

I continue worshiping her, nudging a finger inside. She thrusts harder against me, her breathing growing more uneven, muscles tightening around me. I push another finger inside her, stretching and massaging.

I'm so focused on her, on making her feel good, I barely register when a knock rips through the space. It's not until Nora hoists herself up onto her elbows and stares at the door I realize we're being interrupted.

"Anders, I think—"

"Ignore it." My hand on her chest, I push her back against the mattress.

I return to her, tuning out everything else, thrusting my two fingers back inside her before adding a third. She succumbs to me again, her moans and whimpers growing closer together as she fights her impending orgasm. I suck her clit harder, my motions more frenzied. Then there's another knock, which only serves to aggravate me even more. This never happened back in New York.

"Anders…" Nora attempts to pull away from me again.

And again, I refuse to let her, placing my hand on her stomach, pinning her to the bed. "Ignore it," I tell her, this time louder. More demanding. More desperate.

I continue plunging my fingers inside her, no longer sure if I'm doing this for her or for me. I know what's waiting on the other side of the door. I need this one slice of normalcy before being sucked back into my reality.

When the knock sounds again, this time more incessant, I jump from the bed, growling out of frustration. I toss a blanket over Nora before storming toward the door and yanking it open only enough for Nathan to see my face.

"Will you bugger off?" I seethe, lip curled. "I left explicit instructions I was not to be disturbed, so what is so bloody important that I can't be left alone for one goddamn minute?"

His expression remains even, not so much as a flinch in response to my outburst. He bows his head, as if he'd interrupted my morning coffee, not me on the brink of making love to my fiancée.

"His Majesty has requested your presence at Lamberside. Immediately."

My jaw ticks, hand clenching into a fist as I fight against a tremor.

"Captain Lawson is waiting with the car, sir."

I have an overwhelming urge to tell Bridge I'm not going. Perhaps if I were still a defiant teenager and college student, I might. But in a few years, I'll be king. I need to start acting like it.

"Fine," I huff, not hiding my irritation. "Give me a few minutes and I'll be right down."

"Of course." With another bow, he spins, striding purposefully down the hallway.

I close the door behind him, staring at it for several long seconds, cursing under my breath.

"You have to go," Nora comments. It's neither a question nor a statement, but some ambivalent remark in between.

I exhale as I slowly face her. "I'm sorry, love." I walk to the bed and lower myself onto the corner. "Trust me when I say going to the palace is the absolute last thing I want to do today. I'd much rather spend it in bed with you."

Raising herself to sitting, she bends toward me. "I'll take a rain check."

When her lips graze mine, a current runs through me. Which only increases my frustration.

"This isn't how I pictured your first day here. I thought I'd have time to ease you into things."

"I think we both saw this going differently." She gives me a pointed look. "But it's important you go address our…situation." Her expression turns playful. "You can't tell the king to… What was it you said? Bugger off?"

With a slight chuckle, I bury my head into her neck and inhale her scent. "I'll be back as soon as I can." I meet her gaze. "It's a gorgeous day, so relax. Lounge by the pool. Meditate in the gardens. Whatever you'd like. Try not to fall asleep, or you'll never get used to the time difference. If you need anything, let Richard, the butler, know. Food. Supplies. Anything. They'll get it for you. And when I come back…" I waggle my brows, hovering over her once more, my lips skimming hers, "I plan to pick up right where we left off." I run my hand up her leg, squeezing her thigh.

"Well then," she begins in a breathy voice, "don't be gone long."

After treating her to one last kiss, I stand, grabbing my tie and jacket off the floor. I pull it on, making quick work of redoing my tie, something I can do blindfolded at this point.

As I reach the door, I pause, glancing over my shoulder at her. "I love you."

She smiles that smile that both broke my heart and put it all back together when I first saw her. "And I love you."

I hold her gaze for a beat, then walk out of my private quarters and toward the uncertainty of my future.

Seven

Anderson

The halls of the palace are silent as I follow my father's principal private secretary, Colonel Frederick Winters, toward wherever I'm to speak with him. I'd expected him to lead me toward the private residence, thinking this a personal matter between father and son.

I should have known better. After all, as people have reminded me most of my life, there are no personal matters anymore. All personal matters are also matters of the state, considering I'll one day be the sovereign.

We finally come to a stop outside a heavy, wooden door leading to the conference room in the monarch's executive suite. Colonel Winters knocks once, then opens the door.

"His Royal Highness Prince Gabriel," he announces, then steps aside to allow me to walk into the room.

I wasn't sure what would await me, but as I glance around the large conference table to see not only my father, but also my grandmother, the queen mother, as well as the head of the royal household, Dalton Peel, I know this is a bigger deal than I'd anticipated.

"Your Majesty," I say to my father with a bow, then offer my grandmother the same courtesy, even if it's not technically required. She was once queen. Even though her husband, my grandfather, passed away years ago and the requirement to bow ended with him, it's still protocol to show her the respect she deserves after her years of service to the country.

"Take a seat, Gabriel." My father gestures to the chair at the opposite end of the table from where he, my grandmother, and Dalton sit.

I almost want to remain standing just to maintain some semblance of control in this conversation. I know better than that, though. I've been *trained* better than that. If my father sits, everyone else should, as well. If he stands, everyone must follow. At least in more formal meetings, which I'm quickly realizing this is.

I unbutton my suit jacket as I lower myself to the chair, keeping my back straight. "I apologize for the fact you found out about the engagement this way. If you'll look at your calendar for tomorrow, you'll see I'd requested to speak to you. I'd planned to ask for your approval to marry Ms. Tremblay then. I fully intended to follow protocol."

He studies me, seeming to assess my words for a prolonged moment. His dark hair sports a bit more gray than the last time I saw him, but the combination of his stoic features and tall frame gives him an intimidating presence. There used to be a time I saw the man who gave me life whenever I looked at him.

It didn't take long for that to change.

The minute he walked down the aisle of the National Cathedral and was anointed with holy water in our most hallowed of ceremonies, his family was no longer his priority. His country was. The monarchy was. Since then, every single one of his decisions has been focused on what's best for the monarchy.

Nothing else.

Apart from being the heirs, Esme and I no longer mattered to him. We were no longer viewed as human beings in need of a father's love, but as a necessary commodity to keep the monarchy going. There are times I still feel that way, despite any breakthroughs to mend our relationship my father and I may have had over the years.

Like when he learned I was considering removing myself from the line of succession upon being diagnosed with MS. He convinced me I didn't have to. That I could use my diagnosis to bring attention to the disease. That I could still be an effective leader.

It was one of those rare moments he acted like my father, not the king.

But I haven't seen that human side of him since.

And I certainly don't see it now, especially when he's in the presence of the head of the royal household who, for all intents and purposes, is one of the people who makes the real decisions. My father may not see it, but I do. He's just one piece on a giant chess board, and the members of the royal household are the chess masters moving us around as they see fit in search of victory.

"I appreciate your candor, Gabriel," he begins. "I didn't realize things between you and this American—"

"Nora," I correct him. "She has a name. And it's Nora. I'd appreciate it if you used it." I look from him to Dalton on his right, then my grandmother to his left. "All of you."

My father doesn't respond for several moments. He simply stares at me, as if waiting for Dalton to give him permission to move one square or remain where he is. Finally, he nods. "Nora. I didn't realize things between you and Nora were serious."

"How could you when you never seem to show much interest in my life?" I snip back. "Apart from how it relates to the monarchy."

"Gabriel, darling," my grandmother interjects in a formal, well-practiced tone evidencing her noble upbringing.

I look in her direction, her demeanor as cold and aloof as I've always remembered. Sure, on the outside, she's beautiful, her short, straight, silver hair, piercing, gray eyes, and tall, slender frame repeatedly earning her a place on a popular magazine's list of the most beautiful women over fifty. But her inner beauty could use some work.

"What your father's trying to say is he believed her to be more of a…dalliance," she finishes with a trite smile.

I arch a brow. "A dalliance?"

"Can you blame him?" She narrows her gaze on me. "Up until a year ago, that seemed to be your M.O., so to speak. We had no reason to believe this woman was anything more than another distraction while you sorted through the stress of your diagnosis. We assumed once you got it all out of your system, you'd return and marry someone more…" She trails off, searching for the correct word.

"More what?" I grind out.

This conversation isn't helping to keep my stress level to a minimum, as my doctors have advised. Heat courses through my veins. And not out of desire like mere minutes ago when I was alone with Nora. Instead, it's out of a rage desperate to be unleashed. But I can't do that. I know the rules. Worse, I know the ramifications of showing too much emotion. In this life, emotions are a weakness to be used against you. I have no doubt they'll use the way I feel about Nora against me.

They'll use *Nora* against me.

"Someone more appropriate," Dalton Peel interjects without hesitation.

"If you ask me, there's no one more appropriate to marry than the woman I love."

"This isn't about love, Gabriel," my grandmother states dismissively, waving a bony hand through the air.

"Not about love? How can marriage *not* be about love?"

"For most people, it is. But I don't need to remind you that we're not most people. *You're* not most people. You're the heir apparent. The future king. And you have a duty to produce the next heir to the throne. You can't do so with some American we know nothing about. Especially with the referendum on the ballot this November. And unlike the previous occasions a constitutional amendment to severely limit the powers of the monarchy has made it onto the ballot, it has quite a lot of support this time. If we make one wrong step, we risk it passing, essentially turning the monarch into more a figurehead than an actual leader. And this…" She leans toward me, eyes like ice. "This is a serious misstep, Gabriel."

I grip the arms of the chair, needing it to keep me grounded when I'm ready to lash out at every single person in this room. "*You* got to marry for love," I remind my father.

"He was never supposed to be king," my grandmother points out. As if I need the reminder that my life was once normal. That I once had two parents who loved me and my sister. That I once had all the opportunity in the world.

Not anymore.

People are under the impression we lead a charmed life, because that's what we want them to believe. What we're taught to make them believe. In reality, we're prisoners. Our cage may be gilded, but it's still a cage.

"And look what happened. Your mother was too weak to handle the stress of this life. She very well could have destroyed everything we've built for centuries. Over the decades, there's been increasing sentiment that the monarchy is an antiquated notion. All it will take is enough people to show up on election day who share those sentiments for this all to disappear. We cannot have that. We cannot have the king married to someone weak."

I glance at my father, seeing his own jaw tighten as he seems to hold back what he wants to say in defense of his wife. But he won't. And not because he doesn't want to be disrespectful toward his mother, but because he's been trained.

Thankfully, I haven't been around this life long enough to have all my humanity erased.

"That woman was my mother. And if my wife ends up being half the queen she was, even in her short time at my father's side before her untimely death, I'd consider myself blessed."

"There are a number of respectful women you could marry, Gabriel," she insists. "Especially Caroline DeVries. She's a much better option, in my opinion. From a good family. A *noble* family. Most of the country assumed you'd eventually marry anyway."

"We've already prepared a response," Dalton interjects, extending a file folder toward me. "The king will offer his congratulations, but remain tight-lipped about any forthcoming approval of the marriage. After a few weeks have passed, we'll announce your engagement to Ms. Tremblay has ended. That she wasn't prepared to give up everything she'd have to in order to stay in this life, including her American citizenship. You'll act heartbroken for a while, but we'll stage some photographs of Ms. DeVries comforting you. You'll rekindle your relationship."

"We didn't have a relationship," I retort, my eyes flaming. I glance at my grandmother, giving her a smug grin. "It was more of a...dalliance."

"After sufficient time has passed...," Dalton continues, ignoring my previous comment, "His Majesty will announce your engagement to Ms. DeVries, preferably by November. Before the referendum goes to a vote. The publicity team feels that would have the greatest impact on swaying voters. After all, people love a wedding. Especially a royal wedding."

I can't believe what I'm looking at, but here it is in

black and white. A plan for me to marry a woman I'm not in love with, all because these people think she'll be a better fit.

"As you can see in the report, Ms. DeVries is in optimal health. And is fertile."

I fight to swallow down the bile rising to my throat. "Fertile?"

Is this actually happening? Am I really listening to my father's chief advisor detailing Caroline's ability to conceive a child? How do they even know this information?

This is too similar to the discussions I've had with Esme about some of the horses she's trained that she decided to put out to stud. Is this all we are, too? Something bred with another carefully selected specimen in the hopes of producing offspring that will be at the top of his or her game?

I know the answer to that.

I've always known the answer to that.

"She'll be able to provide you with an heir without complications," Dalton clarifies, as if this is a normal conversation. "We don't know anything about this American."

"*Nora*," I hiss.

"Nora," he corrects, but shows no hint of an apology. "We have no way of knowing whether she can produce an heir."

"She can," I argue.

"Right now," he adds. "I'm well aware of her… history. How she lost her first pregnancy."

"Ember."

"Excuse me?" my grandmother asks.

I pin her with a glare, not caring about decorum or protocol. "Her daughter's name was Ember. She didn't just *lose* her first pregnancy. She went through labor and gave birth, all the while knowing that when her baby was born, she wouldn't have a heartbeat."

"Which is precisely why you should reconsider this course of action," she responds flippantly, her pointed nose upturned. "You don't know if she's still able to conceive after that...trauma." She says the word like it leaves a sour taste in her mouth. She's one of the few people who knows precisely what trauma Nora endured that caused her to lose Ember.

And Hunter.

"She's fine," I insist once more.

"You don't know that. What happens if, by some miracle, this wedding *does* happen and you find yourself saddled with a wife who can't provide you the one thing she's under an obligation to — an heir?"

The longer I sit here and listen to my grandmother speak about Nora as if her only value to me is as a womb, the more my temper rises. The more my hand twitches. The fewer fucks I give about the consequences of my actions.

"You're already well past the age most royals marry. When I was your age, I'd already had five children. But you're not even married. Your uncle was married at twenty-two. Had his first heir at twenty-three. You're nearing forty, for crying out loud. All the more reason to give serious consideration to Caroline DeVries. She's a respectable girl we know can produce an heir. There's a real possibility Ms. Tremblay may never be able to give you an heir, as is required of your wife. She—"

"*Nora's already pregnant!*" I bellow, fists clenching, chest heaving.

The room falls eerily silent.

Eight

Anderson

"What did you say?" my grandmother asks, still the picture of grace and refinement. No matter how angry she may be on the inside, her composure never wavers.

Shit. Shit. Shit.

I shouldn't have allowed my emotions to overpower my rationale. Shouldn't have lost my cool. And I certainly shouldn't have shared that piece of information.

I look away from her and toward the only person in this room who can remotely be considered an ally — my father.

"Nora's pregnant. I'm going to be a father."

"And you're certain the baby is yours?" Dalton asks. "Have you had a paternity test conducted?"

I glower at him, my lip curling in the corner. "Why would I need that?"

"With all due respect, sir, we don't know anything about this woman. She could simply be after your money.

The pregnancy could be a trap. She may not even be pregnant."

Placing my hands on the table, I lean across it, fire in my eyes. "I will not have you talking about my fiancée and your future queen that way," I grind out. I almost *want* him to argue with me on this point. "Not to mention the mother of your future king or queen, as well."

"Not necessarily," he counters.

"Why? Because you think you can sit here and dictate who I can and can't marry? I'm sorry to tell you, but I don't give a damn what you think. I—"

"As it stands," he interrupts, tone icy, his small, dark eyes trained on me in superiority, "even if she *is* pregnant with your child, he or she will not be considered a full heir with rights of succession unless you're married when the baby is born. And the marriage is one approved by the sovereign." He looks at my father.

While Dalton's opinion on the matter is clear, based on the disgust covering his expression, my father's isn't. I can sense his turmoil.

Feel his humanity.

So that's what I need to appeal to. His human side. His *reasonable* side.

"Would you really withhold your approval of my marriage to the woman I love and would do anything for, a woman who's currently carrying your grandchild, because some *advisor* told you to? You're the king, Father. You make the decisions."

He peers at me, torn. As king, he needs to act according to what's best for his country and the monarchy. Right now, that appears to conflict with his role as my father, who should support his son when he's finally found the woman he wants to spend the rest of his life with.

"You've really dug yourself into a hole here," he exhales, breaking the silence.

"I just want to marry the woman of my dreams. Like you were able to."

"That was before anyone thought I'd be king. I wasn't under an obligation to get the monarch's approval because I'd already been pushed down to sixth in line by that time. It's different with you. You *are* the heir apparent. Whom you decide to marry holds a great deal of weight on how people will view the strength of the monarchy."

"And how will it make the monarchy look if people find out I'm forbidden from marrying the woman carrying my child?" I look from him to my grandmother. "I've always remembered my place, stayed quiet about a lot." I return my attention to my father. "But if you allow this to happen, I will not stay quiet about it. You can be damn certain about that."

He pinches the bridge of his nose, the stress of this situation wearing on him. When he looks at me again, his gaze goes to my hand. I follow his line of sight, noticing the tremors.

"I thought you were doing better."

I shake out my hand. "I was."

"You were?"

"Am," I correct. "I am. It's fine. Probably just jet lag."

He studies me for a protracted beat, then sighs. "I won't withhold my approval."

I exhale a huge breath of relief. "Thank you. I—"

"Your Majesty," Dalton interjects, eyes frantic. "You've

seen the reports from the polling the publicity team did. Those numbers don't—"

My father holds up his hand, cutting him off. Dalton quickly falls silent, but it's obvious it kills him to do so, to know the king is no longer following his advice. At least not on this matter.

"I have complete control over my approval," he says, giving Dalton a pointed stare before looking back at me. "But I can't do anything about the law of succession. For your child to be an heir, to be considered part of the royal family, he or she cannot be illegitimate."

"What is this? The bloody 1950s? People have babies all the time without being married."

"The rules on who can and can't ascend to the throne are clear. Granted, they were put in place because some of our ancestors seemed to think it a competition to see how many women they could impregnate."

"That was centuries ago. Times change."

"Yes. But the purpose for it is still valid. To—"

"I know. I know. Protect the monarchy." I run a hand over my face.

It's amazing how I could go from being on cloud nine when I asked Nora to marry me a week ago to being absolutely miserable. A part of me wishes I'd never come home. But I couldn't just ignore my duty, especially with the referendum on the ballot. The people need to be reminded of exactly what they're voting for — having me as their king in a few years when my father voluntarily abdicates, as is the tradition.

"And if we decide we don't care about the baby being a full heir?" I ask. "If we don't want to be rushed to marry before he or she is born?"

"If that's—" my father begins, but Dalton places his hand on his arm, stopping him.

"There's also the Royal Marriages Act to consider."

"All that says is I need the monarch's approval prior to marrying."

"Essentially, yes. But if you recall your schooling, you'll remember it also sets forth restrictions on this grant of approval. The Royal Marriages Act forbids the king from approving a marriage between an heir to the throne and someone of…loose morals."

"Loose morals?" I couldn't have heard him right. This must be some sort of alternative universe. That's the only possible explanation for what's going on right now. "What does that even mean?"

"According to the act, that includes but isn't limited to prostitutes, habitual drug users, and women who bear a child outside of wedlock."

"You do realize it's the goddamn twenty-first century, right?" I seethe. "Someone choosing to have a child outside of wedlock isn't evidence of *loose morals*. It's a personal decision."

"May I ask how far along Nora is in her pregnancy?" my grandmother inquires.

"Six weeks."

She nods, keeping her shoulders square.

"There are…options," Dalton says after a beat.

"Options?"

"We can still fix this situation."

"Fix?" I struggle to say, knowing all too well what he's suggesting.

"It's still early on in the pregnancy. There's still time to…" He waves a hand, "make it go away. I believe that's better for all involved, given the referendum vote."

It takes every ounce of self-control I have to not fly across this table and land a hard blow to his face. I find it ironic they'll forbid me from marrying Nora if she's already given birth to my child, but they'll sit here and suggest I do something unthinkable.

Hypocrisy at its finest.

"It doesn't help you haven't been in the picture much lately, sir," he continues. "People are already concerned about your…condition."

"Condition?"

"Yes. They remember how quickly your mother died from MS—"

"That was because she didn't get the help she needed and took her own life, a detail you've all conveniently kept out of the media."

"Nevertheless, all that matters right now is that the monarchy is in jeopardy. The referendum didn't have much support until you broke protocol and granted an interview to some American magazine. Now, all the people of this country see are the king approaching retirement age and an heir who may not be able to fulfill his obligations. So you need to do everything possible to reinstill their confidence in you. Based on early polling, this leaked engagement…to an American, no less…certainly isn't doing that."

"But a royal wedding may just distract them," my father interjects softly.

Dalton whips his head toward him. "Excuse me?"

My father smiles slyly. "You said it yourself when you shared your plan regarding Ms. DeVries. You claimed people love a wedding, especially a royal wedding. That it gives them something to be a part of. We saw how wrapped up the people of this country were during the latest British royal wedding. They filled stadiums to celebrate it. And *he* married an American, too. If you're so concerned about this referendum, perhaps that's an alternative to your...proposal."

"What is?" I ask.

My father faces me. "That you marry Nora before people go to the polls this November. Preferably before she starts to show."

"Before she starts to show?"

"She's six weeks now. I'd suggest marrying her within the next eight weeks at most. We must consider the public perception. The longer you wait to marry her, the more obvious the reason you *are* marrying her will become."

"I'm marrying her because I love her. Her pregnancy is just an unexpected blessing. Nothing else."

"That's not the way people will see it. If they learn she's pregnant before you're married, they'll think that's the reason."

"Won't people get suspicious anyway?" I argue. "Particularly if we announce we're getting married in a matter of weeks? When the baby is born, they're bound to do the math."

"But by that point, the vote will have already passed and they'll be too excited about the birth of a royal baby."

I blink repeatedly, looking into the distance. Heavy drapes frame the tall windows, portraits of important figures in Belmont history hanging on the walls, as if a reminder of my place in this world.

But what about Nora? This is a completely new world for her. We've discussed taking the next year to adjust to our new life together and being new parents. Now we don't have a choice but to rush into marriage just to be together.

"Listen, Anderson," my father says, turning from the king into my father. "I can give you my approval, and I do so happily. But the second your child is born, I can no longer grant you that approval. If you wait to marry until she's given birth, you'll be doing so in direct violation of a royal act. Which will—"

"Automatically remove me from the line of succession."

"Precisely."

A year ago, I had every intention of giving up my place in the line of succession just to prevent my father from forcing me out, as I'd assumed he did to my mother after she was diagnosed with MS.

Now I know that wasn't the case, that the depression she experienced after her diagnosis made her push everyone away. I tried to do the same thing, but Esme wouldn't let me.

More so, my father wouldn't, either.

Now I'm actually looking forward to the day I'll lead this country. Can bring it and the monarchy into the twenty-first century. Can give it the breath of fresh air it needs.

But at what cost to Nora?

"I can't make this decision without talking to her," I

tell him. "This life is all new to her. The media circus. The spotlight."

He nods, standing. I do the same. "I can hold off on making a statement to the press for a day or two. That should give you enough time to discuss this with her."

"In the meantime," Dalton begins, rising to his feet, as well, "if anyone asks about your status, you tell them—"

"I know. I know. No comment." I force a smile.

"Precisely."

I turn my attention toward my grandmother. She's remained unusually quiet throughout most of this conversation. As I learned from playing chess with her, her being silent is never a good thing. Those long stretches of time when she simply stared at the chess board, mentally playing out all her moves, usually led to her declaring a rather embarrassing victory.

I hope the same isn't true here.

I bow toward her. "Your Majesty." Then I face my father, offering him the same sign of respect, before retreating from the conference room.

My father's private secretary greets me the second I step into the foyer. He bows toward me, then spins, leading me away from the executive wing, as if I'm a visitor, not someone who spent his adolescent years in this building.

Once I'm back in the SUV and the imposing palace walls are far behind me, Creed meets my eyes in the rearview mirror. "How did it go?"

I give him a knowing look as I roll my eyes.

"That good?"

I blow out a laugh. "Worse."

"No matter what, Nora's a strong woman. She'll be okay."

I nod, leaning my head back against the seat, praying he's right. Sure, I'd told her what life would be like as my wife, the things she'd have to give up.

But that was before she saw it for herself.

Before she experienced it for herself.

Will she still want this? Want to be under a microscope for the rest of her life?

Like she told me earlier today, she wasn't thrust into this life like I was. She chose it.

But now that she's had a taste, will she still choose it?

Will she still choose me?

Nine

Nora

I rest my forearms against the railing of the spacious balcony off Anderson's private quarters, inhaling the fresh air, hoping it helps me stay awake when I'd love nothing more than to fall asleep. I doubt I'd be able to sleep, though. My mind is far too preoccupied with what could be going on at Anderson's meeting with his father.

I doubt they're talking about the latest rugby match or polo game. Or whatever it is royal people from Europe discuss.

They're talking about me. About whether I'm good enough for Anderson. Whether I'm good enough to be his wife.

To one day be queen.

Years of being made to feel inadequate by my mother bubble to the surface. I fight to push down her biting reminders that I'm *not* good enough. That I'm a failure. That I'll never amount to anything.

I close my eyes, practicing my breathing, inhaling only

positive energy while pushing out all the negativity.

Or at least try to.

It doesn't work as well as it once did.

Right now, there's a lot of negativity in my life.

A pair of warm lips against my shoulder blade takes me by surprise. In a heartbeat, I no longer need my breathing exercises to relax, my body succumbing to Anderson's soothing caress.

There was once a time when meditating and yoga were the only way I could find peace and quiet my mind.

Now it's Anderson.

His touch is all I need to erase my worry. As long as he's here, everything else is just noise.

Tranquility encompasses me as he runs his hands down my arms, then pulls my body into his, my back to his front. I don't ask how his meeting went. Don't want to ruin this moment. Instead, I bask in the love radiating from his embrace as we peer at the breathtaking view of the magnificent gardens leading to jagged cliffs, miles of ocean stretching out below them. It's reminiscent of Hawaii…if Hawaii had more of a European flair.

I wonder if this is what the French Riviera is like. Or the Amalfi Coast. Two places Anderson said we'd visit at some point.

Will we still have that chance?

Or is everything about to be ripped from under us?

"Want to go for a walk?" Anderson eventually asks.

When I turn around, he drops his hold, and I peer into his eyes for the first time since he arrived home. In that one look, I can tell things didn't go as he'd hoped.

"Is this a good walk, or a bad walk?"

He smiles and reaches for my hand, our fingers interlocking. "That all depends on you."

"Okay." I force a smile. "Let's go for a walk."

He leads me back into the bedroom, through the living area, and out into the hallway. Neither of us says a single word as we walk through his estate, any staff we encounter bowing or curtseying as we pass. I've only been here a few hours, but knowing I'm constantly being watched already suffocates me.

As if Anderson can sense my discomfort, he quickens his pace to the double doors leading to the gardens. Once we step outside, I inhale a deep breath, the chains seeming to cut off my oxygen falling away. I steal a glance at Anderson, his own expression similar to mine.

"This way," he murmurs.

Hand in hand, we stroll along the flower-lined paths. The sweet aroma fills me, making me forget everything, even if for only a minute.

As we near the edge of his property, the breeze picks up, blowing my hair in front of my face. He leads me to a bench and gestures for me to sit. Then he joins me, his gaze focused on the sparkling ocean sprawled out before us. The sun setting on the horizon casts a peaceful glow over our surroundings.

When Anderson gave me a tour of the estate and grounds earlier, he'd remarked that this was the place he often went if he needed to clear his mind. I can see why. The crashing waves of the ocean below coupled with the lush greenery around us is a sight to behold. Makes you forget that only a few hundred yards away sits a building that's more a prison than a place to call home. At least that's the feeling I get when inside its walls.

But out here, I feel…free.

And by the look of serenity on Anderson's expression, I assume he does, too.

"This world is vastly different from what you're used to," he says after a protracted pause.

It's not a question. So I don't respond, granting him this opportunity to sort out his own thoughts.

"And not just the different electrical outlets and the side of the road we drive on," he adds, his voice lightening momentarily. "But *my* world is different from yours." He shifts his gaze toward mine, the glow from the sunset reflecting in his vibrant blue eyes.

"Truthfully, there's a lot I've kept from you. Not because I didn't want you to know, but because I didn't want you to think I don't appreciate the opportunity I have. That I take my position for granted. I don't. I'm grateful to be in a position where I can potentially make a difference in people's lives, as cliché and idealistic as that sounds." His lips press together into a tight smile. Then he turns his eyes forward once more.

"Unfortunately, this world sometimes has its drawbacks. Our lives are under a microscope on a daily basis. People dig deep for any hint of vulnerability or weakness that can be exploited. And that's especially true now with the referendum on the ballot."

I scrunch my brows. "Referendum?"

"It happens occasionally. A referendum to amend the Constitution to either severely limit the monarch's power or abolish the monarchy altogether in favor of a true parliamentary government gains enough support to go to the voters on election day."

"If it's a monarchy, people still get to vote?" I ask, wishing I'd done a little more research on how this form of government functioned.

"In a constitutional monarchy, the king is akin to your president, with the Executive Council having powers similar to that of your Cabinet, all of whom are elected by the people. That's simply the executive branch. Like you, we also have a legislative and judicial branch. The judicial branch is appointed by the Executive Council, with the monarch's approval. And the legislative branch is a unicameral house of elected representatives. Each branch functions much like you're accustomed to. The legislative makes the laws. The executive carries out and enforces the laws, with a limited power to enact certain orders, as well. And the judicial branch adjudicates any disagreements regarding laws that have been passed."

"So you're telling me I should have paid more attention during my World Political Systems class in college."

"Probably not a bad idea." He chuckles, his eyes lighting up in amusement. It only lasts a second, but I'll take what I can get. "As I was saying, there's a referendum on the ballot to limit the monarch's power. We'd still be a constitutional monarchy, but if it passes, the bulk of the executive power will now be placed in a prime minister elected by the people, the monarch only retaining certain limited powers, much like is currently in place in the U.K. This country is one of the last remaining true constitutional monarchies where the monarch still retains quite a bit of executive power. I think it's partly because of an unspoken rule that when a monarch reaches the age of sixty-five, he or she will voluntarily abdicate.

"Because of all of this, every decision must be carefully weighed, all the potential public relations issues evaluated in terms of how it will affect the monarchy. How it will affect the referendum vote." He glances at me. "Even decisions of a more…personal nature."

I lower my eyes, fidgeting with the hem of my skirt, an unsettling premonition forming in the pit of my stomach that this constitutional referendum is about to wreak havoc on our lives. That the leak of our engagement isn't helping matters.

"Your father doesn't like the idea of us getting married."

"He was more surprised by it than anything. He didn't think we were as serious as we are." He sighs, rubbing the back of his neck. "He'd have no reason to, I suppose. I don't have the kind of relationship with him where I share what's going on in my personal life. Most of his updates about me come from his private secretary. It was my grandmother and the head of household, Dalton Peel, who were quite opposed. Particularly the head of household."

"Head of household?" I blink, confused. "Like the main butler or something?"

"No. The head of household is similar to what you know as your president's chief of staff. He's essentially in charge of the entire royal household, which basically means he's in charge of the entire monarchy. He's the only person on the Executive Council who isn't elected, but appointed by the king. And he's also my father's most senior member of his Privy Council."

"And what's the Privy Council?"

"An advisory committee to the monarch. Whereas the Executive Council offers the king advice on matters of state, the Privy Council advises the monarch on matters of, well, the monarchy. Our history. Our traditions. Our public image."

I take a minute to process this new information, my brain on the verge of exploding. Now I really wish I'd learned more about this concept of government. At least that would have given me a foot up, so to speak.

"So your grandmother and your father's most trusted advisor are against us." I glance at Anderson. "Isn't it the king's decision to grant us permission to marry?"

"Technically, yes. But in all matters relating to the monarchy, the king listens to his Privy Council's advice, as well as the advice of certain members of the royal household."

"Like your grandmother?"

"Yes, although she's more accurately a member of the royal family."

I dig my fingers through my hair, pulling at it. "You do realize how confusing this all sounds, right? Especially to an outsider?"

"I'm sorry I didn't bring you up to speed on this ahead of time. *I* still occasionally get confused about how everything works, so I can only imagine how you must feel. Simplest explanation… The royal family includes the people in the line of succession, as well as certain people who were formerly married to a deceased monarch, like my grandmother. The royal household includes everyone who works behind the scenes to make the royal family look good — Privy Council members, private secretaries, publi-cists. In reality, they're the ones who keep the monarchy alive and going. The ones who make a lot of the decisions. Imagine this life is a chess board… The members of the royal family are the game pieces, the royal household are the chess masters."

"I see…" I stare forward, the last bit of daylight slowly disappearing beyond the horizon. "And these so-called chess masters would prefer if I weren't part of the game."

"I'm not going to keep anything from you, Nora."

His firm tone forces my gaze back to his. I survey his appearance…muscles taut, jaw clenched.

"You may not like some of the things I'm about to tell you. I didn't like hearing them earlier. But there are quite a few people in the royal household and royal family who do not support us as a couple. Who think I should marry someone more 'appropriate'. Someone who's been around this life, who grew up in it."

"So this is your way of letting me down easy," I reply in a shaky voice, running my clammy hands along my dress. "Tell me your father won't give his approval."

"Actually, no."

I tilt my head. "No?"

"Getting the monarch's permission is more of a formality. Not to mention, it would look bad if he were to publicly denounce our engagement after it made headlines."

"If he approves, then—"

"I told them about the pregnancy."

"Oh." I shrink into myself, hugging my arms around my body as a sudden chill overtakes me.

He blows out a frustrated laugh, rubbing the back of his neck. "It wasn't my intention. But Dalton and my grandmother kept going on and on about Caroline being able to conceive a child and not knowing whether you were able to—"

"What a second." I furrow my brow, recalling a few reporters shouting that name earlier. "Who's Caroline?"

He smiles sadly. "Caroline DeVries. After Kendall died, we had a…thing. Nothing emotional. Purely physical. She was someone who could help me forget." He turns his gaze in my direction, mouth quirking into a sheepish smile. "I'm sorry."

I rest my hand over his and squeeze. "I did the same thing after Hunter. It's how I ended up marrying Jeremy. He helped me forget."

"We tried to keep whatever we had going on under wraps, but the paparazzi found us together on the French Riviera and the photos went viral. Since then, the entire country assumed we'd eventually get married. Saw her as someone who helped heal my broken heart, even though neither of us were interested in anything serious. We had an arrangement we'd hoped to keep quiet.

"As a royal, if you go public with a relationship — hell, if you're frequently seen in public together with the same person — you'd better be ready to announce your wedding date. We went our separate ways roughly three years ago, right after the photos were leaked. But that didn't stop the rumors from circulating, especially whenever we were photographed together at an event we both just happened to be at." He brings his gaze back to mine as he clutches my hands in his. "I'm sorry I didn't tell you about her sooner. I just—"

"I do know you've been with women before me, Anders. You have nothing to apologize for. As long as you haven't been with anyone since we got together, that's all I care about."

"And I haven't." He cups my cheek. "How could I be with someone when you're the only woman who possesses my heart?"

On a sigh, I angle toward him, my lips seeking his. He tugs me closer, his fingers digging into my hair. A part of me wants to crawl on top of him so we can continue what we started earlier. But we need to finish this conversation. Not remain blissfully ignorant of it, like we've spent the past several months of our relationship.

When Anderson brings our kiss to an end, I straighten, smiling sadly at him. "I imagine nobody bent over backwards to offer their congratulations when they heard about the pregnancy."

"That may be the understatement of the century," he scoffs with a roll of his eyes. "They brought up a few things I absolutely will not repeat to you because their suggestions aren't even an option to me."

"What did they propose?"

He gives me a grave look, and I know precisely what he's referring to. A chill washes down my spine.

"Oh."

"I refused. Told them that to even suggest such a thing was an insult to me and the child who would eventually become their king or queen." He places his hand over my stomach.

I grit out a smile, pretending to have the same enthusiasm over the pregnancy as Anderson seems to. I'm trying so hard to be excited, but I still live with the fear of something going wrong.

Still remember enduring over twenty hours of labor, knowing full well I wouldn't be greeted with a crying baby.

Wouldn't peer into her vibrant eyes and marvel at this human I created.

Wouldn't bask in her tiny hands wrapping around my finger.

Instead, all I had was mere minutes to hold her lifeless body before she was taken from me.

I am absolutely petrified of going through that again.

"Which was when I was reminded about the laws of succession. And illegitimacy."

"Illegitimacy?"

He slowly nods. "If our child is born outside of wedlock, he or she won't be considered an heir. Won't be considered part of the royal family. Won't ascend to the crown."

"So we'll need to marry before he or she is born."

"Not just before the birth. They want us to marry before, well... Before it's obvious. My father suggested within the next eight weeks."

"*Eight weeks*? It won't take a genius to figure it out. Especially once the baby is born. All it will take is some simple math."

"I said the same thing. But he believes people will be so distracted by the wedding, then the pregnancy announcement, that they'll be too excited to do the math. By the time the baby's born and anyone *does* stop to do the math, the referendum vote will be behind us."

"But eight weeks?" I protest once more. "Evie and Chloe are in their third trimester. They can't travel."

"I wish I had an answer, but I don't. This is the only way for our child to be considered an heir and part of the royal family."

I swallow past the lump in my throat, frustration heating my face. I knew whatever kept Anderson at the palace most of the afternoon wouldn't be happy news. I just didn't expect this. I thought we'd have more time. Would be able to acclimate ourselves to this life together in Belmont. Then as new parents. Then as a married couple. Thought I'd be able to have my friends by my side at my wedding to the man of my dreams.

That plan has disappeared in the blink of an eye.

"And if we don't agree to their proposal? If we still want to do things our way? Get married on our own schedule after the baby is born?"

"My father will be forced to rescind his approval."

"*What?*" I exclaim. "Why?"

"The Royal Marriages Act," he says with a shrug. "It automatically revokes any approval the king's given to an heir and a person of 'loose morals'."

"Loose morals? What the hell is this? Puritanical England?"

"It was written in the early eighteenth century in order to ensure only people of the highest standards marry into the royal family. Prevent scandal. Unfortunately, one of the examples written into the act is someone having a child outside of wedlock."

"Unbelievable." The chains around me tighten with every word Anderson speaks.

I haven't even been here a full day and can already say with unequivocal certainty that the fairy tales many little girls grow up obsessing over are a bunch of bullshit. A girl doesn't meet a prince and get to ride into the sunset without a care in the world. No. They must get the monarch's permission, which can be revoked at any time.

"And if you were to marry me without the king's approval?"

"I'd lose my place in the line of succession and would no longer be a member of the royal family."

"So the only way for you to be king and us to stay together is to marry soon."

"I'm afraid so."

I squeeze my eyes shut and draw in a deep breath. *Positive energy in. Negative energy out.*

I could exhale for the next hundred years and doubt I'd be able to expel all the negative energy in this place.

"Nora, listen to me," Anderson's urgent voice cuts through. I turn my eyes toward his. He takes my hands in his, clutching them tightly. "I'm not going to sit here and tell you what to do. Only you can decide if this is really what you want. But I want you to be aware of what you'll have to give up. Your privacy. Your anonymity. Your independence. It will all disappear, and you'll never be able to get it back. Right now, you can walk away. It will absolutely shatter me, but I won't be angry. I will completely understand. After everything you've been through, you deserve to be deliriously happy. Unfortunately, I don't have that same option. I can't walk away. As frustrated as I am at times with the politics at play, especially within the royal household, I still love this country and its people. I want to do right by them. I want to be their leader. But you don't have to sacrifice yourself for me."

I peer forward, watching as the ocean waves crash against the rocky shoreline in the distance. It reminds me of Manderley, the fictional estate from *Rebecca*. The stunning interior cared for by a silent staff. Gorgeous gardens that are home to a fragrant array of blooms. The mysterious ocean nearby where the title character sank to a watery grave.

Will our story end much like that of the unnamed narrator and Maxim DeWinter, who was driven from a home haunted by custom and protocol?

Or will we find our own happily ever after, despite all the forces working against us?

I bring my gaze back to Anderson, admiring his stoic profile. "Is it worth it?"

"I know my answer will probably surprise you, considering everything we're currently facing, but yes…" A subtle smile curves his mouth. "It's worth it. I've probably made this life sound horrible, but it's not all bad. I'm lucky to be blessed with an opportunity to do good. Not only in this country, but in the world. To bring attention to a variety of causes. Truthfully, the majority of the job is great."

"And the rest of it?"

He pushes out a breath. "It can be frustrating. And exhausting. As a royal, you're held to a higher standard. A more…moral standard, I suppose. My mother had this saying when we were kids, especially after my uncle and cousins died. Something she said to me whenever I complained about being in a London boarding school and missing my home and friends."

"What's that?"

"'With great power comes great purpose.'"

Sadness hints at the lines of his face as he recalls his mother. Or at least what he can remember of her after having lost her when he was only ten.

"I'd like to think I've lived most of my adult life according to that motto. That my family may possess a great deal of power in this country, but that we use it for good. For a purpose. And you can, too. But only if this is what you truly want."

He reaches into his pocket before extending his hand toward me, revealing a single penny in his palm.

"What do you say? Should we toss a coin to help you decide?" He narrows his gaze on me.

Nostalgia tugs on my heartstrings. After all, it was a coin toss that led me to join Anderson on our Route 66 adventure in the first place. But I didn't toss the coin so it would tell me what I should do. I did so because, while that coin was in the air, it helped me realize what I really wanted.

I stare at the penny in his outstretched hand, smiling at the memory of the cocky stranger who tried to impress me with his knowledge of the plot to steal Lincoln's body.

How I knew my life would never be the same from that moment.

How I knew I was at a crossroads of my life.

Just like I am now.

I lift my eyes to his, a dozen emotions swirling within his depths. "I'm not going to toss that coin, Anderson."

He briefly closes his eyes, his shoulders falling. "I

understand. I—"

"I don't need to."

He flings his gaze to mine.

"You're my true north." I rest my hand over his heart, the compass tattoo hidden beneath the fabric of his suit. "No matter the obstacles thrown our way, I will always come back to you."

His entire body goes slack as the tension rolls off him. He covers my hand with his, keeping it firmly on his chest.

"They can try to tear us apart all they want. But even when you try to smash a compass to pieces, do you know what happens?"

"It will still point north," he answers with a hint of a smile.

"It will still point north. No matter what happens in these next few weeks or months, you can be sure of one thing. That my heart will always bring me back to you."

His grip on my hand tightens as he presses his mouth to mine, pouring all the emotions he's experienced today into his kiss. Happiness. Worry. Despair. Desperation. Frustration. And love, which shines through above everything else. I have to believe this once-in-a-lifetime love we've found in each other will be enough for us to navigate the rough waters ahead.

When he pulls back, he's no longer the haunted, tortured man he was mere seconds ago. He's back to being the cocky, confident man I couldn't help but fall in love with.

"What do you say we finish what we started earlier?" He waggles his brows, leering at my chest as he lasciviously licks his lips.

"Why, Your Highness..." I bring my mouth back toward his. "That may be the best idea you've had all day."

Before I can utter a single syllable, Anderson jumps to his feet and scoops me into his arms. Laughter falls from my throat as he rushes me through the gardens and into the house, peppering kisses along my neck. My squeals of joy echo through the halls. I doubt anyone on the household staff has ever seen anything like this, considering their stunned expressions as we pass.

They'd better get used to it. Because I'm not going anywhere.

Ten

Anderson

I lower myself to the edge of the bed, pushing a few strands of Nora's hair behind her ear, admiring her as she sleeps. I need to wake her up, but hate the idea of disturbing her. Not when these few quiet seconds may be the last she has for the foreseeable future.

Today, life as she knows it will change.

As if it didn't change when she stepped off the plane yesterday and was bombarded by an angry mob who doesn't think she's good enough to marry their prince.

Now, in mere hours, my father will publicly announce his approval of our engagement, as well as our wedding in eight weeks.

Gone is the quiet life she once led. Her privacy…gone. Her independence…gone. Her ability to go to the local café for a coffee…gone.

From today forward, she will no longer be an unknown woman trying to make her way in the world. She'll become Crown Prince Gabriel of Belmont's fiancée.

The future crown princess and queen consort.

I still question whether I'm worthy enough of everything she's agreed to sacrifice for me — her home, her career, having her best friends at her side as she marries me. But I'll make every effort to prove I am.

As if sensing my eyes on her, she stirs, rolling onto her back and meeting my gaze.

"Do you like watching me sleep or something?" she asks, her voice lazy.

"I just like looking at you." I lower my lips to hers. "Can't believe I'm the lucky bastard who gets to do that every day for the rest of my life."

She moans into my kiss, her fingers raking through my hair. What I wouldn't give to spend all day with Nora in bed. But that's not our life anymore. It's a new world for us, and it starts today.

Reluctantly, I pull back.

"You're up early," she comments, trailing her fingers down my suit-clad chest. "And already dressed?"

"It's officially a workday for me. And *your* first day of work, too."

She briefly closes her eyes, drawing in a deep breath. "We're really doing this, aren't we?"

I blow out a nervous laugh. "Unless you've had a change of heart."

"Nah. I mean, maybe if you didn't make me come… What was it? Three times last night?"

"Actually, four."

She scrunches her brows. "Really?"

"I believe so." I count off on my fingers. "First there was in bed with my tongue."

"Right."

"Then when you rode me."

Her pupils dilate. "That was fucking intense."

"Bloody right it was." I chew on my lower lip, desire coiling in my stomach from the mere memory. "Then in the shower with my mouth again."

"Exactly. And that was the last one. So three."

I slowly shake my head. "Don't even try to deny it, love. I felt you go again when I took you from behind right after that."

"You just said it yourself. It was right after. So that very well could have been merely a continuation of the same orgasm. There must be a rule somewhere about how much time is required between orgasms to classify them as two separate events."

Barking out a chuckle, I grab her exposed nipple between my thumb and forefinger. "Perhaps, but I'm claiming four. We can always test your theory later. See what kind of lapse in time is required."

Her eyes flutter closed as her body warms under my touch. "I really like the sound of that."

"As do I." I cover her mouth with mine, continuing to tweak her nipple, and she whimpers into me. I deepen our kiss, my tongue swiping against hers for a moment before I pull back, dropping my hold on her and rising to my feet. "But for now, it's going to have to wait."

"Grrr…"

"Did you just…growl at me?"

She throws the covers off her body and stands. "Can you blame me? Yesterday afternoon, I was on the brink of a mind-blowing orgasm before you got called away. And now you're getting me all worked up again just to walk away without so much as a quickie before we have to endure a day full of press conferences and media appearances. Does that about sum it up?" She places her hands on her hips in feigned irritation, not caring one bit she's completely naked.

This is one of the many things I love about her. The way she's so at ease around me that she has absolutely no problem walking around our apartment in barely any clothes. Or at least our *old* apartment. I doubt she'll ever feel comfortable enough to do that here. Not with the risk of anyone stopping by at all hours of the day and night.

"Sounds about right." I hook an arm around her waist, pulling her to me. "But think how great tonight will be."

She tilts her head back and skims her lips against mine as she reaches for my crotch. "True, but think how amazing *right now* could be." She moves from my lips to my neck, nibbling along my earlobe. "It would be a real shame if I had to put one of my vibrators to use when I have a perfectly good fiancé. I'd hate to have to ask the butler if he has a charging adaptor for Mr. Rolls."

I pull back, brows furrowed. "Mr. Rolls?"

"Yeah. You know. The Rolls Royce of vibrators."

Eyes flaming, I yank her harder into me and press my arousal against her. "You little vixen. Do you feel what you do to me? A minute ago, I was completely limp. Now, I can't leave unless I relieve some of this…pressure."

"Is that right?"

Her sultry voice sends a thrill down my spine, my hunger for her increasing with every heartbeat.

"You know it is." I nip at her lower lip, eliciting a moan.

"Well, then…"

She pushes against me, freeing herself from my grasp. Swaying her hips, she walks over to the bed and gets on her hands and knees, facing away from me.

This woman constantly surprises me. When I don't think she could possibly do anything else to steal my breath and remind me how damn lucky I am to have her, she proves me wrong. And it's not because she's more than eager to have a quick romp before breakfast. It's because she trusts me enough to expose herself like this to me.

She glances over her shoulder, eyes dark with desire. "We don't want you suffering from a case of blue balls, do we?"

I hastily make my way toward her, only taking the time to discard my jacket before unzipping my pants and thrusting into her.

This isn't how I saw the start of my day going, but I'd be crazy to complain.

***

"Good morning, Your Highness," Richard greets me with a bow the second I sit down at the head of the table in the formal dining room. "Your usual breakfast and coffee?"

"Just coffee for now, Richard."

I do my best to keep my tone as professional and even as possible, despite the fact I'm struggling to catch my breath after the incredible sex I just had. I can only imagine how flushed my complexion must still be, how mussed up my hair is. But it was completely worth it. Anything to make Nora feel loved is worth it.

"Ms. Tremblay will be joining me shortly."

"Of course, sir." He nods, then spins, leaving through the server's door on the far side of the room.

I grab a copy of the *New York Times* from the table and unfold it as I glance around. A few members of the household staff are stationed in the corners of the room, as stoic and unmoving as statues, only coming to life when ordered to do so.

"Here you are, sir," Richard says, placing my coffee mug and saucer in front of me. "Is there anything else I can get for you right now?"

"I'll wait to order until Ms. Tremblay arrives."

"Certainly, sir." He bows and starts to leave.

"And Richard?"

"Yes?"

"Please inform Lieutenant Colonel Bridge to hold off on his morning briefing until Ms. Tremblay is here. Going forward, she'll need to be a part of them, since my schedule will also affect her."

He nods. "I'll make sure he gets the message."

"Thank you."

He bows once more, then retreats, leaving me to enjoy the last few moments of calm before the day becomes one engagement after another. As much as I should find some sort of familiarity in being in the same room I've begun each of my days while in residence here, it's lacking. The one thing that does bring me comfort is turning to the *New York Times*, like I did each morning in New York.

As does the smell of Nora still on my fingers whenever

I bring my coffee to my mouth.

While I wait for her to join me, I peruse the various national newspapers I request be delivered every morning. After nearly an hour, I begin to wonder if I should go check on her when the door to the dining room opens. I snap my head in that direction as Richard enters and stops past the entrance, body stiff, as if at attention.

When Nora steps in behind him, all the oxygen is ripped from my lungs, leaving me breathless, thoughtless…mindless. If I didn't know better, I'd think Grace Kelly herself came back from the dead and just sauntered into my dining room. It's remarkable how much Nora resembles her, apart from her hair having a bit more strawberry in it than the first American princess had.

She glides into the room, as if she's walking on air. As if she were made for this life. Even the few other attendants can't help but stare. I all but forget the manners that have been drilled into me, too stunned by how incredible she looks. It's not until she's within a few inches that I remember to stand to greet her. I brush my lips against her cheek, then step back, admiring the green-and-white floral dress that's slim through the waist, then flares in a style similar to what Grace Kelly once wore. And in typical Grace Kelly style, Nora completed the look with a simple strand of pearls around her neck and one in each ear.

"You look beautiful, Nora. Like a princess."

"Good." She laughs nervously. "Because I feel like an imposter."

I hold her face in my hands, my gaze unwavering. "You're only an imposter if you let them think you are.

And from where I'm standing, you're the real deal."

She gives me a smile as I help her into the chair kitty-corner to me. The second we're seated, Richard approaches.

"What would you like to drink this morning, my lady?"

Obviously taken aback at the way he addressed her, Nora stiffens before recovering, playing the part of my future queen with ease. "Decaf, please. Just a touch of cream and one stevia sweetener, if you have it."

"Of course, ma'am." He smiles, then looks toward me. "What would Your Highness like for breakfast this morning?"

I peer at Nora, silently asking her if she has any preference. Her expression is uneasy as she fidgets with her hands in her lap. She seems overwhelmed enough as it is, so I order for us.

"We'll both have two eggs, over easy, buttered toast, and fruit."

"Yes, sir." He bows, then retreats.

"It's going to take me a bit to get used to all of this," she comments under her breath once he's out of ear shot. "I'm used to being able to eat breakfast in just a t-shirt, my hair knotted in a messy bun."

I fold the newspaper and push it away, grabbing her hand in mine, giving it a squeeze. "And you're just as gorgeous in a t-shirt."

"You're only saying that because I wasn't wearing any pants in that scenario."

I pinch my lips into a tight line. "Perhaps." I waggle my brows as I lean toward her, sliding my hand up her thigh. "But you're not wearing any pants right now, either."

She playfully swats me away. "Fiend."

"Only for you."

Hearing a throat clear, I look up as Lieutenant Colonel Bridge walks up to the table. I'd love to tell him to wait until we've at least eaten, but this morning's…activities have already put us behind schedule.

"Your Highness." He bows, then turns toward Nora. "My lady." He meets my stare once more. "If you're agreeable, I think it's best if we go over today's agenda."

I nod, gesturing to the chair opposite Nora.

He unbuttons his suit jacket as he sits and sets his tablet on the surface in front of him, but his posture is still straight. "Today is a light day because of the announcement." He looks at Nora as Richard places her coffee in front of her. "Tomorrow will be rather hectic for you, my lady. Once you're announced as Prince Gabriel's fiancée, you'll be assigned your own private secretary to manage your daily calendar, which will be synched with Prince Gabriel's. You'll also have your own PR team to take care of any and all publicity. I'm sure His Highness has already advised you, but going forward, it's best if you restrict any of your social media time. In fact, your PR team will most likely advise you to close all your current accounts and start new ones, which they will manage on your behalf."

"But all my profiles are private. Only my friends can see what I post. I—"

"Once His Majesty announces his official approval, there will no longer be anything private about you. The public will want to know everything, and they'll dig wherever they need in order to get that."

I can sense Nora's nerves from a foot away. As if today isn't stressful enough for her. This is why I'd hoped to have a long engagement. Now we're essentially cramming for an exam, and Nora will be doing the bulk of the work.

"Don't worry about any of that," I tell her, her face already several shades paler than when she walked in here minutes ago. "It's all going to be okay."

I want to promise her she'll get used to it, but I'm not sure anyone ever does, even someone who's been around this most of his life.

"Why don't we focus on today?" I suggest to Bridge as Richard approaches with our plates and sets them down in front of us before silently retreating.

"Certainly." Nathan smiles politely.

The last thing I need is for my personal secretary to overwhelm Nora. I know what it's like to wake up in a strange bed and be told to dress in a suit for breakfast when I was used to wearing pajamas. Then to walk into a dining room where everyone addressed me so formally, sitting in the very chair Nora is now as my father's new private secretary ran us through the agenda for his first public appearance as heir apparent and me as second in line. I remember wanting nothing more than to run away. To disappear. To return to my old life.

I reach under the table, gently squeezing her leg. She shifts her gaze toward me, and I give her a reassuring smile.

"As I mentioned...," Bridge begins.

We both turn our attention back to him. But I don't take my hand off Nora's leg, keeping it there while I eat my breakfast with the other, despite the break in etiquette of only using a fork instead of a fork and a knife.

"The schedule is light today. You'll arrive at the palace at ten, where you'll introduce Ms. Tremblay to His Majesty, the king, and Her Majesty, the queen mother. After that, you'll all go to the royal vault where Ms. Tremblay will select her engagement ring."

"I already have a ring," she protests.

"It's a tradition," I explain. "Another one of many you'll learn over the course of the next several weeks, probably years. Wearing a ring from the royal vault is a sign that the monarch approves of the marriage." I lean toward her, but don't exactly lower my voice, not caring who can hear. "It's one of my least favorite traditions. I view it much like I suspect you do. Like you're marrying the monarchy, not me. Which is why I made sure to propose with a ring I purchased. One that has no ties or connection to the monarchy. Because, at the end of the day, I want you to be my wife, regardless of whether I'm a prince or some schmuck you met in a roadside diner. Okay?"

A smile pulls on her lips, momentarily erasing her nerves. "Okay."

"Right then," Nathan says, shooting to his feet in one swift motion. "If you're finished, I suggest we head to the palace. It wouldn't be a good first impression for Ms. Tremblay if we were to arrive late on her first day."

I check my watch. It's already a little after 9:30.

"Are you ready?" I glance at her plate, noting she's only had a few bites of toast. "You've barely eaten anything."

"I'll probably vomit it all up anyway," she says with a small laugh, dabbing at her mouth with her napkin and placing it beside her plate.

I do the same, then push away from the table, helping Nora to her feet.

"Are you sure? I can have them pack some fruit for you to eat on the drive."

"I'm sure." She places her hand on my chest. "I just need to get through this press conference. Then I'll let you feed me a huge meal of your favorite local foods. Okay?"

"Okay." I place a kiss on her forehead, then lead her from the dining room and toward a new life she never could have imagined in her wildest dreams.

I hope it doesn't become a nightmare.

Eleven

Nora

"Just keep your eyes forward and ignore the circus," Anderson says, squeezing my hand in the back seat of the SUV as Creed navigates toward the palace.

People line the streets of Montrose, the picturesque capital city of Belmont, hoping to catch a glimpse of the formal announcement today. Or perhaps they're here to protest the idea of their beloved crown prince marrying an American, some still holding onto hope of a Gabriel-Caroline marriage.

During my snooping this morning, I learned there are some fanatics out there who've even given them a couple name — Gabrieline. I try to not allow that inconsequential fact to eat away at me. She was someone Anderson sought comfort in when his life had been turned upside down. I did the same thing after I lost Hunter and Ember. I didn't realize how passionate some of these people were about their prince. In my eyes, he's an ordinary man who lives an extraordinary life. To everyone else, he's their beloved Prince Gabriel. They adore him.

Which will make my job that much harder.

He leans toward me, his fingers lifting the material of my dress above my knee and grazing my skin. "Just think about all the naughty things I'm going to do to you when we get back home," he whispers, his voice low, dangerous.

It sends a shiver through me, my core clenching. I shift in my seat, squeezing my thighs together as I push down the desire filling me. I don't know how this man does it. One touch, and all my trepidation disappears. He makes me forget about the world. Forget about everything except us and the love that grows stronger every day.

"Naughty?" I murmur, turning my lips toward his, but remaining out of reach.

His leering stare skates over my body, his pupils dilating. "Very." He brushes a gentle kiss to my cheek, at odds with the carnal heat in his gaze. He pulls back as the SUV slows outside a pair of wrought-iron gates, an imposing, brick building looming in the distance.

From the research I've done, Lamberside Palace is over 500 years old and boasts several hundred rooms. It functions as the primary residence of the monarch, as well as the executive offices of the monarchy and royal household.

Cobblestone lines the vast courtyard leading up to the sprawling estate, two smaller wings jutting out on either side of the main building, each impressive in its own right. I've seen large houses before. Hell, Evie's husband, Julian, is one of the wealthiest men in the United States. Or he would be if he didn't donate a huge portion of his annual income to charity. But his stately home in Rye, extravagant villa in the Hamptons, and lavish Columbus Circle penthouse pale in comparison.

And this was where Anderson spent the majority of his formative years.

And once his father voluntarily abdicates in a few years, this will be where I live.

Holy fuck.

If I was nervous before, my anxiety about today just increased tenfold. Hell, a thousandfold.

"So… This is where you grew up?" I say as nonchalantly as possible.

Anderson looks at me, then breaks into a throaty laugh. "Not much to write home about, is it?"

"Doesn't everyone grow up in a building that's featured on postcards?"

His laughter only increases as he slings an arm around my shoulders, pulling me closer and kissing my temple. If I don't make light of this situation, I'll lose my mind.

"If you look closely at one of those postcards, perhaps you might see me giving the photographer a show."

"Is that right?"

"There may have been a few times I invited a few of my mates over and we all decided to go streaking through the gardens and swam in the reflecting pool."

"Gardens? Reflecting pool? What… No orchestra shell? This really is subpar."

"Actually, love, there *is* an orchestra shell on the west side of the palace. Every Friday evening during the summer, the Belmont National Symphony performs. I'll take you one of these days, if you'd like."

"Sure…" My voice is distant as I struggle to wrap my

head around this being my life from now on.

When Creed pulls the SUV underneath an awning, I glance out the window at a pair of ornate wooden doors, a red carpet lining the short flight of steps into the building.

Butterflies flit in my stomach as a man approaches. He wears black pants and a black, high-necked jacket with various pins and medals on the left side over his chest. It's reminiscent of the United States Marine Corps dress uniform, apart from being all black. Two men dressed similarly, but with red jackets, approach both passenger doors.

As if rehearsed, our doors open at the same time, the man outside mine bowing. "My lady." He offers his arm and helps me out of the SUV.

It's still a shock to hear people address me so formally. Yesterday, I was Ms. Tremblay or ma'am. I suppose that's what the king's approval does. I go from being no one to being someone. More specifically, the crown prince's fiancée.

Anderson approaches and links his fingers with mine, leading me up the stairs and into the palace. Creed and Bridge follow behind as the man in the black uniform walks in front of us, his steps measured and in time.

Before we make it more than a few feet into the grand foyer dripping in gold and crystal, a familiar woman wearing a navy blue-and-white striped dress walks toward us, her steps graceful, as is everything about her. I breathe a sigh of relief. Sure, Anderson has a calming effect on me, but it's comforting to see someone else I knew before all of this.

"Nora," Esme says, her accent more prominent than her brother's, since she hasn't spent as much time living in the States.

"Esme," I respond, ignoring the glare the man escorting us gives me, probably for addressing her so informally.

She takes me in her arms, kissing both cheeks before whispering into my ear, "Breathe. It'll all be over soon." When she pulls back, her eyes lock with mine, making sure I heed her advice.

"Thank you."

She drops her hold on me and faces Anderson. "And fuck you very much, big brother," she snips without a care for the decorum of our surroundings. "I have to find out you're engaged from the bloody pappos?"

Anderson chuckles, wrapping his sister in a brief hug, kissing her cheek. "Sorry, Ezzy. I'd planned on telling you in person." He shrugs as he releases her. "Things didn't exactly go as planned yesterday."

"I'd say." She crosses her arms over her chest, glancing between Anderson and me before looking over his shoulder. When her gaze lands on Creed, a blush blooms on her cheeks and she fights a smile.

Most people may not notice it, but I've gotten to know Esme fairly well. That, and Anderson mentioned his sister and Creed had a thing before he was inducted into the Royal Guard, forbidding him from having any sort of romantic relationship with a member of the royal family. But it's obvious there's still an attraction there. I can physically feel the electricity vibrating between them.

"Your Highness," Creed says, bowing.

"Captain Lawson." Her eyes linger on him for several moments, something silent passing between them before she tears her gaze back to Anderson. "I'm having a thing tonight."

"Thing?"

"Yeah." She gives him a knowing look, as if speaking a language only they can understand.

Growing up in this world, I suppose you have to develop a way of communicating only those you trust can understand. And if there's one person Anderson trusts in this world besides Creed, it's Esme.

"Nora needs a bit of normalcy in her life. Especially after today. So be there. Eight o'clock. And for fuck's sake, don't wear a suit, or I'll hang you from your bloody tie. Got it?"

He laughs. "Got it."

"Good."

"Excuse me," the older man in the dark uniform interrupts. "His and Her Majesty are ready for you in the private drawing room. We shouldn't keep them waiting."

"Of course. Thank you, Major General Lawson."

Picking up on the fact that he has the same last name as Creed, I snap my eyes to Anderson. He gives a slight nod, answering my unspoken question. That the man who appears to be in charge of the security of this palace is Creed's father. Talk about some big shoes to fill.

I glance at Creed, then Major General Lawson, noticing a resemblance. Both are impressive physically. Not just their height, but also their muscular build. Both have dark, impassive eyes. Both strong noses and square jaws. The only difference is their hair. Creed still boasts a full head of dark hair, trimmed but not in military precision, whereas his father is shaved bald.

"I won't keep you any longer," Esme says, forcing my attention back to her. "I'll see you out there anyway." She wraps me in another hug, squeezing me tighter than normal. "Congratulations, sweetie. And I promise, it'll be worth it." She holds my gaze before floating away.

Once she disappears, we follow Major General Lawson up the grand staircase. I try not to gawk at my surroundings. It's a little surreal to be inside the palace I've only read about in history books.

Will I also be in those books one day?

The thought is crazy, especially after living most of my life feeling inadequate.

After walking through a maze of corridors, we come to a stop outside a wall that, upon closer inspection, is actually a concealed door. Another man in a black suit hurries to meet us.

"Your Highness," he bows at Anderson before looking to Creed's father. "Major General Lawson."

"Colonel Winters."

"My father's private secretary," Anderson explains under his breath.

I nod in understanding as Colonel Winters gently presses the hidden door, which automatically opens inward. He strides inside, snapping his heels together.

"Your Majesties," he says with a bow. "His Royal Highness Prince Gabriel and Ms. Nora Tremblay."

Panic rises inside me as I glance at Anderson. It's always nerve-wracking to meet the parents of the man you've fallen in love with. But meeting his father and grandmother when they're royalty is a level of anxiety I never knew existed.

What do I do? What do I say? What's the protocol? Who do I curtsey to first? Am I supposed to curtsey to Anderson, too?

As if sensing my unease, he leans toward my ear. "Just follow my lead. After greeting them, I'll introduce you. You need to do a small curtsey when they greet you. Okay?"

I don't even have a chance to respond before he leads me into the room, leaving Creed and his father in the hallway. I want to tell my feet to stop, to carry me back to a less stressful life, but they won't listen, automatically following Anderson.

"Your Majesty." He releases me and bows his head slightly. I watch as an older version of Anderson shakes his hand, the gesture feeling oddly formal and lacking any closeness or affection. As if Anderson's an employee, not a son.

"Gabriel."

Then Anderson turns toward the woman at his father's side. She's tall and slender, much like Esme. Her silvery platinum hair is styled in a trendy pixie cut, reminiscent of Jamie Lee Curtis. In fact, everything about her reminds me of the actress, even down to the penetrating gaze that studies and analyzes every inch of me. She certainly doesn't exhibit any warmth or affection toward me. But as her eyes focus on Anderson, she smiles.

"Gabriel, darling."

"Grandmother." He bows. She inclines her head before offering her cheek, which he kisses.

When he returns to me, he straightens his posture, turning into a person I haven't seen much of since our relationship began. He turns into Prince Gabriel.

"I'd like to introduce you to Ms. Nora Tremblay. Nora." He smiles down at me. "This is my father, King Gabriel."

Nerves spiral through me, piercing and deep. All I can do is pray I get the greetings correct and don't look like an idiot when I curtsey. I haven't exactly needed to curtsey to anyone in the past, oh…lifetime. Now I wish I'd spent last night learning all these archaic customs and rules instead of wrapped in Anderson's arms as we made love. Four times, if he's to be believed.

Doing my best to maintain my balance, I move one foot behind the other, lowering my head slightly as I bend my knees. "Your Majesty."

My gesture seems to pass muster as he offers me his hand, which I take. "Pleasure, Ms. Tremblay."

I smile before Anderson turns toward his grandmother.

"Grandmother, I'd like you to meet Ms. Nora Tremblay. Nora, this is my grandmother, Queen Veronica, the queen mother."

I go through the same motions, even more cognizant of my movements this time. I picture myself losing my balance and stumbling. It would be my luck to do something like that.

When I first met Hunter's parents, I'd spilled my drink across the table at the restaurant, soaking his mother's dress. I'd never been so horrified. Thankfully, she laughed it off. I expected her to forbid her son from ever seeing me again because I didn't measure up. But she didn't. She embraced me, despite what I viewed as my failings. It made me realize my relationship with my own mother had been incredibly unhealthy.

"We'll have to work on that, won't we?" Queen Veronica snips out, her nose upturned.

I open my mouth, unsure how to respond.

"It's my fault," Anderson interjects. "I sprang this on her. I have no doubt once Nora begins her instruction, she'll catch on rather quickly."

I keep my expression neutral, like I used to whenever my mother criticized me in that passive-aggressive way she always did. Much like it seems Queen Veronica does.

"One hopes so. Thankfully, all she'll need to do today is stand there and smile." She turns her annoyed stare toward me. "You *can* manage that, can't you?"

"I'll try not to disappoint," I counter, doing everything to bite back any snarkiness begging to be set free.

"We should get on with it." King Gabriel smiles a congenial smile.

I still don't know what to think about him. He's a bit of a conundrum. Over time, I'll probably have a better read on him, but right now, I sense he never learned how to balance being both a king and a father. It's like he wants to be a father to Anderson right now and celebrate in this moment, but he remembers who he is and the responsibilities placed on his shoulders.

I hope Anderson doesn't turn out the same way.

"Your Majesties, if you're ready." Colonel Winters appears out of thin air.

"We are," Queen Veronica responds.

"Very well." He turns on his heels with precision, escorting us out of the drawing room. Creed and Major General Lawson join us for the journey through the corridors. When we approach a large metal door, Major General Lawson punches a code into it and it swings inward. Once we're all inside, he closes the door, leading us through what feels like an underground network of tunnels.

"These are the palace safe rooms," Anderson explains. "If it's ever under attack, the royal family and staff will be evacuated here. It's pretty much an underground fortress. And is also where the royal vault is located."

Goosebumps prickle my nape. This all seems like a dream. Secret tunnels. Safe rooms. Royal vault.

For the past year, I've kept waiting to wake up in a dingy motel room on Route 66 to learn I dreamed the entire thing. That I imagined Anderson.

But as Major General Lawson unlocks another metal door and leads us into what can only be described as a jewelry vault on steroids, I know I'm not dreaming. No way in a million years would I be able to imagine this.

Thick glass covers the floor-to-ceiling display cases containing priceless jewels. Centuries-old rings. Brilliant earrings. Necklaces of all shapes and sizes. Even dozens of intricate tiaras. You name it, and it's here, everything marked, as if a historical archive.

"That's the coronation crown, scepter, and mantle," Anderson's grandmother tells me, gesturing to a glass case in the far corner.

I take several slow steps toward it, the sound of my heels on the floor echoing in the vast room. When my gaze falls on a mannequin adorned in a military dress uniform, my pulse increases.

Almost from the beginning, I've known Anderson was a prince. I've seen photos of him at official events, dressed in his military uniform, always the picture of poise and authority.

But the reality that he'll one day be king never truly sank in until this moment. Being here, seeing the crown amongst a treasure trove of jewels, makes it all real.

Anderson approaches behind me, his reflection in the glass nearly lining up with that of the crown and mantle.

"You're going to be king," I murmur, the words escaping me before I can stop them.

He smiles, placing his hands on my shoulders as I gawk at our reflection — me a nobody, him a remarkable man whose life somehow intersected with mine.

"First time I came down here, I thought the same thing. And right over here…" He touches a hand to the small of my back, leading me toward the glittering tiaras placed on black velvet, "are the family's tiaras, one of which you'll wear on our wedding day."

He stops me in front of one of them, a thick band of diamonds surrounding a large sapphire in the center, the blue color making my eyes pop even more. My jaw goes slack at the reflection of me in a tiara. And not a cheap costume tiara like I donned when I played dress-up as a little girl.

A real tiara worth thousands of dollars.

"We're running short on time, so if I might suggest we take a look at the rings," Colonel Winters says in an even tone.

"Certainly, Frederick." King Gabriel nods in his direction as a man in a suit appears from the shadows. I'm starting to think that being able to blend into the background and appear only when needed is a prerequisite to work here.

The man approaches one of the cases and removes a velvet-lined display, six rings placed in the grooves. He brings it to a nearby table, and Anderson leads me toward it.

"I did my best to choose a selection of rings my lady might prefer, based on your skin tone and the size ring you wear," the man says.

"Which one do you like?" Anderson asks.

I shake my head, the glittering stones almost blinding me. They're much bigger and extravagant than I pictured myself wearing. I want to tell him the ring he already bought me is perfect, that I can't imagine myself wearing something so…grandiose.

I don't have a choice, though. I need to learn to play by their rules, and that includes wearing a ring from the royal vault as a sign of the king's approval of our union.

Swallowing down my protest, I study the different rings, trying to select one I wouldn't mind wearing the rest of my life, at least at public events. They're all beautiful. Some all diamonds. Others different jewels — sapphire, ruby, emerald.

But there's one that calls to me. A blue stone that reminds me of Anderson's eyes — light around the edges, transitioning to a stormy blue in the center.

"This one, I think." I point to the stone that's flanked by dozens of smaller diamonds.

"Lovely choice, ma'am." The man removes it from the display. "That's an eight carat tanzanite stone surrounded by an additional two carats worth of diamonds. Do you know much about tanzanite?"

"I don't."

"It's one of the rarest stones in existence. In fact, it's a thousand times rarer than diamonds. The stone was named by Tiffany's after its place of origin in Northern Tanzania. It's estimated there's only a thirty-year supply left. In my opinion, it's the perfect choice to commemorate a once-in-a-lifetime love." He beams and hands Anderson the ring.

Anderson takes my left hand in his, his eyes trained on mine as he removes his original engagement ring. When he brings the tanzanite ring up to the same finger, he arches a single brow.

He doesn't make any move to put the ring on my finger yet, giving me one last chance to change my mind. I don't need him to say it. Once we do this, once I walk out of those doors to meet the press for the first time and his father announces his formal approval of our engagement, there's no backing out.

But I couldn't walk away from Anderson even if I wanted to.

My stare unwavering, I nod.

He slides the ring onto my finger, then raises it to his lips, kissing my knuckles. Neither one of us says a word, but I can't help but feel like there's been a shift inside of me.

I pray it's for the better, not the worse.

Twelve

Anderson

"Is it possible to pull a muscle in your face?" Nora remarks later in the evening as Creed drives from my estate on the outskirts of the city and toward the vibrant city center. "Because I'm pretty sure I have."

"How so?" I ask, stealing a glance at her.

There's something different about her now that our engagement has been made official and my father has announced to the world that, in eight weeks, she'll be the Crown Princess of Belmont, and eventually queen consort. But all of that comes second to the most important aspect of my father's announcement. In eight weeks, I'll be her husband, our hearts and souls bound together even more so than they are now. Most men might be nervous. Not me. If possible, I would have married her today.

I truly am the luckiest bastard in the world.

"From smiling all day for the cameras. If this is to become a regular thing, I may have to work face exercises into my workout routine."

Chuckling, I grab her right hand, lifting it to my lips, brushing them against her finger where the engagement ring I got her sits, the family ring on the left. It meant a lot she insisted on still wearing my ring.

"I can think of a few ways to stretch those face muscles." I mischievously waggle my brows.

"I bet you can."

"We'll start when we get home, if you'd like."

"Is that right?" She pulls her hand from mine and shoots me a playful glare.

"You're the one who said your face muscles could use a workout. I'm simply offering my services. Consider me your…personal trainer."

Her lips pinch together into a tight line. "I wouldn't want to burden you. Shouldn't you check with your private secretary first to make sure you have room in your schedule for what I can only assume could be a rather time-consuming task?"

I dip my head toward her, my mouth a breath away from her neck. "I'll make the time to feel your lips on my cock." I linger there for a beat. I don't even need to look at her to know her expression is flushed, her breaths coming quicker. Then I pull away, confirming my original suspicions. "I think two hours a day is a good start." I lean back in the seat, extending my legs as far in front of me as possible and place my hands behind my head, the picture of relaxation. "Feel free to start now."

"Such an opportunist."

"Like I said, I'm simply offering to help."

She curves toward me, trailing her fingers down the t-shirt I changed into, per Esme's instructions to not wear a suit. As her hand approaches my belt, she stops. "Baby, you wouldn't be able to last two minutes."

I raise a brow. "Don't think so?"

"I know so. If memory serves correctly, last time I sucked your dick, you went quick."

I graze my lips against hers, a lightness in my chest at our easy banter and conversation. It reminds me of the people we were back in New York. Gives me hope we'll still be those people, despite the uncertain road we're about to embark on.

"What can I say? You give damn good head, gorgeous."

She seals her mouth over mine, her tongue teasing, giving me a taste of exactly what she can do with that tongue on other parts of my body. "Likewise…" Pulling back, she smirks. "Gorgeous," she adds, mimicking my accent to the best of her ability.

When the SUV comes to a stop in front of a brick row house across from one of the many canals snaking through the capital city, Nora peers out the window.

"No gated drive or elaborate palace for Esme?" she asks as Creed slides out of the SUV.

"Her formal residence has all of that."

"Formal residence? Then where are we?"

"Somewhere she goes to escape it all."

Nora's door opens, and Creed helps her find her footing. When I step out, I glance up and down the quiet street to make sure no one is around to catch a glimpse of us. As expected, I notice a few dark SUVs at either entrance of the block, preventing vehicular and pedestrian traffic from coming this way for the few seconds it takes us to go from the SUV and up the front steps of Esme's townhouse.

"I'll keep an eye on things," Creed tells me. "Call when you're ready to leave."

"Thank you."

"Enjoy your evening, Your Highness." He bows, then looks to Nora. "My lady."

"Creed."

He remains in place, as he's been trained. It's not until I punch a code into the keypad by the front door and it opens that he retreats.

"That's going to take some getting used to," Nora mumbles under her breath as we step inside the house, closing the door behind us.

"What is?"

"Everyone calling me 'my lady'." She plays up the British in her intonation.

"You won't have to get used to it for long," a familiar voice says.

We look toward the doorway off the foyer where my sister stands wearing a pair of ripped, skinny jeans and a billowy blouse. It's a complete one-eighty from the put-together princess she was earlier today.

"In a few weeks, they'll be calling you 'Your Highness'. Then in a few years, it'll be 'Your Majesty'." She approaches, pulling Nora in for a tight hug. "How are you handling everything?" Her concern is clear.

"Good."

"Good." Esme smiles, then looks at me, jabbing my chest. "It's your job to make sure she stays good. Got it?"

"Got it," I reply with a roll of my eyes, feigning annoyance.

"Because you'll have me to answer to if you don't. And you don't want that." She winks and offers me her cheek for a kiss. "Come on. We need to introduce Nora to the people who will remind her she's normal."

I grab Nora's hand and follow my sister into the open living area. Five familiar people sit on the various couches and chairs, sipping cocktails and enjoying a lively conversation.

When we enter, they all stop, glancing in our direction.

"It's about time you got here, you wanker," a man says, standing and heading toward us.

"Good to see you, too, Marius," I chuckle as he pulls me in for a quick hug. He's a tad shorter than me, but still has an impressive physique. After all, he does have Norwegian roots. Most Nords I've met are exactly like Marius — tall, blond, and can drink you under the table.

"It's not like you announced your engagement today or anything." He winks, then turns to Nora. "This must be your blushing bride-to-be."

"Marius Erling, this is Nora Tremblay. Nora, this is a dear friend of mine, Marius."

"Thank you," she replies.

"Although I should probably be thanking the two of you."

"Why's that?" she asks.

"Now we're off the hook." He gestures between himself and Esme as she approaches with a few rocks glasses filled with sparkling water, handing them to Nora and me. "Before your…unexpected announcement, the royal household had the balls to suggest we announce an engagement in the hopes of swaying the vote on the referendum."

"I shot them down, of course," Esme says, a playful look of disgust crossing her expression. "I love you, Mari, but under no circumstances am I interested in you that way."

He raises his glass toward Esme. "The feeling is mutual." He takes a drink, then looks our way once more. "Plus, now they'll get a real wedding, not a sham of one. And people are already eating it up."

"How do you mean?" Nora inquires.

"The headlines, darling. Granted, not everyone likes you. You're bound to have a few haters. A lot of twenty-somethings are convinced you've stolen their prince from them, even though they never had a chance to begin with." He looks over his shoulder, addressing one of Esme's friends lounging on the couch. "Hey, Harri. What did that article you were reading to us say again?"

She smiles as she grabs her mobile and clears her throat before reading. "'If you ask me, Nora Tremblay from America is exactly what this country needs. She's a breath of fresh air. Beautiful and poised, she's the reincarnation of Grace Kelly. Nora gives off the impression of being likable and, dare I say it, one of us. I, for one, am excited about the prospect of an American princess gracing our country with her fresh perspective. In my opinion, any romantic notions that may have existed between Prince Gabriel and Lady Caroline DeVries can't hold a candle to the love I saw radiating between him and Ms. Tremblay this morning. I have no doubt this passion-filled marriage will breathe new life into a monarchy in desperate need of a facelift.'"

She lowers her phone, her dark eyes meeting ours. "And that's just one of many. You chose good, Anders."

I glance down at Nora. "It wasn't even a choice." I curve into her, giving her a soft kiss on her lips.

"Well, fuck me sideways. You two really are in love."

I reluctantly pull away, looking at a blond man, his long legs propped up on the coffee table.

"Of course they're really in love, you tosser." The redhead beside him playfully swats his head.

"That's Jasper and Maggie," I tell Nora. "Jasper was one of my mates from…before."

"Before you became a complete pillock."

"Tosser and pillock?" Nora interjects, crossing her arms over her chest. "I might need a dictionary for some of these words. Or at least a translator. I know wanker, but what's a tosser and pillock?"

"Idiot," everyone says at the same time.

"Same as wanker," I add.

"You have three slang terms for idiot?"

"Actually, we have a few more," another man states.

I give him a smile and nod. "Cody."

"Anders."

"Wait until you find out how many slang terms we have for penis," the woman at his side says. "I'm Penelope, but you can call me Nellie."

"That's because she made the mistake of marrying me. Used to go by Penny, but once she married some bloke with the last name Lane, well…"

As if on cue, everyone breaks out singing the classic

Beatles song, myself included.

Nora looks around, appearing as if she just stepped into some third dimension. I can understand why it would surprise her, especially after all the pomp and circumstance of today. Which is precisely why I needed to bring her here. Surround her with people who won't address her or me using some title. Who knew Esme and me before our lives were forever altered. Through all the changes, they grounded us. Hopefully, being here will help keep Nora grounded, as well.

"So are you going to leave me hanging here or what?" Nora asks once our spontaneous rendition comes to an end.

"About what?" I press.

"These slang terms for penis."

"Right," I answer, glancing around the room. "Well, there's gentleman sausage."

"Twigs and berries," Marius adds.

Harriet raises her glass. "Meat and two veg."

"Knob," Esme says.

"Dobber," Cody offers.

"Bell end," Nellie states.

A brief silence settles as we all share a look. And like the old friends we are, we know precisely what we're all thinking.

"And John Thomas," everyone says in chorus.

"John…Thomas?" Nora arches a brow.

I beam. "You've read *Lady Chatterly's Lover*, correct?"

"You know I have." She gives me a look, reminding me of role playing in her favorite Manhattan bookstore. It feels like a lifetime ago now, instead of mere days.

"Then you're familiar with the gamekeeper's unique ability of coming up with many colorful sayings for penis. Such as John Thomas."

She stares at me for a moment, before she bursts out laughing. "I will never again look at a penis without thinking of John Thomas. Or *Lady Chatterly's Lover*."

"I hope you'd think of me first." I drape my arm around her shoulders, steering her toward my usual spot on the love seat.

"We'll see." She winks.

Thirteen

Anderson

I can't remember the last time I've laughed so hard. Or heard Nora laugh so much. If I had any worries about her meeting my friends, they vanished instantly. Unlike the less than positive reception she received at the palace, my friends happily accepted Nora with open arms, despite the fact that everyone here holds some sort of title, from Harriet, a duchess, to Marius, a lowly baron. At least that's how he puts it.

But in this group, titles are irrelevant. It was a pact we all made years ago. One we maintain to this very day.

One I think Nora's happy to be a part of, as well.

"What did everyone think?" Esme asks, settling into the chair beside Marius as we all sit around the dining room table, bellies stuffed and spirits lifted.

"Horrendous," Cody jokes. "Absolute rubbish, darling. You shouldn't be allowed in the kitchen ever again. I mean, look around you." He gestures around the table, not a morsel left on a plate. "Obviously not a single person enjoyed it."

"Riiight," she draws out. "That's the reason you licked your plate clean? Literally? I actually witnessed you licking your plate." She playfully tsks. "What would your dear old grandfather have to say? That's certainly not behavior becoming of an earl."

"Either is running a bookie business, yet here we are." He winks.

"What did you think, Anders?" Esme turns her attention to me, hopeful, as if my opinion is the only one that truly matters.

After all, I was the first person she used as a test audience when she started experimenting with food. Our grandmother would have a meltdown if she knew Esme once spent her days in the palace's kitchen while one of the head chefs taught her how to make the various dishes they served. Esme always dreamed of opening her own restaurant, spend her life showering people with love through food.

But because of who we are, that's not possible.

Instead, she's resigned to hosting dinner parties for her friends, testing her latest recipes on us. Most people would probably be surprised about Esme's love for cooking. It's certainly not a hobby one typically associates with royalty. But we aren't your typical royals. Probably because this was never supposed to be our lives.

"Exceptional, Esme. Truly some of your best work," I say just as the sound of the door opening and closing cuts through, followed by heavy footsteps that grow closer until Creed's imposing frame appears in the doorway.

"Your Highness." He bows toward me, then shifts

toward Esme, his expression softening a bit, along with his voice. "Your Highness." Creed bows in her direction, his eyes lingering on her before glancing around the table. "Your Graces," he greets the rest of the party. Then he looks my way. "I apologize for the interruption, but there appears to be a…situation."

"Situation?" I tighten my arm around Nora's shoulders as she sits in the chair beside me. I had a feeling something was amiss. Creed wouldn't crash one of Esme's parties without a damn good reason.

"I'm still looking into how it happened, but there's a crowd. Paparazzi. Fans. That kind of thing. We've got it managed for now, but the sooner we get you out of here, the sooner the crowd will disperse."

I blow out a breath, my shoulders slumping. I hate to pull Nora away from this slice of normalcy, especially since I know precisely how difficult tomorrow will be. But the longer we stay, the larger the crowd will grow.

"I'm sorry, love," I say to Nora with a small smile. "So much for giving you a bit of fun tonight."

"I learned a long time ago to always expect the unexpected with you. Plus, I need to get used to this life. Nothing like jumping right into the fray, correct?"

"You'll do fine," Harriet encourages. "Don't pay attention to the rubbish anyone says. They're just jealous hags."

"Thank you." Nora smiles as she pushes back from the table.

I shoot to standing in order to help her, but after sitting most of the night, my muscles are tight, causing me to waver. Quickly, I place a hand on the table to steady myself.

Esme gives me a concerned look, as does Creed, but I subtly shake my head, wordlessly telling them I'm fine and not to press the issue. That's the thing no one warns you about when you have MS. Everyday occurrences you never thought twice about now make you question its cause. Like muscle weakness, dizziness, loss of balance and coordination… All things I've experienced more and more of lately.

Once I'm more confident in my balance, I lead Nora around the room to say our goodbyes.

"You good?" Esme asks when I reach her.

"I'm good."

"Okay." She gives me a quick once-over, then wraps Nora in her embrace. "If you ever need anything, don't hesitate to reach out. And like I always tell Anderson, don't let the man get you down." She winks.

"Thanks, Esme. Tonight was exactly what I needed."

"Then we'll all have to do it again sometime soon."

"I'd like that."

Once we finish saying our goodbyes, we follow Creed into the foyer where another guard waits. He has a similar build to Creed, although slightly shorter, his skin paler, his bright red hair shaved into a crew cut.

"Your Highness." He bows his head.

"Kylian," I respond.

"Lieutenant O'Kelly has been assigned to guard Ms. Tremblay," Creed explains.

"A guard?" Nora presses, glancing between Creed and me. "Is that necessary?"

"It is." I turn toward her, taking her hands in mine. "It goes without saying there's quite a bit about this lifestyle I disagree with. But when it comes to your safety and protection, no amount of guards is too many. So far, you've only had a taste of what's to come. The airport was controlled. As was the press conference earlier. This isn't. There are entire websites devoted to reporting on the royal family's movements in the hopes of snapping candid photos. Among other things."

"Other things?" she asks.

"There have been kidnapping attempts on Her Highness," Creed says stoically, nodding toward the dining room where the lively conversation continues. "Every single member of the royal family is a high-priced target. And I have no doubt there may be threats to you now, as well. That you also have a price tag on your head. It's why you'll always have a guard at your side whenever in public, regardless of any lack of perceived threat. Why you'll soon go through a training class to learn how to conduct yourself if you're ever kidnapped and held hostage."

"Held hostage?" Nora squeaks out.

"It's standard procedure," I assure her, squeezing her hand. "We've all been through it and have never needed to use what we learned because the Royal Guard is the best at what they do."

I steal a glance out the front windows, crowds of people swarming the sidewalks and streets. The only barricade between them and us right now is the Royal Guard blocking the stairwell.

Local police attempt to move people along. This is private property and they're currently trespassing. The threat of arrest never seems to dissuade them, though. In fact, some view getting arrested as a badge of honor. The best course of action is to give them what they came here for — a candid shot as we leave and get into the car. Then they'll continue on with their existence until the next time. And the next. And the next.

"Ready?" Creed asks, looking between us.

Nora draws in a deep breath, squaring her shoulders, her head held high. If this scenario has her on edge, she doesn't let it show, still the picture of confidence. Like she was born to be a star.

"Ready," she states.

I nod at Creed. He presses a finger to his earpiece. "We're coming out."

The instant he opens the door, flashes blind us as we make our way out of the building and toward the SUV parked a few feet away. But those few feet may as well be miles for all the slurs I hear being flung at Nora.

"You're no Grace Kelly."

"He'll come to his senses."

"No one wants you here, so just go home, you American skank."

It takes every ounce of willpower I have to not whirl around and give a piece of my mind to the assembly of mean girls I recognize from several of my public events. All college-aged girls who follow my every movement to the point of obsession.

When we finally reach the car, I glance at Nora. Her expression cracks slightly as more derogatory statements are thrown at her without a single care for the fact that she's a living, breathing human with feelings. Then again, the second I introduced her to this world, she ceased to be human in their eyes. She's their future princess, a thing put on display for them to criticize as they see fit.

I quickly help her into the SUV before jumping in behind her. The instant the door slams closed, the guard behind the wheel, Lieutenant Montgomery, drives the car down the street at a slow pace, the police helping to disperse the crowd.

It's not until we're a mile away that either of us seems to relax, Nora letting out a long breath.

"You okay?" I give her hand a squeeze.

She nods. "'If you can paint, I can walk,'" she answers in a shaky voice, quoting the last line from a movie that has a special place in our hearts — An Affair to Remember.

During our journey along Route 66, we'd often fall asleep watching that movie together. At first, we were drawn to the similarities between the storyline and our lives — two people meeting on a journey who fell in love with each other. But after our journey ended, it held a deeper meaning. That despite the obstacles we face, we'll get through them together. Like Terry McKay tells Nicki Ferrante when he realizes why she didn't show up to meet him at the top of the Empire State Building… "If you can paint, I can walk." It's become an unspoken promise between Nora and me, our vow that no matter what, we won't give up on each other. On our love.

"If you can paint, I can walk," I repeat, brushing my lips against her knuckles.

A thick silence descends on the car as the city disappears behind us, our surroundings becoming more residential. When we're about to turn onto the driveway leading up to my residence, Nora finally speaks again.

"It won't always be like this, will it?"

I open my mouth, unsure how to respond. I could lie to her, tell her this kind of thing doesn't happen often, but it does. I have a feeling it will only get worse in the coming weeks. Nora's fresh meat, and the masses are like a pack of wolves that hasn't had a meal in ages.

Instead of feeding her any lies, I bring her hand to my lips and kiss the ring I gave her. "I'm sorry."

It's the best I can offer right now.

Fourteen

"**D**id you hear what I just said?" a woman's condescending voice cuts through as I struggle to keep pace with everything my PR team has thrown at me in the past several hours, giving what can only be described as a crash course in learning how to act like a royal.

If I thought I'd ease into my new role as the crown prince's fiancée, I was mistaken. Instead of sleeping in this morning, I was woken up before the sun and informed I needed to be at the palace at nine. I barely got to see Anderson for more than a few minutes during breakfast, which Lieutenant Colonel Bridge dominated, running through his packed schedule for the day. Then Lieutenant O'Kelly whisked me away for my day full of meetings with the palace's PR team.

"Something about my image," I say, my response sounding more like a question.

After sitting in this room for the past six hours, my

mind is complete mush. Color-coded schedules. Social media. Etiquette classes. Self-defense instruction with a special ops team.

"Not *something* about your image."

I look at Pippa, the head of my dedicated PR team, which consists of five people with strong opinions about everything. Inadequacy fills me as I compare myself to this group of people who look more like they just stepped off the runway at Paris Fashion Week. They're all beautiful, stunning, the picture of confidence. Tall frames and slim bodies, not a single hair out of place. Even with my own personal stylist doing my hair and makeup in the morning, I feel awkward and frumpy next to them.

"*Everything* about your image." She gives me a tight-lipped smile, masking her obvious annoyance. "Which is why we need to ensure it's squeaky clean. From now on, your social media accounts are no longer controlled by you. In fact, we've taken the liberty of deactivating all your personal ones. The only social media you'll have now will be of your…royal life.

"Tomorrow, after your morning instruction, you'll go out with our team of photographers to spruce up your social media presence. They'll stage photos of you exploring the city. Going forward, you won't go anywhere without my social media guru, Daphne." She nods at the heavily made-up woman to her right. "She'll capture everything you do, from etiquette classes to wedding planning, and everything in between. It's my job to make the public think you're princess material." She gives me a contemptuous smile. "That you're worthy of marrying Prince Gabriel. And this is how we do it. By making you appear likable on social media."

Unable to stop myself, I bark out a laugh. My entire PR team stares at me in obvious disapproval that I'd even dare to question their plan.

"Not to sound rude, but wouldn't it be more beneficial if people saw me connecting with the community? Volunteering perhaps? I don't see how staging photos of me doing things no one can relate to will make me likable. Isn't it more important for them to find me…I don't know…relatable?"

Pippa keeps her back straight. "Making them view you as relatable is the absolute worst thing you can possibly do as a potential new member of the royal family."

I scrunch my brows. "Why? I—"

"Because it's our job to make people think the crown is divine," a firm voice interjects, carrying through the room.

Everyone snaps their eyes toward the source, jumping to their feet, bowing and curtseying with a chorus of "Your Majesty".

I don't even have to look to see who it is. Of course Anderson's grandmother would walk in at the precise moment I'm no longer being the obedient puppet they wish I were.

On a deep inhale, I pull myself to my feet and turn, greeting her with as sweet of a smile as I can muster. "Your Majesty." I curtsey.

"Do you know why the crown is divine?" she continues.

"No, ma'am."

"Because it's a position ordained by God himself. This may be a difficult thing for you to understand, considering your country was founded on the notion of separation of church and state, although one questions the effectiveness of that little experiment. However, in a monarchy, the king is not only the head of the country. He is also the head of the national church. He draws his power from God himself. Not the people."

I part my lips, fighting to bite my tongue. She's right. This is a difficult idea for me to wrap my head around. I've lived my entire life in a country where the people elected who they wanted to lead them. Although you could argue that's less and less true these days, considering the amount of corporate money that finds its way into elections, particularly on the national level. But to say the role of the monarch and royal family in general is divine? I don't fully understand.

"Right then. I believe it's time for a chat." She looks at the man appointed to be my private secretary. Like every other private secretary I've met, he's obviously former military, clean cut and authoritative, yet still obedient to the Crown. "Lieutenant Thomas, would you be kind enough to send word to have tea prepared for us in the rose garden?"

"Ms. Tremblay hasn't been instructed on proper tea etiquette," Lieutenant Thomas interjects, his posture stiff. "Perhaps it's best if—"

"Then I shall take this opportunity to do just that. Tea. Rose garden."

He bows his head. "Yes, Your Majesty."

She fixes her steely gaze back on me. "Come with me." She doesn't wait as she spins on her heel and strides away.

Acting the part of the trained dog I am, I rush to catch up, my steps quick.

"Once you begin your etiquette classes, you'll learn that when Prince Gabriel becomes king, you'll need to remain two steps behind him at all times."

"Does the reason for this go back to the whole divine and ordained by God thing?"

"Yes. And because no one should ever be seen to be on equal footing as the king." She pins me with a glare. "Even his wife. The sooner you dispense with any feminist notions of maintaining equality in your relationship, the better."

I falter for a minute, her statement hitting me hard. Harder than I thought it would. I knew once Anderson took on the role as king, I'd have to show a certain level of deference to him. But to never be able to walk beside him in public? Never be able to hold hands as we stroll the streets? It's borderline sadistic to take that away from a couple.

What other rules will I have to follow? What other rules will dictate our relationship?

I try to not allow my mind to wander. Instead, I remain the silent, obedient future crown princess Queen Veronica wants me to be as we walk through the hallways.

Palace attendants are stationed every few yards, their black and red uniforms blending into the wall. It reminds me of that scene in *Annie* when Daddy Warbucks takes Little Orphan Annie to the movies for the first time. How theater attendants lined the pathway from the doors all the way down the aisle as a show of opulence and overindulgence.

This feels the same.

As we approach a pair of double doors, an attendant magically appears. After bowing toward Queen Veronica, he opens a door, and we step onto the palace grounds.

If it were any other time, I'd take a moment to appreciate my surroundings. Grass so green I question whether it's real. Fragrant flowers of a dozen different varieties. There are even a few butterflies flitting about from flower to flower, as if the famous Lamberside Palace gardens aren't picturesque enough already.

A man in black tails and white gloves escorts us past a large, marble fountain and toward a more secluded area, overhanging trees creating the feeling of a private alcove. A single table with two chairs sits in the center, and the man ushers us in its direction.

"Your Majesty…" He pulls out a chair for her.

"No, Michael. Ms. Tremblay first. I'd like to see how she sits."

I stare at her smug expression, as if she's expecting me to collapse into a heap on the chair, completely uncivilized. I didn't realize there was a proper way to sit.

Apparently there is.

Trying not to let my nerves show, I walk to the opposite chair and lower myself, sitting with my legs at a ninety-degree angle.

"Slant them."

"Excuse me?"

"If you keep your legs positioned as such, it's possible for someone to glimpse what's underneath your skirt. Always sit with your legs slanted down, preferably crossed at the ankles."

I fight the urge to tell her this wouldn't be a problem if I were allowed to wear pants. I do as she asks and slant my legs slightly to my right, crossing them at the ankles. It's not exactly the most comfortable position, but I act as if it's normal.

"Lovely. Now you look a little more polished, although we still have our work cut out for us."

She lowers herself into the chair across from mine, her movements graceful and refined, head raised and back straight. Once she's situated, she nods at the man, who pours tea into her cup before mine. I don't make any move to bring my tea to my mouth just yet, waiting for her.

When she does, I watch her movements, attempting to mimic them.

"Keep your pinky in," she chastises. "Pinch your index and thumb through the handle, using your middle finger to support it. At no time should you ever extend your pinky."

I correct myself, the position awkward at first, but I eventually get used to it. I lean over the table slightly, meeting the cup halfway to take another sip.

"You don't go to the tea. The tea comes to you. Don't lean in. Don't hunch your shoulders. Keep your back straight. If I were to put a book on your head, it should remain there the entire time."

"Yes, ma'am," I respond, squaring my shoulders and doing my best to follow her directions.

Perhaps if she'd instructed me to just pretend I had a giant stick shoved up my ass, I would have known how to sit, because that's how this feels.

"Better." She nods her approval. "Now, return your cup to the saucer."

I do as she instructs, confident I can't mess this up.

Wrong again.

"Three o'clock if you're right-handed. Nine o'clock if you're left-handed."

"Excuse me?"

"It's pardon. By some miracle, you may be royalty soon. You never excuse yourself. You *pardon* yourself." She waves her hand at my cup. "And I was referring to the handle on your teacup. Since you're right-handed, it should always point to three o'clock when on your saucer."

I glance down to see my handle is pointing more to five o'clock and correct it.

"Good."

I sit straight, afraid to even breathe for fear she'll say I'm doing *that* wrong, as well. It seems there are rules for everything.

Do they have rules regarding sex, too? Is someone going to be in Anderson's and my room on our wedding night to critique us?

"Good form, sir. Perhaps a nipple pinch would help. Maybe suck on it, too."

I do my best to push down a laugh at the image of some uptight member of the royal household giving pointers to Anderson in the bedroom, but it's impossible. A snicker escapes.

She sets her teacup on its saucer and levels a disapproving stare at me. "Is something amusing, Ms. Tremblay?"

I adjust my posture, holding my head high. "Sorry, ma'am. I just remembered something Anderson—"

"Prince Gabriel," she admonishes. "You will refer to him as Prince Gabriel. Nothing so…familiar as a middle name. Do you understand?"

"Yes, ma'am."

"This world isn't like anything you're accustomed to. We have strict protocol and traditions for everything. You're already questioning our reason for doing things. However, I can assure you that everything we do, these rules we have in place, are there for a reason."

"And what reason is that?" I ask, despite the voice in my head telling me to just accept what she tells me and not act like an impudent toddler.

"To maintain the illusion."

"The illusion?"

"Precisely. I'm going to give you a piece of advice Queen Angelique gave me when I sat where you are right now. And that's to never let the cracks show. People in this country and around the world harbor a sort of fascination with the crown. It carries a certain mystique, casts a spell over all those who aren't allowed to see behind the curtain. It's our job to make sure they never do. To make sure they don't see that being close to the crown can at times be more of a…burden than a blessing. You've heard that saying 'Heavy is the head that wears the crown'?"

I swallow hard. "I have."

"Do you know what it means?"

I shake my head. I have a feeling, but doubt I'd phrase it correctly anyway.

"It's from Shakespeare's *Henry IV*, although it was

actually 'Uneasy lies the head that wears the crown'. It more or less means that those who are charged with incredible responsibility also carry a heavy weight most people can't even fathom being able to shoulder. That we are…burdened. There's no way around it."

I nod in agreement. I've already had to sacrifice my own needs for the monarchy in regards to my wedding. What else will I have to sacrifice in the future? What else will I be burdened with in the future?

"As royals, we undertake a responsibility to our country, our people, and God," she continues. "We commit our lives to service. To charity. To the betterment of our people. But in order to do that, we must also further the illusion of a charmed life. Of an unburdened life. The king doesn't just rule over the country. He also must reign. That means entertaining the masses with the fairy tale that's always been associated with royal life."

"And if we don't?" I ask. "If we allow them to see behind the mask?"

"We risk becoming a mere footnote in the history books."

She peers into the distance for a beat, revealing a crack in her own armor, despite her warnings I not do the same. In that split second, she appears vulnerable, looking like her almost ninety years. But it vanishes as quickly as it appeared, her expression hardening on me once more.

"Which is why I need to be quite frank with you. The job looming in Prince Gabriel's future won't be an easy one. Not only will he need to manage the running of this country, he'll have to do so in a way that will keep the spectacle alive and well. It's not an easy task. And is one best carried out with as little…distractions as possible."

"Distractions? I'm not sure I understand."

"Love is a distraction."

I blink, my blood pressure beginning to rise, heat prickling my skin. "How can love be a distraction?"

"Feelings make you weak. Make you vulnerable. Force you to lose your focus on what's important."

She brings her teacup toward her mouth and takes a sip. I simply stare at her. I couldn't even drink my tea if I wanted, nausea rolling through me.

"I assume the crown prince has mentioned the referendum that's going to a vote in a few months."

"He has."

"That's a prime example of why he cannot afford any distractions. This isn't the first time such a referendum has garnered enough support to be taken to the people for a vote. And it won't be the last. I'm sure you're a…lovely girl…" The distaste in her expression is evidence she thinks otherwise, "but Gabriel will face enough hurdles with his condition. He doesn't need anything else to distract him. And that's all you'll be. That's all you've been to him this past year. A distraction. You've taken him away from his duties. Made him shun his responsibilities not only to the Crown, but to his country. I have every reason to believe he'll do the same in the future, as well, as long as you're still in the picture. It's generally frowned upon for the heir apparent to marry for love, and for good reason. It causes needless problems. Ones this country cannot afford, particularly right now."

How do I even respond? And what's her reason for telling me all of this? In the hopes I'll walk away? I'm not sure what's more shocking — the words she says or the tone in which she utters them, as if reporting on the latest polo match, not telling her grandson's fiancée to more or less take a hike.

"Rest assured, you will still be provided for. Upon a positive paternity test, of course."

"Paternity test?" I repeat, unsure I heard her correctly.

"The royal family takes its obligations seriously. As long as the child is, in fact, Gabriel's, we will ensure you're both taken care of for the rest of your lives." She narrows her gaze. "Unless you'd prefer to explore…other options."

My jaw drops, her suggestion churning my stomach. I shouldn't be surprised. After all, Anderson told me his father's head of household did the same thing. It still stings to think this woman would propose it, and to her own flesh and blood.

Then again, these people don't have children because they want to share their love with another human. They do so out of duty, to continue the monarchy.

Nothing more.

"There *is* no other option," I say coldly.

"Very well. We just need to confirm paternity before we discuss any sort of financial arrangement."

"That's not what I meant." My voice comes out hard and biting, not a hint of hesitation.

Placing my hands on the table, I slowly rise to my feet. I'm about to break every etiquette rule in the book, but that's the last thing on my mind right now. My chest tightens as disgust bubbles in my stomach, spreading through my veins.

"Under no circumstances will I agree to your

little…*proposition*. You don't want to hear this, but I love Anderson. And he loves me. Our love isn't a burden. It's a goddamn blessing."

Her eyes widen, confirming my suspicion that she's not used to people standing up to her.

"You know what's funny?" I straighten, crossing my arms over my chest. Judging by the look of horror on her face, it's not proper etiquette to stand in such a way in the presence of royalty. "Like all little girls, I once dreamed I'd meet a prince and be a princess. Whenever I caught glimpses of them on TV, I actually envied the royal family. I actually envied *you*. I remember seeing clips of you with your children. Thought you were the type of mother I wish I had. Lord knows, mine left a lot to be desired. But now…" I shake my head and look away, collecting my thoughts. Then I turn my icy gaze on hers. "I don't envy you. I *pity* you. I may not have been surrounded by much love growing up, but I didn't give up on finding love. Instead, I *fought* to find it. Fought for Anderson. I have since I met him." With each word I speak, my passion and determination mounts. "And I will continue to do so every day of my goddamn life. So, with all due respect, you can take your proposal and shove it up your ass."

I whirl around, storming off, my heart pounding so furiously I'm confident it's about to burst through the walls of my chest. I clench and unclench my fists, grinding my teeth…hard.

As I approach the gated arch at the entrance to the rose garden, I stop and turn to face Queen Veronica once more, her eyes still wide in utter dismay.

With a trite smile, I curtsey, my motions more

pronounced than necessary. "Your Majesty." I hold my position for a beat, finding pleasure in her shellshocked expression. Then I continue out of the garden, my entire body vibrating with fury.

And perhaps a hint of regret.

As I stomp toward the palace, my chief protection officer, Lieutenant O'Kelly, appears out of nowhere. If I were in a better mood, I'd ask if they're all wizards, like in *Harry Potter*, and have learned how to apparate.

"If I do say so, ma'am," he begins once we're a safe distance away, "that was a bloody brilliant show."

I laugh under my breath, adrenaline still pumping through me. I can't believe I just told Anderson's grandmother, the queen mother, to shove it up her ass. It's completely out of character for me. Then again, all bets are off when it comes to Anderson.

When we approach the doors to the palace, Lieutenant O'Kelly touches my shoulder, and I stop. He narrows his eyes on me.

"I hope you're prepared, though."

"For what?"

"You just made an enemy out of the queen mother. Rest assured, she's not going to make your life all that easy going forward."

Great.

Fifteen

Anderson

I can barely keep my eyes open as Creed drives along the road leading to my estate. I'd forgotten how draining days like today can be. A ribbon-cutting ceremony. A speech at a charity where my father's a patron. Then heading to the palace for a meeting with my father and some ambassador before being rushed fifty miles in the opposite direction to attend the memorial service of one of our country's last surviving WWII veterans.

As much as I'd hoped to ease back into things, the royal household had different plans. Sadly, this referendum has more support than it ever has in the past, and part of it has to do with my MS diagnosis. I never considered the possible consequences of going public with my diagnosis this past winter. Either did my father when he encouraged me to do so. Perhaps we should have because, not even a week later, a well-known group of anti-royalists started collecting signatures in order to bring the referendum to a vote, using my diagnosis as proof that the monarchy isn't as strong as it once was. So the more I show I'm willing and capable of fulfilling all the duties of king, the more confident voters will be in my abilities, the less likely they'll vote in favor of turning the monarch into a purely ceremonial position.

But after a week of constant appearances and meetings, not to mention preparing for a wedding in seven weeks, I'm drained. Every night I've come home and barely made it to bed before collapsing, I tell myself the next day will be better. That it won't be so exhausting once I'm back in the swing of things. That I've simply been away from all of this for too long.

But it hasn't gotten better yet.

Worse, I've hardly seen Nora, apart from a few minutes every morning for breakfast when our private secretaries run through our busy schedules for the day, which haven't intersected for a single joint public appearance. By the time I get home late at night, she's already asleep.

"We're here, sir." Creed's voice cuts through my thoughts as the car comes to a stop in front of my residence.

"Thanks, Creed," I respond, my exhaustion evident.

He jumps out and runs to open my door. I step down from the SUV, but when my feet hit the pavement, my legs give out beneath me. Creed reacts quickly, wrapping an arm around my waist and keeping me upright.

"You okay, mate?" he asks in concern, switching from my chief protection officer to my closest friend.

"I'm fine." I attempt to push away from him, not wanting to make a big deal of it. "My leg must have fallen asleep on the drive home."

He loosens his hold, yet doesn't let go. "Are you sure?"

I shrug him off, taking a few cautious steps. Once I'm confident my legs won't fail me again, I continue toward the house, hiding any hint of uncertainty in my expression.

Lately, I've seemed to have had quite a few flareups. After the first dizzy spell, I told myself it was nothing, that people get dizzy when moving quickly all the time. That the soreness in my muscles wasn't connected to my MS. But with each muscle spasm and dizzy spell, the lies I tell myself are becoming harder and harder to believe.

"Yes, I'm sure. Good night, Creed."

I expect to hear his typical "Your Highness", but it never comes, making me slow my steps and glance back.

He looks around to make sure no one's nearby to witness him break protocol, then jogs up the steps toward me, his gaze narrowed.

"Do you think this is the best course of action, Anders? You've only been back a week and are already exhausted."

"I told you. It—"

"I know. I know. It's important for people to think you're capable of carrying out the responsibilities of king when the time comes." He licks his lips, hesitant. "But if you keep going like this, you won't be able to. Perhaps you should reconsider infusion therapy. Your current course of treatment doesn't seem to be working. Or, at the very least, go see a doctor who's not being paid by the royal household."

"The palace neurologist is one of the top people in his

field."

"On paper, that may be true. But as your chief protection officer, it's my job to protect you from all threats, including from within." He leans toward me. "Including yourself, Anders. If the palace neurologist signed off on this schedule, which your private secretary claims he did, then he's not the right person to be in charge of your care. Even *I'm* bushed, and I'm not fighting MS. You are. You need to acknowledge that fact before it's too late."

He allows his words to sink in for a beat. "Your Highness." After a quick bow, he retreats down the steps and ducks inside the SUV.

On a long exhale, I squeeze my eyes shut and pinch the bridge of my nose. I know he's right. Know I can't possibly keep this up. But I still struggle with a certain level of denial. Just like when I was first diagnosed, I don't want to admit it's because of my MS. Want to believe it's something else. *Anything* else.

Don't want to believe I'm getting worse.

Sensing Creed's gaze still focused on me through the darkened windows of the idling SUV, I turn and trudge the rest of the way up the front steps, a butler greeting me the instant I walk inside the estate.

"Your Highness." He bows. "Can I get you anything before you retire for the evening?"

"No. Thank you."

"Of course." He stands to the side, posture rigid, as he'd been trained.

My hip muscles still unusually stiff, I do my best to hide any limp as I make my way up the grand staircase. Once I reach the east wing where the private quarters are located, I slowly open the door to the bedroom, hoping it doesn't creak and wake up Nora.

My grandmother tried to insist I move her into the guest quarters at the palace to remove any appearance of impropriety, since we're not yet married. I adamantly refused. I barely see her as it is. If she didn't live here, I'd probably never see her. I won't isolate her further from me, which is exactly what my grandmother wants.

As I slip inside the room, I expect to see that Nora's fallen asleep reading a book, as she's prone to do. To my surprise, when I look at the bed, a soft glow from the side table the only light, her eyes meet mine.

"Hey," she says sweetly.

With that one word, all my troubles melt away. The day is nothing more than a distant memory, her soft voice and kind smile a reminder of what I want to come home to every day for the rest of my life.

"Hey," I reply, dragging my body toward her as I tug off my tie and drop my suit jacket onto the floor. Sitting on the edge of the bed, I kick off my shoes and crawl on top of her, taking the book from her hands. "*Rebecca*?"

She shrugs. "Seemed like a good idea earlier." Her expression falls. "Now it's hitting a bit too close to home."

"How so?"

"A nobody falls in love with a somebody, who then takes her to be lady of his English estate where she's made to feel inadequate at every turn."

I place the book on the nightstand and lower my lips toward hers. "You are not inadequate. How can you be when you saved my life? When you continue to save my life every damn day?"

She moans as I coax her mouth open, desperate for a taste of her. Her fingers scrape against my scalp as her tongue glides against mine, awakening a stirring sensation low in my belly. As I run my hand up her frame and over the swell of her breasts, her nipples straining against the thin material of her tank top, she tightens her grip on me, trying to pull my body even further into hers. But it's still not enough. For either of us. Still doesn't satisfy our unquenchable thirst.

"I need you," she whimpers when I tear my lips from hers, peppering kisses along her jawline and neck. Knowing how much it sets her off, I clamp my teeth onto her earlobe, circling my tongue around the sensitive flesh.

"And I need you, gorgeous. You have no idea how bloody much I need you."

"Then have me."

"I plan on it." I return to her lips, kissing her once more before pulling back. "Just give me ten minutes to clean up. Okay?"

She smiles and nods. "Okay."

"Okay." I leave her with one more kiss, then take my time to stand. Once I'm confident I won't lose my footing, I rush toward the bathroom.

"Anderson?" she says as I'm about to close the door.

"Yes?" I meet her seductive gaze.

"Don't shave. I miss the feel of your scruff between my legs."

"Yes, my lady," I say with an exaggerated bow.

Not wanting to keep her waiting any longer than necessary, I take one of the quickest showers of my life. After today, I need this connection, need to lose myself in

Nora. As long as we're able to leave the outside world behind, even for a few moments every night, I'm confident we'll survive this tumultuous world.

Once I've washed away the day, I dry off, not bothering to dress in anything more than a pair of boxer briefs. I don't plan on wearing them long anyway.

"Okay, gorgeous," I say upon walking out of the bathroom, a wall of steam following me. "I'm all clean and…" I trail off as my gaze falls on her. Her chest rises and falls in an even pattern, lips slightly parted, eyes closed in peaceful slumber.

On light feet, I head to her and take the book out of her hands once more, placing it on the nightstand. I bend toward her, kissing her forehead.

"I love you," I whisper.

After I turn off the lamp, I walk to the other side of the bed and climb in. I set my alarm for thirty minutes earlier than usual in the hopes of taking care of her tomorrow morning instead. I nuzzle close to her, inhaling a deep breath, her comforting aroma carrying me to sleep.

It feels like only a second passes before my alarm buzzes, rousing me. Keeping my eyes closed, I turn it off and reach for Nora. When I don't feel her, I open my eyes to find an empty bed, even at six in the morning.

I toss the duvet off me and stand, wrapping a robe around me. When I step into the hall, one of the members of my staff greets me, waiting to cater to my every need.

"Good morning, Your Highness," the woman says

with a curtsey.

"Did Ms. Tremblay already go down to breakfast?"

"Actually, she left for London early this morning."

"London?" I shake my head, wondering why I wasn't made aware of this.

"It was a last-minute trip. The designer Her Majesty wants for her wedding dress had availability to squeeze her in today."

"Oh." I swallow past the lump in my throat, hating she's in London without me. I promised I'd take her one day.

Yet another broken promise.

I debate canceling my engagements scheduled over the next several days to surprise her with a romantic weekend away. She's only been here a little more than a week, yet I can't help but feel like I'm losing her. Like there's a divide between us when we were once strong and impenetrable.

But when I glance at the copy of the local newspaper left on a silver tray outside my door, the headline reporting the referendum still has strong support, despite the announcement of my engagement, I'm reminded of my obligations to the Crown.

Nora will have to wait.

Sixteen

Nora

"Are you feeling okay, love?"

I look up from the fruit I'd requested for breakfast. I thought it would be the easiest on my stomach, but nothing seems appetizing right now.

"Just morning sickness." I give Anderson a smile, not wanting to ruin the few minutes we have together before we each have to go our separate ways for the day.

"I'm sorry."

I swallow hard, pushing down the acid rising in my throat at the mere thought of eating anything. Sliding the bowl away, I opt for a small bite of my dry toast instead.

"It'll pass," I tell him in the hopes it eases his worry. He has enough to concern himself with lately.

Anderson has spent every day of the past three weeks attending meetings, galas, public events, all to prove to the nation that his MS won't limit his ability to lead when the time comes… *If* the time comes. There's still a possibility this referendum will pass.

By the time he gets home after working for sometimes sixteen hours, I'm usually asleep or, if I do manage to stay awake in order to have a few minutes with him, he's exhausted with only enough energy to shrug out of his clothes before collapsing into bed.

We've barely spent more than an hour together lately, outside of sleeping in the same bed. I can't help but wonder if it has something to do with my impromptu afternoon tea with his grandmother the day after our engagement was made official.

Despite the palace PR team trying to arrange a few public appearances where Anderson and I are seen together, something more important always comes up, causing me to go pick out floral arrangements alone. Or taste cakes alone. Or pretty much do everything alone.

"Are you sure that's all?" Anderson asks after I attempt to swallow down some toast, fighting my body to do so. "That there's not something else bothering you?"

"What makes you think that?" I take a timid sip of water, unsure whether it'll help keep the few bites of food down or cause it all to come back up and destroy the tablecloth that probably costs more than most of the clothes I owned before I met Anderson.

"Because I know you." He grabs my hand, brushing his thumb against the diamond ring on my right hand.

God, I've missed this connection, the roughness of his skin against mine. I miss *him*. Miss spending hours doing whatever we wanted as we roamed New York City for hidden gems.

Like when I took him to the subway grate made famous by Marilyn Monroe, both of us proceeding to pose like the famous actress did.

Or when he showed me the Hess Triangle in the West Village, a small triangle of privately owned property in the middle of the sidewalk that's the result of a dispute between the Hess Estate and the city.

Or when I took him to Grand Central and demonstrated the magic of the Whispering Gallery. How one person could whisper something while standing on one side of the famed arches, the person standing on the other side clearly hearing it over all the noise of the train station. He'd whispered he loved me. Then quite a few things that would make even some of the girls working at the strip clubs blush.

"Remember what I told you before we stepped off that plane?" Anderson presses, pulling me out of my memories. "I need you to be open and honest with me. If I don't know something's upsetting you, how can I help fix it? I don't want to always worry that you're not telling me something that affects your well-being. If you keep things from me, I will be."

I study his own tired appearance. His weary eyes, eyelids drooping, bags underneath. I look at his hand as it caresses mine, noting he's been chewing his fingernails, a habit he only does when extremely stressed. I hate the idea of adding to that stress. Hate the idea of making him feel guilty simply because I'm a little homesick. That I've rarely been able to talk to my friends because of the time difference.

That I wish I saw him more.

All I can hear are Queen Veronica's words she shared with me during tea. That it's my job to continue the illusion, to not let the world see that being near the crown is a burden.

And that means not letting Anderson see being close to him has become a burden.

"I'm just a little nervous about today. That's all."

He furrows his brow, glancing down at his calendar on the tablet in front of him. "Is it something for the wedding? Or a training exercise?"

My heart sinks, and I lean into him. "I told you last week." I keep my voice low. "I have my first appointment with the palace OB/GYN. Even made sure it was on your agenda." I look from him to Lieutenant Colonel Bridge, who sits on the other side of him, as he always does during breakfast in order to review his schedule. Most days, this is the only time I get with Anderson, yet I still must share it with his private secretary.

Am I always going to have to share him?

"Shite." He squeezes his eyes shut.

I pull my hand from his, my shoulders slumping. I don't even have to ask. He either forgot, or my appointment never made it onto his calendar for today.

Possibly both.

"I'm sorry, Nora. I guess I…lost track of days or something."

I swallow down the disappointment bubbling inside me and force a smile, despite being on the brink of tears. It's utterly ridiculous for me to be upset over this. It's only a doctor's appointment.

But after suffering a pregnancy loss as traumatic as I did, I'm constantly worried I'll lose this one, too. Constantly scared of sitting in that exam room all alone.

What if the doctor tells me there's no heartbeat?

I went through that alone once.

I don't want to go through it again.

"It's okay. There will be more appointments," I say, although my voice lacks any conviction.

Hopefully there will be more. But will he be at those? Or will they also be conveniently left off his schedule?

Anderson shifts his gaze from me, pinning Lieutenant Colonel Bridge with a glare. "Why isn't Ms. Tremblay's appointment on my agenda?"

"It was," he begins. "Unfortunately, a few things came up last minute that were deemed a higher priority."

I laugh under my breath. "Of course they did."

I have no doubt his grandmother played a role in this. Maybe I'm being paranoid. But after she all but bribed me to walk away, what am I supposed to believe?

"What do you mean by that?" Anderson asks.

"Nothing." I grab my napkin, dabbing at my mouth before pushing back from the table and standing.

Anderson and Bridge jump to their feet, their own etiquette training kicking in like it's second nature.

"I have a busy day, so I should get to the palace. Am I to assume I *won't* be seeing you at my doctor appointment?"

"I'll be there," Anderson says without a moment's hesitation.

"But, sir," Bridge interjects, "your schedule is quite packed today. I don't see how we can add anything else without canceling something. And, as I mentioned, everything is deemed a high priority."

"I understand that," Anderson responds in an authoritative tone. "But *my* priority is and always will be Ms. Tremblay. Her doctor appointments are the highest priority. Even above anything to do with this referendum." He turns back toward me, grabbing my hand. "I'll be there."

"Don't make any promises you have no intention of fulfilling, Anders. I'd rather go in knowing you won't be there than be disappointed later."

"If I tell you I'll be there, I'll be there." He loops an arm around my waist, pulling me against him.

Out of the corner of my eye, I notice Bridge lower his head and walk away, giving us some privacy, as I expected. After all, overt displays of affection between royalty are severely frowned upon.

"Better yet, I'll cancel all my engagements afterward." He nuzzles my neck, peppering light kisses along my skin. "We'll have a nice, romantic dinner in the gardens. Then a night to do anything we want."

I close my eyes and melt into him. In a heartbeat, all the unease that's consumed me since I woke up this morning slowly vanishes. This is exactly what I've needed. To not feel so alone. To be reminded why I gave up my old life. Now I have something else to look forward to instead of spending all day worrying about my appointment.

"How does that sound, gorgeous?" he asks in a husky voice that should be illegal in public. Or at least in his formal dining room, where we're never truly alone.

"Heavenly."

"Good." He abruptly pulls back, leaving me wanting. Judging by the smirk on his face, he knows it, too. "To be continued later." He waggles his brows. "For now, shall we?" He extends his elbow for me.

"Of course."

I hook my arm through his, allowing him to lead me from the dining room, down the corridors, and out to the front driveway where two black SUVs wait to whisk us away for our morning obligations.

He kisses my cheek before I turn, giving Lieutenant O'Kelly a smile as he holds open the rear passenger door for me. I'm about to climb inside when a hand on my arm stops me. I whip my head up to see Anderson clutching onto me. Then he yanks my body against his.

"Kylian, you might want to turn around, particularly if public displays of affection make you uncomfortable."

"Yes, sir," my protection officer says with a slight laugh, doing as he was ordered.

"And what kind of public display of affection did you have in mind?" I flirt.

"This." Anderson's hold on me tightens as his lips slowly descend toward mine.

It's not a ravenous, desperate kiss. More loving and affectionate, his tongue urging my mouth open and swiping against mine in carefully measured strokes. I sigh and curve into him further, wanting to be as close to him as possible.

His kiss is like that first warm, spring day after a winter of cold and desolation.

Like that first taste of wine after a long, trying day of work.

Like the smell of hot chocolate on a snowy day.

Welcome.

Inviting.

Absolutely beautiful.

"New rule," he says when our kiss comes to an end.

"What's that?" I toy with a few tendrils of his hair. What I wouldn't give to run my hands through it and mess it up so it more closely resembles the man I met in that Chicago diner.

"No more leaving without kissing each other goodbye."

"You kiss me goodbye every morning."

He gives me a knowing look. "A kiss on the cheek is a rubbish way to say goodbye."

"Rubbish?"

"Bullshite. I hate it, all because of some stupid rule against public displays of affection. This is our home, so if we want to make out on the front steps, we're going to bloody make out on the front steps, to hell with who sees."

I laugh, an overwhelming sensation of weightlessness filling me. My chest expands at the love I can physically feel radiating from his heart and into mine.

"From now on, we agree to never say goodbye without a real kiss. Okay?"

I edge toward him, ghosting my lips against his. "I think this might be my new favorite rule."

Seventeen

Nora

Sometimes it's the littlest things that make the biggest difference in your day. One positive thing to change your outlook.

That's precisely the impact Anderson's new "rule" has on my day.

I've had so much positive energy all morning that I've barely thought about my doctor's appointment. I feel deep in my soul it will all work out. That it won't be like the last time a doctor hooked up the ultrasound machine to me, only to quickly turn the screen away so I wouldn't be able to tell there was no heartbeat. This time, I won't have to go through it alone. No matter what happens, Anderson will be by my side.

"Pardon the interruption."

I pop my head up when my private secretary peeks into the conference room where I'm currently in the middle of a meeting with my PR team, all of whom I'm convinced hate me.

"A call just came in for you, ma'am."

No longer having control over who has access to me has been one of the most difficult things for me to get used to. All incoming calls to my old cell phone are forwarded to one screened by my private secretary, who decides whether I should take them or if it's simply something for him to handle on my behalf.

"Prince Gabriel?" I ask.

In the past three weeks, Anderson's the only one he's let through. Everyone else has been told to leave their information for me to call back.

"No, ma'am. It's a nurse from a hospital in New York."

My breath hitches, panic rushing through me. Maybe it's just Izzy reaching out to see how I'm doing. I glance at the clock to see it's only a little past noon here. Meaning it's barely after three in the morning in New York.

Lieutenant Thomas drops his voice. "Mentioned it's regarding your friend, Chloe."

I jump to my feet.

"I'll show you to an office for privacy."

"Thank you."

He quickly leads me from the conference room to a vacant office a few doors down the corridor. But unlike most office spaces I've seen in my life, this isn't filled with florescent lights, a cheap desk, and filing cabinets. The desk is solid mahogany, the walls all built-in bookshelves, containing what appears to be law books and other historical texts.

"Here you go, ma'am." He hands me the phone.

"Thank you."

He bows, then closes the door. Silence surrounds me as I close my eyes, drawing in a deep breath, trying to brace myself for whatever news awaits me.

But nothing could have prepared me for this.

"This is Nora Tremblay."

"Well, look at who is so important as to have somebody else answer their phone calls."

A sudden chill envelopes me, my stomach roiling at the sound of that grating voice. One I would have been happy to never hear again.

"Mom…" On shaky limbs, I lower myself into the ornate chair.

"Surprised? You *are* difficult to get in touch with. Have you not been getting my messages?"

I grit a smile, despite the fact she can't see me. It's become a habit. "I have."

"Too busy to call dear ol' mum back?" She mimics a proper British accent, much like the people speak with here.

I bite down on my lower lip. It would be so easy to hang up on her, tell her to never call again, then order my private secretary to make sure she's unable to get through if she does. After all, there are only two reasons she'd ever get in touch with me. She either wants something from me, or needs to feel superior and wants to use me as a verbal punching bag for a few minutes. Perhaps both.

I need to address this, though. Not ignore it and allow it to blow up down the road. Need her out of my life, once and for all.

"Actually, yes. I am quite busy these days. But that's not the reason I didn't return your call. In case you've forgotten our last conversation, I've turned over a new leaf. I—"

"Yeah. Yeah. Yeah," she slurs, evidence she's been hitting the liquor hard tonight. "You're removing all the negative energy from your life, or whatever New Age bullshit you've been fed."

"It's not bullshit. As a psychiatrist, I'd think you'd be happy to learn I'm taking steps to clear the clutter from my life."

"Speaking of which, imagine my surprise when I turn on the news a few weeks ago and see my very own daughter making headlines across the world. Some call you the new Grace Kelly. You don't want to hear what others are saying about you. Trust me. It's not pretty at all. And it's certainly not pretty for me to be associated with some gold digger American who's only spreading her legs to be a princess."

I clench and unclench my fists, trying to find my calm and serenity again, but it's impossible with this woman.

Worse, she knows it.

I don't know how she does it, but every time I'm having one of the best days in recent memory, she somehow senses it and decides to do everything in her power to make me feel inadequate. It's a talent's she's had all my life.

"As enlightening as I find this conversation, I have a busy day," I say, practicing all the refined speech and etiquette rules I've learned. "Why don't you get to the reason for your phone call."

It's silent for a beat, then I hear the telltale sound of ice against glass, confirming my suspicions that she is, in fact, drinking. At nearly 3:30 in the morning. "I wasn't sure who to call about this, but I wanted to find out my travel arrangements."

"Travel arrangements?"

"For the wedding."

"What wedding?"

"*Your* wedding, of course."

"Oh. I see." A conniving smile pulls on my lips. "Now that I'm about to marry a prince, you actually *want* to come to my wedding. Need I remind you that you showed zero interest in my relationship with my first fiancé, and even less in my wedding to Jeremy. In fact, you got married the same day, just out of spite."

"Oh please, Nora. That's always been your problem. You're so self-centered. The world doesn't revolve around you."

I bark out a laugh. "Me self-centered? Do you even listen to yourself? Since Dad died, you've done nothing but criticize and berate me. You've never supported me. Never loved me. Like I said, I've made it a goal to keep all negativity out of my life. And you've never been anything but negative. So no, you're not invited to our wedding."

She inhales a sharp breath. I can sense her exasperation from across the ocean. "Excuse me? I'm your mother. How do you think it's going to look if you don't invite your own mother to your wedding?"

"It'll look like I've grown the backbone I should have years ago. I will not have you there to ruin the most important day of my life."

"Until the next wedding."

"There won't be another wedding. I'm not you."

"We'll see about that."

"We certainly will. But you still aren't invited."

"I can make life extremely difficult for you. Don't forget. I know all your secrets. I'd hate for the world to learn them, too."

"At one point, that might have been enough to scare me into caving to your demands. But not anymore. Go ahead. Tell the world my secrets. Anderson's the only person I care about, and he already knows everything about me. So you lose. Goodbye, Elaine," I say, refusing to call her mother.

"He's not Hunter," she says before I can end the call.

I grind my teeth, resisting the urge to scream. She always has a way of saying the precise thing that will cut me deeper than anything else.

"That's not why I'm marrying him."

"Are you sure about that? That's why you married the last one. What was his name again?"

"I just mentioned his name," I hiss. "It's Jeremy."

"Right. Jeremy. And he only looked like Hunter. But this one… Well, in my line of work, you learn that relationships born out of a shared tragedy never survive." Her voice softens, oozing with sympathy. Except I know it's about as real as her latest lip enhancement. "It won't bring him back."

"I don't need to bring Hunter back. He'll live on where he's meant to be. In my memories. Which is where I plan on keeping you. At least the memories I have when you cared about me. You haven't in years. So, for the last time… Goodbye."

I punch the end call button on the screen, then shoot

to my feet as adrenaline winds through me. Agitated, I pace the length of the room, trying to work off some of this anxiety.

With every step I take, another painful memory of my childhood comes to the surface. How I was never good enough. How I was never smart enough. How I was never pretty enough.

It all becomes too much. A lifetime of being made to feel incompetent and lacking burns within until the only way I can find relief is to let it all go. So that's what I do.

Forgetting where I am and any sense of decorum, I dig my hands into my hair and bend over, releasing all my pent-up frustration with a piercing scream.

When the door bursts open seconds later, I straighten. O'Kelly's panicked eyes find mine, Lieutenant Thomas close on his heels.

"What happened?" O'Kelly asks, scanning the room for any perceived threat, his hand on the gun in his holster, ready to immediately draw and fire.

Smoothing a hand down my hair, then my dress, I take a moment to compose myself. Grabbing my phone off the desk, I return it to Lieutenant Thomas. Minutes ago, I hated that he controlled who had access to me. Now I'm grateful for it.

"That was my mother," I tell him.

His face blanches. It doesn't take a genius to know precisely what that means. I have no doubt Anderson's already briefed both men regarding her.

"I apologize, ma'am. The incoming call came from a hospital in New York. When she claimed it was about your friend, Chloe, I thought—"

"And I thank you for that. I had the same thought when you told me. From now on, the only people I want you to put through are from the numbers already stored in my phone. Even if it's an emergency, my friends are more inclined to call from their cells."

"Understood," Lieutenant Thomas says, bowing his head slightly. "It'll never happen again."

I nod with an appreciative smile. "Thank you."

———

I tap my fingernails against the arm of the chair as I sit in the waiting room of the palace physician's office.

When I learned I'd be attended to by one of the "in-house" physicians throughout my pregnancy, as is the protocol, I assumed the appointments would take place in a private office located somewhere in the palace, similar to the nurse's office at school, but on a much classier level.

Never did I expect to walk into an entire hospital wing within the palace walls. Apart from having a private waiting area reserved for immediate members of the royal family, it's like every other medical complex I've been to. Sterile surfaces. Fluorescent lights. The smell of bleach and latex. It's a small taste of normal in a life that's anything but.

I steal a glance at the clock hanging over the doorway leading to the exam rooms, every tick seeming to echo and vibrate through me, almost mocking me. I try to tell myself it's not a big deal. He's only fifteen minutes late. Perhaps he got delayed at one event, which caused a ripple effect throughout his day. I know first-hand how one delay can put the rest of your day behind schedule.

But when the sound of a cell ringing echoes through the room, a premonition settles in my stomach that he's not simply running late. I lift my eyes toward Lieutenant Thomas sitting beside Lieutenant O'Kelly in the far corner, remaining as discreet as possible.

He pulls the phone from the inside of his jacket pocket. "Ms. Tremblay's line. This is Lieutenant Thomas." He meets my gaze as his Adam's apple bobs up and down. "Of course, sir." He rises to his feet and walks toward me, holding out my cell. "It's His Royal Highness."

I take the phone and bring it up to my ear. Closing my eyes to fight back my tears, I attempt to collect myself. "You're not going to make it, are you?" I manage to say, my tone even, emotionless.

"Nora..." Regret laces Anderson's voice. "I'm so sorry. I wouldn't do this if it weren't important. And... Fuck!"

I picture him tugging at his hair. I've heard that tone before, and that's precisely what he did.

"I'm so sorry," he repeats. "But my grandmother fell ill and I must cover for her. She was scheduled to appear with the queen—"

"But she *is* the queen."

"No. She's the queen mother. I'm talking about *the* queen. The Queen of England. She flew in to attend a function at Westerly College. It was partly to show her support of the opening of the school of medicine, but also to try to help turn the tide on this referendum. And since my father is currently in Spain—"

"It now falls on your shoulders."

"You have no idea how sorry I am, Nora. I promise to

make it up to you. I'll be at every other appointment, no matter what."

I stare blankly at the wall in front of me. Today started with so much hope. So much possibility.

How could it go downhill so quickly?

"Please, Nora. Say something so I'm not sitting here wondering what's going through your head. I swear to you, I won't miss anything else baby related."

"Like I told you earlier," I begin after a protracted pause, "don't make any promises you have no intention of keeping."

I tear the phone away from my ear, jabbing the screen to end the call. Then I stand, Thomas and O'Kelly remaining stoic and unemotional. I hand the cell back to Thomas, keeping my shoulders squared and expression even.

"Can you tell them I'm ready to go in now?"

A flash of remorse crosses his face. "Would you like to wait? Perhaps call Her Highness Princess Esme to see if she'd be able to join you?"

I vehemently shake my head, never feeling so alone, despite constantly being surrounded by people. "That's not necessary."

I should get used to being alone now.

I may very well be alone for the foreseeable future.

Eighteen

Anderson

"Have you heard from her?" Creed asks, glancing into the rearview mirror as he drives faster than normal on the way back to my estate.

What a crap day this has turned out to be. I had every intention of being there for Nora. Was looking forward to seeing that first ultrasound of our baby, then devoting the rest of the afternoon and evening to her. It's no secret we haven't had much time to ourselves since arriving here three weeks ago.

But the second Bridge's phone rang around lunchtime and he gave me a concerned look, I knew my plans had all gone up in smoke. If it were anyone else, I would have insisted someone other than me attend, perhaps Esme or one of my cousins, all of whom the royal household often calls upon to help when needed.

But the Queen of England is too important to send third or fourth in line to the crown. Hell, she's too important to even consider sending the second in line, which was why it fell on my shoulders.

I check my phone, seeing my texts have been delivered but not read.

"No."

Creed nods subtly.

After a few more moments of silence, I blurt out, "I'm a complete fuckup, aren't I?"

"You had your reasons for missing her appointment," he offers.

"But?" I say, sensing he's holding back.

"Regardless, she also has every reason to be upset with you."

"I know." I squeeze my eyes shut and pinch the bridge of my nose, fighting against a headache, like I have been most of the day. "So what am I supposed to do? How do I make this right?"

He studies me for a beat in the mirror as he slows to a stop in front of my residence. "You grovel." He puts the SUV into park and turns to face me. "And when you're finished groveling, you grovel some more. That woman has not only sacrificed everything for you — her home, her friends, her job — she's now carrying your child. I'm not sure you've ever shown her your appreciation for everything she's done for you."

I open my mouth to protest to the contrary, searching my brain for proof that I've shown her my appreciation. But nothing comes to mind. I've *told* her how grateful I am. I've showered her with gifts, but Nora's not the type of woman who cares about material things.

How would I feel if our roles were reversed?

Probably exactly like Nora feels right now.

Alone.

Lost.

Betrayed.

Creed opens his door and darts around the SUV to open mine. I'm cautious as I step onto the ground, making sure I have my footing before placing my full weight on my legs. Once I straighten, he bows, then stands aside as I walk up the stairs and into the building.

"Your Highness," my head butler greets me with a bow.

"Richard."

"Ms. Tremblay is out back in the gardens. I thought perhaps—"

"Of course. Thank you."

"Yes, sir."

He bows again, then retreats. I pause in the foyer, running a hand over my face as I try to come up with something to say to Nora to make this better. Make this right.

It was only one appointment.

But to Nora, it was more than that.

It was about having me present, something I've done a shitty job of lately. I'm not sure how to balance all these new responsibilities the Crown has placed on me *and* being a good fiancé.

Now I understand why my father never remarried after my mother passed away. It's impossible to balance both a relationship and running a country. No wonder most monarchs don't marry for love but to simply produce the requisite heir and a spare.

But I don't want that life for me.

My mother didn't want that life for me, either.

Exhaling a long breath, I make my way out the back doors and through the gardens. I don't even have to question where Nora is. I know. She was just as drawn to this spot as I was the first time I saw it. So I head straight for the overlook along the rocky cliffs.

As I approach, I slow, pausing to appreciate how beautiful she looks as she sits on the bench, gaze focused on the crashing waves below. The breeze blows through her hair, the moonlight illuminating her silhouette, making her appear ethereal and otherworldly. Like something from a different dimension.

Then my gaze shifts to what she holds in her hand — a grainy black-and-white photo, something that resembles a bean inside a dark space.

If I felt like an asshole earlier, it's ten times worse now that I see the first picture of our baby.

I should have been there when *she* first saw it, too.

"Baby's doing well," she says evenly, not looking at me. "Measuring nine weeks, so that's about right. And the heartbeat is strong, but because of my past…complications, the doctor wants to see me again in two weeks to make sure everything's still progressing well. But don't worry. I won't expect you to make room for me in your hectic schedule to be there."

I advance toward her, my eyes pleading. "You have no idea how badly I wanted to be there today."

"I know." She stands, leaving the ultrasound photo on the bench, taunting me. "Trust me. I know." She faces me, revealing bloodshot eyes from what I can only assume to be hours of crying while I attended a gala thrown for the

Queen of England.

"For the last several hours, I've berated myself for being upset with you for breaking your promise. It's not like you didn't have a good excuse. But what happens next time when some foreign minister comes into town? Or the president? Or someone else more important than me? Lord knows that list is miles long."

"Nora...," I say again, stepping toward her, but she holds up her hand, stopping me.

"I get that you have responsibilities. I've had this 'duty to the crown' edict ingrained into my head every damn second since I stepped off that airplane. I know all about your duty. And, apparently, my sole duty is to provide an heir and a spare, making me feel like I'm nothing more than a walking uterus."

"You're so much more than that. You know that."

"Do I? Because these past few weeks, you've done little to make me feel that, Anders. I've never felt so goddamn alone in my life. I left the only home I've known for you. Left my friends. For you. And now I'm going through this pregnancy, which scares me absolutely shitless. All. For. You."

With each word she speaks, her voice becomes louder and more choked with emotion, tears falling down her cheeks.

"If I want to be with you, I have no option but to give you children. That's part of the deal of marrying the future king, something I wish you'd have told me. After everything I went through last time..." She raises her face to the sky, her eyes glistening against the moonlight. Then she levels a stare back at me. "But I'm willing to put these fears aside. For you. Willing to sacrifice having my best friends at my side when I all but sell my soul to this monarchy. For you. What have you given up to be with me?"

I open my mouth, unsure what to say, but she answers for me.

"Nothing, Anders. You've sacrificed nothing."

The vein in her neck pulses against her skin, her muscles taut, anger and despair mixing in a lethal combination on her face.

"I miss my home. Miss the stench of New York, even on garbage day. Miss my friends. But you don't seem to care about any of that." She pinches her lips together in a tight line as she crosses her arms over her stomach, seeming to shrink into herself. "Maybe your grandmother was right. Maybe I *am* too weak for this."

"What do you mean?" My gaze flames with fury and surprise. "When did she say that?"

She shrugs. "At tea a few weeks ago. The ink on our engagement announcement was barely even dry when she pulled me aside to tell me I wasn't good enough for you."

"She doesn't speak for me. You know that."

"Just the rest of the royal household." She throws up her hands. "Hell, the rest of this entire *fucking* country."

"What do you want me to do? Walk away from this? Because I will. For *you*, Nora, I will."

She swipes the tears from her cheeks. "I would never ask you to do that. As much as I can tell certain things about this life aggravate you, I saw your face as we were landing and you laid eyes on your country for the first time in a while." She smiles sadly. "It's the same way I feel when I see the Manhattan skyline. You love your home. You love your country. And when I walked off that plane on your arm and caught my first glimpse of Prince Gabriel, I realized you were born to be king. To lead. You said it yourself. You have the opportunity to do good not just for your country, but for all of Europe. Maybe even the world. After all…" She swallows hard. "With great power comes great purpose." Her eyes lock with mine, a beat passing between us. Then she lowers her head. "But when I saw the photos of you with the Queen of England today, it finally hit me."

"What did?"

She lifts her gaze back to mine, smiling sadly. "That the man I've seen during public events and in the media is a complete stranger to me." Her chin trembles, her words as difficult for her to say as they are for me to hear. "That I don't know you anymore. That I don't know the man I'm supposed to marry in a few weeks."

I step toward her, clutching her cheeks in my hands, swiping her tears away with my thumbs. "Yes, you do. You're one of the few people who *does* know me. Who knows who I really am. Who knows Anderson North. Everything else, this person who has to cut ribbons, kiss babies, and make speeches… Prince Gabriel… That's not really me."

"That may be true, but lately, that's the only person I've seen. How am I supposed to share my bed with a stranger? How am I supposed to marry a stranger?" She peers into my eyes, begging me for an answer I can't give. Then she steps away and turns toward the house.

"Where does this leave us?" I call after her, biting on

my lower lip to stop my chin from quivering. "I don't want *you* to walk away from all of this, either. If it weren't for you, I wouldn't be here. You saved my life." An ache bubbles in my throat, the pain excruciating.

Why do I feel like she's slipping away with nothing to anchor her to me?

Like I'm losing her?

Like this world is tearing us apart?

"And you saved mine," she admits sadly. "But I'm not sure it's enough anymore. I'm not sure *I'm* enough."

"You are." I advance on her, framing her small face in my large hands once again, holding onto her like she's a lifesaver and I'm being tossed around by a tumultuous sea. "You're more than enough. You claim I was born to be king. There's no doubt in my mind you were meant to be my queen. That you *are* strong enough for this role."

She searches my eyes, as if they contain the answer she's been seeking. Then she pushes out of my hold again. "At one time, I would have believed that."

"And now?"

"Now…" She exhales, licking her lips as she collects her thoughts. "Now I need time to think. I hope you can at least give me that after everything I've given you."

I want to argue that we don't have the luxury of time. That in mere weeks, we're supposed to walk down the aisle of the National Cathedral and get married. But she has a point. After all the sacrifices she's made for me, time to think is the least I can give her.

"Okay."

"Thank you." With a sad smile, she turns from me and walks through the gardens.

"I love you, Nora," I call out after her.

She pauses, but doesn't immediately respond, taking a moment to collect her thoughts. Finally, her purple-blue eyes meet mine.

Eyes I once dreamt about before I even knew her name.

Eyes I've been lucky enough to wake up to nearly every morning for the past several months.

Eyes I've noticed lose more and more of their luster since we arrived here.

"And I love Anderson. With all my heart. But I'm expected to marry Prince Gabriel." She shakes her head. "That man is a stranger to me."

Nineteen

Nora

The sun peeks through the heavy drapes in the bedroom I typically share with Anderson.

Or is it Prince Gabriel?

I don't even know anymore.

All last night, I'd tossed and turned, replaying our argument in my mind. Was I too hard on him? He *did* have a valid excuse for missing my doctor's appointment.

But it wasn't just a missed doctor's appointment. That was simply the impetus that made me realize something I've been struggling with since our engagement was announced.

That I've rarely seen the man I fell in love with.

That in his place is a relative stranger.

That I'm expected to marry a man I feel like I don't even know.

The man I've been sharing my bed with barely resembles the one who approached me in front of Lincoln's tomb and tried to impress me with his useless knowledge of the plot to steal Lincoln's body. I want to marry *that* man. I'm not sure about this other person he's become since we landed in Belmont.

It's times like these I wish I were still in New York. All it would take would be a single text to Evie, Chloe, and Izzy, and they'd drop everything to offer me the advice I need. Or a proverbial slap in the back of the head if they thought I was being ridiculous, as has been known to happen.

Grabbing my old phone, I check my international clock to see it's a few minutes past nine on Thursday evening in New York. While we used to get together every Thursday night at a local bar near Chloe and Evie's work, once they got pregnant and moved out to the suburbs, we opted to trade the local bar for one of our places, usually Izzy's or mine.

Figuring it's worth a shot, I find Chloe's contact information and hit the FaceTime button, waiting as the call connects. I feel like I haven't talked to them in ages, not just the few weeks I've been here. After I FaceTimed them to tell them about our hasty wedding announcement and the reasons behind it, I haven't had much time to get in touch, my days filled from the second I wake to the moment I fall into bed. We've all sent the occasional text, but that's not the same.

A ping from my phone brings my attention back to it, Chloe's bright, gray eyes and brilliant smile greeting me.

"It's about dang time you called!" she exclaims. "We were starting to think you'd forgotten about us."

"I could never forget about you girls." My throat constricts at the sight of Izzy's familiar townhouse in the background. It reminds me of home. *They* remind me of home.

Chloe moves from the kitchen island, setting her phone onto the coffee table in front of a couch I'm all too familiar with, Evie's and Izzy's faces popping into view.

"We miss you so much!" Evie states.

"When are you coming to visit?" Izzy inquires.

"Is that why you're calling?" Evie beams. "To tell us you're coming soon? Girls' night isn't the same without you. It's like we're missing an important member of our gang."

"I know," I sigh longingly. What I wouldn't give to be there with them right now. "I'm just so exhausted lately."

"You have a lot going on," Chloe encourages. "You're in a new place. New country. New life."

"You're also pregnant. That puts a lot of strain on your body," Izzy adds, always the nurse. "You need to make sure you get plenty of rest and take care of yourself, regardless of everything else you have to do."

"I am," I tell her, although nothing could be further from the truth. I don't have time to take care of myself.

As has been ingrained into my brain these past several weeks, my needs will always come second to the Crown's. That, from now on, I serve the monarch and the country. It's a noble idea, but I would love nothing more than to be selfish and put myself first, even for just a day.

"How's Anderson?" Chloe asks, a touch of hesitation in her voice.

When I don't immediately respond, she eyes me warily, somehow able to pick up on the tension. I should have expected nothing less. She's always had a unique ability to read me, even when I tried to hide my feelings from everyone, including myself.

"What happened?" she pushes.

"I just…" I expel a long breath. "Everything came to a head last night, and I snapped. Since we arrived here, we've barely had time for each other. Between all the pre-wedding planning, public engagements, and princess training—"

Izzy holds up a hand. "Wait a hot second. What's *princess training*? Is that really a thing?"

"Of course." My voice oozes with sarcasm. "The future of this very nation depends on whether I know how to hold my teacup properly."

In a way, it does. Like Queen Veronica told me, it's all about the illusion. Once the illusion disappears, once people see us as normal, the monarchy risks becoming obsolete.

"We haven't had sex since right before the king announced our engagement," I admit softly. "Over three weeks ago."

"When you say *right* before," Evie states, "are we talking in the throne room before? Or…"

"No. Not the throne room," I giggle, already feeling better and a little less homesick.

"Pity." Chloe smirks. "But getting back to this unusual dry spell… What's going on with you two? Why no hanky-panky?"

For some couples, three weeks wouldn't be long at all. We've gone longer, but not when we were living together. And certainly not when we shared a bed every night.

"We haven't had time. Our days are filled with obligations. Even on the weekend, we're torn in two different directions. There have been a few nights I've tried to stay up until he got home, but I'm constantly exhausted. Plus, morning sickness has kicked my butt. Most days, I can barely stomach more than some dry toast or crackers. And let's not talk about how much the royal family hates me."

"Esme doesn't hate you," Izzy reminds me. "At least the few times I've met her, she seemed quite nice. Not like a princess at all."

"Oh, Esme's great. It's Anderson's grandmother who worries me."

"God, that woman." Chloe rolls her eyes. "She's been known to make even some paparazzi cry, and they usually have thick skin. You have to in order to not give a shit about invading someone's personal space in their moment of vulnerability, all for a buck. I wouldn't be surprised if she has a jar where she stores all their tears. Or souls. Or hearts."

"Either would I. Pretty sure she tried to get me to cry when she invited me for tea."

All my friends lean closer to the screen, hanging on to my every word.

"Do tell." Evie grins mischievously.

"You guys can't repeat a word of this conversation. Or really anything. My PR team wouldn't like the idea of me talking to you at all, since you two work for a magazine." I point between Evie and Chloe. "But that's not going to happen."

"Damn straight," Evie snips. "We'd hunt you down. Plan a rescue mission if we had to. Bust you out of there."

I bark out a laugh at the image of a very pregnant

Evie and extremely pregnant Chloe being part of any sort of rescue attempt.

"Plus, you know we'll never share things you tell us in confidence," Chloe adds. "That's not how we work. We may love our jobs, but we value our friendship more. We've kept you out of the headlines so far, haven't we?"

"Yes. You certainly have." I smile, although my heart squeezes, emotion overwhelming me. I love talking to these girls, but every minute I do makes me miss them more than I thought I would. Makes me want to pack my bags, hop on a plane, and never look back.

But if I did that, I'd be leaving a piece of my heart here.

I'd be leaving *Anderson* here.

"So what happened at tea with Queen Veronica?" Evie presses.

"She tried to bribe me."

Their eyes widen.

"As long as they're able to establish paternity, of course. They won't pay if I'm not actually carrying Anderson's child."

"Bribe you? So you'd…leave?" Izzy's voice rises at the end.

"Yup. Unless I opted to 'eliminate' the problem," I tell them using air quotes.

All their mouths drop open simultaneously.

"That hag!" Evie exclaims once her shock wears off.

Hag isn't a word I'd use to describe Queen Veronica. At least not regarding her outward appearance. She's the picture of beauty and grace. But I can attest to the fact that the inside doesn't match the outside one bit.

"What did you tell her?" Izzy inquires.

"I told her to shove it. And not just metaphorically. Word for word, I told her she could take her bribe and shove it up her ass."

The line goes silent, my friends staring at me in shock, mouths agape. Then Chloe laughs. Soon, everyone joins in, including myself. I can't remember the last time I've laughed. The last time I've felt this happy, even if it's fleeting.

"Wait a minute. Wait a minute. Wait a minute…" Chloe clutches her protruding stomach as she struggles to breathe. "You told Queen Veronica, Anderson's grand-mother, *the queen mother*, to shove it up her ass?"

I shrug, my lips quirking into a small smile. "Then I got up and stormed out of there. But not before curtseying and saying 'Your Majesty' in an overly dramatic way." I swipe at the tears streaming down my cheeks, unsure if it's from laughing or crying. Possibly a combination of both.

"It's official," Chloe says. "You're my hero."

"What was I supposed to do?" I counter. "Accept her offer to leave? Not an option."

"And now?" Izzy interjects. "Is leaving *still* not an option?"

The frivolity filling our conversation mere seconds ago vanishes, all our expressions becoming serious.

"I don't know," I answer honestly.

"What did you and Anderson fight about last night?" Evie asks.

I glance toward his side of the bed, the covers still drawn up, evidence he didn't sleep here last night.

"It all started because he missed my doctor's appointment yesterday."

I don't even have to explain why that's a big deal. They know. To most women, that first appointment with your OB is a big deal. But for me, for someone who's experienced an excruciating loss in the past, it's even more important.

"Did he tell you why?" Izzy asks.

"Wait…," Chloe interjects. "He had an appearance with the Queen of England, didn't he?"

It doesn't matter that she was promoted to the current affairs desk at the magazine a few years ago and is no longer working on the celebrity news column. Chloe still likes to keep an ear out for gossip. Then again, this is probably more current affairs than gossip.

"Queen Veronica was supposed to greet her and appear with her at Westerly College," I explain, "but she woke up with a head cold and didn't want to get the queen sick, so she asked Anderson to fill in on her behalf. I know how it sounds," I add quickly. "He definitely had a valid reason, so I didn't go all crazy on him because of one isolated incident."

"But because of everything else, too," Chloe states matter-of-factly.

"It was just the catalyst. The event that drew into focus something I've felt since our engagement was announced."

"And what's that?"

I look up at the ceiling, taking a moment to collect my thoughts. "As I stood next to Anderson, his arm around my shoulders, while his father announced to the media that he'd granted us his permission to marry, it felt like a stranger's arm was around me. It wasn't Anderson's. It was Prince Gabriel's, this man I know nothing about. I brushed it off, though, because I still saw bits of Anderson, too. But in the past few weeks, as I've learned more and more about the royal family, its history, seen coverage of his public appearances, it feels like I'm sharing a bed with a man I don't know. That I'm about to marry a man I don't know."

Evie offers me a sympathetic smile. If any of my friends can empathize with what I'm going through, it would be her. She dealt with something similar with her husband, Julian. Maybe not to the level of Anderson and me, but she can certainly relate.

"Do you want to know what changed my mind about Julian?" she asks, her green eyes awash with compassion.

"What's that?"

"I realized how lucky I was. When I first learned that Julian kept this huge secret from me, that he was the subject of the article I'd been writing for the magazine, unbeknownst to me, I was absolutely furious. It was the worst kind of betrayal. But then I realized the truth."

"The truth?" I repeat, swallowing hard through the ache burning my chest.

"I was one of the few lucky people to know Julian. The *real* Julian. Not this other persona he'd created. Just like you're lucky enough to know the real Anderson, the side of this highly sought-after prince that no one else gets to see. Who cares if you don't know Prince Gabriel? What you have is infinitely more special. Sure, when his father was up there announcing your engagement and upcoming marriage, Anderson may have not been the same man.

But I guarantee you the love he has for you *is* the same. Don't throw it away because you don't think you know him. You do. You know him better than anyone. And I'm not saying that because you own his cock."

I burst out laughing, swiping my tears from my cheeks.

"It's because you own his heart," Chloe adds. "Regardless of whether he's the Anderson you met on Route 66 or the Prince Gabriel the public adores, his heart is still the same. There's no doubt in my mind that it beats for you, and only you."

Emotion swells in my chest, and I choke out a sob. "God, I hate all these pregnancy hormones."

"Oh, don't get me started," Evie says. "I was watching *Schitt's Creek* the other day and couldn't stop crying."

"Was it the series finale?" Izzy asks. "Because I cried during that, too."

Evie slowly shakes her head. "No. It was that scene where David and Stevie are buying wine and equating the wine to David's sexuality, like how he likes red wine *and* white wine, and sometimes a red wine that used to be a white wine." Her lower lip quivers. "It was so beautiful how accepting Stevie was of that."

The line falls silent for a moment before we all laugh once more. Unfortunately, my moment of happiness is cut short by a knock on the door.

"Ms. Tremblay, you need to be at the palace in ninety minutes."

I groan, cursing under my breath. "Thank you!" I reply in a bright voice.

"You have to go?" Chloe presses.

"Duty calls," I sing. "It was so good to see you girls."

"It was great to see you, too," Izzy offers.

"Let's make a plan to do this every week," Evie says. "You need some normalcy in your life. Let us be that for you."

I beam. "I'd really like that."

"We would, too," Chloe states. "Now go. Be a fucking princess."

"Okay. I'll go be a fucking princess. Love you girls."

"We love you, too."

I blow a kiss to my friends, then end the call before dragging myself from my bed for another day of learning how to be a princess.

Or, as Chloe puts it, a fucking princess.

I like the sound of that much better.

But that still doesn't solve my Anderson/Prince Gabriel problem.

Can I really promise my life to a man I barely know just for the brief glimpses I get of Anderson?

What if those brief glimpses become fewer and fewer until Prince Gabriel swallows him up entirely?

Is Prince Gabriel a man I *want* to be with?

I wish I knew how to answer that.

Twenty

Anderson

"If you ask me, it was kind of a dick move," Esme snips out, not holding back at all. I didn't expect her to. She never does.

"What choice did I have?" I throw up my hands as I sit in the director's office of a local children's home where we'll play with some of the kids and read them a story, all to promote literacy and bring attention to the need for more families to open their homes to foster children, a cause Esme champions regularly. "Grandmother fell ill. Someone had to meet the Queen of England."

"It didn't have to be you," she argues, arms crossed.

"You know damn well it did, Esme. When the Queen of England comes, either the queen mother or the highest-ranking member of the royal family must go. Since Father was out of town—"

"It wouldn't surprise me if she wasn't sick at all and only canceled to keep you from going to Nora's appointment."

I wave her off, not voicing that I had the same concerns. "It wasn't just the doctor's appointment. That was merely the straw that broke the camel's back, so to speak." I pull my lips between my teeth, resting my forearms on my legs as the previous night's conversation plays on repeat, like it has all morning. "She claims she doesn't even know who I am," I manage to say through the lump in my throat.

"And rightly so," Esme agrees.

I furrow my brow, darting my eyes toward her. "What do you mean?"

She smooths a few strands of her golden blonde hair behind her ear, then saunters toward me. Always one to shun expectations and protocol, she's dressed in a sleeveless blouse tucked into a pair of skinny jeans that make her long legs appear even longer. And as a big middle finger to the establishment, she wears a pair of wedge sandals with her toes peeking through — two big no-nos.

Then there's me, the picture of conformity — crisp suit, cleanly shaven face, tie that's begun to feel more like a noose than an accessory.

"Since the news of your engagement broke, she's been immersed in this world she's had absolutely no previous experience with. She's expected to jump right in, feet first, and become a princess, wife, and royal in mere weeks? Remember how you felt when you were pulled out of school, sent to London, and forced to learn a new way of life almost overnight?"

I lower my head, nodding slowly.

"Well, for Nora, it's even harder. At least we had some exposure to all of this first. She never has. When we were ripped from our world, what was the one thing we had that helped us through it all?"

"Each other," I admit, looking around the room. The linoleum floor is cracked, and some of the tiles in the ceiling show signs of water damage. Books fill the shelves lining the far wall, many of their bindings worn. It's a rude awakening to visit places like this. Makes me even more grateful for all the opportunities I've had.

"Precisely, Anders." She sits on the couch beside me, taking my hands in hers. "We had each other. With everything else in our world turned upside down, we were able to find comfort and stability in the idea that we were still the same people we were back in the country, riding horses and getting covered in mud. But Nora…" She shakes her head. "She boarded that plane expecting to start a life with Anderson North, but instead came face-to-face with Prince Gabriel of Belmont."

"We're the same person," I argue.

She smiles sweetly, resting her hand on my bicep. "No, you're not. You may think you are, but Anderson immediately turns into Crown Prince Gabriel when the cameras are rolling or there's a crowd. You can deny it all you want, but in your heart, you know it's true. The second you're back in this country, you're different. It's not a *bad* different," she adds quickly. "I adore you, and that includes all the different versions of you. Nora's lucky to know the side of you most people don't get to see. As am I."

"How do I make her see that?" I ask in frustration, jumping to my feet and digging my hands through my hair.

Dizzy from the sudden movement, I place my hand on the armrest of the sofa as I attempt to maintain my balance. I take several deep breaths, blinking repeatedly in an attempt to clear my vision, but everything's still slightly blurred.

Esme eyes me warily, her attention focused on my hand gripping the armrest. "Are you okay, Anders?"

I take a moment to steady myself before straightening. "I'm fine." I grit out a smile, ignoring the ache in my hip, something else that's become more prominent lately.

"So, how do I make her see that?" I repeat in an effort to shift the subject back to Nora and me.

She levels a stare on me, then sighs. "I don't think your problem is showing Nora she's lucky to know Anderson. She knows she is. She wouldn't have agreed to marry you if she didn't." Her expression softens. "Maybe she needs to get to know Prince Gabriel."

I grind my jaw in irritation. "But I *am* Prince Gabriel."

"To her, you're Anderson. This man you've become is a stranger to her."

"But—"

She places her hand on my arm, cutting me off. "Do what all strangers do when they like a girl."

I blink, shaking my head. "I don't follow."

"Jesus Christ, Anders." She throws up her hands in frustration. "Are you that out of touch with reality?" she retorts playfully. "You see, in the real world, when a guy likes a girl, he asks her out on something called a date."

"You want me to ask my fiancée out on a…date?"

"Not a regular date. A date with Prince Gabriel."

"And you think that will fix this?"

She shrugs. "I don't know, but it's worth a shot. At the very least, it'll show her you acknowledge her concerns. That you're *trying*. That's all people want out of a relationship. To know your worries don't fall on deaf ears. To know the other person is listening. So show her that."

A knock on the door cuts through, and Bridge peeks his head into the office. "We're ready whenever you are."

"Thanks, Nathan. We'll be right out."

He bows. "Sir." Then he does the same to Esme. "Ma'am."

She acknowledges him with a smile before he disappears.

"Shall we?" I look at my sister.

"Absolutely."

I begin toward the door, the stiffness in my hip and leg causing me to lose my footing and nearly topple over. I grab onto the desk as Esme rushes toward me, helping me upright.

"Anders, you need to go to a doctor."

"I have," I argue.

"And not the bullshit neurologist on the royal household's payroll. A *real* doctor."

"I'm fine," I grind out.

"You are *not* fine. Stop being such a stubborn ass. There's something going on."

"It's just stress. I haven't been sleeping well, either, so that doesn't help. You know as well as I do that stress can exacerbate some of my symptoms. Muscle strain. Dizziness. That's all this is. I promise. I'm fine. Once things settle down and this vote on the damn referendum is over, I'll be as good as new."

I straighten, pushing through the pain in my hip as I step away from her, demonstrating that I'm fully capable of walking unassisted.

"See? I'm as good as gold. Now, let's go. Don't want to keep the kids waiting." I hold out my elbow for her to take.

She studies me for a beat, then exhales, walking toward me. "If you say so." She lifts her eyes to mine. "But you'd tell me if it wasn't stress. You wouldn't keep me in the dark about your prognosis. Right?"

My smile cracks as I peer into her vibrant, blue orbs that mirror mine. The one piece of our mother we both have. Her concern is well-founded. After all, our mother suffered from a more severe form of MS, but kept most of her symptoms from us — physical and psychological — until it was too late.

I hate the idea of lying to my sister.

More than that, I hate the idea of her worrying about something she has no control over.

That I'm quickly learning I have no control over, either.

"Of course I will, Esme."

"Good. Because I can't lose you, too."

I lean down, placing a soft kiss on her forehead. "You won't. Promise. I'm not going anywhere."

She wraps her arms around my waist, clinging tightly to me, resting her head against my chest. "You'd better not." She pulls back, pointing a finger in my face. "Because if you do, I swear to God, I'll strike a deal with the devil to make sure you're tortured for all eternity."

"That's assuming I'm going to hell when I die. A

pretty lofty assumption, if you ask me."

She places a hand on her hip. "Trust me, my darling brother. I know all your secrets. And if you go to heaven, provided such a place *does* exist, mankind is worse off than I originally believed."

I bark out a laugh, the sound filling the room.

At my lowest moments, I can always count on Esme to lift me up, to remind me what it's like to feel normal. She grounds me when I feel as if my world is spinning out of control. And it's this bond that helps me finally understand Nora's concerns.

She hasn't had anyone to count on as her world spun out of control, threatening to throw her off. It used to be me, but as Anderson. Now, while we're here, it needs to be Prince Gabriel.

"Hey, Esme?" I ask.

"Yes?"

"Can you do me a favor?"

Her smile turns conniving, as if able to read my thoughts. "Anything for you."

Twenty-One

Nora

"What are your plans now?" Esme approaches as I make my way out of the palace conference room where I just sat through yet another morning full of etiquette classes.

I come to an abrupt stop, momentarily surprised to see her. Then I glance at my private secretary, almost positive I have a meeting with my publicists to go over a few events leading up to the big day, all staged to paint me as a woman worthy of marrying Prince Gabriel.

It hasn't escaped my notice that everything planned is to make me appear worthy, to give off this image of perfection. I'm held up to impossible standards, whereas Anderson is revered and adored, regardless of what he does. It's such a double standard that no one can live up to, but I'm expected to do just that.

"Actually, ma'am, your next appointment has been canceled."

I furrow my brow. "My publicists canceled?" I repeat,

making sure I understood him and pregnancy brain hasn't taken over already.

"Scheduling conflict, I believe. You're free and clear for the rest of the day."

"Perfect." Esme claps excitedly. "Then we're going out."

"Out?"

"There's this great little café in the plaza by the canals." She grabs my hand, tugging me down the corridor. "They have the best tea and cakes around. You could use a break. Go somewhere other than home or the palace."

"You mean there's a world outside of these walls?" I shoot back, only half-joking.

She leans toward me. "Shh. Don't tell anyone I let you know." She winks. "We'll stop by your place so you can change."

"Change?"

"I'm sure you'd love nothing more than to put on a pair of jeans. Or really anything that doesn't require you to wear bloody pantyhose."

"You have no idea," I say, avoiding a few pointed stares from other members of the royal household who appear to believe the rules should be strictly adhered to. I can only imagine what they think of Esme's jeans and open-toed sandals. Wedges, no less. But if they disapprove, Esme doesn't seem to care.

She doesn't seem to care much for any of the rules.

"Then let's blow this joint." With a devious grin, she hands me a pair of oversized dark sunglasses.

Why do I feel like a prisoner about to break free from

captivity?

Because that's exactly what I'm about to do.

"I'd love to."

"He's not lost," Esme explains as her chief protection officer, Captain Walsh, drives around the same few blocks a couple times. "I didn't give them much notice to advance the café."

"Advance the café?" I repeat.

She smiles, but it's more out of annoyance than amusement. "Welcome to life as a royal. You can't go anywhere in public without a shadow." Her eyes meet the man driving. "No offense, Archie."

"None taken, ma'am."

She looks back at me. "There's no more popping down to the local Starbucks for a quick coffee with friends. No going for an early-morning run before the city comes to life. No strolling along the canal bridges to see the flowers on that first nice, spring day. Every single one of your movements must be approved and organized with a security team. Anywhere you want to go needs to be scouted ahead of time to make sure there are no dangers hiding within."

I nod. I may not be as accustomed to this as Esme, but I've had a little taste of royal living. People think it's a fairy-tale life. That with a crown comes the ability to do anything you want.

Nothing could be further from the truth.

"It's not optimal, but like everyone else, all you can do

is try to make the best out of the hand you've been dealt. Although saying it like that makes me seem ungrateful. I'm not. I appreciate having a platform to bring attention to causes I believe in. Just like you will. But everything in life comes at a price. You have to decide what yours is." She gives me a knowing look.

"He told you about our…disagreement, didn't he?"

"He did."

"And you think I overreacted," I say, filling in the blanks.

"Actually, I don't. This life can sweep you up in its current until you can no longer fight the riptide pulling you under. If you don't fight for yourself, no one else will. So I'm proud of you for fighting for yourself. Trust me. I know this isn't an optimal situation for any relationship. It will test you." She reaches across the seat and squeezes my hand. "But if there's any couple who will persevere, it's you two. I feel it in my soul."

She holds my gaze, then breaks away when the SUV comes to a stop. "Here we are."

Captain Walsh gets out of the SUV and swiftly makes his way to the back passenger door, opening it. Esme places her sunglasses over her eyes, then slides out grace-fully. I put my own dark glasses on and join her, a few onlookers pointing and whispering. It doesn't take a genius to figure out who we are. Esme's supermodel appearance, coupled with the security presence, is a dead giveaway. But I don't care. I'll take a group of onlookers pointing and snapping photos over being locked behind the walls of the palace any day.

"This way, ma'am," Captain Walsh says, leading us

toward an outdoor table with the perfect view of the plaza and canals. Men in casual clothes sit at a few nearby tables, drinking coffee or reading a newspaper, but I have no doubt they're part of the security team. They have the same look as every one of the protection officers I've met. Stoic expression. Built physique. Analytical eyes looking everywhere for a possible threat.

I sit beside Esme, noticing all the chairs face the canals instead of each other, encouraging people to take in the beautiful surroundings.

"It reminds me of Paris," she remarks, placing her sunglasses on the table. I do the same. "This is how many sidewalk cafés are set up there, especially along the Seine."

"I haven't been."

She straightens. "You haven't?"

"Anderson promised he'd eventually take me." I shrug. "So we'll see."

"Well, if he doesn't, I will. Everyone needs to experience the City of Lights." A peaceful expression washes over her, as if the mere thought of Paris reinvigorates her. "Don't tell anyone, but it's my favorite place on the planet."

I smile. "Your secret's safe with me."

"Good," she replies as a man approaches. Unlike the rest of the waitstaff here, who wear just a white shirt and black pants, he's dressed in a crisp suit, making me think he's the owner or manager.

"Your Highness." He performs a slight bow. "So wonderful to see you again. Would you like your typical order?"

"Yes. Except let's do a green tea, one with a touch of

ginger and peach, if you have one."

"Of course, ma'am." After bowing once more, he retreats.

"Don't worry," she says in a low voice. "It's caffeine-free. And the ginger does wonders for any morning sickness. At least that's what I'm told.

"Now, if you'll excuse me for a minute…" She pushes back from the table and stands. "I need to go freshen up. I'll be right back."

"Okay." I watch as she retreats, a protection officer following, then shift my attention to my surroundings. I inhale the fresh air, feeling like a caged animal that's finally been reintroduced into her natural habitat.

Since the engagement announcement, I've barely spent any time in public. The only times I've been allowed to leave the palace, aside from being at Anderson's estate, have been for pre-wedding planning or on a photo shoot with my publicist. Since the night the paparazzi found Anderson and me at Esme's dinner party, we haven't been seen together once.

Almost like someone doesn't *want* us to be seen together. Doesn't want people to think we're actually going to be married.

Doing my best to push down the negative thoughts, I turn my attention back to the canals in front of me, marveling at the sheer number of people riding bikes here. When I sense a presence looming beside me, I look to my right, expecting to see one of the waitstaff approaching with our tea.

Instead, my gaze falls on a suit-clad body, debonair smile, and enigmatic blue eyes.

"Anderson? What are you—"

"Shh," he hushes me before I can finish. "How about some role play?" He winks.

Role play? Here? Sure, we once did just that at least once a week in New York to keep things fun, meeting at various spots in the city and pretending to fall in love as different people all over again. But how is that going to help our situation? I'm not interested in falling in love with a stranger.

I inhale a sharp breath, the realization washing over me.

"Or perhaps *real* play might be more appropriate right now," he says.

"Real play?" I repeat.

He nods slowly, keeping his hopeful eyes locked on mine. "Yes. Real play."

I blow out a small laugh. "I think that's exactly what we need."

"As do I."

Twenty-Two

Anderson

"My name's Gabriel." I extend my hand, pleading with Nora to take it. Like she holds my entire future in her hands.

In a way, she does.

Finally, she places her hand in mine. "Nora."

"Nora," I croon in a husky voice that sends a visible shiver through her. She can try to deny it all she wants, but her body still responds to me the same way it did the first time our eyes locked in that Chicago diner. "That's a beautiful name."

Gaze trained on her, I gradually lift her hand to my lips. Her complexion reddens, chest heaving with her increasing breaths. When I brush my mouth against her knuckles, I swear a tiny moan escapes her throat.

God, that sound does things to me.

I release my grip on her before I can't resist the temptation to yank her from the chair and pin her against the wall as I give her a taste of precisely what she'll miss if she leaves. But I don't, remembering the part I'm here to play.

"Would you like some company?" I gesture to the empty chair.

"I'd love some."

"Wonderful." Unbuttoning my suit jacket, I lower myself into Esme's chair. "I get the feeling you're not from around here."

"What makes you say that?"

"Just a hunch, although that adorable American accent of yours is a dead giveaway."

She's about to respond when the owner of the café approaches. Noticing me beside Nora, he straightens, my presence obviously taking him by surprise. But he recovers quickly and bows.

"Your Highness."

"Good to see you, Lewis."

"Here are the tea, scones, and sandwiches Her Highness ordered, sir."

"Lovely. Thank you."

"Of course." He gives Nora a smile and, after another quick bow toward me, retreats.

I grab the pot and pour liquid into the two small teacups before adding a bit of sweetener to both. I slide her cup and saucer toward her, ensuring the handle points in the correct direction.

"A toast." I lift my teacup.

"With tea?"

"Why not?"

"What shall we drink to?" She raises her cup.

"What do you say to second chances and fresh starts?"

A shy grin tugs on her lips, her eyes gleaming. "I think

it's perfect. To second chances and fresh starts."

We clink teacups and take a sip. After returning my cup to its saucer, I grab her plate, serving her a few finger sandwiches from the three-tiered presentation.

"I should probably tell you," I begin once I have a plate of my own, "I'm kind of a big deal around here."

"Is that so?" She places the cloth napkin over her lap.

"I can see why you wouldn't know, considering you're not from here."

"And why are you a big deal?"

"Truthfully, it's rare that I lead with this information. Not because I'm trying to hide who I am," I add quickly. "I simply don't want it to cloud someone's opinion of me. Most of my relationships have been…superficial. People only tend to spend time with me because of who I am. To this day, I can count on one hand the number of authentic people in my life." I narrow my gaze on her. "The number of people who know the *real* me."

She averts her eyes, a hint of remorse tugging on her expression.

"But something tells me you don't have a superficial bone in your body," I continue, pulling her attention back to me. "That despite who I am, you'll decide whether I'm worth your time based on my merits. Nothing else."

"I'd like to think I'm not one-dimensional enough to only want to be with someone because of any alleged clout they may have. Trust me. I was raised by one of the most superficial women out there. The last thing I want is to turn into my mother."

"Fair enough." I straighten, inhaling a deep breath. My stomach flutters, hands growing clammy.

Why am I nervous? She already knows the truth. But I'm desperate for this to go right. Desperate for today to be the first page in this new chapter. Not the end of a story cut too short.

"Here goes nothing." I take a deep breath and lift my eyes to meet Nora's. "I'm a prince."

Silence fills the air between us. I barely even register the background noises of the city around us, my confession lingering. Much like it did when I told her the first time.

And just like that first time all those months ago, she makes light of my admission.

"Is that just some cheesy pickup line? If so, you've got your work cut out for you, buddy, because I've heard better."

I throw my head back and laugh. "Trust me, gorgeous. I wish it were just some cheesy pickup line. But it's true. My name is Gabriel Anderson Joseph Xavier Wellingston, and I'm next in line to the throne here in the beautiful country of Belmont."

"Is that right?"

"'Fraid so."

"Then tell me, Prince Gabriel…." She edges closer, the gentle breeze wafting her perfume toward me.

It reminds me of the miles we drove together in a Jeep Wrangler with the top down. For weeks after our adventure ended in heartache, I smelled her everywhere. I thought it was the penance I was forced to pay for my sins. That I'd forever be tormented by my brief slice of heaven while I roamed the depths of hell.

"Why is a prince talking to a girl in a sidewalk café? I

imagine you must have no shortage of women vying for your attention."

"That's certainly true. And I'd be remiss if I didn't mention that quite a few people in my inner circle already have a strong opinion on who I should…associate with."

"Associate with?"

"Date. And eventually marry."

"You make it sound like a professional connection. Not a romantic one."

"In my world, that's all a marriage is. A strategic decision."

"But that's not what you want." It's more a statement than a question.

"No."

"Then what do you want?"

"Love," I answer without a moment's hesitation. "And not some promise or assurance that I may eventually learn to love someone. I want the real thing. That butterfly-inducing, heart-racing, soul-fulfilling love most people think only exists in fairy tales. Which is why I had to come over here and talk to you. Because the second I looked up and saw you, I…" I trail off, words feeling grossly inadequate to relay how I felt the first time I noticed her.

And how I felt when I saw her walk into this café with Esme moments ago. We may not be the strangers we once were, but my feelings are the same. The way my heart aches for her is the same.

"Yes?" She leans closer, desperate for my next words.

"I couldn't shake the feeling that you were put in my life for a reason. And despite what happens, I knew I'd always regret it if I didn't…"

"Didn't what?" Her breath dances on my lips, taunting and teasing, making my mouth salivate with an unquenched thirst.

As much as I want to kiss her, I can't rush this. I need to sweep her off her feet. Need to give her the fairy tale she deserves.

But as Prince Gabriel this time.

"Ask you out." I abruptly pull back.

She blinks repeatedly, mouth slightly agape. Then she smooths a hand down her shirt, adjusting her composure. "Ask me…out?"

"People do go on dates where you're from, correct?"

"Yes, but—"

"Then, Nora from America, would you do me the honor of accompanying me to dinner tomorrow night?"

"Dinner?"

"Yes. Dinner."

"How will that work?"

"I'll pick you up and—"

"I get that." Her voice drops to barely a whisper. "But what about any prior engagements? Mine *and* yours."

"Consider them canceled."

"Canceled?"

I smirk. "I managed to get your afternoon meeting canceled, did I not? As well as mine. I'll simply do the same tomorrow."

"*You* planned this?" Her tone isn't accusatory. More appreciative with a touch of awe.

"I did." I clutch her hand, running my thumb over her diamond ring. "We may not be able to be as spontaneous as we were in New York, considering every move we make here has to be properly planned. But I wanted to make this seem as…authentic as possible."

Her smile slowly builds, lighting up her entire expression. A glow I haven't seen in too long washes over her. "Thank you," she squeaks out. "That means a lot."

"It's the least I could do."

I hold her gaze for a moment, then clear my throat, falling back into my Prince Gabriel persona. "So what do you say? Can I take you on a date? Get to know you better? Allow you to get to know Prince Gabriel?"

"I'd really like that." A weight seems to lift off her, allowing me a glimpse of the carefree girl I once made scale a fence so we could check out an abandoned drive-in along Route 66, despite the 'No Trespassing' signs.

"I'd really like that, too. I promise to do everything to make it a first date you'll never forget." I slide my chair back and stand, buttoning my jacket. "I'll pick you up at seven." Grabbing her hand, I bring it up to my lips, savoring the feeling of her smooth skin. "Until then, gorgeous, I'll be counting down the minutes." I reluctantly release my hold on her and turn, one of the protection officers jumping up from a nearby table and following.

As I approach the sidewalk, a dark SUV pulls up, the officer opening my door for me. I'm about to get in, but hesitate, meeting Creed's gaze behind the wheel.

"Give me one minute."

"Yes, sir."

A man on a mission, I stride back toward Nora's table, ignoring my sister as she sits beside her.

Nora shoots her wide eyes toward mine. "Did you forget something?"

"Yes."

She glances around the table. "What? I don't——"

"This."

In one swift move, I pull her up from her chair and yank her body against mine. Not giving her a moment to protest, I dig my free hand into her hair and lower my mouth toward hers.

"Anderson," she says quickly, placing her hand on my chest, stopping me.

I search her face, petrified I'll see the same woman who left me alone in the garden last night. Instead, a sly smile greets me.

"What about the rules forbidding public displays of affection?" she teases. "From where I'm standing, we are most certainly in public right now." She gestures subtly with her head.

I look where she indicates and see an interested group of onlookers. It's not a huge mob, but people are taking pictures. I have no doubt our location has already been leaked on social media.

All sense of reason tells me to retreat, to remember the rules and my place. But why should I have to hide my love for this woman? Because some prude centuries ago thought it improper to show the world what love looks like? I'm done with that.

Eyes narrowing, I tighten my grip. "Fuck the rules," I growl, my lips covering hers.

She's uncertain at first, seemingly at war with how to respond, what kind of backlash she'll face. I respond by holding her tighter. My tongue swipes against her mouth, begging her to kiss me back.

That's all it takes for her to relax, parting her lips for me. At that first taste, she moans, running her fingers through my hair and tugging at it.

Cheers and whistles echo around us, but neither one of us seems to care. All we do care about is this moment. Of not permitting anyone else to dictate how we should love each other. Of no longer hiding our love from the public.

I pull away and stare at her in awe, my skin tingling. This time, it's not from the MS but from the effect this woman has on me. I want to drag her home and lose myself in her for the rest of the night. But as much as I want her right now, especially after the dry spell of the past several weeks, her needs are my priority. Before I can make love to her as Anderson again, I need her to figure out where Prince Gabriel fits into her life. It's the only way this will work.

I rest my forehead on hers, our heavy breaths echoing around us. I lick my lips, the taste of Nora still on them.

"Seven o'clock tomorrow," I tell her.

"Seven o'clock tomorrow."

"Good." I release her, about to retreat once more, but stop. I curve into the crook of her neck. "And do me a favor."

"What's that?"

I drop my voice. "Don't wear any panties."

I allow my request to sink in, then meet her stunned expression. Leaving a chaste kiss on her cheek, I head toward the waiting SUV, waving to a few onlookers who call my name.

"Did it work?" Creed asks as he pulls away.

"Only time will tell," I answer, taking one last look at the café, Nora still in a state of shock. "But if I were a betting man, I'd be all in."

Twenty-Three

Nora

"Why am I so nervous about this?" I glance at Esme as she expertly applies some liner around my lips.

As I stare at the drawers upon drawers filled with more makeup than most people think necessary to own in a lifetime, I can't help but be impressed. I always considered myself fairly experienced with hair and makeup, but my skills are no match for hers. After all the people who worked on me for the official engagement announcement, not to mention a stylist who helps me pick out my wardrobe and get ready every day, I assumed she also had someone to do it for her.

Instead, she told me she learned how so she could have time to herself before being put on display. To most, it would seem a crazy notion, since so many women look forward to being pampered at the salon, myself included.

But that was before I had a taste of this life. Of always having people do everything for me, right down to helping me dress…and undress. As if I'm a child, not an adult capable of taking care of myself.

Now, her expertise has allowed me to escape the estate to get ready for my date with Anderson. Or, more appropriately, Prince Gabriel.

"I think it's cute. He's nervous, too." She winks, stepping back and spinning me so I face the mirror.

I felt completely out of my element when choosing what to wear, unsure where he planned to take me. He didn't give me much direction, aside from not wearing any panties. I debated whether to go with something casual, but considering he's taking me out as Prince Gabriel, I opted for something a bit more formal. It's not at the level of the dress I wore for the official announcement, but it's still sophisticated, yet something not in my "approved" wardrobe. Something I brought with me from New York.

I'm fairly certain the sleek, curve-hugging black dress would break all protocol rules. From the off-the-shoulders neckline that makes my cleavage appear even more pronounced, to the slit running up my thigh, to the leopard print strappy heels that show off my bright red toenails, it is most definitely not royal family approved.

But like Anderson…Prince Gabriel said last night… Fuck the rules.

When a chiming cuts through, my pulse skyrockets, butterflies flittering in my stomach.

"Sounds like your date's here," Esme teases in a singsong voice, spinning from me. I follow her out of the dressing room, down the hallway, and toward the stairs leading to the foyer.

Hand on the railing, I do my best to keep myself from

tripping over my own feet, something that's been known to happen. With every step I take, more and more of Anderson's tall frame appears, starting with his dark shoes, up to his perfectly tailored tan pants, then his matching suit jacket. I expect the look to be finished with a crisp, white button-down shirt and coordinating tie, similar to what he typically wears. Instead, he's sporting a V-neck, black t-shirt, his chest muscles prominent against the material.

Like he wore during our time together on Route 66.

It's a reminder that, despite his public persona as Prince Gabriel, underneath all the glitz and glamor is the man I fell in love with.

When our eyes meet, I can't look away. Just like I couldn't when I heard a deep, accented voice tell me to rub Lincoln's nose for good luck as I stared at the bronze bust outside the final resting place of the sixteenth president.

Lips parted, he barely blinks as he drinks me in. He starts at my feet, my toes grateful to finally see the light of day after being covered up these past several weeks. His gaze only grows more heated as it travels up my legs, jaw tightening. When his eyes return to mine, they're no longer a mixture of every shade of blue, but a dark midnight, raw hunger swirling within.

"Goddamn, am I a lucky bastard," he hisses under his breath.

"And don't you forget it," I respond with a nervous laugh.

"Never."

His stare lingers on me in a way that makes me think he's about to pin me up against the wall and kiss me, much like he did the first night we slept together. But he doesn't. There's time for that later, though.

He clears his throat, briefly looking away. "I know most men bring flowers on a first date, but I'm not most men."

"You don't say."

He flashes a brilliant smile, the white of his teeth bright against his tanned complexion. "So while I don't have any real flowers for you, I do have something I hope you'll find just as acceptable." He reaches into his jacket and produces a small, black velvet box.

"Anders…," I begin.

"Gabriel," he reminds me.

"Of course." I nod, playing along. "Gabriel."

At one time, the name felt foreign on my tongue, the man in front of me not resembling a Gabriel. But in this moment, I actually see the crown prince and future king. But that's not all I see. Mixed within the pieces of the man who will one day rule this country, I still see bits of Anderson. More than I have recently.

"You didn't have to get me anything," I admonish, as I always do whenever he spoils me with something he just couldn't resist buying.

"I know. But I still wanted to do something for you. A token of my appreciation." He extends the box toward me.

When I pop it open, my hand flies to my chest. All the air is ripped from my lungs as I stare at what I can only assume to be Prince Gabriel's version of buying flowers for his date. Technically, they *are* flowers. But instead of something that will wither and die in a few days, it's something I can keep forever — a pair of earrings in the shape of a flower.

"That's a yellow diamond in the center with five pear-shaped diamonds around it. Total weight of each is about a carat."

"They're gorgeous."

"I bet they'll be even more gorgeous on you. May I?" He extends his hand again. I nod, passing him the box before quickly removing the simple diamond studs I'd been wearing. He takes them from me and drops them into the inside pocket of his suit jacket. Then he steers me toward the large mirror in the foyer of Esme's townhouse.

There's something inherently intimate about watching our reflection as Anderson secures the earrings to each ear. Once he's finished, he stands back to appreciate them, his hands on my shoulders.

I cover one of his hands with mine, squeezing. "Thank you."

"Anything for you, gorgeous." He holds my gaze in the mirror for a beat, then releases me. "What do you say we get this date started?" He offers me his elbow.

I face him and hook my arm through his. "I'd love to."

"Have fun, kids!" Esme calls after us as we walk toward the door.

I stop abruptly. I'd forgotten she stood just a few feet away. That always seems to happen whenever I'm around Anderson. And now Prince Gabriel, too.

Excusing myself, I rush to Esme and hug her. "Thank you."

"I only did your hair and makeup."

I pull back and shake my head. "No. You did a lot

more than that."

She holds me at arm's length, squeezing my biceps. "You both deserve to be happy. If you'd both just get out of your own way every once in a while. Now go. Enjoy your fairy tale. And come midnight, neither one of you better turn into a bloody pumpkin, or you'll have me to answer to."

"We won't. Promise." I give her one last hug, then allow Anderson to lead me down her front steps and into the back seat of the idling SUV.

Once I'm situated and Creed pulls away, that same nervous energy returns, a heat caressing my skin. As I steal a glance at Anderson, I know exactly what's causing it. His eyes flame as his gaze rakes over me, exploring, craving. The hair on the back of my nape stands on end, my pulse picking up with each longing stare.

"Did you do as I asked?" His voice is low and seductive.

"What's that?" I squeak out.

He glances at my legs and leans toward me. His hand caresses my flesh, starting above my knee and leisurely moving higher before disappearing up my slit. His breath heats my neck, my libido screaming at him to keep going and not stop until he touches me between my thighs.

The poor girl's been quite neglected these past few weeks.

"Did you wear any panties?" he murmurs.

I close my eyes, my breathing becoming more ragged with every inch his fingers creep toward my center. Swallowing down a moan, I curve into him. "A little farther, and you can find out for yourself."

He pinches his lips together. "True." He moves his hand farther north, then suddenly retreats. "But not yet."

"No?"

He slowly shakes his head. "No."

"Then when?"

"Soon. And don't worry. I plan on making the wait worth your while, love."

"You'd better." I cross my arms over my chest. "Because my libido is in rare form tonight."

"Is that right?"

"She's had a bit of a dry spell lately."

"Let's see what we can do about putting an end to that sooner rather than later."

I bite my bottom lip. "I like the sound of that."

After a short drive filled with sexual tension, Creed pulls up in front of a restaurant. When I notice the paparazzi already waiting, I assume he'll continue around to the back. He doesn't, though.

I look toward Anderson, a single brow raised.

"Part of dating a prince is cameras and paparazzi following us. Since I've had a penchant for breaking the rules lately, I figured I'd break one more. Instead of waiting for the paparazzi to find me, as they always do, I had my people tell them where I am so my security team could control the situation from the beginning. See?"

He nods out the window. Police barricades are set up, much like at pre-planned engagements. It's a marked difference from the last time I'd encountered the paparazzi. There's no frenzy of people shouting and grab-bing. It's orderly. Manageable. Safe.

"Better to take control of the situation before it

controls you. Now, shall we create some headlines?"

I look from the crowd and back to Anderson, my mouth growing dry. I thought we'd go somewhere private where no one would be able to see us. But to walk through the front entrance of a restaurant where there are actual diners? To do something normal people do?

This is exactly what I need. What I've needed since I first landed in this country and my life was turned upside down.

"Absolutely."

"Good."

When Creed opens the door, Anderson steps out to a chorus of cheers and camera flashes. He buttons his suit jacket, giving a quick wave to the crowd before turning back toward the car, offering me his hand.

I slide across the seat, praying this isn't a repeat of the night we were chased from Esme's dinner party. After the past few weeks, I'm not exactly in the mood for a bunch of jealous girls to point out every single of one of my imperfections and tell me all the reasons Caroline DeVries is better suited for Anderson. Especially after my unexpected phone call from my mother yesterday.

But like Anderson said, this is part of dating Prince Gabriel. That's what I wanted. And that's precisely what he's giving me.

On a deep inhale, I carefully step out of the SUV. The instant my feet hit the pavement, the camera flashes increase, people shouting my name. But that's not all. They're begging Anderson to kiss me like he did yesterday, a few photos having made the rounds on social media, much to my publicist's chagrin.

Anderson smirks, playfully waggling his brows. "What do you say, love? Should we give them what they want?"

I place my hand on his chest, tilting my head back. "I wouldn't want to disappoint your adoring fans."

"See, that's where you're wrong." He yanks my body against his, lips descending toward me. The cheers grow louder with every inch he erases. "They're *your* adoring fans now, too."

As his mouth covers mine, cheers and applause echo around us, cameras clicking even more hurriedly in an attempt to capture the perfect shot of our kiss.

The evening's barely begun, yet there's no doubt in my mind.

This is the perfect date with a prince.

Twenty-Four

Nora

"What is this place?" I ask later that evening when Creed pulls the SUV in front of a three-story, industrial-looking brick building, not a soul in sight, the only sound that of the occasional dog barking and the lapping of ocean waves in the distance, indicating we must be somewhere near the water's edge.

"You'll see," Anderson answers with a devilish smirk.

"It's where you hide the bodies, right?" I joke. "This whole prince thing is just a front, a way to lure unsuspecting young women to your lair?"

He leans toward me, midnight blue eyes undressing me. "You figured out my secret. Although the only woman I hope to lure to my lair is you, gorgeous." He winks as Creed opens my door.

Once my feet hit the cracked sidewalk, I look up at the building.

It's a complete one-eighty from the picture of perfection of Anderson's estate and the palace. Not somewhere

I'd ever imagine him spending any meaningful time. Or bringing a date.

After the extravagant five-course dinner that oozed with sophistication and romance, I expected more of that. Not to end up in an area of town that's more akin to Jersey City than Central Park West.

"This way." He places his hand on the small of my back and steers me toward a large metal door. After punching a code into the keypad, the door buzzes.

A musky, woodsy scent surrounds me as I warily step into what appears to be a vast, empty space. The only light comes from the full moon shining in through rain-spotted, grimy windows.

Anderson takes my hand in his, leading me to the far corner of the room. Despite the relative darkness, he seems to know precisely where he's going, as if he can navigate this path blindfolded.

When we approach a pair of gated doors, he opens them, revealing a cage-like elevator.

"I've seen rickety elevators like this in the movies, and it never ended well for the woman who stupidly got in it."

"Come on. Live a little." He waggles his brows as he pulls me inside, then tugs the door closed. After he presses a few buttons, it starts with a jolt, moving at a languid pace.

"Where *are* we?" I press once more.

"I told you…" He erases the distance, pinning me against the wall. "I'm bringing you back to my secret lair."

"Is that right?" I reply in a sultry voice.

Throughout the night, there's been a flirtatious vibe between us, even more so than usual. Probably because it's been so long since we've been intimate, both of us ready to snap at any moment. But despite the fact Anderson insisted on sitting as close to me as possible during dinner, he's barely touched me, leaving me squirming.

The anticipation is driving me mad.

"You're about to find out."

The elevator comes to a stop, but he doesn't retreat, his gaze searing into me, warming me from the inside out.

"Aren't we going to get off?" I ask in a shaky voice.

His eyes flame in the darkness, jaw clenching. Then he nuzzles the crook of my neck as he grinds his hips against me. "God, I really fucking hope so. You have no idea how badly I need to get off."

"I think I do." I run my hand through his hair, pulling him closer. "I've been on edge all night long."

He pulls back. "Any reason for that?"

"You know the reason for that."

"Do I?" he counters, feigning innocence.

"You're the one who told me not to wear any panties, then barely laid a hand on me all night."

His conniving grin returns as he rakes his gaze down my body. "In my experience, delayed gratification can be quite...pleasurable."

"And sadistic," I retort.

"Trust me, love. I'll make it worth your while." Winking, he opens the cage door and steps into yet another dark space.

I take a moment to compose myself, drawing in a shaky breath to calm my raging hormones.

Everything about tonight has been perfect. From going out in public as Prince Gabriel's fiancée, to the amazing dinner, to the even more amazing conversation as Anderson and I reconnected after weeks of being torn in two different directions.

But right now, I don't want to be wined and dined. I don't want to be romanced. I want Anderson. More than I think I ever have.

"Welcome to my secret lair," he says once I step off the elevator. "Or, as I like to refer to it, my studio."

He flicks a switch on the wall, bathing everything in light. Pipes and beams run the length of the ceiling, the walls exposed brick. A variety of different light stands have been arranged in the corner, as well as cables and a few fans. Framed prints and canvases are interspersed throughout, some on easels, some hanging on the walls. From what I know of Anderson's style, they're all his work.

"You have a studio?"

"I do."

"Why isn't it at your house? You have enough space there."

"Because sometimes you need an escape. Esme's cooking is hers. This is mine. Where I come when things get to be too much. When I need to feel…" He trails off, searching for the right word.

"Normal," I finish his statement.

"Exactly." He pushes a strand of hair behind my ear. "When I need to feel normal."

"Who knows about this?" I pull away from him and continue into the room, studying the photographs.

"Just Esme and Creed. And now you. This is a part of myself I don't share with many people. But I want *you* to know this side of me. Give you another peek into who I am." He gazes around the dimly lit space. "There are a lot of pieces of me sprinkled around here."

I survey the various images. If I know anything about Anderson, I'd assume each of the photos he chose to display here holds a special place in his heart. Has a deep meaning for him.

"When did you take this?"

I move toward a mostly black-and-white image on canvas. The only color is a red balloon against a cloudy sky, a young, blonde girl standing on the beach watching it float away. There's a sadness in its simplicity that draws me to it.

"Is it recent?" I glance over my shoulder as he approaches.

"Actually, no. That was the first photo I'd ever taken. At least with a professional camera and using some of the techniques my instructor taught me. That's Esme."

"Esme?" I whip my attention back to the canvas, squinting. "But this girl... She couldn't have been more than seven or eight."

"Seven."

"You started learning photography at eight?"

"My therapist thought it would be good for me."

"I remember you telling me that. I assumed, well... I guess once I learned who you were and that your girlfriend had passed away unexpectedly..."

"You assumed my therapist suggested it as a coping mechanism after Kendall's death."

"Yeah."

"It was to cope with, well..." He waves a hand around. "All of this, I suppose. Going from a nobody to suddenly being on everyone's radar. Being chased by paparazzi at only eight years of age. Coming to terms with the fact that my life was no longer my own."

I study him, my heart aching for the little boy who had to grow up overnight. I may not have had the best mother, but I was still able to be a child. He was deprived of that.

"Did it help? Photography, I mean."

"It did. Knowing that I had photography, had this hobby… It was and still is something that's just for me. A part of me the rest of the world doesn't get. I'm probably not making any sense, but—"

I place my hand on his cheek, and he lifts his gaze to me. "You make perfect sense. I understand now. Prince Gabriel's more a mask than a person, something you need to don to protect yourself from everything that goes along with the job."

He smiles sadly as he nods. "And you'll have to do the same. You'll have to be a different person when you're in public. You can still give them parts of you, don't have to be this uncaring machine, but if you give them all of you, there will be nothing left for me." His Adam's apple bobs in a hard swallow. "Worse, there will be nothing left for you."

Eyes impassioned, he grips my cheeks so I'm unable to escape, unable to avoid this conversation, forced to face the reality of my future.

"I'm sorry I kept Prince Gabriel from you for so long. It's not because I didn't want you in my life, Nora. I do." He licks his lips, a contemplative look crossing his face. "I guess I was so used to people only wanting to be with me because of *what* I am. Not *who* I am. So I may not have given you Prince Gabriel." He brushes his thumb along my bottom lip, sending a shiver through me. "But it's because I wanted you to see the best part of me. The *real* part of me. Although, I must confess…"

"Yes?" I tilt my head back, my breathing growing uneven.

"*You* are the best part of me."

My heart expands more than I thought possible as his declaration fills me with love. "And *you're* the best part of me."

He leans down, erasing the last bit of space between us. When his lips touch mine, I sigh into him, his kiss like an electrical jolt, sparking me back to life. It's not a passion-filled exchange like in front of the restaurant earlier. That one was for them. But this one…a gentle meeting of our mouths…is just for us.

"Anders," I exhale.

"Yes?"

"I need you to take me home and make love to me."

"Putting out on the first date?" he jokes with a sexy lift of his brows.

"I didn't think you'd complain."

"True." He pauses. "But I'll have to respectfully decline."

"Decline?" I wiggle free of his grasp, mouth agape. "You can't be serious. You—"

He wraps an arm around my waist, tugging me against him. I initially try to resist his kiss, but it's a losing battle. Has been since the beginning.

"I have to respectfully decline," he repeats against my lips, "because we don't need to go home."

"We don't?"

With a sly smile, he shakes his head and steps back, extending his hand toward me. "Let me show you."

I eye him cautiously, but curiosity gets the better of me and I link my fingers with his, allowing him to lead me back into the elevator.

When we arrive on the third floor, Anderson opens the cage doors into yet another space. But unlike his studio, this is more like an apartment. An open-concept kitchen, dining, and living area greet me. It still has an industrial feel, but is more homey.

"So *this* must be your secret lair."

"Oh, most definitely." He chews on his bottom lip, giving me a seductive look that makes me nearly combust in my panties. If I were wearing any, that is. "Last chance to make a run for it."

"I doubt I'd be able to work that elevator." With a shrug, I lift myself onto my toes, my mouth a breath away from his. "I guess I'll have to take my chances."

"I guess you will."

He clutches my hip, yanking me against him. Our chests heave as we peer into each other's eyes. Anticipation coils deep within, all the pent-up frustration from these past several weeks threatening to spill over like lava.

Finally, he crushes his lips to mine, momentarily relieving the pressure inside me. But only for a heartbeat. When his tongue swipes against mine, lust consumes me, urging me to kiss him harder, deeper, faster, begging him to give me what I need.

Not breaking the contact, he steers me backward until my spine hits the wall. He grips my ass and, much like the first night we spent together, lifts me up, forcing my legs around his waist.

I throw my head back, moaning when I feel his erection. I pulse against him, my breath coming quicker, the combination of my lack of panties and our weeks-long dry spell winding me tighter than I have been in recent memory.

"God, baby…" He nuzzles me, nipping and sucking at the sensitive spot where my neck meets my shoulder. "You have no idea how badly I want you."

"I feel how much you want me." I slide my hand down his chest, landing on his crotch.

He hisses in a breath, briefly closing his eyes. Then he brings his thumb to my clit and slowly circles.

"And I feel how much you want me. Have been dying to do this all fucking night. You have no idea how badly I wanted to reach under the table during dinner and make you come right there."

"Anders…," I moan, moving in time with his motions.

"But I won't let anybody else have that. Your moans, your whimpers, the look on your face when you come…" He growls, rubbing me faster and faster. When he pulls back, his eyes swirl with pure animalistic hunger. "It's all mine. *I'm* the only one who gets to see that."

"Yes…" I move more frantically against him, out of my mind with lust. His words are possessive and dominant, but damn, I love it. "Only you, Anders. Oh god…" I struggle to catch my breath, my orgasm so close I can practically taste it.

"Put one foot back on the floor," he orders, readjusting his grip on me.

I do as he instructs, keeping one leg wrapped around his waist while I lower a foot to the floor. I don't feel him as hard against me as before, but that all changes when he slips a finger inside me, his thumb still circling my clit.

"This reminds me of Tucumcari." His motions quickening, he adds another finger. "Do you remember?"

"How could I forget?" I pant. "That was the night you told me who you really are. Then fingerfucked me in the alley outside of the bar."

"Because I couldn't go another minute without having you." He brings his lips to mine. My body burns hotter and hotter with east thrust and pinch. "Because I couldn't go another minute without making you come."

He covers my mouth with his as a bomb detonates inside me, swallowing my cry, waves and waves of my orgasm washing over me.

But that doesn't make him stop or pull away. He only kisses me harder, taking everything I have to offer, giving me everything he has in return.

As my body and mind come back to earth, our kiss transitions from one of desperation and hunger to one of affection and respect. It's slow, but still makes me feel all the things this man brings out in me.

My tremors waning, he lowers my other leg, maintaining his hold on me until I have my balance.

"*That's* why I asked you to not wear any panties."

"So this was all part of your plan?"

"More or less." He shrugs. "I wanted to recreate what I consider our first date, but give you the Prince Gabriel version. That first night in Tucumcari might not have been a date in the traditional sense, but I think that was where we truly began. Where we both decided to take a risk on each other. While I can't take you out to a dive bar here, then fingerfuck you in an alley, I'd like to think I've given you a taste of what that kind of date with Prince Gabriel would be like."

"I suppose…," I draw out.

"You suppose?"

"You seem to have forgotten one rather important part of that 'first date'."

"What's that?"

"That after you fingerfucked me in the alley, you all but bolted with me back to the hotel room so you could fuck me for real." I give him a coy smile. "If we're recreating that first date, but the Prince Gabriel version, you can't neglect that. Otherwise, how am I to judge which version of you I like better?"

His pupils dilate, jaw clenching. "Is that what you want, Nora? To be fucked by a prince?"

A shiver rolls through me, a new wave of moisture pooling between my legs. I swallow hard, chest heaving as he leers at me with a look that drives me wild with need.

"I…"

"Tell me you do." He leans his forearm against the wall behind me and brushes his lips against mine. "Tell me you want to be fucked by a prince."

Holy shit.

This may be the hottest thing we've done in a while. Even hotter than the quickie fuck the morning of our engagement announcement when he screwed me still dressed in his suit, the one he wore in all the photos that day. But this… This game is infinitely better.

Doing my best to keep my voice steady, I look at him with an unwavering gaze. "I want to be fucked by a prince."

Twenty-Five

Nora

Neither one of us moves as my plea hangs in the air. God, the anticipation will be the death of me. Worse, Anderson knows it, yet is still torturing me to the point that I'm pretty sure this could be considered cruel and unusual punishment.

Yes, he's already given me a mind-erasing orgasm, but I need more. Need him in all the ways I can have him.

As a prince.

As Anderson.

As both at the same time.

At the end of the day, he's all these things and more. My beautiful, mysterious, duplicitous prince.

Finally, Anderson slowly curves his lips into a devious grin. "I bet you do, my little vixen."

Grabbing my wrist, he yanks me down the hallway, his steps quick, stride purposeful. When he reaches the last door, he opens it and flicks on the switch, the low light illuminating a large room, a king-sized bed in the middle. It's not nearly as extravagant as the one I've been sleeping in the past several weeks. This one is more simple, modern, blacks and whites accented with hints of lilac and plum. It's reminiscent of Anderson's beachfront condo in Santa Monica. A peek at the man beneath the crown.

He kicks the door closed. I face him, the space between us crackling with tension. Stare resolute, he stalks toward me, shrugging out of his jacket and dropping it to the floor. My mouth goes dry at the way his muscles stretch the fabric of his black t-shirt. I haven't seen him in anything other than a suit and tie since we arrived here. It only makes my hunger for him increase.

"Turn around," he orders.

Too desperate to disagree, I obey, spinning to face the bed. My heart pounds as I wait to feel his hands on me, my skin tingling with anticipation. But I don't feel anything right away. Or even several moments later.

When I don't think I can wait another second, his breath caresses my nape. I sigh, my body becoming momentarily lax as he presses soft kisses along my shoulders.

"God, I love your skin. So smooth. So creamy. So bloody perfect."

He rests a hand on my stomach, pulling me against him, his front to my back. I whimper when he circles his hips, his erection prominent.

"I could bend you over the bed right like this and fuck you. Would you like that?"

I lean my head back against his shoulder, moaning as his hand brushes my nipple. When I don't immediately answer, he squeezes. I yelp, a shockwave of electricity rushing through me.

"Tell me, Nora."

"Y-yes."

His grip on me tightens, his arousal pressing harder against me.

"And, god, what I wouldn't give to do just that." He wraps my hair around his fist, forcing my head to the side, leaving my neck completely exposed.

It's official. This may be the hottest experience of my life. And I don't give a fuck who I'm with. Prince Gabriel. Anderson. It doesn't matter. I love all the parts that make up this man. I *want* all the parts that make up this man. The good and the bad.

When his teeth skim against my neck, I cry out.

"But I'm not." He abruptly pulls away, leaving me wanting. I should be used to this by now. It's a typical Anderson move. But damn if it doesn't frustrate me to no end. Which is precisely why he keeps doing it.

I whirl around, panting. "Not what?"

"Going to fuck you."

He's so nonchalant about it, as if talking about the weather.

He slides off his shoes, then untucks his t-shirt, pulling it over his head.

It doesn't matter how many times I've seen this man naked. I still marvel at his physique. He's lost a little muscle tone over the past year, but he still has an incredible form. Broad shoulders, sculpted chest, that chiseled V around his abdomen.

"But I just told you I wanted to be fucked by a prince," I protest.

"You also asked me to make love to you." He unbuckles his belt and slides it out of the loops.

My attention is drawn to the tufts of hair just above his waist. It's like I haven't spent the past year becoming acquainted with every part of his body. Like it's our first time all over again.

"So what's it going to be, Nora?"

I chew on my lower lip, considering my options. Why does it have to be one or the other? Why should I limit myself to only one? He can fuck me *and* make love to me at the same time. Just like my heart can love Prince Gabriel *and* Anderson North.

Sauntering up to him, I brush my lips against his. "I've finally realized I can have both." I pull back, my eyes locking with his. "I can love both."

A hint of relief flashes across his expression, the meaning in my words not lost on him.

"Just because you only see one side of me doesn't mean the other doesn't love and admire you."

I cup his cheek. "I know. I understand that now."

He loops his arm around my waist, erasing the last bit of space separating us. "You've possessed the most important part of me all along." He takes my hand and brings it to his chest, covering his tattoo of a compass. "My heart, Nora. You own it. Regardless of whether I'm putting on a show as Prince Gabriel or revealing my innermost secrets to a complete stranger I met on Route 66 as Anderson North…"

I blow out a tearful laugh at the memory.

"My heart will always belong to you."

His mouth meets mine in a searing kiss. It's not the

affectionate-filled kiss like when we first arrived here. But it's not the lust-filled kiss from mere minutes ago, either. It's a combination of both. Ravenous, yet ardent. Greedy, yet satisfied. Eager, yet content.

He grips my hip and steers me toward the bed. When the back of my legs hit the mattress, we stop, but he doesn't retreat. Instead, he finds the zipper on my dress and lowers it with ease. I help him push the sleeves down my arms, allowing the material to fall over my hips and pool at my feet.

He gradually brings our kiss to an end, his eyes flaming as they take in my black lace bra. I doubt this is on the approved list of royal attire.

"Sit on the edge of the mattress," he says in a low voice.

I nod, doing as he asks.

He drops to his knees and takes one heel-clad foot in his hand. He plants kisses from my knee down to my ankle before unfastening the strap, sliding off my shoe. I don't know how he does it, but he makes this mundane act extremely erotic, my pulse increasing when he gives my other leg the same treatment.

Not looking away, he stands, pushing down his pants and briefs before kicking them off.

"Like what you see?" He flashes me a flirtatious smirk.

"You know I do."

I grab his hand, yanking him on top of me as we both collapse onto the mattress. When I wrap my legs around his waist and feel skin against skin, I whimper.

"I need you," I murmur. "Need to feel you."

Using the element of surprise, I manage to flip him

over, straddling him. As I straighten and unclasp my bra, tossing it to the side, his eyes go even darker. His chest heaves through his unsteady breathing. With slow motions, he takes a breast in each hand, kneading. I arch into him, closing my eyes as I relish in the sensation.

From the moment I met him nearly a year ago, I knew there was something different about him. After I lost Hunter, I didn't think I'd ever find love again. Didn't think I *wanted* to find love again. How could I love another man when my heart belonged to a ghost?

Then Anderson walked into my life. In a matter of days, he managed to break down the walls I'd built around my heart. Crept his way under the mask I'd erected after a lifetime of being made to feel inferior. He did something I didn't think another man would be able to.

Made me feel beautiful.

He still makes me feel beautiful.

Fingers burrowing into my hair, he coaxes my mouth toward him. But I fight against it, remaining just out of reach as I circle against him.

"You know you're driving me crazy, right?" he growls, digging his fingers into my scalp.

I waggle my brows. "I can *feel* that."

He brings both hands to my hips. Before I can react, he swiftly flips me onto my back and slams his mouth against mine. Resting his weight on one forearm, he reaches between our bodies and brings his arousal up to my center.

But like the tease he is, he doesn't push into me. Instead, he tortures me by getting so close before retreating. I'm about to take matters into my own hands when he finally inches inside me.

Euphoria washes over me and I moan, momentarily sated at the connection of our two bodies. The connection we've both been deprived of for too long now.

"Look at me," he demands when he's barely inside me, teasing me with this small taste.

I do as he asks, focusing my eyes on his. He keeps his stare trained on me as he pushes deeper, slowly torturing me with his languid motions until he's fully seated.

He doesn't move for a protracted moment, neither one of us so much as breathing.

Then he exhales, his body going slack before he pulls back and thrusts into me again.

"Goddamn," he grunts, pupils dilating.

I wrap my legs around him, my fingers digging through his hair. He withdraws once more before driving inside. This time, he continues thrusting. It's not hard and punishing, but not gentle and tame, either. It's both Anderson and Prince Gabriel in this one amazing connection.

I've known the truth of who Anderson is almost from the beginning. He didn't trick me into sleeping with him and then reveal his true identity. Before I invited him into my bed, I knew he was a prince.

But this is the first time it feels like I'm sleeping with all of him. That he's finally allowing me to have all of him. To have not just the person he wishes he could be, but also the person he wishes he didn't have to be.

"I love you," I say as I cup his face in my hands, holding him tightly. "All of you."

He briefly closes his eyes as he moves faster, yet still

reverently. "And I love you, Nora," he chokes out. "So goddamn much."

His lips press against mine, and I succumb to him. Not just his kiss, but everything about him. All his faults. His regrets. His fears. His imperfections. They're all pieces of him, and I wouldn't change a thing.

Not anymore.

With each thrust, my body is propelled higher and higher. A wave of desire slices through me as I fight against that familiar sensation. But it's more pronounced than before. More intense. More…everything.

My breathing grows more uneven as I struggle to make sense of the myriad of emotions rolling through me. I want to fall apart, but don't want to without Anderson.

As if sensing my inner war, Anderson pulls out of our kiss and cups my face in his hands. "Wait for me," he begs, increasing his rhythm.

"Always." I tighten my legs around him, that familiar tingling starting low in my core.

His pants fill the room, his increasingly frantic thrusts pushing me closer and closer to the point of oblivion. When I dig my nails into his spine, he reels back, roaring like an untamed beast as his orgasm sneaks up on him. He collapses on top of me, his teeth clamping onto my neck as he keeps thrusting, the pain mixed with pleasure setting me off yet again.

Lights flashing before my eyes, I fall apart with my prince, wave after wave of bliss washing over me and erasing every last doubt I've ever had.

Our heavy breathing fills the room as we attempt to come down, neither of us wanting to move, to put any space between us. There's been too big of a distance between us lately. I don't want to go back to that.

When he manages to lift his head, he peers at me with reverence, at odds with the carnal lust that blanketed his expression mere minutes ago.

"I wish I could promise you that I won't fuck up again. But chances are I will. And probably worse than I did this week. Despite popular opinion that the royal family pisses rainbows and shits unicorns, we're not perfect. Far from it."

I laugh slightly, averting my gaze, but he pinches my chin, drawing my eyes back to his.

"Better yet, we don't have to be perfect. And neither do you. You can tell me when shit just really bloody sucks and you miss home. I may not be able to whisk you away on the next flight to JFK, but I can at least do something to try to fix it, even if the best I can do is recreate an outdoor movie in Bryant Park, or have a pastrami and rye from Katz flown in."

I shoot up, pushing him off me, mouth agape. "You can do that?"

"What? Recreate an outdoor movie? Of course. I—"

"No." I quickly shake my head. "Have Katz flown in. Do you have any idea how badly I've been craving some pastrami and matzo ball soup? And pickles. Lots and lots of pickles."

He laughs as he pulls me into his arms. "And here I thought pregnancy cravings didn't start until the second trimester. At least that's what the book I've been reading says."

My brows furrow. "You've been reading a pregnancy

book?"

"I figured it was the least I could do, considering we've barely been able to see each other lately. Thought if I read a bit on what happens every week, at least I'd have some frame of reference." His expression falls. "I should have started in the chapter about dealing with pregnancy loss." He cups my cheek, his hold resolute. "If I had known how difficult that first appointment could be, especially after what you went through, I never would have missed it. I knew it was important. You told me as much. I should have fought harder for you. For your needs. From now on, that's exactly what I plan on doing. Okay?"

I part my lips, about to argue that he had a legitimate excuse, but he won't hear it, erasing my protest with a kiss.

"Okay?" he repeats.

With a small smile, I nod. "Okay."

"Good."

He pulls me against him again as I process this new piece of information. Try to picture Anderson in his office, a stack of pregnancy books piled beside whatever important things are on his agenda for the day.

"What is it?" he asks, his voice borderline accusatory.

"What do you mean?"

"I can hear you thinking."

"I didn't know thinking made a sound."

He runs a finger along my back, the gesture comforting. "Not for most people, but I can hear your brain." He places a kiss on my head. "Tell me. No more secrets."

I tilt my head back to look into his eyes. "I'm just trying to picture you reading a pregnancy book. I have to admit, it's not easy, especially when the only things I've seen you read are the newspaper and books on World War II."

"It was actually quite interesting."

I shift toward him and prop my head in my hand. "Oh yeah? What kinds of things did you pick up on?"

He pinches his lips together for a beat, peering into the distance in contemplation. I can't help but admire the strong lines of his face, the proud nose, square jaw, not to mention full mouth that brings me more pleasure than should be legal.

"Babies drink a lot of pee."

I grimace. "Ummm… Okay."

"Not once they're born, but when they're developing. Amniotic fluid is pretty much all pee. I found that interesting. I was actually wondering about that."

"I'm glad to know the heir to the throne stays up at night wondering about baby's pee while in utero."

He shrugs. "What can I say? I'm a pretty complicated guy."

"You've got that right." I run my hand through his hair and muss it up. "What else did you learn?"

"That your uterus can press more weight than some bodybuilders."

"Really?"

"Yup. Apparently, the force of your contractions can equal up to 180 kilograms per square foot."

"And in U.S. terms, what's 180 kilograms?"

He scrunches his brows, doing the math in his head. "A little less than 400 pounds."

"Wow. My vagina deserves a medal."

His lips lift in a playful smirk. "Damn straight it does.

Or maybe an award in the shape of my cock."

When he thrusts against me, I swat him, trying to fight my smile. It's impossible, though, especially when he turns into the flirt he is now.

"Okay then. What else did you learn?"

His eyes darken as he brushes a finger against my nipple, then squeezes. It instantly hardens, sparks shooting through me. "In the third trimester, nipple stimulation can bring on labor." He pushes me onto my back, covering a nipple with his mouth as he continues to tease the other one. "So, when you're on the cusp of popping from carrying our baby for forty weeks, I'm your guy." He circles my pert bud. "Hell, I'm your guy now."

I close my eyes, basking in the sensation. That's all it takes for my libido to put out her cigarette and jump back into the fray, ready for round two. Or is it three?

When he slips a finger back inside me, his mouth still on my chest, I murmur, "I think I can get on board with that."

Twenty-Six

Anderson

The scent of baby powder and lavender surrounds me as I approach the gardens near the edge of my estate. I could be blind and still know Nora's out here. Thankfully I'm not. I may eventually need help walking, but at least I have my eyesight.

At least I'll always be able to appreciate Nora's beauty.

And right now, as she sits in a lounge chair, the sun warming her milky skin, a pile of letters stacked on the table beside her, I don't think I've ever seen her so beautiful. Because she's also finally found her peace.

Found her place in this world.

Over the past few weeks, things have turned around quite a bit, especially for Nora. No longer is she kept out of the spotlight for fear she'll do something wrong.

Since I informed the palace PR team that I planned to do things my way from now on, the country has finally gotten a chance to know their future queen. During our public appearances together, Nora absolutely shines.

Not only is she the picture of poise and grace, but she also takes time to talk to people. And not just about approved topics. Nora engages in meaningful conversations, a gift that continues to marvel me every day.

But what really endeared her to the people of this country, as well as across the world, was the day we visited a pediatric oncology wing. Despite having another engagement immediately after, she insisted on staying to play dress-up with a few of the younger patients. Suffice it to say, the media remained behind to cover that story instead of a photo op I had to attend with my father and a few foreign dignitaries. Now, the press is much more interested in the future crown princess' public appearances than anyone else's.

The royal household hates it.

I love it.

Once I stopped blindly following their advice simply because that was the way things had always been done, Nora began to soar, a caged bird no more.

The people adore her, as evidenced by the hundreds upon hundreds of letters she receives every day not only from people in Belmont, but around the world. Little girls who see a real-life fairytale coming true. School-aged children who wish her good luck on her upcoming wedding. Even some older women who have also suffered a pregnancy loss, thanking her for bringing light to miscarriage and stillbirth, something that continues to carry a stigma, as ridiculous as that sounds.

"I know you're standing there watching me like a creeper," she says, her eyes remaining focused on the palace stationary as she responds to another piece of fan mail, as I call it.

Although the royal household hates that term. Hates the idea that Nora was able to accumulate adoring fans, despite all their efforts to the contrary.

Initially, she had hoped to respond to each and every letter. However, that proved to be a challenge, particularly as the number of letters increased to the point where the staff now has to choose which ones they'll give her.

"What can I say?" I retort, taking slow steps toward her. "I like looking at you. Especially when you're in it."

"In it?" She signs her name, another thing the royal household despises, since they view it as an autograph, which is against the rules. Then she glances over her shoulder. Brilliant blue eyes meet mine as joy radiates from her. Weeks ago, I didn't think this level of happiness was possible. Instead, I was prepared for her to walk away from this world.

But she hasn't.

Granted, it hasn't all been unicorns and rainbows. There are still quite a few people who don't like the idea of me marrying an American. But we've stopped caring what anyone else thinks, which was a huge feat for Nora, since she's lived most of her life doing everything to live up to her mother's impossible standards. Of always trying to be perfect in everyone's eyes. She's finally realized she'll never make everyone happy, that there will always be someone critical of something she says, does, or wears.

"In it," I repeat as I slide into the chair beside her. "Like when you're so immersed in what you're doing that you forget there's a world outside of it all. You're in it." I shrug. "It's something my mother used to say whenever she noticed I was deep in thought."

She leans toward me and treats me to a kiss that leaves me wanting so much more. "I like it." She lingers near my mouth for a beat, then pulls back, grabbing the next letter and unfolding it.

"To what do I owe this pleasure?" she asks as she reads a letter I can only assume to be from another young girl, based on the disjointed writing. "I thought you'd be stuck in meetings the rest of the day."

I extend my legs in front of me and cross them at the ankles as I place my hands behind my head and lean back. "That's the good thing about being in charge. I can reschedule if I want."

She gives me a playful look of disapproval before grabbing a fresh piece of stationary to respond to another letter. Just seeing her pile of responses makes my hand ache.

"You're not in charge yet. Your father isn't officially going to abdicate until a few months after Little Pickle is born." She pats her stomach.

While it's still not obvious she's pregnant, I'm the lucky bastard who gets to share my life with her. Every night when I fall asleep with Nora in my arms, my hand always seems to find its way to her stomach, a little bump becoming more noticeable, at least to me. I can't help but marvel that a tiny life we created grows within. I don't want to rush the process, still enjoying this time with Nora when it's just us, but I can't wait to meet "Little Pickle", as Nora has nicknamed him or her, after her latest craving. One I try to satisfy as much as possible by having her favorite New York treat of pastrami on rye and pickles flown in from Katz.

"Then maybe I'll head back to the palace and not take you to Paris for the weekend," I say nonchalantly as I stand, resecuring the button on my suit jacket.

"*Paris?*" she shrieks, scrambling to her feet, letters falling onto the ground around her. "Did you say you're taking me to Paris?"

"I was thinking about it. Ya know, give you an immersive experience after all your French lessons. But you're right," I continue in a forced serious tone. "I should absolutely go back to work."

"No!" She flings her arms around me, squeezing me tightly, bouncing on the balls of her feet. "Take me to Paris!"

I chuckle, placing my hand on her back and pulling her closer. "If that's what you wish, my lady."

She looks at me, smiling brightly. "Oh, it is. It really, really is."

I lower my mouth to hers, our lips skimming. "Then let's go to Paris."

Twenty-Seven

Nora

Paris. I'm in fucking Paris. Home of the Notre-Dame Cathedral, the Arc d' Triumph, and the Eiffel Tower.

Of croissants and eclairs.

Of love.

For as long as I can remember, this has been a dream of mine, but it always seemed so unattainable. Hunter and I had discussed coming here after our wedding. Then I got pregnant, so our Paris honeymoon was changed to something not so far away.

When I met Jeremy, he promised to eventually take me, too, but something always came up. After we divorced, I considered coming here as part of my divorcation, the term my friends and I used to refer to a honeymoon for a divorcée.

Instead, they insisted I take the trip along Route 66 I was supposed to do with Hunter. Fulfill the promise I made his parents that I'd spread his ashes along the route.

Which was where I met Anderson.

It's funny how life works sometimes. I may have fore-gone my trip to Paris to finally say goodbye to the ghosts of my past. But in doing so, I found my way to Paris anyway.

"What do you think, *ma chèrie?*" Anderson asks as we stroll along the Seine, the setting sun casting a magical glow over the city that's still alive with a mixture of locals and tourists.

The Eiffel Tower reaches for the heavens before us, Notre-Dame Cathedral behind us, romance surrounding us. Artists sit along the river, hard at work at capturing whatever catches their eye. We even passed several couples dancing along the promenade. This city truly is romance personified.

"It's even more beautiful than I imagined. The perfect weekend getaway."

Since we arrived earlier today after a flight that lasted less than an hour, Anderson showed me a few of his favorite spots around the city.

The Sacre-Coeur Basilica atop the hill in Montmartre, which has one of the most amazing views of Paris.

Rue de la Paix, with all its exquisite shopping, where we struggled to resist the temptation whenever we saw anything baby related, since we still need to keep that a secret.

The Pantheon, where some of the greatest French minds are buried — Rousseau, Voltaire, Dumas.

And Pere Lachaise Cemetery, where we paid our respects to Héloïse and Abelard, the famous star-crossed lovers who were forced to carry out their love through letters.

"There's nothing like Paris," he admits, his own eyes alight with a renewed energy.

I wasn't the only one who needed this little getaway. He did, too. While we've made an effort to spend more time with each other these past few weeks, Anderson rarely attending any engagements in the evening unless I'm with him, life behind the proverbial palace walls can still be exhausting, especially with the wedding in just two weeks.

It's been refreshing to be a normal couple. Granted, a few people *have* recognized us as we explored the city, a team of plain-clothes protective officers flanking us. But we haven't been chased by the paparazzi, who seem to have become obsessed with capturing our every movement back home.

"My dad always dreamed of coming here," I murmur absentmindedly as a breeze wraps around me and kicks up a scent that can only be described as Paris — food, history, and love.

"You were five when he died, correct?" Anderson asks, his voice hesitant.

Throughout our relationship, I haven't spoken of my dad in any detail. Doing that would inevitably lead to my mother, which is always a touchy subject.

"I can't remember much about him, especially since he was still active military and was on deployment quite a bit, but I do remember that. Promised that one day, when we had enough money, he'd take me."

"I'm sorry he was never able to."

"Don't be." I shrug. "My father taught me how to

dream. Here was someone who came from nothing. Literally. He had no one."

He tilts his head, his interest piqued as I speak of this man who's remained a mystery to him most of our relationship. "What do you mean?"

"His parents were addicts. He was neglected a lot growing up. Most of the time, the only meal he ate during the day was the lunch the school provided. When school was on break, he either had to steal food or hope one of his teachers felt bad enough for him that they'd drop off something."

"Why didn't the authorities get involved? If his parents weren't feeding him, were neglecting him…"

"I don't know. I only learned this from my brothers and a few of the members in his unit who stayed in touch with us."

He nods. "And they're all much older than you, correct? Your brothers, I mean."

"Charlie's seven years older, Michael's eight, and Joshua's ten. Because of the age difference, I always felt like an only child.

"Anyway, my dad could have very easily followed in his parents' footsteps, started doing drugs, repeating the cycle."

"But he didn't," Anderson remarks.

"No. Thanks to his French teacher."

His eyes widen. "His French teacher?"

"Why does that surprise you?"

"I could see a football coach getting him on the right path, but a French teacher? It's just unusual."

"Well, his French teacher was also his wrestling coach,

so you're not totally off-base." I wink. "My dad grew up in a small town in rural North Carolina that consisted of maybe 2,000 people, so culture wasn't high on their list of priorities. Hell, most people in town had lived there since birth. Had probably never ventured too far away from the town line. So his French class was my father's first exposure to a different culture. An eye-opening experience to a world outside the one he'd been living. That became his dream. His motivation to do whatever it took to get out of that small town and not repeat the cycle."

"So he joined the military."

"It was the only way out for him."

A silence passes between us. Then he glances my way. "How did he meet your mother?"

I smile nostalgically. When I first heard their love story, I thought it was beautiful, the kind of story we all hope to have.

Unfortunately, their happily ever after was short-lived.

"At a funeral."

"A…funeral?"

I nod. "When my father left town for boot camp, he swore he'd never come back. Until he learned his French teacher had passed away. So he requested leave and went home to pay his respects. His teacher's name was James Harcourt. His daughter's name is Elaine."

"Your mother…," Anderson breathes.

"Yes. My dad told his navy buddies it was love at first sight. Unfortunately, she had a boyfriend at the time. And three young boys."

"But they weren't married? Your mother and this boyfriend?"

"No." I furrow my brows. "I never figured out why. One of my dad's navy buddies thought my mom was a romantic at heart, at least back then. That she knew her boyfriend wasn't her soul mate. But my father was. After the funeral, they stayed in touch. Sent letters to each other, which I find extremely romantic, especially nowadays when most couples send texts asking to hook-up. Over the course of a year and dozens of letters, they fell in love. My mom left her boyfriend, married my father, and three years later, I was born." I give him a smile.

"Wow…" Anderson blinks, seemingly surprised by this. "That sounds incredibly…sweet."

"You didn't expect that?"

"Based on what I know of your mother? No."

"She wasn't always the way she is now. She used to be…nice. Loving. It wasn't until my father passed away that she changed. When he died, a part of her did, too. She became a different person, someone I barely recognize. And it's only gotten worse with every man she marries and realizes he isn't my father. Will never be my father. I think that's why…" I trail off.

"Why what?" he presses.

I shrug sheepishly. I haven't told him about my most recent conversation with my mother. I didn't think it mattered. It still doesn't.

"Remember. No secrets."

I draw in a breath, slowly shifting my gaze toward his. "Why she accused me of doing the same thing with you after she learned of our engagement."

"When?"

"She called me a few weeks ago."

He forces me to stop walking and peers at me with frantic eyes. "I'd left explicit instructions with your private secretary that she was not to get through to you. I—"

I place my hand on his cheek, placating him. "She manipulated him. Made him think it was a call from the hospital about Chloe."

He takes a deep breath, then slowly lets it out. "What did she say?"

"Other than being pissed about not receiving an invitation to our wedding, she claimed I'm only marrying you because of a shared traumatic experience."

He blows out a laugh. "That's why you *shouldn't* marry me."

"True. But the heart can't be reasoned with. And despite it all, my heart still wants you."

He leans down, our lips meeting in a soft kiss. "My heart will always want you."

I link my fingers with his once more as we continue along the river, a comfortable silence between us. It reminds me of the miles we traveled together along Route 66, neither one of us saying anything, simply enjoying the serenity. I once hated silence, needed to fill it with conversation, particularly around someone I didn't know well.

But from the beginning, I didn't feel that way around Anderson.

He truly became the stranger I recognized, as a fortune teller predicted would be the man who owned my heart.

"How about you?" I ask after a while. "How did your parents meet?"

"My mum was jumping one of her horses at competition and my dad happened to have a polo match on the next field. When the match was over, he headed back to his car and saw my mum. Said he was mesmerized. Couldn't look away. So he stayed. Then he found out her name and the rest of her competition dates. Made sure to be there. It was a slow-build romance, much like your parents. They started as friends, I suppose, although there was always something else there. But my father couldn't date publicly without the media going crazy over it, even though he was second in line at the time.

"So they dated in private for a while because they both understood once they went public with their relationship, they'd be pushed toward marriage. My father knew she had strong ambitions and respected those."

"What kind of ambitions?"

While I've learned quite a bit about his mother through all my princess training, they didn't go over any personal aspects of the woman who gave Anderson life.

"She loved animals. Was studying equine science and wanted to eventually work with horses. By the time she finished her schooling, my aunt and uncle already had four kids. So my father was now sixth in line to the crown and didn't need my grandfather's approval to marry any longer. Regardless, he asked for it, and they were married about a year later. But despite the fact she was now a princess, she never stopped caring about her horses. Even when she became queen consort, most of her time at the palace was spent in the stables."

"I wish I could have met her," I say after a beat.

"She would have loved you. You have the same…attitude toward this life."

I chuckle. "The same disregard for the rules, you mean?"

"Exactly." He pulls me to a stop and loops an arm around my waist, yanking my body into his. "But I wouldn't change anything about you."

"And I wouldn't change anything about you."

Digging his free hand through my hair, he presses his mouth against mine, coaxing my lips apart. Even his kisses feel different in this city. More poignant. More powerful. More potent.

"What do you say to going to my absolute favorite spot in Paris?" he murmurs against my mouth.

"And what's that?"

"The view from our suite, of course."

While I've enjoyed roaming Paris with Anderson, this entire day has been one big tease, my desire for him increasing with every second. I want nothing more than to lock ourselves in our suite and never come out.

"I'd love to," I answer.

I barely utter a single syllable before he clutches my hand in his and hurries me in the direction of our hotel.

Twenty-Eight

Anderson

The door to the room doesn't have a chance to close before I slam Nora against the wall, my mouth claiming hers. Maybe it's this city. Maybe it's being away from my responsibilities for the weekend. Maybe it's just Nora. I don't know. But an animalistic craving unlike any I've ever experienced overtakes me. I grind my hips against hers, my tongue plunging deeper into her mouth, an addict desperate for his next high.

"Did you bring your camera?" Nora pants when I pull away, peppering hungry kisses along her jawline, nipping at her flesh. Gripping her thigh, I force her leg around my waist.

"My camera? Why?" I tug her closer, squeezing her ass.

"Because…" She moans when I cover her nipple with my mouth through her dress and bra. "I want you to take my photo. Like you did in Santa Monica."

My muscles tighten at the memory of snapping her

photo as she slept. How a few innocent photos turned into one of the most erotic experiences of my life.

I pull back, peering down at her. "Really?"

Her sultry eyes trained on me, she nods. "Yes. But even naughtier."

"I'd be a fool to say no to that."

Releasing my hold on her, I stride farther into the suite. I unzip my camera bag and retrieve the body, attaching a lens to it.

By the time I face Nora, she's already naked, her dress and sandals lying in a heap. I expect her to head toward the bedroom and climb onto the bed. Instead, she brushes past me toward the French doors leading to the balcony.

"Nora, what are you doing?"

"What good are these photos if you can't tell where we are? All bedrooms look the same. But there's only one Paris." She smirks flirtatiously, then steps onto the balcony without a care in the world that she's naked, that somebody might see her.

It's official. Paris has infused into her blood.

And I love every second.

I follow her out onto the balcony. A few blocks away, the Eiffel Tower shines brightly against a midnight blue sky. I cautiously glance around, concerned some paparazzi discovered our location and booked a nearby room. But we're secluded on this balcony on the top floor of the hotel, the night sky offering a curtain not possible during the day.

Swaying her hips, Nora walks toward the bistro table and lowers herself into the chair. She crosses her legs, her posture and confidence reminiscent of Sharon Stone in

Basic Instinct. Then she stiffens.

"What am I thinking?" she says playfully, uncrossing her legs and slanting them to the side, crossing them at the ankles. "That was no way for a royal to sit. I really should pay more attention to the rules."

I can't help but laugh at the irony. "I'm fairly certain we're currently breaking every rule in the book."

"I didn't see any rule against allowing my fiancé to photograph me nude."

"Pretty sure it's an unspoken one covered by the prohibition against indecent or immoral behavior."

"Are you going to reprimand me?" she asks in a husky voice. "Maybe spank me for being so…naughty?"

"Jesus," I hiss under my breath, my hands trembling with the excitement of an inexperienced teenager before he cops his first feel. "What's gotten into you?"

"Hopefully *you* will soon." She straightens. "Now, how would you like me?"

"That's a loaded question," I mutter under my breath, trying to concentrate on adjusting the aperture and focus on the camera, not the fact that the woman who will be my wife in just two weeks currently sits on the balcony of our Paris hotel room completely naked.

"I'm sure it's not the only thing that's loaded."

I can't fight the smile crossing my lips. This woman constantly surprises me. I never know what to expect with her, every day a new adventure.

"Come on, Anders. Tell me."

I inhale, returning my gaze to her, doing my best to switch from horny male to professional photographer. I study the background and ambient light from the city, which casts a glow on Nora's peachy skin as she sits with her back straight, expression even. There's almost something…haunting about her.

"Like that," I answer softly, bringing the camera up to my face and snapping a few photos. "Don't move a muscle." I squat, capturing her from a lower angle, the moon highlighting her sinful curves. "Look off to your left," I say, entranced.

She does as I ask, peering into the distance, her chest rising and falling in a quicker pattern.

"Lift your chin a bit," I tell her.

Again, she obeys my request, elongating her neck.

"My god, you are so beautiful."

Right now, with Paris behind her, I see what so many others have commented on since I introduced her to my world. She is the new Grace Kelly. And not simply because she's an American about to marry a prince, but because she bears a striking resemblance to the actress, especially now as I capture her silhouette. If I put this picture beside one of Grace Kelly, I doubt anyone would be able to tell the difference. Dainty nose, heart-shaped lips, milky skin.

"Hold on." I quickly straighten. "I'll be right back." I hurry back into the room. Opening my suitcase, I grab a black velvet box. I'd planned to wait to give it to her tomorrow, but this is the perfect accessory right now.

Returning to Nora, I hand her the box, to which she responds with a playful look of disapproval.

"You spoil me. You know that, right?"

"If I can't spoil my wife-to-be and mother of my child, who can I spoil?"

She attempts to reel in her smile, to no avail. When she opens the box, a gasp escapes. "Anders…"

I extend my hand, an unspoken request for permission. She nods. I take the box from her, removing the bracelet.

"Every woman needs a pearl bracelet." I take her wrist in mine and attach the string of pearls.

"I already have one," she reminds me.

"True. But this one is made up of all-natural pearls."

Her eyes widen. "These are all-natural?"

I slowly nod.

"Jesus, Anders. How much did this cost you?"

"You don't want to know."

"You're right. I don't think I do."

"Do you like it?"

She admires the glistening stones with appreciation. "It's perfect."

"Good." I smile at her, my heart expanding. "Now, where were we?"

"You were taking dirty pictures of me."

"They're not dirty. They're beautiful. *You're* beautiful."

"You make me feel beautiful."

She cranes her head toward me. I meet her lips, kissing her sweetly, but don't deepen it. If I do, I won't be able to control myself. And I want this night to last forever.

"Come this way." I help her to her feet, leading her toward the ledge. "Bend a little at the waist and lean on the railing."

She follows my request, but the angle seems wrong.

"Here."

I move behind her to reposition her. The second our skin touches, the atmosphere shifts, sexual heat crackling and sizzling. I curve toward her, inhaling her perfume as I smooth a hand down her arm, linking my fingers with hers and moving it farther away from her body.

Then I straighten her so she's putting her weight on her hands, yet not leaning too far over the railing. Content with her form, I grab her chin and position it so she's looking down at the bracelet and sparkling diamond ring.

I step back to check her placement, everything about her just so damn perfect, right down to the slight swell of her stomach. I grab my camera, snapping several photos, wanting to capture everything about her. Her poise. Her confidence. Her grace. I've never met anyone else like her in my life. I doubt I will again.

"Is something wrong?" she asks once the shutter stops, glancing over her shoulder, her eyes locking with mine.

I set my camera onto the table and walk up to her. I smooth her hair back from her nape and plant warm kisses along her skin.

"I can't wait another damn second." I spin her around in one quick move.

She's not able to get out a surprised gasp before I cover her lips with mine, my tongue tangling with hers. Hand firm on her hip, I steer her back into the suite. She moans into my mouth, running her fingers through my hair. When her nails dig into my scalp, igniting me on fire, I kiss her even harder.

Once we reach the bed, I carefully lower her onto it, my motions quick as I shrug out of my jacket and kick off my shoes. Then I yank my t-shirt over my head before shoving my jeans and boxers down my legs, stepping out of them.

Joining her on the mattress, I seek out her mouth once more, desperate for another taste of her sweet nectar.

"I need you," she murmurs breathily.

"And I need you. Need to bury myself deep inside you." I pull back, framing her face in my hands. "But I need to taste you first. Need your cum on my tongue."

"Fuck, Anders."

She writhes beneath me as I snake down her frame. I take one of her nipples in my mouth, gently nibbling. "Can I do that?"

"God yes."

"Mmm…," I moan as I inch farther south, my tongue trailing down her torso. Her stomach rolls through her increasingly ragged breathing, especially as I grow closer to her center.

When I settle between her thighs, I steal a glance at her, a look of delicious anticipation on her face. She squirms and pulses, her body telling me to give her what she craves.

The instant my tongue makes that first contact against her, she moans, temporarily relieved as she loses herself in my touch. I start slowly, teasing and torturing her, slightly pressing a finger inside her before retreating, which only frustrates her.

"Please," she begs, her plea sounding like a combination of a mewl and a pant.

I grin, inching my finger a bit farther inside her as my tongue circles her clit. When I finally push all the way in, she whimpers, begging me to go deeper and faster. I continue my ministrations, adding another finger, then another, stretching and massaging her.

"Anders…," she moans again, lost to the sensations.

I love watching her like this. So sexy. So needy. So out of her mind with lust.

"Do you want to come?" I ask, increasing my motions.

"Yes."

"That's my girl."

When I nip her clit, she releases a noiseless gasp. Her motions grow more frantic and desperate until she cries out, her body pulsing through her orgasm. But I don't pull away. Instead, I do everything I can to draw out this sensation of bliss as long as possible.

Once her tremors have subsided, I crawl up her frame and slam my lips against hers. "God, I love watching that. Love being the one to make you come like that."

"And I love when you make me come like that." She waggles her brows. "So why don't you go for two."

I chuckle, reaching down and stroking myself, but my dick doesn't seem to get the message that there's a beautiful woman in my bed.

"Oh, come on. Not now."

"What's wrong?" Nora hoists herself onto her elbows.

"Nothing," I grind out, frustration forming in my throat as I stroke myself harder, to no avail. "Goddammit!"

"Here." Nora sits up, reaching for me. "Let me." She presses her hand against my shoulder, pushing me onto my back.

I squeeze my eyes shut, trying to focus on the warmth of Nora's fingers wrapped around me, not the fear that this is yet another one of the side effects of MS coming to rear its ugly head at the worst possible moment. I push down the thought, remembering Nora posing on the balcony, so confident and sexy. But nothing seems to work, not even this incredibly provocative woman attempting to jerk me off.

"Fuck!" I roar, shooting upright. "It's useless." I bolt off the bed, grabbing my jeans and sliding them on.

"It's okay. We'll try again in a little while."

"No." I tug at my hair as I pace. "It is *not* okay. I'm fucking useless, Nora. I can't even keep my goddamn fiancée happy because of this bloody disease."

She scrambles to her feet, placing a hand on my bicep. "You don't have to sleep with me to make me happy, Anders," she says with all the sympathy I've come to expect from her.

It still makes me feel inadequate, though. Like I'll end up not being able to give her what she needs. What she deserves.

Like I'm less of a man.

I shrug her off, making her gasp, the sting of my rejection seeming to burn her hand. But that doesn't make me stop.

"Today, I can't get an erection. Tomorrow, who knows? Maybe I'll start pissing and shitting myself. Is that really what you want? You really want to be saddled with someone who can't even control his own fucking body?"

"Yes. A million times yes. Like I've told you repeatedly. I don't care about any of that. All I care about is *you*. And I love *you*, Anders." She grabs my hand in hers, not bothering to cover up. Instead, she exposes herself to me in all her raw vulnerability, as if hoping I'll do the same.

But it's different. This wasn't supposed to happen to me. I'm going to be king one day. How can I lead an entire nation if I can't even control my body?

"Anders, talk to me. Don't shut me out."

"I'm not—"

"You are. Do you honestly think I haven't noticed something off lately?" she retorts. "You're pushing your-self too hard. You need to take time for yourself. For your health. You don't have to be everything for everyone."

"Yes, I do!" I roar, my voice louder than I anticipated. "That's exactly what I have to fucking be, Nora!"

Breath hitching, she straightens, eyes wide in surprise. And a hint of fear. It's this fear that hits me hard. I scrub a hand over my face, my mind cloudy as I attempt to collect my thoughts.

Stepping toward her, I cup her cheek. "I'm sorry. I just… I can handle the occasional tremor and dizzy spell. But what happens when I can no longer walk? Can no longer fuck?" I choke out, my frustration turning to despair.

She places her hand over mine as I continue to hold her face. "I'll still be by your side."

I pinch my lips together, shaking my head. I should find comfort in her reassurance that she loves me regard-less of whether I'm able-bodied or bound to a wheelchair. And a part of me does. But there's this other part of me that thinks it's selfish of me to ask that of her. To force her to stay by my side while my body slowly deteriorates.

To force her to watch me die a little more every day.

She's already lost so much.

Can I really ask her to lose even more?

"I need to go for a walk." I retreat from her.

"Anders, *please*. Don't push me away," she begs again.

This time, I respond a bit more calmly. "I'm not. I just need to take a minute to clear my head. Try some of your meditation exercises. They always seem to help," I lie. "Maybe by the time I return, the general will finally be awake." I blow out a laugh, hoping my joke will console her, but she still looks at me with sympathy. And perhaps even a little pity.

I hate it.

"I won't be long." I place a soft kiss on her forehead, then tug on my shirt.

Once I slide on my shoes, I grab my wallet and mobile, firing off a quick text to Creed before walking out of the suite. I don't even acknowledge him when he steps out of the next room and follows me toward the elevator. He doesn't say a word the entire ride down to the lobby, being the good friend he is. Or perhaps trained protection officer.

I'm about to make my way onto the sidewalk when I spy a lounge in the corner of the lobby. I haven't had a drink in nearly a year. Controlling my diet was supposed to help slow down the progression of my MS and prevent any flareups.

Apparently not.

"Sir." Creed touches my bicep, eyes narrowed, sensing my thoughts. "Don't."

I know it comes from a place of concern, whereas most people would accuse me of behaving like a spoiled rich kid. I can't shake the feeling that my world is falling apart around me. If I can't feel pleasure, I'd rather be numb.

"Fuck you." I shrug him off, then storm toward the lounge.

Twenty-Nine

Nora

The sound of a slamming door stirs me from a restless sleep. As I blink my eyes open, I glance at Anderson's side of the bed. Still empty.

Hearing a thump, followed by a curse, I sit upright, wrapping my silk robe tighter around me. Considering our suite is surrounded by a team of protection officers, there's only one person it could be. And based on the fact it's after two in the morning and he seems to be running into every piece of furniture, Anderson's been drinking.

He finally manages to stumble into the bedroom, eyes slits, hair disheveled. The stench of alcohol is strong, even from a few feet away. I want to remind him of the negative effects drinking can have on his MS. I don't want to spend the rest of our time in Paris fighting, though. Don't want that to be the memory I take away from this magical place.

Not saying a word, he yanks his shirt over his head. When he attempts to kick off his shoes, he nearly topples over, grabbing onto the dresser. Steady once more, he refocuses on me. His lust-filled gaze causes an ache to stir deep within me. It shouldn't. Not after the way we left things. But as he slides his jeans down his legs, revealing his rock-hard erection, my body betrays me, mouth growing dry, breathing becoming ragged.

I part my lips, words on the tip of my tongue. Words I can't bear to say, especially when I recall the utter despair that covered every inch of him earlier.

He needs this. Needs to know he's not the broken man he thinks he is.

And I need this, too. Need to know he won't let this come between us.

I loosen the sash of my robe, allowing it to fall open in invitation. His eyes flame, the swirls of turquoise and sky blue becoming darker as he crawls onto the bed, spreading my legs. He brings his erection up to me, moving my slickness around before plunging inside.

I cry out at the invasion. I'd anticipated it, but didn't expect it to be so…rough. So desperate. So anguished. There's no other word to describe the way he buries his head in my neck and fucks me ruthlessly, each thrust more hopeless and frantic.

I should put a stop to this, make him talk to me about what's going through his brain instead of fucking away his anger. But when he peers at me, his gaze begging me to take away the pain, I don't have it in me.

I dig my hands through his hair, wrapping my legs around him, allowing him to take whatever he needs. I don't know what else to do to fix this. I wish there were a magic pill that would make his body strong again. Reverse the deterioration I've already witnessed in just the past year. But there isn't. I've seen him grow more tired and weary as he tries to balance the fate of the country on his shoulders against this debilitating disease that takes more and more from him with every breath.

His pace quickens, each thrust furious and brutal. I scrape my nails along his back, and he arches. His carnal gaze spears me as he drives into me even faster. This isn't making love. This is fucking, pure and simple. He's not interested in pleasure right now. Just to prove a point. Prove he can do this.

Sweat beads on my brow, my breathing labored as I attempt to keep pace with him. Finally, a roar slices through the room and he jerks, eyes scrunched closed, his orgasm coming hard and fast. He rides the waves until he physically can't keep himself propped up any longer and collapses on top of me. His heart hammers against my chest, muscles trembling as he sucks in breath after breath.

I run a light hand up and down his sweaty back, hoping the calming motion will help him regain his faculties, snap him out of whatever trance he was in when he stepped into the hotel room.

Then a cry rips from his chest, tortured and afflicted. It stops me cold, clawing through my soul and shredding my heart.

Tears spill from my eyelids as I search for the words I need to tell him it will be okay. But I've come to realize we have two vastly different definitions of okay. His is being normal again. Mine is standing by his side no matter what.

Will that be enough for him?

Will *I* be enough for him?

In the past few hours, I've witnessed him go through nearly all the stages of grief — denial, anger, bargaining. There's no doubt he's in depression right now.

All I can do is hope he makes an upward turn toward acceptance and doesn't fall deeper.

Thirty

Nora

I stare at the Eiffel Tower as the sun heats my skin, the sounds and smells of Paris surrounding me. I hate to leave this place. Not just because I fell in love with this city, but because I fear what awaits us back home.

Since Friday night, Anderson hasn't been the same. On the surface, he seems like the Anderson I remember from our early days. Flirtatious. Endearing. A bit cocky. But I can tell it's all a way to make me think everything is the same.

Whenever he gazes at me, turmoil swirls in his blue eyes.

Whenever he kisses me, it's restrained and lacking.

Whenever he tells me he loves me, the words are laden with reluctance.

As much as I want to bring up the other night, I don't want to taint our time in Paris any more than it already has been.

Don't want my memories of this city to be clouded

with the fear that we've turned down a dark road neither of us will ever come back from.

Don't want Paris to forever be associated with the beginning of our end.

Then again, I could be overreacting.

But every time I peer into Anderson's eyes, all I see is that same remorse-filled expression he wore during our final days together on Route 66. He'd known those were our last hours together. Not because we were about to go our separate ways, but because he'd been keeping a secret from me. One that would shatter me into a million pieces.

I can't help but feel like he's doing the same here. Like he knows something horrible is about to happen and is protecting himself against the inevitable catastrophe.

"Are you ready?" Anderson peeks his head out of the balcony doors.

I take one last look at the Paris skyline, then nod, turning toward him. "Of course."

He places his hand on the small of my back as I step into the suite. We don't make it too far before the door flies open, Creed and Lieutenant Colonel Bridge hurrying inside, eyes wide with panic.

"What's going on?" Anderson asks, his posture stiffening.

"Your Highness." Bridge glances in my direction before returning his attention to Anderson. "Something's happened."

When he floats his gaze to mine yet again, I sense this has to do with me. But what could it be? I've done everything to follow the rules lately. The most risqué thing I've done has been stripping and encouraging Anderson to photograph me nude.

Oh god…

My heart drops to the pit of my stomach. Did somebody see me? Maybe a photographer at a nearby hotel while he was checking one of his zoom lenses? It's a long shot, but if I've learned anything over the past few months, it's that nothing is impossible, especially where the paparazzi is concerned.

"I can explain." I step forward, frantic. "It was purely some innocent fun. It's not the first time he's done it, but those photos are just for us. I—"

"This isn't about any photos, ma'am," Bridge interrupts, shifting from foot to foot, clearly uncomfortable.

"Then what—"

"It's your mother, ma'am."

"What about my mother?" I ask, voice shaking slightly. After thirty years of dealing with her, I doubt whatever he's about to tell me is happy news.

He licks his lips. "She was just interviewed on a popular morning show back in the States."

My legs weaken. I gingerly lower myself into a nearby chair, dread balling tightly in my stomach.

"The focus of the interview was you, ma'am."

"Me?" I manage to squeak out through the thickness in my throat.

"Hey."

I peek up as Anderson sits beside me, his eyes sincere.

"I'm sure she didn't say anything you have to worry about."

"On the contrary, sir," Bridge interrupts. "There's a whole slew of photographers and reporters camped out in front of the hotel right now who believe otherwise. I'm guessing a hotel employee probably saw the interview trending on social media and decided to make a quick buck by selling your location."

"Fuck," Anderson hisses under his breath, pinching the bridge of his nose before lifting his steely gaze back to Bridge. "Well, get on with it. What newsworthy gems did that sham of a shrink drop? I hope she's ready to be sued, because that's exactly what I'll do if she said one negative thing about Nora."

I place my hand on his arm, trying to settle the fury I can feel radiating off him. The last thing I need is for him to have another flareup. Since Friday night, he's been relatively okay, apart from an occasional finger twitch.

Then again, he's barely touched me all weekend, as if worried he'll have a repeat of that night and would rather remain celibate than deal with the reality. Would rather resort to prescription drugs in order to have sex, like I surmise he did on Friday night, especially when I discovered a bottle of little blue pills on the bedroom floor, obviously having fallen out of his jeans.

"It's okay." I smile at him, then look at Bridge. "What did she say?"

I square my shoulders, trying to appear calm, despite the fear bubbling inside of me. My mother wouldn't go out of her way to espouse all my positive qualities. The only reason she'd do this interview was if she could publicly humiliate me, which is why I don't want her at my wedding.

I should have realized she'd find a way to do that anyway.

"Perhaps it might be best if you show them," Creed suggests. "That way, they'll get the full picture."

"Very well." Bridge pulls a laptop out of his briefcase and sets it on the coffee table in front of us.

My nerves kick up when my eyes fall on Carly Hart, one of the most popular and well-liked morning talk show hosts, my mother sitting in a lush chair beside her. Bridge hits the spacebar, and Carly's voice fills the room.

"Here in the US, we've all been wondering who exactly Nora Tremblay is, the woman who captured Prince Gabriel of Belmont's heart. Up until now, everyone we've spoken with has refused to give an interview, claiming to respect her privacy. But a few days ago, the future princess' own mother, Dr. Elaine Harcourt, finally agreed to give us an inside peek into the new American princess."

I laugh to myself as I cross my arms over my chest. "I guess she's back to her maiden name. Things with husband number five must not have worked out. Or maybe it was six."

Anderson gives my leg a reassuring squeeze.

"Thank you so much for taking the time to talk to me, Doctor. I understand you're extremely busy, so I appreciate you shifting your schedule around for us."

"As I discussed with your producers, I'm a psychiatrist. Normally, my patients come first and I'd only reschedule on them if it were of the utmost importance. But I felt it necessary to let the world know precisely who Nora Tremblay is. Particularly the fine people of Belmont. Particularly Prince Gabriel."

Carly tilts her head. *"What makes you say that? Nora appears to have charmed people all across the globe. They're calling her the new Princess Grace. You have to admit, she does resemble the actress. The first time I saw her photo, I had to do a double take."*

My mother grits a smile. *"Yes, she does."*

I can sense her aggravation over Carly's compliment even from halfway around the world. It's been a sticking point with her for ages. At least since I hit puberty and people started paying more attention to me.

"Nora is quite beautiful. Unfortunately, she often uses that beauty to the detriment of others."

"How so?"

"Perhaps it's my fault, but during Nora's formative years, I was a single mother. My husband, Nora's father, died on deployment."

Carly covers her heart with her hand. *"Oh, I am so sorry."*

"Thank you." My mother blinks back fake tears, her lower lip quivering. I must admit, it's quite the Oscar-worthy performance. *"I did the best I could at the time, but somewhere along the way, I guess I missed the signs."*

"What signs are those?"

She peers into the distance for a beat before returning her attention to Carly. *"How on days she had a history test, she'd wear clothes that were slightly more revealing. I should have questioned how she could have possibly brought her C average up to an A in a matter of weeks, but I figured perhaps she buckled down. The following year, the same history teacher was dismissed for improper relations with a student. We were never told the exact details, but a mother just knows."*

I blink, my breaths coming deeper and more shallow. I can't wrap my head around the lengths this woman will go to in order to paint me in a negative light.

I was the one who went to the principal on my own about the ongoing series of unwanted advances my teacher made on me.

I was the one who had to prove that he purposefully downgraded my papers to trick me into attending private tutoring sessions with him.

I was the one who had to stand up for myself when my own mother simply claimed I was overreacting, that a mature man of nearly forty wouldn't want anything to do with an awkward sixteen-year-old like me.

"It started with her grades in high school. Then college. She even cost me every single one of my husbands."

I bark out a laugh, rolling my eyes at the ridiculousness of her assertion.

"Why would she do that?" Carly asks.

"Like I said, I take full responsibility. She grew up without a strong male figure in the household. That always affects a child's development. Yes, her father's death was tragic, but somewhere along the way, Nora started seeing his death as abandonment. As such, she's always craved attention. And once Nora was able to gain it, she mastered the art of manipulation."

"How so?"

"Simple. She always knew exactly what to do and say to get someone to do whatever she wanted. Hell, she manipulated me for years. Made me believe she was the perfect, well-adjusted teenager, then young woman. That's how good she is. So what started as her manipulating her teachers in order to give her passing grades eventually turned into manipulating men for...other things."

"Other things?"

"A job. Apartment. Money."

Carly considers my mother's story for a beat, then shifts through a few of the papers in her hand. *"I don't doubt you know your daughter better than anyone, but I have trouble reconciling your side of things with a story I was able to dig up from approximately seven years ago.*" She slides her glasses onto her face. "*Your daughter almost died in a fatal car accident on Long Island, correct?*"

"*She was in a fatal car accident. She was the only person to walk away.*"

"*And her fiancé at the time, Hunter Copeland, did die.*"

"*Yes.*"

"*And Nora was six months pregnant, but lost the baby.*"

Anderson grabs my hand in his, but it does nothing to comfort me. Nothing can right now, especially with the grave expression on both Creed's and Bridge's faces. I may not know either men well, but I can tell when something's about to go wrong. That everything my mother said up to this point was simply a warmup.

"*I suppose that's one way of looking at it,*" my mother replies, her tone pinched.

"*What do you mean?*"

"*Hunter's family was quite affluent. I have no doubt she targeted him, just like she's now targeting Prince Gabriel. I find it curious that a week before Hunter was ki— I mean, died in that crash, he took out a rather large life insurance policy. And guess who he named as the primary beneficiary.*" She grins smugly.

"*He was your pregnant daughter's fiancé,*" Carly argues on my behalf. "*It's entirely reasonable to make sure your family's provided for in the event of a tragedy.*"

"*I'm not disagreeing with that,*" my mother says sweetly, as passive-aggressive as ever. "*And perhaps it was innocent. But my daughter never displayed any desire to settle down and get married. Then she's suddenly engaged and about to have a kid?*" She shakes her head. "*I struggle to believe the girl who had complete disregard for everyone in her life had a change of heart overnight.*"

"*So what is it you're suggesting?*" Carly presses.

"*I don't know. All I do know is that when I learned about the accident, I couldn't shake this feeling in my gut. The car erupted in flames, but Nora just so happened to be able to get out? I saw photos of the aftermath. The car was practically incinerated. Not to mention it hit a tree off the embankment with a force no one would be able to walk away from. Not without help. Yet the police were never able to corroborate Nora's statement that a Good Samaritan had pulled her to safety. It's just…suspicious.*"

"*So is it your contention that Nora…killed her former fiancé, then somehow terminated her pregnancy when she was six months along, all to collect a substantial life insurance policy?*"

"*I'm simply saying it's suspicious. That's all,*" she responds, evasive as always.

"*My producer discussed with you the potential ramifications for defamation, correct?*"

"*Yes. And like I reminded him, since Nora can now be considered a public figure, to succeed in any suit, she'd have to not only prove this is all a fabrication, which it's not, but that I also acted with malice. That's not my intention here. It's simply to share the truth about the woman who's manipulated her way into being days away from marrying one of the most powerful men in all of Europe.*

"*I'm more than aware that, after a thorough investigation, the police ruled out foul play. And perhaps I'm wrong Perhaps it did unfold as Nora claimed. But, unfortunately, I've never been able to believe much of what she's said. If I didn't come forward and something horrible were to happen to her current fiancé, well… I'd never forgive myself. I want to warn him personally, but I have no doubt Nora's tricked him into believing the worst of me. Which is why I felt it important to come on this show. To warn him and the entire royal family about the woman he's about to marry."*

Bridge hits the spacebar, pausing the video, then closes the laptop. "I think you get the gist of it," he says solemnly.

I blink, processing everything my mother just said on national TV, my stomach churning.

She inferred I killed Hunter.

And our baby.

How could she do such a thing? Why?

Because that's who she is. Everything she claims about me could be said about her. *She's* the manipulative one.

I'm the one who couldn't bring boyfriends home because she'd hit on them.

I'm the one who had to move from town to town every time my mother's latest husband realized just how warped and twisted of a person she was.

I'm the one who suffered her wrath whenever she noticed one of her boyfriends looking at me in a way she didn't like.

Yet *I'm* manipulative?

"Nora, love." Anderson's voice cuts through. "Talk to me."

I can't look at him. I'm numb. Sick. So fucking tired of getting close to having it all, only for that woman to take it away from me in a perverted game.

Not saying a word, I stand, practicing a few calming breathing techniques as I walk across the living room. The heat of everyone's stares prickles my skin, but I don't glance back or offer an explanation. I couldn't give them one right now anyway. Not without screaming.

Keeping my head held high and spine straight, as I

was instructed in my etiquette classes, I make my way into the bathroom, neither walking too fast nor too slow. I shut the door behind me and turn the lock, the click echoing in the vast space. Then I stride toward the double vanity and lean my hands on the counter, hanging my head.

I inhale a deep breath and close my eyes, trying to quiet the rage bubbling to the surface after years of keeping it buried deep within me. I learned early on that my emotions were another thing for my mother to exploit. That it was best to lock it all inside.

But what's the point when she'll find another way to get her revenge. To keep me trapped.

Muscles tightening and jaw hardening, I bring my gaze up to the mirror and study my appearance with the same scrutiny my mother always seemed to.

Eyes that are a few sizes too big for my face.

A nose that's a bit too pointed and could benefit from reconstructive surgery.

Cheeks that, despite the passing of years, are still cherub-like.

Heart-shaped lips that should be a tiny bit plumper.

For years, I listened to her call me too fat. Too skinny. Too plain. Too boring. Too uptight. Too carefree. All I wanted was to rid her from my life. To forget about all the ways she's tormented me, everything I did either too good or not good enough.

My body shaking more violently the more I recall everything that woman put me through, I scream. Unable to stand my reflection, all my imperfections glaring at me, I grab the metal tissue box off the vanity and hurl it against the mirror, the glass shattering.

A loud knocking thunders on the door, followed by someone trying the handle, but I ignore it, screaming again as I take off one heel, then another, throwing them at the mirror, more glass falling to the floor. I step on the shards in search of something else to throw, the pain on my feet a welcome distraction to the storm brewing within me. I grab the hair dryer and toss it, followed by the soap dish, Anderson begging for me to let him in.

I continue throwing everything I can find — shampoo bottles, vase with flowers, and even a few towels. When there's nothing left, I allow my tears to overtake me as I lean against the wall and slump to the floor, hugging my legs to my chest, blood covering my feet.

The door flies open and Creed barrels inside, frantically scanning the room. But his worry is no match for Anderson's. Glass crunches beneath his shoes as he hurries toward me and crouches down, pulling me into his arms, my sobs echoing in the sudden silence.

"It's okay," he soothes, kissing my temple. "It'll all be okay. She won't get away with this."

I wish I could believe him. But she already has. The truth is irrelevant. In the court of public opinion, I've already been judged guilty.

Nothing anyone says or does will change the verdict.

Thirty-One

"Are you sure you'll be okay?" I ask Nora as we stand in front of my residence. The dark SUV that drove us from the airfield idles behind us, waiting for me to get back into it.

She lifts her eyes to mine, but they're as empty as they've been all afternoon, all signs of life gone.

I'd never seen Nora as broken as when Creed burst through the bathroom door and my gaze fell on her defeated frame, her feet cut up, glass everywhere.

From the beginning, she had a habit of hiding behind a mask of perfectly groomed hair and impeccably applied makeup. But I was able to see it for what it was. A cry for help. A silent plea for someone to finally set her free. And not just from her sorrow over losing Hunter and her baby. But also from her mother's torment.

Now I can't help but think I dragged her back into the darkness. Forced her into this life where she lost another piece of who she was daily until it got to be too much and she snapped.

Thankfully, we were able to get out of the hotel without incident, the French police dispersing the assembled paparazzi almost as soon as they showed up. During the short, tension-filled flight back to Belmont, I'd grown hopeful it would all blow over. That the people here wouldn't buy into the lies. That they'd focus on the woman who captured their hearts these past few months.

Who joined in on a nationwide search for a missing child, tromping through fields alongside a volunteer group looking for any clue as to her whereabouts.

Who donned a baseball hat and sunglasses to serve meals at a soup kitchen when she saw they were desperate for help. Something no one in the royal family would ever do, except for Esme and myself.

Who spent hours trying to respond to every letter she received, not wanting anybody to think their messages fell on deaf ears.

But when our plane landed to a swarm of media and outraged locals, I knew that wasn't the case.

It didn't matter the OB who delivered Ember gave an interview painting Nora in a vastly different light, claiming she'd never seen a patient so distraught.

It didn't matter the local police chief where the accident happened also made a statement that there was no physical evidence to support Dr. Harcourt's inferences regarding foul play.

It didn't matter that Hunter's parents also made a statement in support of Nora's strong character and sympathetic nature.

The die's already been cast. Nora's mother gave

everyone a sensational story. In the court of social media, the people are the judge, jury, and executioner. The truth is completely irrelevant.

If I thought Nora was broken before, having to drive through a city entrenched in protests, people holding signs calling her a murderer, gold digger, and baby killer, destroyed her last remnant of life.

The last thing I want is to leave her in such a fragile state, but I don't have a choice, not after being summoned to the palace.

"I'll be fine," she says, her voice defeated. She lowers her head as she turns from me, her steps sluggish.

I pull my lips between my teeth, rubbing the back of my neck. I hate this. Hate watching her break down. Hate I can't stay to comfort her. What good would it do, though? I fear our fate has already been decided.

"O'Kelly," I bark out at Nora's chief protection officer as he starts to follow her into the house.

He pauses, glancing at me.

I walk toward him and lean in, dropping my voice to barely a whisper. "Do not let her out of your sight. Got it?"

He nods. "Yes, sir."

"I mean it, Kylian. Not for so much as a heartbeat." I hold his gaze, hoping he picks up on the importance of my request. When he nods once more in understanding, I turn, sliding back into the SUV.

Creed doesn't utter a single word during the drive to the palace, simply studies me every so often through the rearview mirror. I'm grateful for it. I'm not sure what I'd say to him even if he asked how I'm holding up. I have no fucking clue. This interview came out of left field, leaving all of us unprepared.

Although I shouldn't have been.

Should have known this woman wouldn't sit back and allow Nora to be happy. She's now succeeded in doing what she's tried to do for years.

Breaking Nora to the point where I barely recognize her.

As we approach the front gates of the palace, I keep my eyes trained forward in an attempt to ignore all the protestors assembled outside. I'd give anything to admonish each and every one of them, remind them how, mere hours ago, they adored Nora.

How quickly the tides turn.

They have fresh meat for the slaughter, and they're more than happy to roast Nora on a spit.

During my schooling, I was often fascinated by the Salem Witch Trials. How it was possible for mass hysteria to spread so quickly, a sham of a trial being the only thing standing between the accused and a date with the gallows. Now I understand. It has nothing to do with who's right. All that matters is who has the loudest voice.

And the mob outside the palace gates is deafening.

When Creed pulls the SUV to a stop in front of the entrance, I glance up at the building, my stomach roiling. My hand twitches, head throbs. I squeeze my eyes closed, pinching the bridge of my nose.

"You okay?" Creed asks.

"Fucking peachy," I snip out as one of the palace valets opens my door. I slide out and button my suit jacket, about to walk up the steps when I pause, popping my head back into the car. "Listen, mate. I'm sorry. I'm—"

"It's fine. It's been a trying day. Just don't forget what's important to you. What you fought so hard for."

It's like he can read my mind. Like he knows the war I've been waging these past few days.

"I haven't," I tell him.

"Good."

I turn and follow my father's private secretary toward the executive wing of the palace. This is all distressingly similar to when Nora and I first landed in Belmont a few weeks ago.

But I have a feeling the outcome this time won't be as positive.

When we reach the same conference room, Colonel Winters knocks once, then opens the door, stepping inside. "His Royal Highness Prince Gabriel," he announces, then moves to the side.

I'd expected to be greeted by my father, the head of household, Dalton Peel, and my grandmother, as is typically the case whenever something like this happens.

I didn't expect to walk in to see all the members of the Privy Council assembled around the conference table, my father at the head.

"Your Highness," they all murmur as they stand and bow.

I nod in acknowledgment, then look back at my father, bowing. "Your Majesty."

"Gabriel." My father bows toward me, then gestures at the chair at the opposite end of the table. "Have a seat."

I make my way through the room. With every step I take, the knot in my stomach grows tighter. Things must be bad if the entire Privy Council is here. I have no doubt I'm not going to like what my father has to say.

I sit, back straight, steeling myself for the proverbial bloodbath that's about to ensue.

"I assume you know why I called you here today," he says, as if I had any question.

"I do."

"Then you're already aware that the interview has had quite a disastrous effect. And not just on Nora, but also you. Hell, on the entire monarchy. There's no other way to put it. This is a bloody catastrophe."

"It was all a lie," I remind him, my jaw tight. "Every single word that woman spoke was a fabrication." I narrow my gaze on him. "And you know that."

"What I know is irrelevant." He waves a hand, as if it will relieve him of any liability. "What's important right now is that this story, whether true or a fabrication, is out there. Is being eaten up by the tabloids. Unfortunately, we no longer live in an age of responsible journalism, where reporters are respected and revered for giving people the truth. The truth doesn't matter. In this day of clickbait and social media, all that matters is what's sensational. And Dr. Harcourt just gave the world a story that's prime gossip fodder."

He squares his shoulders, swallowing hard. I know this expression. Know I won't like whatever follows. It's the same look he wore when he called Esme and me into the library at our family home in the country and told us our uncle had died, as did our cousins. That we would have to move to the capital city of Montrose.

That I'd be shipped off to boarding school in London.

That I would one day be king.

But instead of manning up to the new responsibilities placed on me as the future monarch, I reacted like an eight-year-old boy.

I cried. Screamed. Shouted.

I knew it wouldn't change anything, though. Knew the wheels had already been set in motion and I had no choice but to accept it.

Just like I fear is happening now, too.

"Right now, our best course of action is to come up with a plan to…" He glances to his right where Dalton Peel sits. "Save face," my father finishes.

"Save face?" I repeat in disbelief.

It was a fool's wish to think I'd come to my father's office and learn he and the royal household would stand behind Nora. A part of me had hoped that would be the case. That my father would stop taking the council members' advice simply because that's the way things have always been done. I've seen first-hand what can happen when you stop doing that. The people of this country fell in love with the idea of Nora and me as a couple because, instead of appearing out of reach and untouchable, we became relatable.

But as the saying goes… You can't teach an old dog new tricks.

My father has never truly felt comfortable in his role as king, having been thrust into it unexpectedly.

As such, he continues to allow his council and the royal household to control most of his decisions. Including this one.

"Why would we need to save face when Nora did

nothing wrong?" I argue. "When that woman went on national news to spread lies? Rest assured, I will be pursuing legal action against her."

"A lawsuit will take years," Dalton reminds me. "Threatening legal action is like putting a Band-Aid over a gunshot wound. It won't fix the underlying problem. It will only become more and more infected until it destroys you from the inside out. If a person has an infection in a leg that could kill him, the doctor doesn't put a bandage on it and hope for the best. You want to know what he does?"

"What's that?"

He leans across the table, eyes narrowed slits like the snake he is. "He amputates the leg. So that's what we need to do. Amputate the leg. Rid us of this…infection."

"Infection?" I grind out.

"After the interview this morning, the publicity team conducted some preliminary polling." Dalton stands from his chair and makes his way toward me, placing a folder in front of me.

I reluctantly open it, charts and numbers staring back at me. By now, I'm accustomed to this sort of thing. All of my life's big decisions have been reduced to bar graphs and statistical probabilities.

"As you can see, the most favorable outcome for the monarchy remaining as it is would be if the royal family, yourself especially, were to distance itself from Ms. Tremblay."

Bile rises in my throat as I flip through the pages, a half-dozen different scenarios presented, ranging from continuing on as if nothing happened to doing what Dalton suggested — walking away from Nora.

It was an easier idea to wrap my head around when I contemplated doing just that in order to save her from being saddled with a lifetime of being married to a man who may one day lose the ability to walk, to control his bladder, to make love to her.

It's harder to consider when I'm being ordered to end things.

"Most of the interview was speculation, no concrete evidence," I remind them, grasping at straws.

"The preliminary research indicates that a large majority of our representative sample believed Dr. Harcourt made a compelling case," one of the Privy Council members replies. "Especially when she'd mentioned Nora had somehow miraculously walked away from that car wreck with barely a scratch."

"Unfortunately for us, photos from the accident report were leaked and are currently circulating on social media," Dalton adds. "Everyone's offering their opinion, regardless of their knowledge about this topic. It doesn't look good. For Nora. Or the monarchy."

I run a hand over my face, shaking my head as my shoulders slump, sitting in a way that's incredibly unbecoming of a future monarch. "She was *in* that car."

"So you say, but according to records we obtained, she lived nearby. Her fiancé's parents also lived in the general vicinity. It's not a huge leap to assume she knew the area well. And do you want to know what I learned after doing minimal research?"

I don't respond, knowing he'll tell me regardless.

"That the curve where their car was allegedly run off the road is a common area for drivers to lose control of their vehicles and go over the edge, so much so that there were yearly petitions to put in a guardrail. The town had recently granted the request and were slated to begin installation the following week, another suspicious coincidence. When the police interviewed her in the hospital, she claimed to have been pulled from the wreck by a Good Samaritan, yet even after her fiancé's family offered a reward of over $10,000 for information as to who it was, no one came forward."

"Maybe the Good Samaritan had no need for the money," I say through a clenched jaw.

"Gabriel," my father warns, eyes narrowed.

"But even if we somehow *are* able to track down this alleged Good Samaritan," Dalton continues, "our polling shows it won't matter. There is no scenario in which you'll be able to save the monarchy and have the girl, too. It's one or the other."

I close my eyes, trying to use some of the breathing techniques Nora taught me to calm myself down, prevent myself from doing something I'll regret. With every word Dalton speaks, it becomes more and more difficult.

"The local police chief already made a statement dismissing any claims of foul play."

"The people don't care about that. That's akin to the editor of a newspaper issuing a retraction on page fifteen a week after publishing a shocking front-page story. And that's precisely what this is. A sensationalized story, the stuff tabloids are made of. The only thing that can compete with it is if the truth is even more sensational, even more headline worthy. Which it's not. So the best course—"

"It was me!" I shout, jumping from my chair, chest heaving, fists clenched.

"Excuse me?" Dalton asks.

"Me," I repeat. "It was me."

He studies me for a moment, then smiles, shaking his head. "I see what you're doing. You think you can fix this by coming forward with some romantic tale about how you pulled her from the wreck. Make people forget her mother's version insinuating Ms. Tremblay planned it. I—"

"No. That's not it at all, although I *did* pull her from the wreck. If you were thorough with your research, weren't giddy with excitement over the prospect of finally getting rid of Nora, you would have noticed the date of the wreck."

He blinks, shifting through some papers, pulling out what I recognize to be a police report.

"It's the same night Kendall Davies passed away," I tell him. "At a hospital in Long Island."

"Gabriel…," my father cautions again. This time, it feels more out of obligation, as if he knows there's no stopping this runaway train.

"I don't—" Dalton begins.

"*I'm* the reason they crashed in the first place." I point to myself. "*I* caused the wreck. *I* forced them off the road." My voice wavers as a half-dozen eyes stare at me in utter shock. "*I* killed Nora's fiancé and their unborn child!"

Thirty-Two

Nora

A breeze blows a few tendrils of hair around my face as I stare at the miles and miles of glistening, blue ocean below me. I've never walked this close to the edge of Anderson's property before, choosing to remain at a safe distance. But now I'm drawn to the swirling depths. Wonder how it would feel if I were able to summon up the courage to leap.

I imagine I'd feel free again.

Then nothing.

What I wouldn't give to feel nothing. To be numb.

But I'd never be able to do that. Not only because of Little Pickle, but also because Lieutenant O'Kelly lingers nearby, watching my every move, as if I pose a danger to myself.

After the way I destroyed the bathroom in Paris, I suppose everyone has good reason to think I do.

"My lady." A voice cuts through over the ocean waves crashing below.

I turn around, facing the butler. I can't even remember his name. Charles… Richard… It probably won't matter much longer anyway.

"Her Majesty is here and requested an audience."

I close my eyes, drawing in a steadying breath.

The last person I want to see is that woman, who I'm sure believes every single word my mother said.

"If you're not up for it…," O'Kelly says, expression awash in concern.

It touches me that, even though he's employed by the monarchy, he still shows loyalty to me first.

"Thank you, Kylian. But I'll be fine."

"Are you sure?"

"I'm not sure about anything right now." I smile sadly, then follow the butler out of the gardens and into the house, O'Kelly remaining only a few steps behind me at all times.

As I walk down the corridors, it feels like all the portraits stare at me as they would a condemned prisoner heading to her execution.

With pity.

With disgust.

With just plain revulsion.

From the first time I stepped inside this house, I always felt they were judging me, silently thinking I didn't deserve to be here. That I'd never measure up.

They were right.

"Ms. Nora Tremblay," the butler announces.

I give O'Kelly one more reassuring smile before stepping into the study.

The space is mostly dark, dust from the hundreds of

books clinging to the air. If it weren't located in this house that's more like a prison, I might like this room.

I focus on where Queen Veronica currently sits at a table by the window, a chess board resting on it.

She doesn't get up when I walk in, simply stares at me with those cold, judgmental eyes.

"Your Majesty," I say with an awkward curtsey.

It may be the last one I ever do. It's probably why she's here. To break the news so Anderson doesn't have to. Doesn't have to look into my eyes and tell me we gave it a shot, but it just didn't work out. That he had to make a choice between the Crown and me. That as future king, he will always have to choose the Crown.

"Sit, Nora," she says in an even tone, gesturing to the chair across from her.

There's a part of me that wants to remain standing, one final act of defiance. But there's nothing left. I do as she requests, peering at her with a vacant expression. Nothing she says can hurt me. I don't think anything can now.

We sit in silence for several moments. It once unnerved me. Not anymore. Now I welcome it.

"I'm sure you know why I'm here," she begins.

"It's not to discuss who I favor in the upcoming derby?"

She gives me a reproachful glare, her distaste for my sarcasm obvious. "You've put this family in a difficult position."

"I believe that honor should be given to my mother."

"Perhaps." She waves her hand at the chess board. "Do you play?"

"I know the basics."

"Very well."

She grabs two pawns, one black and one white, closing her hands around them. She hides them behind her back and mixes them up. When she extends her hands back toward me, I tap her left one. She opens it, revealing black in her palm.

I take the black pawn and return it to the board, awaiting her first move. She pushes one of her pawns forward two squares, which I also do when it's my turn.

"Regardless of the veracity of your mother's claims," she continues, her focus mostly on the board, "her version of events is out there, and there's only one person who can clear your name in this so-called Kangaroo Court that appears to have convened in this country."

"Who's that?" I ask cautiously after taking my turn, unsure how much she knows about that night.

According to Anderson, his father ordered Creed to keep the truth a secret from everyone, including Anderson himself. Until a year ago, he had no recollection of his involvement in the crash due to several moments of temporary blindness that caused him to swerve the car he drove into the wrong lane, forcing Hunter and me off the road. It wasn't until Creed realized who I was that he finally came clean to Anderson. But I'm still not sure how many people Anderson has shared the truth with, apart from Esme. And, of course, Hunter's parents when he confessed his involvement to them. But being the kind, forgiving people they are, they never went public with it.

"We both know who that is, Ms. Tremblay." She pins me with a glare before returning her attention to the board. "I wasn't involved in the initial aftermath. Following Ms. Davies' death, Gabriel wasn't in a good spot. So my son handled the situation as best he could with as minimal blowback on the royal family as possible."

"He kept his involvement quiet."

"Yes. There was a referendum vote that year, as well, much like now. Granted, it didn't have as much support as it does this year, but still… It was a risk we couldn't afford. And now we find ourselves in the unique situation where clearing your name would entail throwing one of our own to the wolves. And despite the opportunity this life has afforded him, I have no doubt Gabriel would happily sacrifice himself for you."

I nod, no question in my mind he'd do just that. That he's probably contemplating doing it at this very moment.

"Unfortunately, doing so would complicate matters. Not only will the people of this country essentially learn that the royal family was involved in covering up a crime seven years ago, but we also have an extradition treaty with the United States, which would require us to hand Gabriel over if the district attorney decided to charge him with any crime in connection with his arguably reckless driving that resulted in the death of two people. I'm not certain of the penalties for manslaughter in New York, but I assume it will most certainly include prison time."

"Prison?" I squeak out, my mouth growing dry. That thought hadn't even crossed my mind. "It was seven years ago. Surely, any statute of limitations has run out."

"Unfortunately, it hasn't. While the statute of limitations would generally be five years, in many jurisdictions, it's suspended during any period the alleged offender isn't physically present in the state."

I look up from the chess board, my breathing growing shallow as dread settles deep in my stomach.

"You're most likely doing the math in your head right now," she remarks, making her next move with confidence and determination, her white pieces beginning to circle my king like a shark. But I still have a few moves up my sleeve.

I hope.

"He hasn't been in New York for a total of five years," I murmur.

"Precisely."

"So if he were to come forward…" I trail off, shaking my head. "Isn't there some sort of immunity?"

"To some extent, yes. As you *should* have learned during your training, the royal family does enjoy *some* immunity. But there's no diplomatic immunity for causing a car accident and fleeing the scene of a crime. It's irrelevant that he may have also saved a life that night. In the eyes of the law, he took a life. Technically, two."

"But his MS," I argue, grasping at straws. "He had temporary blindness. That must be a defense."

"It's possible. But not a guarantee. That would be up to the judge or jury to decide. Who can very well decide that Anderson was negligent in getting behind the wheel in the first place upon leaving the hospital where his girlfriend had just died. Even went so far as to threaten and assault his chief protection officer in order to do so."

I study the board, trying to strategize several moves ahead on both our parts, searching for a way out of this corner I seem to be stuck in.

"I can tell you His Majesty and the Privy Council are having the same discussion with Prince Gabriel as we speak. And they're also telling him the choice he has to make."

"And what's that?"

"The one we must make every day of our lives. Between *our* wants and our country's needs. He can either love you or love his country, but it appears he can't do both." She leans closer. "Do you really want to be the reason he throws away everything he's worked so hard for?"

I rest my elbows on the table, despite my etiquette training that I shouldn't, and dig my hands through my hair, searching for an alternative, both in life and on this board.

"Do you really want to be forever remembered as the woman who destroyed Prince Gabriel's career?" She leans closer. "Who forced his hand? Who sent him to prison? Because if he comes forward with the truth of that night, there's a strong likelihood of that happening. Not to mention, this entire monarchy could become ancient history." She pauses, lifting her eyes to mine. "Unless…"

"Yes?" I press, hope building inside me that she has another way out of this mess. An option that will allow me to keep Anderson *and* clear my name.

"What's the sportsmanlike thing to do when there's no path to victory in chess?"

I blink, my throat tightening as I look between her and the board where she has my king caged in with no possible way of winning.

From the moment I heard my mother's interview, saw

the vitriol spewed against me online and in protests here in Belmont, I feared this was how it would end. But now that it's here, that reality has sunk in, that there's no way to untangle myself from this spider's web, it pains me in a way I didn't think possible.

"Of course, my original offer from several weeks ago still stands. The royal family takes care of its obligations." She glances at my stomach before returning her eyes to mine. "In the game of chess, my darling girl, sometimes you have to sacrifice your queen in order to save the king."

I blink, staring past her, the room feeling like it's closing in on me.

When I was younger, I had a dog named Max, a goofy Golden Retriever. After my father died, Max was always by my side, offering me the support and compassion my mother refused to bestow upon me. When Max got sick several years later, it felt like I was losing my dad all over again. At least with Max, I had time to prepare. I was able to have a few good days with him before the vet came to our house to put him to sleep.

At the time, I thought it would make things easier.

It didn't.

It doesn't matter how much you prepare for an inevitability. When you reach that point and have no choice but to say goodbye to someone you love and cherish, it rips you to shreds.

Just like this is ripping me to shreds right now.

My hand trembles as I gradually bring it toward my king, placing my pointer finger on top of it. The instant I do, I know there's no going back. I've touched the piece, so I have to play it. Anywhere I move will eventually put me in check. So I make the only move I can.

My eyes trained on hers, I carefully place my king on its side.

Tears stream down my cheeks, but Queen Veronica doesn't seem affected in the least by the fact that she's all but asked me to rip out my heart and present it to her on a golden platter.

"I resign," I manage to choke out.

Then I push back from the table, keeping my head lowered as I storm out of the room, not so much as looking back to curtsey.

I have no obligation to do so now.

Thirty-Three

Anderson

Weariness fills me as I trudge through the halls of my residence after what felt like a marathon meeting with my father and the Privy Council. No matter what I proposed in order to dig the royal family out of the mess Nora's mother created, it still boiled down to the same thing.

Nora or my country.

I can't have both.

If I choose Nora, come forward with concrete proof of her mother's lies, I'll put my freedom at risk, which would eventually fall back on the monarchy for covering up the death of a young man and his unborn child.

But if I choose the monarchy, I lose part of who I am.

I'll lose my heart.

As I step into the formal living room of our private quarters, I have no idea what I'll walk into. No idea what choice to make. No idea if Nora will even still be here or if she's already been forced out during my absence, my decision made for me.

Thankfully, that's not the case, a lone light illuminating her on the couch, back straight, shoulders squared, legs at an angle and crossed at the ankle.

Just like she was trained.

Then I notice the suitcase beside her, the blue tanzanite ring sitting on the side table. My heart squeezes, throat closing up.

"I contemplated leaving a few hours ago," she says flatly. "But I thought I owed it to you to say goodbye in person."

"I assume someone updated you on, well...everything."

"Your grandmother came to see me." She stands. "We played chess."

"Chess?"

"Yes. Chess. But even before her visit, I knew how this would end. I think I've known for a while but was too stubborn to admit it." She smiles sadly. "I think we both were."

"It doesn't have to," I plead, stepping toward her. "We'll figure out a different way. In chess, you can't just look one move ahead. You plan for the next four or five. If we just do that—"

"There is no move, Anders. Someone must be realistic here. Someone has to admit it's over. That it's been over since that plane touched down."

She laughs under her breath. "It's been a while since I've played chess." A small smile tugs on her lips as she swipes away a few tears. "Hunter loved to play. He's the one who taught me. Do you want to know why he loved the game so much?"

"Because it involves strategy."

"Yes, but that's not the only reason. It's because it mimics life. Like you said, it's not about making a decision based on what's in front of you at this very moment, but on things you can foresee happening down the road. Because of that, I know this is the only option."

"It doesn't have to be." I clutch her arms, clinging onto the last shred of hope.

"Chess is a game of absolutes. How you use those absolutes to dominate the board is where the strategy comes in. But no matter how you use those rules to your advantage, one thing remains absolutely certain."

"And what's that?" I ask softly.

She peers up at me through tear-filled eyes. "You can't sacrifice your king and still win the match."

Dropping my hold on her, I hang my head, the ache in my chest excruciating. It doesn't matter that I've been at war with my diagnosis lately, torn between not wanting to saddle Nora with a husband who will become increasingly dependent on other people every day and selfishly wanting to keep her with me. It's one thing to end things on our own terms. It's another when that decision is made for us.

She touches my cheek, pulling my eyes to hers. "But you *can* sacrifice your queen to save the king."

I shake my head, wanting to tell her again it doesn't have to be this way, but it does. We both know it. "I don't want to lose you," I choke out.

"And I don't want to lose you, but this is the only move we have left. We gave it a shot, Anders. I thought our love would be strong enough. We both need to face the cruel reality that it isn't. At least not to survive your world. If we don't do this, if we don't walk away now, there will be nothing left of either of us to salvage."

I knead at my chest in an effort to stop the pain, but I doubt anything ever will. Returning my gaze to hers, I cup her cheeks in my firm grasp. "You will always own my heart," I declare passionately. "Always."

"And you will always own mine," she squeaks out. "Always."

I seal my mouth over hers, pouring everything I have into the kiss. All my anger. All my sorrow. All my fears. All my love. She grips me tighter, desperation and anguish consuming her, consuming me. I'm not sure what has my tears falling more steadily. That this is goodbye, or because I'm not fighting harder for her.

I now understand why my mother pushed people away after her diagnosis. It wasn't selfish. It was self*less*. She didn't want to burden those she loved with taking care of her.

That's what I'm doing now, too.

At least that's what I try to convince myself.

When she pulls away and peers into my eyes, I nearly beg her not to go. I hate the idea of not waking up to those eyes every day. But I hate what she'd miss out on more. After all the grief I caused her, after everything I took from her, she deserves a normal life.

She'll never have that with me.

I clear my throat. "What are you doing about your flight?" I ask, switching into problem-solver mode, doing my best to keep my emotions at bay.

"Your grandmother arranged for me to use the jet one

last time. Kylian… O'Kelly will accompany me. He'll make sure I reach my destination safely."

"Do you want me to come with you, too?" I ask before I stop to consider the ramifications.

Even if she agrees, I won't be allowed. As the Privy Council instructed, it's imperative I not be seen with her. Not if we stand a chance to keep the monarchy intact.

"I don't think that's a good idea," Nora replies. "The best thing for us is a clean break."

"Why do I get the feeling there's nothing clean about this?"

She lifts her glossy eyes back to mine, tears threatening to escape once more. "Because there isn't. This is as messy and dirty as can be. But I don't see any other option. Do you?" Her voice carries a twinge of hope.

I avert my gaze. "I don't."

Spine straight, she re-secures the mask she wore for years. The same mask she wore when we met. The one I chipped away at. And the one I forced her to put back on when I introduced her to this world.

"I'll keep you updated on Little Pickle. Despite every-thing, I'd still like you to be in his life, at least as much as you're able. He won't have to know who you are. I mean, he'll know *who* you are, but not *what* you are, if that makes sense."

I arch a brow. "He?"

Sadness covers her expression as she rests her hand on her stomach. "Just a feeling I have."

When she first told me she was pregnant, I was beyond excited about the prospect of having a child. But I sensed an unease within her. A fear. I couldn't quite explain it, but for several weeks, it felt like she purposefully avoided any reminder that she was pregnant, not even touching her stomach, probably out of fear she'd get attached to this life growing inside only for it to be taken away.

But lately, she's gotten over that fear.

If she can get over hers, why can't I get over mine?

"I'd like that," I tell her. "If it's not too difficult, I'd like to be there when he's born. Maybe schedule a few trips out there for some of your appointments."

"As long as it won't interfere with your schedule. You're still his father. I won't cut you off just because we didn't work out." She blows out a choked laugh, looking at the ceiling. "Although if you come to visit one day with a new wife you were forced to marry just to produce a real heir, I may have a complete breakdown."

I frame her face in my hands so she can see the truth behind my words. My fingers dig into her skin, an intensity buzzing through me as a new wave of tears falls down my cheeks.

"Our child will *always* be a real heir." I rest my forehead on hers. "And you will always be my queen." My voice cracks as I struggle to speak through the agony enveloping me, mind, body, and soul.

"And you will always be my king."

I press my lips against hers, torturing myself with one last kiss. One last taste of her. One last moment of happiness.

It reminds me of the last time I kissed her before telling her about my involvement in the crash that cost her everything. I knew once I did, there would be no turning back.

But like Esme so succinctly put it back then, I was torn between having a clear conscience and a broken heart. Despite knowing I could have very well kept it to myself the rest of my life, I told Nora the truth. She deserved to know.

Just like she now deserves to be free of the cage this life has trapped her in.

She deserves to fly, and she can't do that with me.

To keep my conscience clear, I break my heart and let her go.

Thirty-Four

Nora

The airplane jostles as I stare out the window, the familiar skyline of Manhattan lit up at night zooming by. The engines roar, the plane gradually slowing down at the end of the runway before turning and taxiing toward the fixed-base operations office where I'll disembark and leave this life behind.

"Ready, ma'am?" Lieutenant O'Kelly walks up to me from his seat toward the front of the plane, the crew bustling around to prepare the cabin to return to Belmont, minus one passenger.

I nod, forcing a smile.

Despite having eight hours to prepare for my return to New York, now that I'm here, it's more difficult than I imagined. I once looked forward to coming home after a long time away. Now I fear anywhere I go in the city will remind me of Anderson.

Then again, I have a feeling I'll find pieces of Anderson no matter where I go.

O'Kelly helps me to my feet, following me down the aisle, the cabin crew bowing and curtseying as I pass. It strikes me as odd. After everything my mother said in that interview, I assumed they'd be happy to see me go. They certainly wouldn't show me any sort of respect or deference. Instead, many of them look at me with sadness.

When I reach the door, I hold onto the railing and take a deep breath, drawing in the city air for the first time in months. It's still the same briny sea air mixed with fuel and something distinctly New York. But it feels different. *I* feel different.

I descend the steps for the last time and allow O'Kelly to lead me into the main office, where a customs officer greets us.

"Passport, please."

I hand it to the woman. She cross-references the photo to make sure it matches.

"What was your purpose for your trip abroad?"

I part my lips, wishing she didn't have to ask that question. "I—"

"She was previously engaged to the Crown Prince of Belmont," O'Kelly interjects, saving me from having to answer.

The woman looks at him before scrutinizing me, realization kicking in. "Oh, of course. I apologize. I didn't initially recognize you."

"It's okay."

After she types a few more things into her computer, she returns my passport. "Welcome home."

I wish this place felt like home, but it doesn't. I'm not sure anywhere will ever feel like home again.

"Why did you go through customs just to essentially walk me to catch a cab?" I ask O'Kelly as he steers me through the FBO office where a few well-dressed men wait for their private jet or charter to take off.

I guess I should be grateful Queen Veronica showed me a sliver of kindness toward the end and arranged my use of the jet. Otherwise, I would have not only had to attempt to get through the Belmont airport with no one recognizing me, but here, too. At least this way, I don't have to worry about people coming up to me and accusing me of being a murderer.

"Because I promised His Highness I would make sure you arrived home safely. Not just in New York. So I'll be accompanying you to your final destination."

When we step out of the small terminal building, a black SUV already waits. O'Kelly opens the back passenger door for me, helping me in. Then he runs around and slides in beside me.

"Do you want to stay in the Upper West Side apartment? His Highness wanted me to tell you that he'll be signing it over to you once the lawyers draw up the paperwork. And not to concern yourself with the property taxes or any other expenses. He'll cover those, too."

"Tell him that's generous, but I can't go back there. He can sell it if he wants. I've already reached out to my friends to tell them I'm coming home. I'll be staying with Izzy in Gramercy Park while I figure out where to go from here."

"Are you sure it's safe? You're not just recognizable in Belmont, but also across the world. *Especially* here."

"Her husband is Asher York. He's——"

"I know who he is," he says with a laugh. "The rock star. Pretty sure you'd have to be living under a rock to *not* know who Asher York is."

"Exactly. So their house has adequate security. I'll be fine there."

"Okay." He meets the driver's gaze in the rearview mirror, giving him a nod.

During the drive from JFK and into the heart of Manhattan, I keep my eyes trained out the window. I should find comfort in the fact that I'm minutes away from seeing the friends I've missed these past six weeks, two of whom are on the brink of giving birth. But I didn't expect the first time I returned to be so…permanent.

After a traffic-filled drive that takes over an hour, despite only being twenty miles away, the SUV finally pulls up in front of Izzy and Asher's townhouse. I glance up at the five-story brownstone a block away from the exclusive, private park in Manhattan.

Lieutenant O'Kelly slides out of the SUV and heads to my side, helping me step down onto the sidewalk. After retrieving my small suitcase, he carries it up the front steps for me, then turns to face me. It's sad to think that my entire life can fit into just one suitcase.

I once marveled at people who got rid of most of their belongings and decided to live more of a nomadic lifestyle, never staying in one place long enough to set down roots.

Now the idea is quite appealing.

"It was an honor, ma'am," O'Kelly says stoically.

"Thank you. This entire ordeal would have sucked if I didn't have you helping me, Kylian."

He grits a smile and is about to retreat when he stops, lifting his gaze to mine. "Can I... Can I give you a hug?"

Tears well in my eyes once more and I nod. He wraps his arms around me, my body tiny compared to his huge bulk.

"You'll always be a princess to me."

I draw in a breath, allowing myself to find a hint of comfort in his words. "Thank you."

He pulls back, keeping me at arm's length as he stares intently into my eyes. "And I think once the dust settles and the noise dies down, you'll find most people feel the same way. The loudest voice in the room is seldom the wisest. And is often the most scared. Just some food for thought." He holds my gaze, then nods, making his way down the steps.

Just before getting into the SUV, he bows his head. "My lady." Then he climbs into the car.

I expect them to drive away, but they don't. Instead, he keeps his eyes trained on me, which I imagine he'll do until he sees me disappear into Izzy's house.

Turning toward the keypad, I enter the code and the door buzzes, granting me entry. I walk into the small foyer, setting my suitcase by the entryway table, the place filled with light. I close the door behind me, then look out the window, watching as the last tie to my life in Belmont drives off.

"Nora?" Izzy's voice carries from the top of the stairs.

I turn toward the staircase to see Izzy, Evie, and Chloe standing there.

"Welcome home," she says with a sad smile.

I make my way up the stairs and into their

outstretched arms. I burst into tears, all the emotions I've kept to myself since walking away from Anderson one last time washing over me. They don't ask me if I'm sure I did the right thing. Don't try to goad me into talking about my mother. Don't bring up anything that would make my heart splinter even more than it already is.

They just hold me and let me get it all out.

Just like any loyal friends would.

Thirty-Five

Anderson

I stare at the empty chair beside me in the formal dining room of my residence while Lieutenant Colonel Bridge reviews my agenda for the day. I somehow manage to nod when it's expected, but my attention is elsewhere. It's focused on the ghost of the woman who once sat in that chair every morning.

I knew I'd miss her when she left. But I didn't expect to feel her everywhere in this house.

Her laughter still echoes in the halls.

Her smile still tortures me every time I close my eyes.

Her perfume still permeates the sheets of the bed we once shared, despite the fact the household staff changes them regularly.

When the room falls silent, I snap out of my daze, bringing my attention back to Bridge. "Thank you," I say, assuming he's done telling me where my presence will be required today.

A trained monkey once more, I simply go through the

motions and do what I'm told. Like I did when I silently stood by as the royal household made an official statement, claiming Nora left voluntarily in response to her mother's interview. As is always the case, they left out any indication of the role they played in forcing her out, remaining neutral instead.

At least I didn't have to stand by my father's side as he shared this with the press. But in the week since, the media has certainly been hounding me, asking for a statement.

No longer prone to shun the rules, I give them the response ingrained into my subconscious at this point… No comment.

"Of course, sir." Bridge stands from his chair, but doesn't bow or retreat.

"What is it?" I ask, sensing his hesitation.

"It's just… Carly Hart's people reached out to see if you were interested in appearing on the morning broadcast at some point to give your own insight into Ms. Tremblay." He raises a single brow. "To possibly counter what Dr. Harcourt claimed."

I stare at him for a beat, my expression impassive. "You know as well as I do it's against protocol for the royal family to give an interview, especially when it would involve information that directly contradicts a statement made by the royal household."

"That's true. And I'd probably be fired if anyone knew I'd brought it to your attention. But I thought perhaps you'd want to make up your own mind about this."

"I'm not allowed to make up my own mind," I say evenly. "Now, if you'll excuse me, I'd like to enjoy my breakfast in peace."

He doesn't move.

"Did you not hear me? You're dismissed."

He opens his mouth, then snaps it shut, straightening.

"What?" I growl.

"With all due respect, sir, I thought you'd fight harder for her." Then he bows. "Your Highness." He spins on his heels, hurrying from the room.

I check my appearance in the mirror, making sure my medals are lined up perfectly, nothing out of place on my military dress uniform, my required outfit for the state dinner tonight. I've always hated these things. Being forced to make small talk. Feigning interest in things like polo and yachting. Pretending my heart isn't still in pieces.

But I particularly hate the idea of being required to attend, considering this event is the first step in the royal household's plan to rekindle any appearance of romance between Caroline DeVries and myself. And like the puppet I am, I've gone along with it, despite my conscience screaming at me to fight. No thanks to Bridge's statement at breakfast this morning that's played on repeat all day.

I thought you'd fight harder for her.

Hell, I didn't fight at all. At the first sign of attack, I sacrificed my queen.

But I had to…

Didn't I?

"Are you ready, sir?" Creed peeks his head into the dressing room of the private quarters where I spent my adolescent years.

I squeeze my eyes shut, wishing I could rewind the clock to the day I looked up from my coffee at a downtown Chicago diner and saw Nora for the first time. To the freedom we felt when we scaled a fence and explored a run-down drive-in. To the way the wind whipped her hair around her face as I drove with the top down on the Wrangler.

To when I was still happy.

To before this life stole that from us.

"Are you okay?" Creed asks.

I open my eyes, pinning him with a glare as I start to push past him. "I'm fine."

"You're such a bloody liar, Anders," he grinds out, grabbing my arm, yanking me to a stop. "Nothing about this is fine. The sooner you stop pretending—"

"I told you!" I tear my arm from his, my eyes on fire. *"I don't want to talk about it!"*

He leans into me, not letting me ignore this conversation any longer. "Oh, I know what you've said, but I've also heard what you *don't* say."

All week, he's attempted to get me to open up about what happened between Nora and me. And all week, I've insisted I'm fine, that our hand was forced and the only option was for her to leave.

"You. Miss. Her."

I glower at him, chest heaving, jaw tight. Then I throw up my hands. "Of course I miss her!"

"Then why are you still here? Better yet, why isn't *she*?"

"You know why! This was the only way!"

He studies me for a beat. "Bullshite, Anders! That's complete bullshite and you know it. Are you really going to stand there and have me believe the only possible way out of this was to do nothing? To simply let her walk away without a fight? That doesn't sound like the Anders I know."

I grind my teeth, my jaw ticking in an attempt to keep my emotions in check. But something inside of me snaps. Everything I've kept from Creed for months burns like lava as it flows from me.

"That's because the Anders you knew is dead, Creed! The Anders you knew used to be able to run. Could fly a fucking helicopter. Could fire a rifle and hit a target 300 meters away. Now I can barely even hold the thing steady, and that's on a good day. My legs and hips are constantly sore from just walking. Oh, and this morning? I had to sit down to take a bloody *piss* because I was so damn dizzy. So excuse me if you don't think I'm the same Anders. I'm not. The sooner you wrap your head around that fact, the easier it'll be when part of your job assignment is cleaning up my shit and piss.

"You can stand there and judge me for not doing enough to keep Nora here, like everyone around me seems to think. But at least I saved her from spending the rest of her life married to a goddamn cripple." I slink to a nearby chair, collapsing into it, fighting against another dizzy spell. They seem to be happening more and more lately, especially since Nora left. I lower my voice, sounding defeated. "I sacrificed my happiness so she can have a chance at being happy. So she could be free."

"Anders...," Creed begins, slowly walking toward me

and sitting in the chair beside mine. "You don't believe that, do you? Do you honestly think she wouldn't be happy with you simply because you don't live up to this ideal of perfection you have in your mind?"

"You don't know what it's like, Creed. To want to make love to your fiancée and aren't able to. To feel like half a man. Not even. To feel…" I shake my head, gradually lifting my gaze to his. "To feel like a fucking burden."

"I won't say I know what you're going through, because I don't. I have no idea what it's like to constantly have my body betray me. But I *do* know that Nora doesn't care about that. Hell, she found it in her heart to forgive you even after everything you took from her. That's how deep her love for you runs, Anders. She doesn't care if you'll be stuck in a wheelchair one day."

He licks his lips, studying me for a beat. "Do you remember your last night together in Los Angeles after driving Route 66? How you asked me to arrange a private showing at the drive-in."

I swallow hard. "I do."

"And what movie did you ask they show? What movie was absolutely non-negotiable in your mind?"

"*An Affair to Remember*," I say grudgingly, sensing what he's getting at.

I'd originally requested that movie because the main characters fell in love while traveling. Much like Nora and me, they came from different worlds, had other commitments and obligations. But regardless of all the complications, they fought to make their dreams a reality. Nicki Ferrante even promised to start painting again, despite destroying all his previous work because it didn't meet the level of perfection he'd hoped to attain. Those were the lengths he was willing to go to in order to pursue his dream of being with Terry McKay.

But now, the story has a deeper meaning than just two strangers falling in love aboard an ocean liner.

"In the final scene," Creed continues, "when Nicki Ferrante sees Terry McKay and finally realizes why she doesn't get up from the couch, does he simply shrug and say, 'Well, it's been swell, but have a nice life, you daft cripple'?"

I chuckle, grateful for the break in tension. "No. But—"

"But what? This is *different*?" he taunts, knowing precisely what my argument will be. "A few of the details might be, but the gist of it remains true here, Anders. He didn't care she couldn't walk. Didn't care she was stuck in a wheelchair. That she might be a 'burden' in some people's minds. What did she tell him?"

"Creed...," I beg, the mere thought of those words like a knife to my chest.

"What. Did. She. Say?" he repeats, firmer.

I blow out a long breath. "'If you can paint, I can walk.'"

"Exactly. What happened the night of that accident was a tragedy. But that's precisely what it was. An accident. You weren't drinking. You had what we now know was an MS flareup, which caused you to momentarily lose your vision. I can't guarantee how the police will respond, but I'd be hard-pressed to believe they'll hold you accountable when any accident is involuntary. When you didn't even know you'd caused that crash until a year ago. So, for the love of *Christ*, stop moping around here because some crusty old men told you to. Do you remember what happened the last time you stopped doing things the old way?"

I blink, not answering.

"People fell in love with Nora. The entire country went nuts over the idea of you two together. You may think your hands are tied, but I have no doubt if you broke a few more rules…" When he narrows his gaze, there's no question he's referring to sitting down for the interview with Carly Hart, "they'll do so all over again. Everyone loves a story of redemption and forgiveness. And that's certainly what yours is. Sometimes you have to break a few rules to break new ground. It worked before. It can work again."

I look straight ahead, mentally going through everything that's transpired since I left New York. The engagement leak. Being reminded of the laws of succession and the Royal Marriages Act. Nora agreeing to marry me in two months instead of next year, as we'd planned. Nora going through all her princess training without a single argument. Rekindling our romance, even with everything else going on. Taking her to Paris, where it all fell apart.

But despite it all, there's no question my happiest times involved Nora. Making love to her at night after a long day of work. Waking up to her every morning. Photographing her on the balcony of our hotel.

She's repeatedly told me she doesn't care about my diagnosis. That she fell in love with my heart, not the body holding it. Hell, she's *shown* that to be true. So why was I so eager to throw it all away, especially after everything she gave up for me?

The argument we had in the garden after I missed her first doctor appointment replays in my mind. She'd asked me what I sacrificed in order to be with her. To my utter dismay, the answer was nothing.

It still is.

But it no longer has to be.

A revitalized energy coursing through me, I jump up. For the first time in ages, I don't waver on my feet, don't have to hold on to some nearby piece of furniture to steady myself.

With determined strides, I stalk into the hallway, Creed close behind. As I turn the corner, I stop abruptly when I see my grandmother walking toward me.

"Your Majesty," Creed says, bowing. I mirror his greeting and movement.

"Heading somewhere?" she asks, holding her head high, her shoulders squared, posture exuding the same distinction and poise one would associate with her title.

"I…," I stammer, unsure what to tell her.

"Why do I get the feeling you're not planning on attending the dinner tonight?"

I look at her with an unwavering gaze. "It was just brought to my attention that I have somewhere far more important to be right now."

She pinches her lips, her dark, analytical gaze tracing over me. I expect her to argue that there's no place more important than being here and serving the Crown.

"It's about time you pulled that enormous head out of your arse."

Creed laughs, but quickly covers it with a cough.

I'm stunned. This is a woman who's always followed every etiquette rule and royal protocol to the T, never straying for so much as a second.

"You *are* planning on going to America to patch things up with Nora. Yes?" she says when I don't immediately respond.

"Well… Yes."

"Then what are you doing still standing here?"

"You *want* me to go?"

She huffs. "Of course I do."

"But you don't even like her."

She rolls her eyes. "Oh, I like her fine. Truth be told, I didn't at first. It's always been unheard of for someone in your position to marry an outsider. And for love, no less. But I must admit, the girl certainly grew on me, especially when I tried to pay her off to walk away and she told me to shove it."

"You did what?" I blink repeatedly, not sure what surprises me more. That Nora told my grandmother to shove it, or that my grandmother attempted to bribe her to get her to leave. Actually, now that I think about it, neither should shock me.

"It was simply a test. I needed to make sure she wanted this. That she wasn't just after you for your title. When she told me to shove it, and up my *ass*, no less," she says, emphasizing the word in an American accent, "I knew she had the backbone required to survive in this life. Not to mention quite a sense of humor."

"Sense of humor?"

The ghost of a smile plays on her thin lips. "No one has ever spoken to me in such a disrespectful way as your fiancée has. Not only did she tell me to shove it, she also stormed off, but not before stopping to curtsey."

I bark out a laugh, able to picture Nora doing that with striking clarity. It's one of the things that drew me to her from the beginning — her somewhat twisted and irreverent way of doing things to make a point.

"But last week, you encouraged her to leave," I argue, confused. "Made her think there was no other option. Why are you changing your mind now?" I wave my hand toward the large windows to my right. "Is it because the so-called circus has finally moved on?"

She pulls her brows together in contemplation, then says, "Walk with me for a minute, Gabriel."

When she offers me her elbow, I loop my arm through it. Creed nods, retreating to my old room to give us privacy. We walk together in silence for several minutes, the only sound that of her evening dress rustling with her steps.

"Watching your grandfather in his role as crown prince, then king, I've learned quite a bit. One of the things that stuck out in my mind is that part of being an effective ruler is knowing when you're wrong and being able to admit your mistakes. When that interview aired and I heard that woman talk about Nora, I knew she was full of shite, pardon my language."

"Trust me. I understand how difficult controlling your language can be when talking about her mother."

She smiles, then faces forward once more. "The problem with being groomed almost from birth to hope-fully marry someone of royal blood is that we're not trained to think for ourselves. Once you enter this life, we're told what to do. If someone were to ask why these rules are in place, they'd say—"

"That's how it's always been."

"Precisely."

We walk in silence, heading in the opposite direction than we need to be. Or at least my grandmother needs to be. For the first time in a long time, I know where my place is. And it's not here.

"These past few days, I haven't been able to stop thinking about the game of chess I played with Nora. She's quite a good player. For an amateur, of course."

"Of course."

"As you know, I've always loved chess. When I was a little girl, I would watch my brothers and father play. I'd asked to learn several times, but my father refused to teach me. Refused to allow me anywhere near the board. Told me it wasn't something for girls, especially girls of noble background. I was supposed to study piano, practice my needlework, learn different languages. Things like that to make myself more 'marketable' to a husband."

"It's so antiquated, like something you'd hear about in the 1800s, not the twentieth century," I remark, glancing at the centuries-old portraits of the royal family eavesdropping on our conversation.

"This was the 40s and 50s, so gender stereotypes were still happily embraced, particularly in upper-class society. When I asked why, I'm sure you can guess the response I was given."

"Because that's the way it's always been," I say in an even voice with a hint of annoyance.

"Precisely. But that didn't stop me from learning about

the game in other ways. After everyone went to bed at night, I snuck into my father's study and read the books he had on chess. Learned about strategy. About different techniques. But since my father didn't want me to play, I was never able to practice." She stops walking and faces me. "When I married your grandfather and he shared his enthusiasm for chess with me, I was finally able to put everything I'd read into practice. But do you know what I learned?"

"What's that?"

"That you can study theory, can study past games, can study openings, mid-games, and end games until your eyes bleed, but there's always a move you don't foresee. Some things you can't prepare for. So yes, when that interview broke and I foresaw the potential ramifications to not only you, but also the monarchy if you were to come forward with the truth of that accident, I did what all the books tell you to do. Protect your king at all costs. I failed to take into account what many chess masters say is infinitely more important than knowing the mechanics of chess, what makes the greats who they are."

"And what's that?"

She places her hand on my cheek. "Intuition, my dear boy. Some of the greatest chess matches of all time would have turned out differently if the players only went by the book. If they made their moves because that's how it's always been." She gives me a knowing look as she pulls back.

"By protecting the king…," she begins, looping her arm through mine again as we stroll through the palace, "what I really did was protect an antiquated way of life that is becoming more and more irrelevant. Looking back at how you and Nora bloomed as a couple made me finally realize that. You two had the courage to question the establishment when they told you to do something simply because that's how it's always been done. You went against the rules and principles. And people loved you for it. When you sit down with Carly Hart, I have no doubt you'll have the same unwavering support." She turns, grabbing both my hands in hers. "You will always have mine. Both of you. I apologize it took me so long."

"Thank you, Grandma."

"You're more than welcome, my dear boy. Now go." She fixes her expression into one of feigned severity. "And don't come home without the mother of my great-grandson."

I tilt my head. "How do you know it's a boy?"

She kisses my cheek, then turns from me, heading back in the direction of the ballroom. "It's just a feeling I get."

Thirty-Six

Nora

"Oh, Chloe," I breathe as Lincoln hands me the little pink-wrapped bundle. "She's absolutely beautiful."

I pull back the blanket, admiring little Eloise's chubby cheeks and fuzzy, blonde hair. Bringing her closer, I nuzzle her as she sleeps, inhaling that addictive smell of a newborn.

"She just couldn't wait to make her appearance, could she?"

"She certainly couldn't." Chloe adjusts herself in the hospital bed. "It's probably a good thing she came three weeks early, considering she's already eight pounds. I don't think my body could have handled anything bigger." She looks up at Lincoln. "I blame you for that."

Leaning down, he feathers a kiss against her temple. She closes her eyes, basking in the touch. Even from a few feet away, I can physically feel their love. It makes me long for the way Anderson would kiss me like that right before

I'd drift off to sleep. Now the only thing remotely close to that is when Izzy and Asher's dog, Treble, curls up next to me and licks my face, treating me to his stinky breath.

Since I returned to New York nearly two weeks ago, Treble's been my shadow. Normally, he's indifferent to my presence. But instead of sleeping in his bed in Izzy and Asher's room, he sleeps with me every night, as if he can sense I need his comfort when the tears find me.

And they do, especially at night.

Especially when I notice my stomach growing a little bigger each day and think about going through all of this alone. But as my friends have reminded me, I won't be alone. It takes a village to raise a child, and they've sworn to be my village. To be with me every step of the way.

"You did awesome, baby," Lincoln says. "You deserve a gold star."

"Thanks, Professor," she jokes. "But the true hero was the anesthesiologist. That epidural was heaven. I couldn't feel a damn thing. Until it wore off. Now my vagina is officially on fire."

I roll my eyes. "Thanks for the visual, Chloe."

"What are friends for?"

"Knock, knock," a sing-song voice says.

I peek up from smothering Eloise with kisses to see Evie and Izzy standing in the doorway, a few bags in their hands.

"Do you have room for two more?" Izzy asks.

"For you girls? Always," Chloe answers.

They barge into the hospital room that now feels on the small side. Visiting rules typically limit it to the spouse and two additional people, but since Izzy's a nurse here, still wearing her scrubs from her shift last night, I doubt anyone considers her a visitor.

"I'll let you all have some time together," Lincoln states. "I could use a shower anyway. It's been a long night."

"Get ready," Izzy taunts. "They're *all* going to be long nights from now on."

"If Eloise is as much of a handful as this one…" He hitches a thumb toward Chloe, "I have no doubt." He gives her one more sweet kiss before turning toward where I sit with Eloise.

I stand, allowing him to take her from me.

"See you soon, baby girl." He kisses his daughter's forehead, lingering for a beat to breathe her in, then hands her back to me.

I hold her in my arms once more, making sure to cradle her head. Then I look at Evie and Izzy. "Who wants her next?"

"Me! Me! Me!" Evie waddles across the room, ready to pop any minute herself. "At least before I need to pee again, which will probably be in mere seconds at the rate I've been going lately."

She lowers herself into one of the chairs. Once she looks as comfortable as she can when eight months pregnant, I hand her little Eloise. Much like me, she nuzzles her, inhaling that fresh baby smell.

"What's in the bags?" Chloe asks.

"We brought some essentials," Izzy states, handing over a bag. "When Lincoln called to say you'd gone into labor while at dinner and didn't have time to head to Rye, then back to the city again, we figured you might need a few important things. Like nipple cream. Breast pads. Lotion for your hands."

Chloe exhales in relief. "You guys are a godsend." She grabs the lotion, smoothing it on her hands and arms. "I swear. The air in hospitals is so damn dry."

"How do you feel?" Izzy asks.

"Some irritation, but surprisingly okay. She's worth it."

I beam at my friend, marveling at how far she's come since our freshman year of college. Back then, she ran as far away from anything remotely resembling any sort of committed relationship. Now she's officially a mother, something she swore she had no interest in being. It's amazing how meeting the right person can change your outlook on things. Soon we'll *all* be mothers — Evie in a matter of weeks, me in about six months, and Izzy a month or so after that, having shared the news of her pregnancy with all of us last week.

"I'm happy for you." I squeeze her arm and give her a sincere look when the television catches my attention.

I blink, my heart dropping into the pit of my stomach, all my focus drawn to the man on the screen.

"What is it?" Chloe asks, noticing my expression. When she glances at the TV, she sucks in a breath.

I'd purposefully avoided all social media and any cable television since returning to New York, not wanting to flip through the channels and stumble across some news story about me. Or, worse, Anderson.

"Can you turn that up?" I ask softly, although part of me doesn't want to listen to whatever this is, especially when I notice Anderson sitting in the same chair as my mother did a few weeks ago during the interview that cost me everything.

But it's not just Anderson who has my curiosity piqued.

It's who's sitting beside him.

Mary and Benjamin Copeland. Hunter's parents.

Chloe grabs the remote, raising the volume.

"Thank you so much for being here today, Prince Gabriel." Carly's voice grates on my skin, especially considering the last interview of hers I saw. *"I have to admit, I was a bit surprised when my producer told me you'd agreed to sit down with me."*

Anderson laughs. *"I almost didn't. But then I realized something."*

"And what's that?"

He looks from Carly to the camera. People may think he's talking to them. But I know that look. It's his Anderson look, the one reserved for me.

"Sometimes you need to break the rules."

"And being here today is breaking the rules for you?"

"Giving an interview like this is generally frowned upon for members of the royal family. Sure, I've done a few interviews with the occasional magazine, but a live television interview is a big no-no. But I needed to set the record straight, despite strong opinions from within the royal household that I not. That I continue to allow them to use Nora Tremblay as a sacrificial lamb of sorts."

"And what do you have to say about Nora Tremblay? As you're aware, her mother gave quite an explosive interview. Claimed her daughter is a known manipulator, someone only out for money. Voiced her suspicions that Nora had killed her ex-fiancé, making it look like an accident, as well as intentionally ended her pregnancy."

I watch as Anderson fights to keep his anger in check.

His jaw ticks. Fists clench. Muscles tighten. But he does his best to remain calm under pressure, offering Carly a smile that's a mixture of forced and annoyed.

"*I didn't come on here today to badmouth anyone. Although there's quite a bit I'd love to say to Dr. Harcourt if she ever dares show her face around me. I came here today to tell the truth about the woman I love. The woman I'm still desperate to call my wife, my queen…*" He turns back toward the camera, his eyes pleading. "*If she'll forgive me for being such a daft knob.*"

I choke out a laugh through my tears, my heart brimming with an emotion I can't quite explain — a blend of love and forgiveness, and everything else that makes us who we are.

"Daft knob?" Chloe asks.

"Stupid dickhead."

She processes this for a moment, then nods. "Sounds about right."

"*The truth is, Nora had no involvement in the accident that took her fiancé's and unborn daughter's lives.*"

"*How do you know that for certain? After Dr. Harcourt sat down with us, I did some digging of my own. Spoke to some law enforcement professionals familiar with the accident. According to them, the police reports were inconclusive. There was no evidence that her version of events was true. But also no evidence it wasn't.*"

"*I can't argue with that.*"

She looks at Hunter's parents. "*Her fiancé, Hunter Copeland, was your son. You put out a reward for any information about a so-called Good Samaritan Nora claimed pulled her from the car moments before it burst into flames, killing Hunter. Isn't that correct?*"

Mary swallows hard, the loss of her son still affecting

her. *"We did. To the tune of $12,000. But no one came forward. At first, we questioned why someone would want to remain quiet about it, especially with a reward of that amount of money."* When she glances at Anderson, a grateful smile pulls on her lips. *"But it turns out the Good Samaritan truly had no need for the money."*

You can practically see the lightbulb go off in Carly's head, her wide eyes returning to Anderson. *"It was you,"* she breathes. Then she quickly rummages through the pages of notes in front of her. *"Of course. It makes sense now. Your girlfriend at the time, Kendall Davies, died the same day in a hospital mere miles away from the scene of the accident."*

He nods. *"That's correct. I pulled Nora from the car. But that's not all I did."*

I suck in a breath and shake my head, my hand covering my mouth. "No. Nonononono. Please, Anders. Don't do this."

But my pleas fall on deaf ears.

"I caused the crash."

"What is he doing?" I mumble to myself, heart hammering in my chest.

"Remember what you told us your first night back?" Izzy asks. "That there were too many obstacles between you?"

I meet her eyes.

She crosses her arms over her chest. "Well, Nora, it looks to me like he's removing those obstacles."

Speechless, I look from her to Evie, who simply nods in agreement. Then to Chloe, who does the same.

When Anderson and I said goodbye, I thought that was it. That there was no path forward for us. That no one would allow him to do something like this. That they'd protect the king at all costs. That's what every chess rule book would say to do.

Then again, Anderson and I have never been a couple to follow the rules.

"What does this mean?" I ask frantically.

"We can't tell you that," Chloe replies. "But the one person who can is only a quick cab ride away. If I were you, I'd get moving."

"But you just had a baby," I protest. "I can't leave you."

She throws up her hands. "Oh, shut up and get out of my room. I'm officially revoking your invitation to be here."

I glance down at my wardrobe. It's not exactly anything remotely close to what I should be wearing if going to see Anderson. I'm fairly certain the royal household would lose its mind if they saw me in my jeans and Mets t-shirt, my unwashed hair in a messy bun, face mostly devoid of makeup, apart from a bit of powder and eyeliner around my eyes. This is how I've blended in this past week. How I've gotten away with no one recognizing me. People are used to seeing the future princess with her hair perfect and makeup impeccably applied. Without those things, no one gives me a second glance.

"Go!" my three friends shout at the same time, Izzy pushing me out of the room.

I pause as a few brief thoughts of inadequacy run through my mind. Can I really put myself through all of this again? Allow myself to have hope? Is Anderson worth it?

When his voice fills the room as he shares our love story, I have my answer.

He will *always* be worth it.

"I love you girls," I say quickly, then whirl around, ignoring the demands from the nursing staff to slow down.

But I can't.

I race out of the building as quickly as I can. Luckily, there's always a line of cabs nearby, and I dart into one.

"Rockefeller Plaza," I say breathlessly. "As fast as you can."

The driver nods, starting his meter. He merges into traffic, then steals a glance at me in the rearview mirror. "Do you know who you look like?"

"Grace Kelly?" I mutter under my breath, having gotten that most of my life.

"No. The American girl who was supposed to marry that European prince but her mother sabotaged it. Probably out of jealousy."

I pull my hair out of the bun, allowing it to fall to my shoulders. "I *am* that American. And that prince is being interviewed by Carly Hart right now. So I *really* need to get to Rockefeller Plaza as soon as possible."

His eyes widen in surprise. Then he turns into the New York cab driver I know he is in his soul. "Of course, ma'am." He presses his foot on the gas, not paying much attention to the rules of the road.

I pull my phone out of my purse and bring up a browser so I can keep watching the interview. For all I know, it may already be over.

But when I tune into the live feed, I blow out a relieved breath to see Anderson's still there. I turn up the volume, keeping my hand on the door handle to prevent myself from sliding all over the back seat as the car's tires squeal around a corner.

I listen as Anderson shares how he was unaware he'd caused the crash until a year ago. How he'd experienced temporary blindness, what he now knows was a flareup of his MS, which was undiagnosed until last year. Then he shares how we met, something that's been kept under wraps from the beginning. How he was on the brink of taking his own life after receiving his MS diagnosis, but saw me sitting in that Chicago diner. As he discloses how he felt when he realized who I was, a text pops up.

CHLOE:

#TeamNora is the top trending hashtag right now. This interview is going viral, more so than your mother's. Nora, people LOVE your story. So go get your man! And don't give up until you have him!

I beam, typing out a quick reply.

ME:

I don't plan on it. No more obstacles.

I look up from my phone to see how close we are. There are still a few blocks to go, but with Midtown traffic what it is, it'll probably be quicker if I just run.

"I'll get out here." I reach into my purse and toss a $20 his way, then hastily push open the door, skirting through three lanes of traffic. People fill the sidewalk like ants, Rockefeller Plaza feeling so close but still so out of reach. Like it gets farther away with every step I take.

Now I know how Terry McKay felt in *An Affair to*

Remember when she was on her way to the Empire State Building to see Nicki Ferrante after their agreed upon six-month separation. Nothing else mattered except getting to Nicki. Just like right now. Nothing matters except getting to Anderson.

When I'm two blocks away, I break into a jog, looking down at my phone every few seconds to see the interview still going. A few people look my way, seeming to recognize me. Some whisper and point, others begin chanting my name as I run past.

By the time I reach the Plaza and can see the open windows of the studio on 49th Street, more and more people have joined in the chant. But I tune out most of them, all my attention focused on the large screens outside broadcasting the interview. Anderson's voice fills the area as he confesses how he didn't fight hard enough for me. How the reason wasn't because of my mother's interview but because he thought he was saving me from a lifetime of living with a cripple.

I stop dead in my tracks, his words hitting me hard, knocking the air from my lungs.

"My god, you are such a bloody wanker," I muse, to which a few people around me laugh.

"Men usually are, sweetie," a woman says, encouraging me forward.

I jog the last block to the studio, the growing crowd stopping to watch, their cell phones pointing in my direction, all of them cheering me on. It invigorates me, an infectious smile tugging on my lips. Days ago, I assumed I was hated. Maybe I never was. Maybe that was all in my head.

Maybe I'd allowed my mother to manipulate me yet again.

Shaking it off, I approach the windows of the studio. My pulse increases when I peek through them and see Anderson under the lights, his hair a bit more wayward than normal, a dusting of scruff on his face.

Now that I'm here, I realize I haven't thought this through. He's on national television right now. What are the chances he'll see me out here? Do I try to find the stage door? I doubt they make it easily accessible.

Instead, all I can do is send him a text message, then watch. And wait.

And hope.

"Are you really her?" a woman asks me, eyes wide in excitement. "Are you really the American princess?"

I smile. "I am."

The woman turns toward her friends. "It really *is* her!"

The crowd cheers, several people asking me to sign their posterboards, some of which were obviously made with Anderson in mind. I can only assume these women are big royal watchers.

While I'm more than aware that signing autographs is frowned upon, I no longer have to live by those rules. So I happily agree to sign their posters, taking their marker and scrawling my name on each. In the background, I hear Carly ask Anderson what he hopes to achieve by finally coming forward with the truth.

"*Nothing,*" his voice booms in the Plaza. "*But I couldn't sit aside and let the world think the worst of Nora. She doesn't deserve that. Her mother painted her in a horrible light. But that's not Nora. Maybe that's the Nora her mother wishes she were, but nothing could be further from the truth."*

"*Why don't you share who Nora Tremblay is then,*" Carly suggests.

"*She's the love of my life,*" he answers without hesitation, his voice wavering slightly.

Hunter's mother reaches for his hand and grabs it, giving him a reassuring smile. It melts my heart to see these people on the same stage together. Connected by tragedy but united for a bigger purpose… Love.

The frenzied sounds of the city seem to disappear as everyone's eyes remain glued to the giant screens overhead. It's as if the world has stopped spinning to listen to the elusive Crown Prince Gabriel give an interview and speak from the heart, something no royal has ever done.

"*Nora Tremblay doesn't have a vindictive or manipulative bone in her body. She's one of the most honest and real people I've ever met. She doesn't pretend to be something she isn't, which I think was one of the hardest things for her about acclimating to life as a royal. Everyone tried to tell her how to act, how to think, how to dress. But Nora isn't the type of woman you can fit into a mold. She's warm, caring.*" He laughs to himself, his brilliant, blue eyes sparkling. "*This is a woman who saw a dog get hit by a car and made me pull over so we could take it to a vet, then paid for all the medical care he needed.*"

With each word he speaks, the more impassioned he becomes, his determination unwavering. Whereas my mother could barely look Carly in the eyes as she spouted her lies, Anderson's gaze remains resolute.

"*This is a woman who has spent the past month taking the time to respond to each and every one of the hundreds upon hundreds of letters she's received from across the globe, not wanting anyone to think she doesn't care. I've never met any other royal who's done that, who's taken the time to interact with people."*

"*That's Nora,*" Mary says from beside him. "*Always giving. Never taking.*"

Anderson gives her a small smile before returning his attention to Carly as tears fall down my cheeks.

"*This is a woman who spent nearly four hours in a pediatric oncology unit playing dress-up with a few of the young girls who are longtime patients there. She had other engagements that day, but that didn't matter to Nora. She didn't care about going to dinner with whatever celebrity we were supposed to be seeing that evening. All that mattered was staying with those kids as long as possible, making them happy.*"

"*I remember seeing that on the news,*" Carly says. "*She certainly won over quite a few hearts with how she interacted with all those kids.*"

His expression falls slightly, his Adam's apple bobbing up and down in a hard swallow, his facial muscles pinching. "*And this is a woman who's suffered an immeasurable loss. Who watched as the car holding the man she hoped to spend the rest of her life with went up in flames. Who was then told their baby no longer had a heartbeat. Who had to give birth knowing there would be no baby's cries greeting her. There would be nothing but silence.*"

I feel an arm wrap around me and glance at one of the women through my tears. She squeezes me, offering an empathetic look, making me think she's no stranger to the pain of child loss.

"*Despite all that,*" Anderson continues through his own emotions, "*despite enduring something I couldn't even begin to fathom, she never lost hope. Never gave up. Which is why I'm not going to give up on her. I'm not—*" He stops abruptly, lips parting as he stares at something over Carly's shoulder.

I look away from the large screens and through the studio windows, wondering what caught his attention, our gazes locking.

He blinks, once, twice, as if worried he's hallucinating. As if he's been seeing me everywhere lately and wants to make sure I'm really here.

Suddenly, he shoots to his feet, ripping his microphone off his shirt as he darts from the studio. At first, Carly's surprised. But when she peers out the windows, her eyes finding mine, she smiles. Then, being the opportunist she is, she waves a camera man over. After a brief conversation, he takes off running, a camera in his hand. Suddenly, the shot of Carly transitions to the backstage area, Anderson darting through the maze of a studio, people scrambling out of his way.

The crowd gets louder and louder as we watch him navigate through hallway after hallway, someone in a page's jacket escorting him out of the stage door. Finally, he steps into an alley before turning onto the Plaza.

Knowing exactly where he is, I spin, the crowd parting so I can get through, my legs not carrying me nearly as quickly as I'd like.

After what feels like miles instead of mere yards, I turn the corner toward the Plaza and skid to a stop when my eyes fall on Anderson for the first time in two weeks. To most, it may not seem that long. To me, it was a lifetime.

His gaze focused on mine, he takes several slow steps toward me, chest rising and falling quickly, not a hint of the uneasiness he sometimes experiences when walking.

When he reaches me, he stops and smiles. "Hey."

"Hey," I manage to squeak out. An electricity buzzes in the air between us. But it's even more poignant than it's ever been. "I though you—"

"Nora, I—" he says at the same time, both of us laughing nervously.

He treats me to that sly smile of his that's always been reserved just for me. "You first."

"I thought you'd be arrested if you told the truth. That's why I left. Didn't want you to have to come forward and implicate yourself."

His expression remains stoic. "I know. But I couldn't let you take the blame anymore. Not for something I should have disclosed." He licks his lips, still standing a foot away. "Do you want to know why I didn't fight harder for you when this all went down?"

I nod. "Because of your MS."

"Yes. But there's a deeper reason." He steps toward me, but still doesn't touch me. "Because I thought by saving you from a lifetime of being with someone like me, it would keep my conscience clear. So instead, I broke my heart." He averts his eyes as he draws in a deep breath. "But how could I have a clear conscience when I allowed them to throw you to the wolves?" He smiles sadly. "So I did what I felt necessary to finally clear my conscience, once and for all."

"And what's that?" I ask shakily.

"Went to the police. Told them the truth."

My shoulders fall as I squeeze my eyes shut, swallowing hard past the lump in my throat. "You didn't have to. You—"

"Yes, I did."

"Will they be arresting you?" I ask, although I don't want him to answer. Don't think my heart can take it.

His expression sobers. Then a brilliant smile tugs on his mouth. "No."

I blink. "No?"

He shakes his head. "I did what the royal household didn't want me to do. Told the truth. Despite everything I shared, the DA declined to pursue charges. Apparently, his sister has MS, too, so he's more than aware of some of the complications. And thanks to the foundation I started last year was able to receive treatment she otherwise couldn't afford."

I blow out a small laugh. "With great power comes great purpose."

He nods, advancing toward me and cupping my cheeks in his hands. "With great power comes great purpose," he repeats, slowly edging his lips toward mine. "*You* are my purpose."

I sigh, bringing my own hands to his face. "And you're mine."

He starts to erase the last remaining distance, but stops, something catching his attention. Taking my right hand in his, he exhales a tiny breath when he sees his ring prominently displayed.

"You're still wearing it," he says in awe.

"I couldn't find the strength to take it off. Wasn't ready to admit we truly were over." I bring my hand back up to his face, and he melts into my touch. "Wasn't ready to give up my faith."

Closing his eyes, he momentarily basks in my declaration. Then he loops an arm around my waist, yanking my body against his. I faintly make out people in the assembled crowd begging Anderson to just kiss me already, but I tune them out, all my focus on this man. On the promise of his kiss.

On the promise of us.

"I'm going to kiss you now. And once I do, there's no walking away."

I run my hands through his hair, mussing it up. "Is that a promise?"

"You bet your arse it is."

Without a moment's hesitation, he covers my mouth. The entire Plaza erupts in cheers, but I don't care about any of them. All I do care about is this man who just flipped the game on its head. Who made a move everyone told him was foolish. A move that would cost him everything.

He put the king at risk to protect his queen.

And, in that one move, won everything he ever wanted.

Epilogue

Anderson

The comforting aroma of cinnamon and apples clings to the walls of the palace, growing stronger the closer I get to the private living quarters. This has always been my favorite time of year. The grand halls decked out in Christmas decorations, everyone in a more joyful mood. It was a time of year my mother always made special.

I remember spending hours in the kitchen with her frosting cookies, decorating gingerbread houses, rolling out dough for pies. The memories we made as a family over food was something I'd always look forward to all year long. As was the feeling I'd experience when we went to a local shelter to donate all the food we'd made to those less fortunate than us.

That all changed when my uncle died and we were ripped from the life we once knew. Then it changed again mere months later when my grandfather also passed away, making my father king and me heir apparent. There were rules about everything, from the way we styled our hair to the way we celebrated Christmas. There were no more hours spent in the kitchen baking and laughing with my mother. Instead, my family had to do what my grandfather did on Christmas, and his father before him, and so on — host a large dinner for the family and other important people on Christmas Eve, then attend midnight mass.

All my mother wanted to do that first Christmas was bake cookies.

She wasn't even allowed to step foot into the kitchen. That wasn't the way things were done around here.

If they knew it would be one of her final Christmases, would they have granted her this wish?

Based on centuries of always doing things the same way, I'd assume not.

As I step into the private residence, my heart warms at the unmistakable scent of cookies and pie, coupled with the sound of Christmas music and joyful voices. I shrug off my suit jacket and loosen my tie, tossing them onto the oversized sofa. I continue toward the sounds and smells, careful not to trip over the myriad of toys scattered around.

Approaching the kitchen I had built when we moved in earlier this year, I pause, leaning against the doorjamb, taking a moment to appreciate the scene in front of me, something I never imagined could be a reality years ago.

But that was before I laid it all on the line for Nora.

Before I stopped living according to the rules.

Before I took a risk.

After the interview where I shared the good, bad, and heartbreaking truth of Nora's and my story, people rallied behind us, despite the powers that be predicting the truth would be disastrous not only for me, but also the royal family.

Instead, the world fell in love with us all over again. I was once able to travel to certain countries without being noticed, particularly away from Europe. That was no longer the case. In the days following the interview, everyone wanted a piece of me. Of Nora. Of us. And not because of some scandal. But because of what our story embodied.

Forgiveness.

Redemption.

Love.

Because I'd been so candid about everything we'd been through, people found us to be an extremely relatable couple. More importantly, they found me to be relatable as this country's future king, the voters overwhelmingly rejecting the constitutional referendum to limit the monarch's power.

Since then, we've experienced a lot of changes. Not only in our personal lives, but also in our royal lives. Nora's no longer merely Nora Tremblay, but Queen Nora Jean Wellingston of Belmont. And I'm now officially king, having been crowned a few weeks after our son's first birthday, who we named Hunter William Anderson Gabriel Wellingston.

Naming our son after Nora's former fiancé hadn't even been on her radar, but I felt it a fitting tribute. Not only to him, but also to our love. After all, it was Nora's journey to say goodbye to Hunter that brought her into my life. It won't bring him back, but maybe he'll look down upon us and smile at the thought that one day, a little boy named for him will become king. Even though little Hunter was born after we finally got married, with the new Royal Marriages Act and law of succession that was passed before his birth, he's considered a full heir.

But since he's only a few months shy of his third birthday, all he really cares about are trucks and trains. He doesn't realize who he is or what his future holds, and we're happy with that. He deserves the childhood I had before it was taken from me. Deserves happiness. Deserves to be a kid, not an heir.

"Papa!" Hunter squeals, looking up from where Nora stands over him at the kitchen island. She peeks up, too, a bit of frosting on her temple.

The room more closely resembles a disaster area — mixing bowls containing the remnants of batter, cookie sheets and pans piled high in the sink, flour covering the kitchen island. It certainly isn't what one would expect a room in a palace to look like.

And I love every bit of it.

"Hey, little man." I walk toward them and scoop Hunter off the step stool, giving him a big hug before pulling back. "Have you been good for your mama?"

"Yes."

"And how about your great-grandmimi and grandpapa?"

"Yes."

"Good. Because you know who's coming tonight."

"Santa!" he replies with all the enthusiasm of a little boy.

"That's right."

I press one last kiss to his cheek, then place his feet back onto the floor, tousling his blond hair before turning my attention to Nora.

"Hey, gorgeous."

"Hey yourself," she responds, lifting herself onto her toes and brushing her mouth against mine. "How was your day?"

"Better now." I hook an arm around her waist, pulling her tighter against me. "Much better now." I press my lips more firmly against hers, coaxing her mouth open so I can have a taste of her before our home is overrun with friends and family.

But this year, there won't be a formal dinner at the palace to celebrate the holiday. No putting on a show for the people of this country. Instead, it'll be a private, low-key affair. Only close friends and family. Like my mother wanted.

Like Christmas should be.

"Kiss kiss! Kiss kiss!" Hunter exclaims.

"They sure do that a lot, don't they?"

We pull back, darting our eyes toward the doorway to see Esme, my father, and grandmother.

Unlike previous years when Christmas was a formal affair and everyone would be dressed to impress, it'll be more casual this year. Much more casual. Our instructions were for everyone to wear an ugly Christmas sweater.

My father probably went as conservative as possible, opting for a red sweater with the infamous leg lamp from *A Christmas Story* on it.

Esme, being the snarky and irreverent woman I love, wears a black sweater that says *Feel The Joy*, two red gloves covering her chest.

But I think my grandmother actually wins for best sweater. Or at least best execution. Leaves and ivy, along with a few sleigh bells, cover the shoulders and arms. On the front are what appears to be reindeer footsteps in the snow.

"You guys look great!" Nora exclaims. "Especially you, Grandma."

"You get it?" she asks.

"Of course! 'Grandma Got Run Over by a Reindeer'! It's genius."

"I have to admit, it was quite fun making this."

"I'm glad."

I watch Nora and my grandmother, the warmth and affection both women have for each other obvious. It's no secret Nora never had a strong mother figure in her life. But my grandmother seems to have become that for her, the two often spending hours playing chess in the study.

When I first brought Nora here and my grandmother was so against the idea of us together, I never could have imagined that possibility. However, my grandmother has relaxed quite a bit over the past few years. She now cares less and less about her role as queen mother, something that used to be her sole identity. Something she clung to out of fear that if she didn't, she'd cease to exist. Not anymore. Now, her focus is little Hunter.

Truthfully, I think she quite likes not following every little rule and requirement of royal protocol anymore. It gives her freedom to do things she actually wants. To follow her passions. While she can still be a stickler for decorum and etiquette every so often, she's let go of certain traditions that only served to keep the idea of the royal family antiquated. My goal as king has been to allow us to be seen as a modern family, one that's no longer resistant to change.

Immediately following Nora's and my return to Belmont, my father cleaned house, starting at the top with Dalton Peel, who he discovered had actually paid Nora's mother quite a large sum of money to give the interview that nearly cost us everything. Instead, he brought on people who could modernize the Crown, make it relevant even in this day.

As for Nora's mother, she finally got what was coming to her, something that should have happened ages ago. After my interview, her license to practice psychiatry was revoked. Not only did she lose her means of making a living, but when her latest divorce was finalized, the judge refused to award her alimony. With no other way to maintain the lifestyle she'd grown accustomed to, she reached out to Nora, pretending to be the caring mother she'd never been. So Nora bestowed the same compassion on her that she'd shown Nora all her life — absolutely none. Last I heard, she's working as a cashier at some grocery store in Florida and living in a rundown trailer park.

As my mother once said... Karma is like a rubber band. You can only stretch it so far before it comes back and smacks you in the face.

Nora's mother has finally gotten the smack in the face she's always deserved.

"Why don't you all head into the living room," I suggest. "I just need to change, then I'll be right down." I give Nora a kiss on the cheek and tousle Hunter's hair before dashing up to our bedroom.

Thanks to the infusion treatments I've started, I *can* dash most days. Some are still better than others. There are times I do need to use a cane to help me get around. I've finally accepted my diagnosis, though. I thought I had years ago, but there was still quite a bit of denial at play. Especially when I refused to try a different treatment plan and constantly pushed myself to my limits just to prove to everyone I could do things. That there was nothing wrong with me.

Because of that, I almost lost Nora.

Never again.

I may have MS, but MS doesn't have me. I won't let it.

After changing as quickly as possible, not wanting to be gone from my family longer than necessary, I follow the sound of laughter and merriment through the halls. When I round the corner, Esme barks out a laugh from where she sits on the floor with Hunter, my father and grandmother sitting on the couch behind them, playing with him like the toddler he is, not the future king.

"'*Birthday boy*'?" she remarks, reading the print on my sweater of Jesus in a birthday hat, a noisemaker in his mouth.

"What? Technically, he is." I shrug, stepping farther into the room.

A large tree stands tall in front of the windows, the plaza outside covered with a fresh coating of snow. Unlike years past when the tree in the private residence was designed by professionals, Nora, Hunter, and I decorated this ourselves with ornaments the palace receives from various schools throughout the country, as well as personal ones — Hunter's handprint, a piece of cement from Route 66 I'd picked up, and even that first ultrasound photo of Hunter when he was still Little Pickle.

That's when I notice something I hadn't before. Another framed photo just below Hunter's first ultrasound. It's nearly identical to that one, except for one very important detail.

Slowly, I make my way across the room, eyes focused on the tree. The world seems to go quiet as everyone watches me.

I unhook the ornament from the branch, squinting as I try to make sense out of what I'm looking at. I glance from this black-and-white picture to the one of Hunter, then back again, my heart hammering in my chest.

"Congrats, Daddy," Nora murmurs from behind me.

I whirl around to see her wearing a Christmas sweater of an oven over her stomach. But instead of only one gingerbread man inside, there are two.

"Are you telling me..." I swallow hard.

"I guess we're overachievers. We've got the heir. But now we're about to have *two* spares."

My eyes widen as I sweep her into my embrace, kissing her deeply, wishing I could show her in some other way how much I love and appreciate all she's done for me.

"Twins," I say, a mixture between a statement and a question.

"Twins," she confirms.

"Two at the same time."

"That's usually how twins work, Gabriel dear," my grandmother interjects with a smile.

I shake my head, pulling Nora back to me once more.

"This may be the best Christmas gift I've ever received. I'm sorry the rest of the girls weren't able to be here to celebrate and share in the news."

"They'll be here for New Years. I won't be able to really celebrate, but it's okay. All I care about is having time with my friends. That's celebration enough. And so is this."

"What?"

She places her hand over her stomach. "Our growing family."

I kiss her again, pulling away when I feel a familiar tug on my shirt.

"Mama has cookies in her belly." Hunter points at Nora's sweater.

"She sure does, bud. Do you know what that means?"

"Mama likes cookies!"

"That's one way of putting it," Esme mutters under her breath, to which everyone chuckles.

"No. It means you're going to be a big brother."

He looks between us for a beat, seemingly deep in thought. Then his expression brightens. "Okay. Can we open presents now?"

I blow out a laugh, marveling at how easy-going he is. "Of course."

As I gaze around the living room at a scene I could have never imagined a few years ago, my heart expands, much like the Grinch's did when he discovered the true meaning of Christmas.

When Nora forgave me after learning the truth of the role I played in the car accident that took her fiancé and unborn child from her, I thought I knew what true love was. When she agreed to move her world for me and acclimate to a life no one can adequately prepare for, I fell even more in love with her. Then even more when we stood in front of God and all our friends and family, promising to cherish each other the rest of our lives. But those are the big moments.

Love is also found in the small moments. In my opinion, those are infinitely more important. I find pieces of our love sprinkled throughout our history. In the memory of her smile as I pulled her hair free of her ponytail as we drove along Route 66 together as two strangers. In the memory of spending a lazy Sunday at Central Park, lounging in the grass as we talked about everything and nothing at the same time. And now as she looks up at me with more admiration than I think I deserve.

I remember what Esme told me when I first grappled with my feelings for Nora. "'Maybe it won't work out. But maybe seeing if it does will be the exact adventure you need to remind you what it's like to fly.'"

There's no doubt in my mind that my time with Nora so far has been the adventure of a lifetime.

I have a feeling the adventure is just beginning.

Thank you so much for reading *Tangled Games*. Want more of these characters, especially Creed and Esme? Start the Broken Crown Trilogy today with Royal Creed and save on the full trilogy. Just scan the code below and type the address into your web browser.

She wants to be my first. I want to be her last. But she's royalty. And I'm just the hired help.

https://geni.us/BCTrilogy

SIGN UP FOR MY NEWSLETTER to receive a
BONUS EPILOGUE of Tangled Games, featuring
Anderson and Nora, as well as all the girls you've grown to
love in this series. Claim your copy today!
Just scan the code below or enter the web address into
your browser.

https://geni.us/TG-Bonus

I appreciate your help in spreading the word about my
books. Please leave a review on your favorite book site.

ROYAL CREED

Our love is strictly forbidden. But every person has their breaking point. And we're about to reach ours.

The last time I saw Creed Lawson was the morning he left for basic training. After eight years apart, I thought I'd gotten over my innocent crush on my brother's best friend.

But when he walks back into my life, there's nothing innocent about the way he looks at me.
Or the thoughts that enter my mind.

I try to ignore the obvious chemistry between us. After all, I'm second in line to the throne. And he's a career military man who's about to be sworn into the royal guard.

Even if I weren't being forced to marry a man I don't love, Creed would never act on his attraction.

Or so I thought…

Until we reach our breaking point and finally succumb to our desires.

There may be no future between us, but that doesn't stop us from being together, despite the risk. And with each day, that risk becomes more dangerous, especially when I learn there's more at stake with my arranged marriage than I'd been led to believe.

My grandmother always told me there's no place for love in a monarchy.
Maybe she was right…

Playlist

Royals - Lorde
Have I Told You - Matthew Mole
Your Lips Are Mine - Connor Duermit
Leaving Home - Cody Fry
Dreaming - Emily James
Grand Canyon - Matt Kearney
Ghost in the Wind - Birdy
Lonely - Violet Skies
Quite Miss Home - James Arthur
If You Love Her - Forest Blakk
Only Everything - Jake Etheridge
Sailboat Bed - The Devil Music Company
Rush - Lewis Capaldi featuring Jessie Reyez
Take it One Day at a Time - Jennifer Chung
Let It All Go - RHODES, featuring Birdy
Up in Fire - McKenna Breinholdt
The Good in Goodbye - Alexander Wran
Closure - Hayley Warner
So Beautiful - Ed Prosek
Memories Crash - Maisy Stella
Here's to You - Sara Phillips

You Have My Heart - Emily Sage featuring Stephen Day
Lucky to Know You - SayWeCanFly
The Good Parts - Andy Grammar

Acknowledgments

Writing acknowledgments is always difficult. It's always the last thing I do before publishing. (Although if I'm cutting it close to deadline, I sometimes have another round of editing or proofreading to do as well.) In my mind, writing acknowledgments means saying goodbye to the characters and this story, which I always hate doing. But it's even more difficult in the final book of a series.

I started this journey with this group of woman back in 2018. That was the year I'd published both my Inferno Series and the Redemption Duet, both angst-filled, emotionally-driven stories. Whenever I write a lot of heavy books, I feel the need to write something lighter, which was when I got the idea to finally write one of my favorite tropes to read - a fake relationship romance.

When I sat down to write *Dating Games*, which was actually titled *Dear Gracie* at the time, I never could have imagined it would turn into this series. It was just supposed to be a standalone romantic comedy before I switched gears to write my first interracial romance in Possession. A pallet cleanser, more or less.

But this group of women had different plans for me.

And I'm so glad they did. In the past 2 1/2 years, they've become close friends. I know I probably sound crazy, since they're all products of my imagination. But they've been with me these past several years. Hell, writing Anderson and Nora's journey together on Route 66 helped me through quarantine, being able to travel vicariously through them.

So it's with a very heavy heart that I say goodbye to this incredible group of women so I can focus on other stories that need to be told… Like Esme and Creed's story! (Stay tuned! It's coming next year!)

With that being said, I'd like to take this opportunity to thank all the people who help me behind the scenes.

First and foremost, a huge thanks to my husband, who's supported me in this author world since day one. And big thanks for helping me come up with the angle of Nora's mother's interview. It really turned the book around for me when I'd hit a wall, so to speak. On that same note, a big thanks to little miss Harper Leigh who makes me laugh and smile every day.

To my wonderful PA, Melissa Crump — I couldn't do any of this without your unwavering love and support. Thanks for keeping this train on the tracks.

To my fantastic beta readers — Melissa, Stacy, and Vicky — thanks for reading and offering your feedback on this story. Sorry about all the angst. Actually, I'm not. You should be used to this by now.

To my amazing editor — Kim Young. Thanks for always treating my manuscripts with care. You're the only one I trust to work on my babies!

To my girl, A.D. Justice. This author world would suck

without you in it. Thanks for always being there for me.

To my review team. Thanks for always taking the time to read and review my work. Your support means the world to me.

To my reader group. Thanks for giving me a place to go when I need a break from writing and the real world.

And last but not least, a big thank you to YOU! My amazing readers. Whether this is your first T.K. book or you've read all of them, I'm so grateful you took a chance on my stories. I still can't believe this is my life, but I'm eternally grateful you've all made it possible for me to write stories for a living.

And I have lots more stories planned, so stay tuned!

Love & Peace,

~ T.K.

About the Author

T.K. Leigh is a *USA Today* Bestselling author of romance ranging from fun and flirty to sexy and suspenseful.

Originally from New England, she now resides just outside of Raleigh with her husband, beautiful daughter, rescued special needs dog, and three cats. When she's not writing, she can be found training for her next marathon or chasing her daughter around the house.

facebook.com/tkleighauthor

instagram.com/tkleigh

tiktok.com/@tkleigh

bookbub.com/authors/t-k-leigh

amazon.com/T.K.-Leigh/e/B00EU3X26C

pinterest.com/tkleighauthor